EDDY N

and the

MAP OF AFRICA

Eddy Nugent

Monday Books

© Eddy Nugent, 2009

First published in the UK in 2009 by Monday Books

The right of Eddy Nugent to be identified as the Author of
this work has been asserted by him in accordance with the
Copyright, Designs and Patents Act 1988

All rights reserved. Apart from any use permitted under UK
copyright law no part of this publication may be reproduced,
stored in a retrieval system, or transmitted, in any form or by any
means, without the prior written permission of the publisher, nor
be otherwise circulated in any form of binding or cover other
than that in which it is published and without a similar condition
being imposed on the subsequent purchaser

A CIP catalogue record for this title is available from the British
Library

ISBN: 978-1-906308-11-7

Typeset by Andrew Searle

Printed and bound by Cox and Wyman, Reading, Berks.

www.mondaybooks.com
http://mondaybooks.blogspot.com/
info@mondaybooks.com

Contents

In memory of Lance Corporal Anthony (Tony) Hannigan,
Royal Corps of Signals, Feb 1969 – Jan 1992
– A lovely bloke, fondly remembered by all who knew him

Preface

Welcome to the second instalment of the adventures of Eddy Nugent... and those of you who enjoyed *Picking Up The Brass* will be glad to hear that *Eddy Nugent and the Map of Africa* is more of the same.

British servicemen and women are asked – for not very much money – to face hardships and horrors that most folks never even have to think about.

One of the principal coping strategies of the British soldier is humour – the ability to laugh at dangerous and even life-threatening situations. The BBC recently broadcast footage of British soldiers under heavy Taliban fire which summed this up perfectly. As the rounds flew overhead, one young squaddie turned to look into the lens of the hand-held camera that his mate was operating, smiled and said, in a faux-Geordie accent, 'Day thirty-six in the Big Brother house!'

We were fortunate to have served in the British Army during slightly more sedate times. During the late eighties and early nineties – when *Map of Africa* is set – the main danger zone was Northern Ireland. Although we both served for two years in the Province, we've steered clear of taking Eddy there. Lots of hilarious things happened to both of us during our time 'over the water', but it's hard to be funny about a period that caused so much pain to so many people. The Gulf War – a conflict that saw huge deployment by British forces in the same timeframe – is omitted because we were both in Belize and watched the whole thing on CNN. (We liked to claim that we were protecting our expeditionary forces from a sneak westerly flanking attack by that notorious scourge of the high seas, the Iraqi Navy.)

Like us, Eddy goes to Belize. He also makes his way over to join the British Army of the Rhine in what was then West Germany, at a time when the Cold War was limping to a close. It turned out that the millions of Russian shock troops poised to flood over the borders weren't quite as well-equipped as we'd been led to believe, and The Third World War would probably have been more like closing time on Plymouth's infamous Union Street.

1

With this in mind, we've tried to put together a book to enlighten the reader about the day-to-day hilarity generated by putting together lots of young men in a camp far away from home, then adding alcohol, women and armoured vehicles.

As with *Picking Up The Brass*, all the antics happened to us or someone we knew. But given that this is a soldier's story, there's been some embellishment – for inauthenticity's sake. As per usual, the names and places have been changed to protect the guilty.

Those who read the first book – we mean the original, self-published version which fell apart on contact with the slightest amount of water – will be familiar with the Belize chapter, but we hope you enjoy it nonetheless.

Lots of love to Carol and Alison, our wives, who've supported us tirelessly, whilst we nipped off to reminisce about old times under the guise of 'research'

Thanks to our GLC (Geordie Linguistic Consultant) Mark Bloxham, whose excellent analyses allow us to get away with North-East murder and to Martin (DS) Beattie for lending his expertise in the strange language of pidgin-German.

Thanks to everyone who supported and encouraged us on *Picking Up The Brass*, by buying it, spreading the word or interviewing us. Special mention goes to Simon Smith for passing it round *The Apprentice* house, so that they too could learn words like 'buckshee', 'deathpack' and 'screech'.

Cheers to Andonis Anthony, Mark Whitely, David MacCreedy and Daniel Rogers for their brilliant short film of the Recruiting Office scene from the first book.

Thanks to everyone at the Army Rumour Service, from Good and Bad CO down to the newest posters, for getting behind us and providing us with a great sounding-board for our writing.

Finally, best wishes to all the men and women of the British Armed Forces. Whether you're in the front line in one of the world's hotspots, or on the skive, smoking a roll-up in a blanket store somewhere near Salisbury Plain, good luck to you.

Charlie Bell and Ian Deacon, October 2009

EDDY NUGENT AND THE DALEK OF DONCASTER

MY NAME'S Eddy Nugent, and here's the story so far. I spent my early years in South Manchester as an only child, surrounded by a loving extended family. I was academically bright at school, but my school reports tended to focus on my desire to be the class clown rather than any concrete achievements. In my last year, fate found me in Fountain Street in the city centre, where I chanced upon the Army Careers Office, an attractive building bedecked with flags and pictures of men with big guns. The staff inside convinced me that a glittering future was mine for the taking; the way they explained it, all I had to do was show up and I'd be a Brigadier in no time at all. That was good enough for me, so I joined the British Army in September 1985. I was 16 years old: let's just say that it seemed like a good idea at the time.

To say that military life came as something of a culture shock to me would be an understatement on a par with Hitler's 1945 bunker admission to Goebbels that he 'might have been a bit of a control freak'. But, like hundreds of thousands of soldiers before and after me, I eventually got used to the sheer lunacy of the Army, to the point where I almost forgot what normality was.

I spent two years at the Army Apprentice College in Harrogate learning my trade as a Radio Telegraphist in the Royal Corps of Signals. Towards the end of my training, I volunteered for service with the prestigious 5 Airborne Brigade. To become a fully-fledged member of this unit, I had to negotiate the dual hurdles of the fearsome 'P Company' and the Basic Parachute Course at Brize Norton. Over the next couple of years, my attempts to achieve the physical and mental levels required to get through P Company met with unqualified failure. Regularly at the back of runs, and a frequent passenger in the Jack Wagon, it seemed that only a complete mind and body transplant would see me succeed.

I was promoted to lance corporal shortly before I was due to embark on another futile attempt on the course. Then chance intervened in my life again, and I found myself being earmarked as a hasty replacement on a tour of duty in Belize.

I case you're like I was at the time, and you haven't got the foggiest idea where Belize is, it's a little country of around 300,000 people stuck just below Mexico on the land bridge linking North and South America. It's on the east coast, facing out into the Atlantic, with the Cayman Islands, Jamaica and then Cuba some 400 or 500 miles distant. It shares a border with Guatemala to the south and west, and below that you've got your countries commonly associated with tinpot dictators and bad Steven Seagal films – like El Salvador, Nicaragua, Honduras and so on. Back in the 1800s, we'd owned Belize – it used to be called British Honduras – but it had been given independence in 1981. Unfortunately, the Guatemalans reckoned it belonged to them, so 1,500 British squaddies were permanently based there to hone their jungle-fighting, rum-drinking and prozzie-shagging drills, just in case things ever turned nasty.

I was posted there in September 1990. We flew out of RAF Brize Norton on a ragged old RAF VC10 which attempted to shake itself to pieces as it thundered down the runway. After refuelling in Washington, we landed in country at around three o'clock in the afternoon, local time. Apart from its beautiful women and that unusual penchant for military dictatorships, central America is perhaps best-known for its humid, cloying fucking heat, and although the sun wasn't high in the sky, it must have been in the early 80s as we walked down the steps from the plane. Before I'd even touched Belizean soil, dinner-plate sized sweat patches were already forming under my arms.

A four-tonner was waiting for us, and once we'd got all our bags we clambered aboard for our journeys to the various parts of the island where we'd be based.

The squadron manned three Rear Link Detachments (RLDs) whose job was to maintain VHF and HF radio links from the smaller, satellite camps back to the main base and then on to the rest of the world. This enabled us to keep headquarters up to date with jungle patrol reports and make any logistical requests.

There were two Signals personnel at each RLD. Myself and Sig Derek 'The Dalek' Dale were to take care of Holdfast Camp, located a couple of miles down the road from the main western town of San Ignacio, not far from the Guatemalan border.

Corporal Mark Smith – the highest in rank, and therefore responsible for our lack of welfare – was to be located with Sig Rich Keogh at Rideau Camp, a mind-and-arse-numbing 14-hour journey south.

Lance Corporal Herbie Naysmith and his mate, Sig Kev Laithwaite, were going to Salamanca camp, which was even further south than Rideau.

We didn't know it then, but myself and The Dalek had got by far the best of the bunch.

We dropped the other four lads off at Airport Camp (APC), the staging post for their trip south, and lobbed their kit out after them. We said our goodbyes in the traditional squaddie manner of a smattering of swearwords accompanied by various offensive hand signals, and trundled off into the humid afternoon on our journey to Holdfast. There were only the two of us now, with the whole of the back of the four-tonner to ourselves, and we sat near the tailgate and took in the scenery. This was my first trip out of England and I was bowled over by the sights, sounds and smells of the place. We rumbled along miles of red mud roads, through thick jungle and patches of farmland, little towns and villages full of rickety houses or brightly-painted wooden shacks, little kids running everywhere with big grins on their faces. Fuck me, it was like the movies, or something: finally the Army was meeting its part of the 'See the world' contract.

I turned round to say something profound to Derek, but he had a thumb and forefinger shoved up his right nostril. He removed a clump of nasal hairs and impacted snot with a theatrical yank and examined it closely. I'd met a few lads with dirty habits – some would pick their noses, others would pick their noses and eat the proceeds, still others were scab-munchers, nail-biters or toe-jam flickers – but only Derek had the lot, and all the lads loved him for it. He'd only been posted in the year before, but had quickly become a popular figure of fun; the 'Dalek' nickname, awarded for the staccato, monotone Doncaster accent in which he delivered his pronouncements, had followed him from the Apprentice College. But all that aside, he was a perfectly competent tradesman, and would, I felt sure, give me no problems.

The distance from APC to Holdfast was about 70 miles, and we arrived at about 5.30pm, just in time for tea.

We were met by the two lads from 216 who we were to replace. Andy Roundtree and Jase Geaney had been in Holdfast for six months and it showed: both were mahogany in colour and wore nothing but shorts and flip-flops.

'Alright lads, welcome to paradise,' said Andy, as we jumped from the truck and started pulling our bags off. We all shook hands. 'Right, Eddy, Derek, this is the script. I'll show you your bedspaces and take you over to tea. It'll be getting dark in a bit, so you need to get your longs on or the mozzies will eat you. I won't bother giving you the work briefing tonight, you look ballbagged.' He was right. It had been a long haul since we'd left Brize. I could have done with a good night's sleep, but Andy wasn't finished. 'What we'll do is we'll have a few in the NAAFI, then go down to San Ignacio.'

My heart sank. The lads would be going back home to their families in seven days and they were in the mood for partying. I knew a proper Saturday night sesh lay in store.

We were shown in to a bright, cool and well-lit room. There were seven beds down each side, separated by lockers, and a few of the beds were occupied by blokes sleeping off a big tea. Three ceiling-mounted fans turned lazily. I was given the space nearest the door, and Derek dropped his bags in the pit straight across from me. Andy and Jase waited for us outside and then hurried us over to the cookhouse. Despite the exotic locale, it could have been in any UK barracks: the same, sour-faced sloppies behind hotplates full of the same scran. I can't believe anybody wants to eat jam roly poly in the middle of the jungle.

Despite promising not to talk shop until the next morning, Andy couldn't help himself. He gave us a bit of a briefing about the camp and its inhabitants while we were eating. 'It's a spot-on place,' he said. 'You're the only two Signals blokes here, so you'll get left alone. You're the only people allowed in the Commcen, so if anyone's giving you a bit of jip you can just go in and lock the door behind you.' He broke off suddenly, a look of abject horror on his face. 'Fucking hell, Derek,' he said. 'Give it a rest.'

The Dalek had just pulled his finger out of his nose and was reaping the nasal benefits of 70 dusty miles. The thing on the end of his digit looked like a green Monster Munch. For once, he thought better of it, and wiped it on the underside of the table.

Andy shuddered, and continued. 'The Glosters are the duty infantry battalion. The lads are sound, but the seniors and rodneys are dicks. Just try and keep away from them as much as you can. Aside from that, there's a battery from 29 Commando. They're a great laugh, all mad bastards. There's a troop of Engineers, nice fellas but they tend to keep themselves to themselves, and there's another troop of Blues and Royals. They're the same detail as the Glosters, watch out for anyone higher than your rank, Eddy.'

I nodded. 'Is that everyone?' I said.

'More or less. There's a handful of REME lads and there's an RAF geezer who refuels the helicopters. He's a good bloke, but he stinks of AVTUR. Most of the units have got their own little bar. They don't like lads from the bigger outfits coming in, but 'cos there's only two of you, they won't mind.'

'So there's plenty to do on camp?' I said.

'It's not too bad. They show shit films in the NAAFI bar every weekend. The usual thing to do is have a few beers in one of the bars and then head down town. San Ig's a good laugh. There's loads of restaurants and bars, and a couple of nightclubs. The Blue Angel's probably the best. We'll show you that one later. Any questions?'

Before I could say anything, Derek jumped in. 'Is there an 'ooer'ouse?'

Andy smiled. 'Oh yes, my friend. It's called Caracol Farm, just a bit down the road. It's out of bounds, but nobody really gives a fuck as long as you don't cause any trouble. The going rate is seven US dollars for a shag and 20 for the whole night. We'll go later if you want.'

I'd never been in a brothel and was as keen as any normal bloke to expand my knowledge in that direction. But Derek looked so excited I thought he was going to get his money and knob out there and then. To be fair, his unsavoury habits meant he hadn't got much action in Aldershot.

'Jesus, Davros, calm down,' said Jase, laughing.

We finished eating and headed back to the block, where Andy looked at his watch. 'Right it's half-six. Get scrubbed up, and we'll see you in the NAAFI at half-seven.'

With that, they shot off back to their own room. We did as instructed, and arrived in the bar just after Andy and Jase. There was a huge TV in the corner blaring out CNN news, and we got ourselves sat down at a table in the opposite corner. Andy remained standing. 'Right then,' he said. 'Me in the chair. You've got a choice, beer or rum?'

I'd only drunk spirits once before and the experience had taught me to keep well clear. 'Beer please, mate,' I said.

'Yeah, I'll have a beer, Andy, cheers,' said Jase.

'Fucking both,' said Derek.

'Roger, out.'

Andy headed off to the bar. He came back with the round and we started drinking; we hardly stopped for the next eight months.

* * * * *

After an hour or so in the NAAFI, we got a cab down into San Ignacio. The plan was to grab a bite to eat first, so we plotted up in a little restaurant near a bar called the Red Rooster and wolfed down huge plates of steak and chips, bought for next to nothing. This was one of the many great things about Belize – you could have the sort of night out which would cost you upwards of 80 quid in Britain for 20 or 30 US dollars.

Then we headed out into the streets. It's a bit bigger now, but back then San Ig was a town of about 10,000 people, and they all liked having a good time, all the time. The ramshackle bars lining the narrow streets were heaving with rum-soaked clubbers, and the music boomed and echoed through the hot night air. After calling in at one or two of them, we found ourselves outside a big club called The Blue Angel. We manoeuvred our way past the crowds of punters and street vendors milling about and headed inside, where I was immediately assaulted by the heat of 300 or 400 bodies bouncing around to an immense wall of bass pumping out of a monster PA system. I remember they were playing a brilliant reggae tune, a big local hit entitled, *I Wanna Wake Up Wid' Whitney Houston*.

We made our way to the bar. Beer was pretty expensive but a bottle of rum and a couple of cans of Coke cost peanuts, and I quickly moved away from my 'no spirits' policy. Bearing in mind I hadn't slept since leaving Oxfordshire 24 hours earlier, I got drunk pretty quickly. For a while, I just stood and gawped at the scene around me. The clientele was representative of Belizean cultural diversity – with a history of slave-trading and colonisation by the Spanish and British, the country is a real melting pot of Mayans, Creoles, Caucasians, Hispanics and all possible combinations of the above. Everyone was very friendly and you couldn't help but pick up on the vibes generated by the clubbers.

Eventually, I drummed up enough Dutch courage to introduce my clumsy, fused-joint dancing into the melee. I have vivid memories of staggering about to the other big hit of the period, *Me Donkey Want Water*, another great track done in the style peculiar to Belize known as 'punta-rock'. To my young Mancunian ears, this sounded like a combination of ska and reggae, though its roots came from the music of Carib Indians and African slaves. *Me Donkey* was the first of a trilogy of songs which all topped the Belizean charts and dealt with the ongoing fortunes of the aforementioned animal; in the second, *Work De Donkey*, the donkey had obviously received the required water, and was now expected to pay for it. In the concluding hit, the donkey had outlived its usefulness and was about to be traded in for a newer model. Its title, *Shoot De Donkey*, made clear that he had featured in his last punta-rock track.

Somewhat bizarrely, the other tune that was rocking Belize at the time was the unbearable *Sacrifice* by Elton John. Going to that from punta-rock was like changing gears from fifth to reverse, but it was played at least three times and each time it came on I found myself weaving my way back to the bar to rejoin Andy, Jase and Derek. They were occupying a corner that gave them a good view of the entire joint. I recall Andy grinning and nodding in Derek's direction. 'Fuck me, Eddy,' he shouted. 'You're going to have a right laugh with that dirty cunt.'

'What's he done now?'

'He's not shut up about going down The Farm since we got here.'

I looked over his shoulder. The Dalek was using rhythmic pelvic movements to demonstrate his shagging technique to Jase.

'I wouldn't fucking mind,' said Andy, 'but he could have copped off with a girl earlier on, and it wouldn't have cost him a penny.'

'Who was that, then?'

'One of the Yank Peace Corps birds. She was chatting him up. I was quite impressed. They're never normally interested in us lot.'

'What happened?'

'She was mid-sentence, when the grotty fucker stuck a finger over his right nostril and blew a big oyster out of the left. It landed on her shoe.'

I grinned. 'That's Derek.'

'Lucky for him the prozzies aren't that choosy.'

* * * * *

Half an hour later, half-deaf from the sound system and with several gallons of rum and coke sloshing around our insides, we jumped into a cab. It was an enormous white 1963 Chevrolet Impala, with enough room for three passengers on the front seat. The driver was a powerfully-built black guy, with shoulder-length dreads.

'Alright, James?' said Andy. 'These are the two new guys that are replacing me and Jase. This is Eddy, and that's Derek. We thought we'd take a trip down The Farm.'

'Andy, Andy, Andy… you are one *baaaad* maan,' said James, laughing and shaking his head. He looked in the rear-view mirror and smiled. 'Hello, fellas. You'll like The Farm. Mimi will look after you.'

He and the two old hands started laughing conspiratorially as the car pulled out into the road and set off. It was about a 20 minute drive from town, and I remember it so vividly it could have happened yesterday. The windows were down, allowing the relative cool of the humid early hours to blow in, and James was playing a mellow reggae tape and nattering away. There was lots of laughter and good-natured ribbing. As we turned down the long driveway to our destination, Derek started tidying himself up, as if he was going on a date. James noticed in the mirror and started laughing. 'Don't worry 'bout your appearance, my good man,' he said. 'If he had seven bucks, them girls would fuck a scarecrow.'

Caught in the act, Derek stopped what he was doing and sat there nervously. As we pulled up, three or four more taxis were disgorging military personnel in various states of disrepair. Andy squared James away with a couple of Belizean dollars and we jumped out. He gave a friendly wave and drove away, and then I met my very first prostitute. She was a meeter-and-greeter, and she was quite beautiful. 'Welcome,' she said, with a smile.

I managed to keep enough cool to say, 'Thank you,' and we all walked in.

Behind me I could hear Derek pumping Andy for information. 'So, can we shag *any* of 'em Andy? Even 'er at the door?'

'Jesus, Derek,' Andy was saying. 'Take it easy. We'll go in and have a drink and a game of pool first. It's only twelve o'clock. The place is open 'til the last man leaves. We'll be here until at least four.'

I waited so Andy could take the lead, and we followed him inside. It was a decent-sized place, with enough space to have 15 or 20 tables dotted around the main room. Off to the right there was a smaller area, with a bit more seating and a pool table. The lighting throughout was just right – low but not *too* low. There were about 30 lads sprinkled around, drinking beer from the bottle or rum from a glass. The majority of the punters were soldiers but there were a handful of local boys as well.

Andy parked his arse at an empty table near the bar and we all followed suit. One of the girls came over, ostensibly to take our drinks order. She was wearing a black mini skirt, a red bra and a broad smile, and would have been in her early 20s – she looked a bit like Gloria Estefan.

'*Ola*, Andy!' she said, in a lovely Latino accent. 'Can I get you and your friends a drink?'

'Yeah, cheers Mariana. Beers all round?' We performed a synchronised nod. '*Quatro cerveza, por favor.*'

She wiggled off to fetch the drinks, with myself and Derek taking the opportunity to ogle her backside as she went.

The Dalek turned back eagerly. 'Was that Mariana a prozzie, lads?'

'No, Derek,' replied Jase. 'She's the MP for Harrogate.'

'Eh?'

'We'd better get him in quick,' said Jase, 'or he's going to ruin his trousers.'

Mariana returned with the drinks. 'Hey, Mariana,' he said. 'The new guy's taken a shine to you.'

She laughed as she put the bottles of beer on the table, then turned to Derek with a smile. 'Would you like to fuck me, new guy?' she said.

'Er,' said The Dalek, his eyes on stalks. 'Er… I think so.'

Jase snorted and spat out his first mouthful of beer, but Mariana ignored him and took Derek's hand and placed it on to her right breast. 'What about now?'

His voice moved straight from low-pitch Yorkshire to cartoon-chipmunk. 'Yes,' he said, his Adam's Apple bobbing up and down.

'Good,' she replied. She turned to face the rest of us. 'You enjoy your drinks, while I enjoy your friend.'

13

Derek stood up and allowed Mariana to lead him away. His nerve had taken a severe pasting, and he looked like a naughty schoolboy getting taken to see the headmaster. They went past the pool table and disappeared through a purple curtain into the nether regions of the bar.

Andy winked at Jase and then rounded on me. 'What about you then, Eddy?'

'Erm, I think I'll have a few more beers first.'

'Nervous?' said Andy.

'Are they all as...' I searched for the word. 'Are they all as *confident* as Mariana?'

'More or less. Best thing is get your first one out of the way. You'll be back all the time, then. I'll have a word with Mimi for you.' He shouted over to a woman playing pool. 'Mimi!'

I got an attack of nerves. 'Leave it, Andy,' I said.

'You're too late, mate,' he chortled. 'She's on her way over.'

I watched her sashay the 15 feet to our table. She was maybe three or four years older than Mariana, but a little taller, much curvier and even prettier. You could tell she was going to be a bit of a porker in the next couple of years, but right then she was just stunning. She sat down next to me and smiled.

'Hello, Andrew, Jason. And who is your friend?'

'Mimi, meet Eddy. He's a bit nervous. And Eddy, meet Mimi. She's the sexiest woman in Belize.'

'Andy, you're too kind.' She turned to me. 'Well, Eddy, how do you like Belize?'

Conscious of Derek's unsuccessful attempts to play things cool, I tried extra hard. 'It's great. Do you live here?'

The words were hardly out of my mouth before I was groaning internally. *Do you fucking live here*? That is fucking *rubbish*, Eddy.

She ignored my embarrassment.

'I'm from Guatemala originally. I'm just here for a couple of years to make my fortune.' She beamed, exposing a set of perfect white teeth. 'If you come with me, Eddy, I can help you to like Belize even more.'

She stood and started heading towards the curtain, beckoning me to follow.

I took a big gulp of my beer and got out of my chair. Andy and Jase cackled as I stumbled after her. 'Marks out of ten, give 'er one,' shouted Jase, and both fell about laughing at their comic originality.

As we approached the curtain, Mariana emerged. She looked completely unflustered, and was smoking a post-coital cigarette. Derek was a few paces behind her. In contrast, he had a wild stare in his eyes and looked like he'd done a couple of laps of a steeplechase. His eyes locked on mine as he walked past, but all he could say was, 'That were fucking great.'

He'd only been in the room for five minutes, a fact not lost on the occupants of all the other tables. Hoots of derision peppered him from all directions, but he seemed oblivious. I watched him sink heavily into his chair and take a long pull on his beer as Andy and Jase started debriefing him. As I turned back, Mimi was disappearing through the curtain. I took a deep breath and followed.

Beyond was a dimly-lit corridor with a row of doors on each side. Mimi had gone into the first room on the left and I went in after her. The room was sparsely furnished, unsurprisingly – just a single bed and a small vanity unit. Subdued lighting gave the place a sultry ambience, though this was marred slightly by the strong smell of disinfectant, the prostitute's friend. Mimi sat on the bed and patted the sheet next to her. I sat down stiffly, facing straight forward, hands on my knees, like I was posing for the front row of the squadron photograph. I was completely at Mimi's mercy, and she knew it.

'Stand up, Eddy,' she said. I did as I was told. In one quick movement, she moved off the bed and knelt directly in front of me. With the speed of a pickpocket, she undid my belt and jeans and quickly dropped them to my knees, closely followed by my Johnny Fartpants boxer shorts. My penis had never been so erect: it felt like it was about to burst. As she moved her mouth forwards, I adopted the standard blow-job recipient stance of clenched fists on hips – kind of like Superman surveying Metropolis from a hill above the city – and picked a spot on the far wall, about a foot below the ceiling, trying to think of something to stave off the inevitable. All I could dredge from my memory was a drill session in Harrogate. I clenched my eyes shut and started trying to imagine the grizzled instructor barking, 'BY THE LEFT, QUICK *BARCH*.'

Just as I thought the drill thing might help me out, I felt a peculiar sensation around my genital area. I made the fatal mistake of looking down. For a second I couldn't suss it out, but then realised that Mimi had my entire wedding tackle in her mouth and was subjecting my dick and both balls to what felt like the spin cycle of a washing machine. The only way it could have been any more mind-blowing was if she had started humming *Me Donkey Want Water* at the same time, but that was all academic as about two seconds later she brought me to climax with a roar of 'Bloooodddddy *hell*!' (from me, not her).

After my eyes had stopped spinning round in my skull, I collapsed on the bed, panting heavily. After a bit of post-nosh admin, Mimi lit a cigarette. 'You can leave the seven dollars on the table when you're ready,' she said.

'No problem.'

My trousers were still round my ankles, so I leaned down and fished around for the fee. As I started tidying myself up, something suddenly occurred to me. I looked at my watch. Christ, I'd only been in there for about two-and-a-half minutes. The blokes out there would make mincemeat of me – even Derek.

'Er, Mimi,' I said. 'I couldn't ask a big favour, could I?'

'What is it?'

'Do you mind if I hang around here for a few minutes?' I flicked my head back in the direction of the main room. 'Do you know what I mean?'

She laughed. 'I can make you a cup of coffee for a dollar?' She whacked a small kettle on and made brews for us both. She asked me a few questions about England, and I made a couple of ham-fisted attempts at small talk, the best of which was, 'So what's it like being a prostitute, then?' Mimi must have endured thousands of conversations with knobbers like me whilst maintaining a façade of rapt interest and, by the time the coffee was finished, I'd managed to spin out a more than passable 15 minutes. We went back through the curtain. As she headed back to her unfinished game of pool, I made my way to my compadres. They all saw me coming, and I was given a cheer to celebrate my fraudulent longevity. It put a bit of a spring in my step, and I adopted a *Saturday Night Fever* swagger until I got to the table.

'Not fucking bad, Eddy,' said Andy. 'Quarter of an hour with Mimi is good going.'

'Well, you know, bit drunk an' all that,' I replied, furtively.

'Still, mate, you did better than Johnny Two Squirts here.'

Derek still looked wiped out, but he had enough energy to tell Andy to fuck off.

Jase leaned over conspiratorially. 'I'll tell you what, though, the first night I went in with her she ripped me to bits. I didn't last much longer than Derek.'

'Really?' I asked.

He started laughing loudly. 'Yes. She made me a cuppa so I didn't have to come back out too quick.'

We all joined in the laughter, though mine was identifiably more hollow.

It was now 12.30am, and we carried on drinking and taking the piss out of each other for the next hour or so before the combination of long flights, strong rum and professional sex took its toll on me and I started to hear my bed calling. Fortunately, the other three had had a good skinful and wanted to get off as well. It was about two o'clock when our taxi pulled up outside and beeped. We dragged ourselves away from a half-full beer, and made for the exit. Some of the girls were hanging around the pool table, including Mariana and Mimi. Mariana called over to us, winking. 'See you soon, Derek… for a little longer next time maybe?'

After the laughing died down, I felt confident enough to shout goodbye to Mimi. 'See you next time, Mimi,' I called, nonchalantly.

'I can't wait, Eddy,' she cooed. 'And I'll have the kettle on.'

EDDY NUGENT AND THE FLIP-FLOP BLOW-OUT

NEXT DAY BEING Sunday, I had a lie-in until about 11am. Eventually, I sat up and spent a few seconds waiting for my hangover to kick in.

Remarkably… nothing. I felt fine. Pleased at this unexpected bonus, I got out of my clothes and stuck my Belize uniform on – flip-flops, shorts and a clean t-shirt would be my off-duty clobber for the next eight months. Across from me, Derek was also stirring, though he seemed a bit more the worse for wear.

The plan for the day was to meet Andy and Jase over at the HQ, so we could go through the Rear Link Det and do a handover of all the gear. As The Dalek pulled himself together, I wandered over to the ablutions and toilets, where I settled into a trap and perused the graffiti. Two-line jokes and rudimentary drawings of female genitalia formed the bulk of the work, with the gags mainly coming at the Glosters' expense. They were all geared towards the usual suggestion that the Infantry are brainless. It's not true, of course, but it does provide endless wind-up opportunities. I remember a couple of the better ones:

What do you call a section of Glosters in a tank? Tinned mixed veg.
And
Why don't the Glosters get NAAFI breaks? Cos it takes too long to re-train them.

After I'd got ready, I waited for Derek and we both wandered over to the HQ building. The weather was absolutely beautiful – sunny and baking hot, with not a wisp of cloud in sight. Andy and Jase took us through our duties. We were required to send by HF RATT any signals that authorised personnel gave to us.

19

They would be transmitted back to APC, and forwarded on to their destinations from there. We could expect two or three a day, including a Sitrep which was sent at 1800hrs every day. Derek and I would work day on, day off, and the 'day on' sounded like about two hours' work. Concerned I might be missing something, I put this to Andy.

'You've got it, mate,' he said. 'It's a complete doddle. I've spent the last few months grafting for two hours every other day.'

For the first time in my young military career, the '*All this and pay as well*' man from the old recruitment posters swam into my mind's eye without a trace of irony.

Our little Commcen was about the size of a large toilet, but it had air-con to keep all the radios cool and, best of all, we were the only ones allowed in there, due to the presence of cryptographic material. I scanned the kit, which was the same as RATT Delta, only not vehicle-mounted.

'Where are the batteries, Andy?' I said.

'Thought you might ask that,' he frowned. 'Follow me.'

We went outside and walked along the side of the building to a little brick shed with a small red door fastened with a large padlock.

'They're in there,' said Andy. 'But we haven't touched them since day one. It's fucking horrible. Some wise old owl thought that it'd be a great idea to stick them in a four-by-two-foot pitch dark cubby-hole, but it's like something out of *Scooby Doo*. I've only opened it up once to see if they needed topping up, and there were loads of little yellow eyes staring back at me. Fuck knows what they were... spiders, rats and snakes, the lot. I had the padlock back on two seconds later. Fancy a look?'

I shrank back, but Derek wasn't as fazed. 'Go on, get the fucker opened,' he said.

'If you want it opening, do it your fucking self,' said Jase, tossing over the key.

Without a hint of trepidation, Derek walked forward and started fiddling with the lock. After a moment or two, it snapped open and he undid the hasp and pulled the door ajar. The outside light poured in and it took my eyes a second or two to adjust to the interior. You could see the batteries, but they were under a mass of little squirming bodies. I saw a couple of snakes, and an enormous tarantula sat across one of the front lugs, and that was enough for me. Derek was already shutting the door, his face a shade or two paler than before. 'Right,' he said. 'That's battery maintenance done for the next eight months.'

With the Commcen inspection complete, they took us on a little tour of the camp. It had all the usual barracks buildings and a 20-metre outdoor swimming pool where there were a couple of lads lounging around sunbathing and listening to a Proclaimers tape. The pool looked great and I planned on spending quite a bit of time round it, though not before the Proclaimers had fucked off.

The final stop was the NAAFI. We'd only spent half an hour in there the previous night and I hadn't really looked around. It was quite packed, with a stack of lads necking soft drinks and eating toasted egg banjoes.

'Scoff's pretty good,' said Andy. 'Rancid makes a mean banjo.'

'Who's Rancid?' said Derek.

'Rancid Flip-flop,' said Andy, nodding towards the cash till, where a tall, middle-aged gentleman was scowling at one of the Engineers who was trying to pay for his lunch with a small mountain of five cent pieces. When Andy looked back, he could see that we were waiting for an explanation. 'His feet are honking,' he said. 'His toenails are like extra large tortilla chips... one of the 29 Commando lads reckons he can smell 'em from across the road. I don't think anyone even knows his real name. It's just Rancid, or 'Mr Flip-flop' till you get to know him.'

Derek took himself off to get a round of Sprites in, and we watched a bit of telly while we waited for him. A few moments later, raised voices at the bar caused us to turn round. Mr Flip-flop was verbally terrorising The Dalek in a strong Mexican accent.

'Honest, Rancid, it was a fucking twenty.'

'Fuck off, you fucking soldier bastard. It was a ten, and my name is not fucking Ranceed.'

'Alright, alright, fucking calm down, Rancid. My mistake. Fuck's sake.'

'I don't know you, and you try to cheat me and call me *Ranceed*. Fuck *you*, you bastard.'

Derek picked up his four bottles of Sprite and scrabbled for his change. 'Jesus, Rancid,' he said. 'It was a *ten*, then. Sorry. They all look the same to me.'

His placatory efforts only ratcheted up the anger levels to near-nuclear status. 'My name is *not* fucking *Ranceed*,' screamed Rancid, slamming the till violently shut and storming in to the back room to sulk.

Derek bimbled over to us put the drinks on the table, and looked at us with a hurt expression. 'Touchy bastard, in't he?'

'Yeah, Derek,' replied Jase. 'Some people, eh?'

Over the Sprites, Andy explained the various workings of the camp. For the purposes of discipline, we would come under the authority of the Glosters. All our admin would be taken care of by 633 Signal Troop in APC, our parent unit. There was PT to do on Tuesday and Friday mornings, but if we'd had a big night beforehand we could always play our joker and lock ourselves in the Commcen whilst conducting an imaginary 'Crypto-check'.

It sounded too good to be true: this was actually going to be a real swan.

We quickly fell into our routine. By the time Andy and Jase hopped on the transport back to APC the following Friday, myself and Derek were on top of all our duties. On my days off, I'd either lounge around the pool all day or shoot off into San Ig. We tried to stay off the beer on the weekday nights, usually limiting ourselves to a couple of bottles in the NAAFI, but we got to know a few of the lads from the other units and, being the Billy-no-mates of the camp, generally got invited to any piss-ups.

The most fun was had in the 29 Commando bar. They were all absolute head-the-balls. Despite being as fit as fiddles, and spending half their lives in the pool or on the multi-gym, they got drunk most nights and had a penchant for naked bar frolics; if you were a guest, you were expected to disrobe accordingly and any hesitation would result in four or five of the fuckers helping you out of your clothing.

It was on my way back from one of their evenings that I experienced the horrible trauma of the drunken flip-flop blow-out. Most of the guys on camp had thought to bring decent sandals with them, but I was making do with the cheapest flip-flops on sale from the Aldershot NAAFI. They'd only cost 45p, and they weren't even worth that. On my way back from the said do, I broke into a bit of a drunken jog down the main road past the ablutions, the idea being to get back to my scratcher that bit quicker and avoid the powerful stench wafting out of the windows. The blow-out occurred when the front of my right flip-flop caught on the road. As the paper-thin foam curled under itself it took my toes with it, and I dragged them along the ground under my full weight for the two seconds it took me to stop. The pain was phenomenal – it felt like someone had taken an industrial sander to my toe-knuckles, and I shrieked like an eight-year-old girl. Two Glosters coming out of the NAAFI looked at me rolling round in agony, and quickly assessed the situation, nodding wisely to each other like two aerodynamics experts.

'Flip-flop blow-out,' said one to the other, before they walked off chuckling, without any offer of assistance.

I hobbled back to my room and went to bed, feeling very sorry for myself. I was even sorrier the next morning when I awoke to find my sheet stuck to my foot by dried blood. After minutes of fruitless probing, and long deliberation with Derek, we agreed that the best course of action was for him to rip it off as quick as he could, in the style of a magician leaving all the cups and plates standing on a table. He could hardly wait. I pleaded with him to be gentle with me. 'Stay still, you shitbag,' he shouted, before ripping the sheet away with a flourish. It hurt even more than the original blow-out, and I bought a pair of sandals from Rancid's small selection as fast as I could hobble there.

* * * * *

Sadly, no swan lasts forever, and a signal came in from 633 which burst our happy little bubble. They needed a temporary replacement after one of the lads from the troop had been posted out at short notice. Apparently, he'd gone nuts in the bar one night and had run round smashing all the windows with a golf club. Although this seemed like fairly standard behaviour to the rest of the blokes, the Army brass were sufficiently worried about him to have him sent back to UK to be assessed at Woolwich, the forces' booze clinic. I found out later that he was a well-known turps-nudger. He'd had a few discipline problems at his working unit, so his Troop OC had decided that the perfect course of treatment involved sending him to Belize for six months. Given that the main pastimes in the country were fucking about and drinking rum, this was like sending an arsonist to work at Bryant and May. Perhaps the daft rodney thought that if his charge were supplied with unlimited amounts of alcohol he'd get bored with it, like when your dad made you smoke a load of cigars after catching you tabbing. But if that were the case, his over-exposure therapy had backfired monstrously, resulting in the soldier being bundled out of the country unceremoniously and the Troop OC failing his Open University Psychology degree.

I was going down to stand in at APC, leaving Derek to look after Holdfast on his own for a while. All things are relative, and an outraged Derek believed himself to be the victim of a huge miscarriage of justice. At a stroke, his working week had been increased from seven to fourteen hours, and he complained bitterly until the moment I got on the transport to take me back down the highway to Belize City.

The duty clutch was a talkative kind of guy, and he gave me a blow-by-blow account – quite literally – of his activities at The Farm. He was just in the middle of a tale about the time an invasion of jungle toads had put him off his stroke when a sign for Mile 33 came into view and we pulled over. Mile 33 was the home of JB's, a roadside café in the middle of nowhere along the Western Highway. It was quite nice inside with an open bar/eating area and walls adorned with plaques from almost every unit that had served in Belize. To top it all off, they did a great cheeseburger which, along with chips covered in the local 'Melinda's Hot Pepper Sauce', really hit the spot. Wash this lot down with a freezing cold stim and you would be more than ready for the final half of the journey to APC.

Back on the road, we flashed through the ramshackle, galvanised metal suburbs of BC and were soon approaching what looked like a large roundabout with an open centre that you could drive straight across. There were no road markings, let alone any signposts, and the traffic that was negotiating the roundabout had no discipline. It began to look suspiciously like it was every man for himself. I looked at the driver. 'Fucking hell,' I said. 'This is a bit disorganised. I bet it takes ages to get across, doesn't it?'

At which point he turned to me, wild-eyed, and screamed, 'Fuck that shit! This here's Kamikaze Junction, baby!'

He then looked ahead, floored the accelerator and closed his eyes. Just as we crossed the point of no return, he called out the horn noise from the *Dukes of Hazzard*'s 'General Lee' and performed an ear-splitting rebel yell. 'Dada da da dada dada da da da da... YEEEEEEEEEEEEEEHHHHHHHHHHHHHAAAAAAAAAA!'

We rocketed across the junction, scattering people, cars and bikes in all directions. I pulled my feet up onto the seat whilst grabbing hold of anything I could get my hands on, all the time saying *Jesus-fucking-H-fucking-Christ-Jesus-fucking-H-fucking-Christ...* Somehow, we made it to the other side and the strangest thing was that all the other drivers, even the ones who'd had to swerve or brake violently, just carried on as if this was the norm.

The driver eventually opened his eyes and turned to me with a big cheesy grin and said. 'Not bad, eh?'

I just called him a fucking knobber, and we laughed a nervous laugh.

We arrived at Airport Camp without further incident; once through the gates, we turned left and drove for about 400 metres before parking up next to a bar called 'The Blackbird Club' and a swimming pool surrounded by sunburnt, tattooed blokes in dodgy trunks. I said my farewells to the mad driver, and he pointed me towards the 633 offices before executing a high-revving three-point turn to head back the way we had come. In one last valiant effort to cement his reputation as a crazed maniac, he sped off as fast as he could and gave a thumbs-up out of his window. He'd only got about 100 metres up the road when a Warrant Officer pounced out from behind a bush and waved his pace stick at the speeding vehicle. The driver slammed on the anchors and, even as the blue tyre smoke billowed out from the locked wheels, I could hear the WO start to scream abuse at him.

Still smiling, I picked up my baggage and headed to the troop office.

* * * * *

The OC wasn't around, so the troop staff sergeant gave me the welcome speech and the mandatory laying down of the law. He was very old and spoke with a gravelled, northern voice. 'Right, Corporal Nugent, I'm Staff Stone. It's nice and relaxed here, but PT is Tuesdays and Thursdays at 05:00 hours so don't get too pissed the night before. Also, try to stay on top of your malaria tablets. Your weekends should be free most of the time, but again try to stay out of the shit.' He went on for some time covering the admin side of troop life, before wrapping his speech up. 'Finally, don't forget that some blokes bring their wives over here for R&R. So when you do go down to the pool, just remember the last thing they want to see is some fucker climbing out of the water in his 10-year-old Speedos with his Black Forest Gateau spilling out all over the fucking place. Do you get my drift?'

'Sensible swimwear, Staff?'

'Egg-fucking-zactly!'

With his points made, Staff Stone summoned in the troop clerk who showed me to my block. It was one of three on the edge of a cricket pitch, all joined by a concrete walkway covered with corrugated iron that offered protection from the elements during the monsoon season but amplified rain to the level of machine gun fire and kept you awake all night.

In between the blocks was a communal ablutions with a dhobi room. There were rumours that if you left 20 bucks on your bedside locker and pretended to be asleep, one of the cleaners would nosh you off but one look at the toothless monster doing the cleaning soon drove any such thoughts from my mind.

The laundry employed the age-old method of thrashing clothing off an immovable object until the cloth became so ravaged that the stain disappeared: I know of at least one officer who threatened to sack a cleaner if she didn't put his shirts inside a tom's to reduce the amount of damage caused to his clothes while braying them against the rocks. Even that kind of abuse didn't always work, and one of the guys had complained about the washer woman not removing a stain from the leg of his jeans. Her reaction had been to take the garment away for a few minutes and then return, with the dirty leg cut off. The bloke had to convert them to a pair of shorts.

The clerk showed me to my pit space, and took me to the radio sergeant, past the NAAFI and the cookhouse. The clerk pointed the buildings out to me as we approached them. Just as he identified the kitchens, the biggest rat I have ever seen obligingly hopped out from a doorway and disappeared into the swill bins. 'Fuck me,' I said. 'Did you see the size of that fucker?'

'What, the rat?'

'Well, it was either a rat or an Irish wolfhound.'

'Yeah, that's Bubonic Trev. He's a permanent fixture around the kitchens.'

I made a mental note to stay on Trev's good side.

Our walk took us over a small bridge and past a line of five half-moon Nissen Huts. The centre hut was The Sunspot Club, the bar for 633 and my spiritual home for the next few months – along with Raoul's Rose Garden (of which, more later).

Past the huts, we took a dirt road off to the right that led into a swamp and, eventually, the transmitter site and the radio stores. The transmitter site consisted of a huge antenna field and a building containing powerful radios that carried all of the high-level traffic to the rest of the world. Attached to this building were the radio stores, where we found the sergeant to whom I had to report. The clerk introduced us and left.

The sergeant was called Jim Dale and he was a very relaxed individual. He told me that he would try to rotate me between working in the camp radio room, helping him in the stores and doing the occasional stint up at the Cooma Cairn Rebro. I was to start the next day in the force HQ radio room, but first Jim squared me away with the low down on APC life. He gave me a once-over in the stores where, from what I could gather, work involved doing fuck all except bumming around all day drinking stims, eating sausage sandwiches and watching pornographic videos with the blokes who maintained the transmitters.

After an hour or so of lounging about, I picked up my bedding and unpacked my kit into my new pit space. Then I headed to the cookhouse and joined the queue for scoff, with a watchful eye out for Bubonic Trev.

By the time I got back to the block, the guys who worked the day shift in the Commcen had knocked off and the accommodation was buzzing with blokes squaring their shit away for a night on the lash. I said hello to some of my new roommates, then got a shower.

Two of the guys, Tony Jenkins and Paul Whittaker, were decent enough blokes and had waited for me so as to make sure I got down to the Sunspot alright, and the three of us walked down there, sweating in the dying heat of the day and gassing about Holdfast, how long I'd been in theatre and all the usual. Somewhere in the distance, a swingfog was blaring away, fighting a losing battle against mozzies and all the other horrible beasties that would bite us to death in the night.

Opening the door to the Sunspot was like walking into the boiler room of the *Bismarck* – my senses were overwhelmed by a wall of heat and noise from the 30 or so blokes packed into the small space, crammed around the dart board and playing Mickey Mouse, chatting and laughing in groups or lounging by the bar. I followed Tony and Paul up to the bar and ordered three cans of Charlie. Carlsberg was the preferred brew in Belize; when that ran out we'd drink Miller, and – worst case scenario – if the Miller went dry we'd move on to

Schlitz, which sounds like 'shits' for a reason. There was one thing worse than Schlitz, a local beer called Belikin – or Bellyache. It was fucking gipping stuff, brewed from the local swamp water in which Bubonic Trev and his pals would regularly wazz.

Halfway along the hut was a door leading outside to an atap, a kind of palm frond lean-to, where there were even more blokes drinking. The atap was cooler and less confined than the bar, but the mozzies and sandflies that frequented it were like particularly determined kamikaze pilots. Every so often, one of drinkers would slap themselves and shout, 'You fucking bastard!' before peering at the splash of blood left by the dead insect. Despite the trauma of the blood suckers, we headed for the atap. I noticed a throne made from sandbags to one side. 'What's that all about, Paul?' I asked.

'Gazomes, mate.'

'What's a gazome, then?'

'It's a piss up for when someone goes home. Every Friday night before people fly out on the Wednesday, we have a gazome. They sit on the throne wearing a ceremonial sombrero, and we tell stories about all the nobbish things they've done and lob cans at the poor fuckers. If anyone's been a real dick the odd full one goes in for good measure. It's a good crack, Eddy, and we also have some other weekly awards. But you'll see those later, mate.'

As the night progressed, we got steadily drunker and drunker. I'm sure you get pissed quicker in the Tropics – probably because you're dehydrated through sweating, not to mention very thirsty and prone to drinking more. Also, you have less blood to dilute the booze, because all the shit bag mosquitoes have drained you dry.

At half past ten that night, Paul was in the middle of an extremely animated anecdote that had us in stitches. I can't remember the exact details, but he was describing a game called 'Slap Cock Treacle Belly', the rules of which involved lying on your back naked, smearing jam on your stomach, then getting wood and forcing your panhandle down away from your body. You stay in this position until a fly lands on the jam, at which point you let your erection go and it comes flying up at Mach 3 to slap on your belly. If you've got it right, the inbound woody kills the fly. That's worth one point, and whoever kills the most flies by this method wins. The punchline involved a lad accidentally launching his penile attack on some strange jungle wasp, and spending the following week bedded down with a poisoned knob. As Paul delivered the final line, Tony leant against the atap wall, with his arm outstretched, and disappeared as if sucked into a time portal. With the wall being constructed merely from over-laid palm leaves, they'd parted to let him through and once he had gone they'd closed back up behind him, thus giving the appearance of him vanishing like Roger Moore in *Live And Let Die*. A minute or so later, Tony reappeared via the main door, but this time he reeked of shit and was covered in some ghastly green slime. It turned out that there was a monsoon drain on the other side of the wall. He was a good sport about the whole thing, and stayed on the piss for the rest of the night without going for a shower; to be fair, we encouraged him to stick around, because it kept the flies away from the rest of us.

EDDY NUGENT AND THE ROCKET-POLISHING RODNEY

MY FIRST SHIFT in the Force HQ radio room was working alongside another lance jack called Nick Bush, known variously as 'Kate' or by an inventive series of descriptors for the female reproductive organs. Kate was a PTI, but on this tour he did normal trade work like the rest of the guys, and he showed me the ropes – the in-house procedures for the processing and documentation of official signals and so on. He also briefed me up on the workings within the HQ. 'Most of your dealings will be with the Duty Officer, The Watchkeeper,' he said. 'There's four of them, and they spread the duty between themselves. Three of them are OK – keep themselves to themselves, only come in here when it's really necessary. But the fourth's a total rocket-polisher.'

As luck would have it, I encountered the polisher for myself that very day. He was called Captain James Peterson-Smythe, though he was universally known, behind his back, as 'Knob'. A Royal Artillery officer on detachment for four months from Germany, he hadn't earned that soubriquet because he fucked us around – discipline-wise, he was no worse than anyone else. His high twatometer rating was awarded for his habit, when bored, of wandering into the radio room and meddling with things beyond his knowledge, or talking out of his arse, or doing both at the same time.

That evening we were hit by a particularly savage tropical storm which left the radio networks in shit state. I was trying to engineer-in the links for the daily sitreps and, just in the middle of everything going tits up, Peterson-Smythe strolled through the door, put his hands on his hips, and said, 'Ah, Nugent. Do you know what I miss about Germany the most?'

I looked at the flashing red lights on the radio equipment, and listened to the wailing alarms. Then I turned to him. 'No, sir. What would that be, then?'

'Nightclubs, Nugent. NIGHTCLUBS! I am a superlative dancer you know.'

Then began one of the worst displays of dancing I have ever seen. It started with a sort of hand-clapping, arse-sticking-out twist, the kind of thing Chubby Checker might have attempted after suffering a serious head injury. From there, he morphed into a series of terrible, bolt upright robotics. All the time, he had a big, happy smile on his face and occasionally he would close his eyes, clearly imagining he was back in some boxhead disco. He finished by flicking his hair back, exhaling deeply and letting out a loud, 'Woooooooo!' I watched as he shook off his limbs like Mr Motivator warming down from a workout. I don't know what he was dancing to – the only sound in the shack was the chugging of the teleprinter, the warning beeps from the radios and the occasional roll of thunder from the storm outside.

Panting slightly, he sat down and looked over at me, expectantly. I tried to smile appreciatively, which seemed to satisfy him, and he began casting about for something to do. I was standing over the teleprinter, watching what looked like the first successful message of the night come through. Clearly driven by the mundane curiosity of a bored ape, he leaned across and said, 'What does this do?' I watched in abject horror as he unplugged the printer's power cable. The three quarters-complete message – which I had just spent the last hour trying to get in – immediately ceased printing out. I jerked upright and lost it. In a fit of rage, I smashed both fists down onto the printer and roared, 'WHAT THE FUCK? YOU FUCKING CUNT!' at the machine.

Peterson-Smythe was gazing up at me like a scared rabbit, stunned by my insane outburst. In his hand was the printer lead.

'Er, I think this may have come loose,' he stuttered.

I took it from his hand, plugged it back into the printer and got onto the engineering network. 'Hello, Hotel Three Zero,' I said, in a voice leaden with anger. 'Hello Hotel Three Zero. This is Zero. Re-transmit your last on the other means. I say again, re-transmit your last on the other means. Over.'

The bloke on the other end was just as pissed off as I was, and clearly thought I'd fucked up in some way. 'Roger that, Zero,' he said. 'Sending now. Out.' What he *meant* was, 'You fucking *wanker.*'

By now, The Watchkeeper was staring up at the ceiling. The printer leapt back into life, and the message starting coming through again as I raced between each bit of kit to make sure that they were still 'all green'. Suddenly, Peterson-Smythe piped up with renewed enthusiasm. 'Did I tell you about my car, Nugent?'

I didn't reply. All my attention was on the incoming message. He didn't allow that to stop him.

'She's a real beauty, I can tell you. Peugeot 205, GTI, 1.9...' He started making 'brumm-brumm' noises and making driving motions, complete with steering wheel, gear stick and foot pedals. He looked like an escaped mental patient, although to give him his due his timing was brilliant. 'Brrrrrrrrrrrrrrrrrrrrrrrmmmmmmmmmmmmmmmmm.' Then, a gear change. 'Brrm Brrm Brrrrrrrrrrrrrrrrrrrrrrrm.' I noted the double clutch in there. His imaginary tyres even screeched when he turned the invisible wheel. The whole sad shambles went on for several minutes, and it was painful to behold. Eventually, he snapped out of it when the final message came through and I handed it to him. 'There you go, sir. These are the patrol sitreps for the last 24 hours.'

By the grace of God, he didn't unwind the window to receive them. Instead, he just cleared his throat, stood up, and in his most formal voice said, 'Oh, ah yes. Well done, Nugent. Carry on.' With that, he disappeared.

I suppose, if you could put up with his sheer idiocy, Peterson-Smythe wasn't too bad. He rarely gripped anyone, and in fact I only suffered at his hands once. Typically, I was completely innocent. I had just taken over shift from Kate, when The Watchkeeper came striding into the radio room in his best attempt at an intimidating manner. Before I could say anything, he said in stern tones, 'Ah, Nugent! Why have you been boiling your handkerchief in my kettle?'

Fucking hell, I thought. *He's finally gone mad.* But all I said was, 'I'm sorry, sir. I don't know what you mean.'

'Well,' he said. 'When I commented to Lance Corporal Bush about the water in my tea tasting *off,* he informed me that you have been boiling your handkerchief in my kettle.'

The bastard. Kate liked to boil eggs in the kettle to make himself a snack on night shift, and his scoff-related activities had obviously tainted it. He'd been challenged and had dropped me in it with some deft quick-thinking. Still, I could see the funny side and I didn't want to get Kate in any shit. 'Er, I think there must have been some kind of misunderstanding, sir,' I said. 'I haven't even got a handkerchief.'

Peterson-Smythe eyed me suspiciously for a second or two.

'Well, er... don't let it happen again,' he said, and turned on his heel.

* * * * *

That Friday, I attended my first gazome in the Sunspot, and had my first night out in BC.

Things started off as per normal with drinks in the troop bar. Then the Troop OC called out above the hubbub, 'Right, gents. We'll get straight into it. Let's have our first nomination for Chopper Of The Week.'

This prestigious award, decided by popular vote, went to the man behind the biggest fuck-up of the previous seven days. The recipient was handed an axe made from a broom handle and a cardboard head, emblazoned with the words 'I am a Chopper', which he was required to wear slung across his back for the remainder of the evening. That night it went to one of the Commcen wallahs who had screwed up in some way, I forget how.

Then we set about voting on the second award, 'The Brown Bottle', which went to the bloke responsible for the previous week's best act of drunken aggression. The winner here was made to carry around a four-foot high inflatable bottle of Newcastle Brown, or 'Dog', and on that first Friday the honour went to a driver called Scouse Richards. Scouse had got pissed the Saturday night before, and pretty much offered out everyone in the bar, all at once. Amusingly enough, on hearing his name called out, the already inebriated Scouse became massively indignant, lurched forward and shouted, 'You what? Yous' can all fuck off, you cunts! I don't get gobby when I'm pissed! And if you've got a problem with it, you can fuckin' step outside for a chat! Alright?'

He then staggered out of the hut, bouncing off several walls on the way, shouting abuse at invisible objects and shaking his fist at everything in general.

I didn't know whose gazome it was, but I joined in the canning of the poor chap nevertheless. It all passed off pretty much as the guys had explained it would, though the departing soldier also had to drink a yard of ale. The stories about him all had a common theme, involving drunken idiocy, deranged sex pestery, or both. The tale that stuck in my mind was the one where he'd got pissed in San Ig and had staggered around town looking for a place to lay his head. He'd eventually broken into the bedding store of one of the few hotels and promptly fallen into a deep sleep on his stash of sheets and pillows. The chirping of the birds woke him up early – that and the vile stench from his 'Grand Slam'. He quickly made himself scarce, but not before finding a pen and paper from somewhere and locating within himself the common decency to leave a note on the pile of soiled linen for the hotel staff to find. 'Sorry,' it said.

After the gazome we stayed in the bar for a few more hours, and the sloppies did their normal Friday night thing of bringing down some chilli con carne and rice. Then I joined the mass exodus into town. We exited through the guardroom, with everyone grabbing a slack handful of johnnies from the tray next to the booking-out sheet in the vain hope that they might actually get some sex for free later on; if that didn't happen, the condoms could always be put in storage for a rainy day and a 'posh wank'. As we waited outside camp for the next Batty's bus, Scouse Richards dropped a load of coins and rubbers onto the deck. When he bent down to pick up his belongings, Kate nudged me with his elbow and pointed at Scouse's arse. 'Look at the state of that catcher's mitt,' he said, with a rueful shake of his head. 'He ain't gonna make it.'

Scouse heard this and promptly challenged us all to a fight, thereby ensuring he would retain the Brown Bottle at the following Friday's ceremony.

The bus eventually rolled up and we all piled on board. A mile or so out of camp, the lumbering old charabanc clattered over a rickety bridge and past a single storey building with an illuminated sign showing a peacock and a peahen having it off.

'That's Raoul's, hombre,' said Kate, in an exaggerated Mexican accent. 'Numero uno fuck shop. We'll have us a nightcap in there later on, dude.'

The lights of Raoul's faded into the distance and we were soon pulling up in the centre of Belize City. The bus stopped near a cast-iron swingbridge and about a dozen blokes from the troop took it upon themselves to inform me that it had featured in *The Dogs of War*. To reinforce their point, several of them started running down the road making machine gun noises, whilst the others started arguing about who played the best nutter, Christopher Walken or Robert De Niro. Tony Jenkins tried to draw me into the discussion on his side. 'What do you reckon, Eddy? It's gotta be Bob hasn't it?' He pulled out an imaginary pistol and tried to look all mad whilst badly reciting lines from *Taxi Driver*. 'Are you talking to me? Well, there ain't nobody else here!' He looked over his shoulder and then back to his invisible assailant. 'Are you fucking talking to me? Yeah, I got you, you shit heel!'

By the time he snapped back into the reality, we were half way down the street. 'Oi, wait for me, you fucking jack bastards,' he yelled. As he drew level, Kate was putting across the case for Walken. 'It's got to be Chris, Eddy, because let's face it, he is actually mad in real life.'

Both Kate and Tony stared at me, awaiting my verdict, as if it would bury the subject forever. I scratched my chin in a thoughtful manner for a bit. 'Well, gents,' I said. 'After much deliberation, I can say that, without a shadow of a doubt, the ultimate film nutter is…' Theatrical pause. 'Big Ken Williams.'

'Who the fuck's Big Ken Williams?'

'You know, Kenneth Williams. Off the *Carry On* films?'

They called me a cunt, and I received a few dead arms for my troubles. By the time the pain had subsided, we were walking up some steps to a bar, the real name of which I still don't know to this day – being the first port of call in town and situated on the first floor, it was always known as The Upstairs Gaddafi. It was a nice enough place, which served cold beer and played punta rock, and one of the Donkey trilogy songs was on as Kate got the beers in. We filtered out of the bar and onto a balcony that overlooked the street. Below us was the typical nightlife of Belize City: food vendors, shoe-shine boys and a constant stream of worse-for-wear soldiers in various stages of mental and physical decomposition. Not long after, in fact, The Upstairs NAAFI had to install chicken wire over the balcony after a spate of pissed squaddies taking accidental headers over the railings.

After a few, we made our way to the Hard Rock Café. I don't think it was a *bona fide* member of the famous worldwide chain, but it was certainly the best bar in BC. A good-sized place, with a big dance floor and a roof garden which was ideal for cooling off whilst waiting for your raging panhandle to subside after a sweaty dance with a local lass, it was like a bigger, newer version of the Blue Angel. From there, much of the night subsided into a blurred memory of flashing lights, punta rock and Appleton's 151% proof death rum.

Kate found me at about two in the morning, wobbed out in a chair, my clothes soaking in Belikin and sweat. It took him five minutes to get me *compos mentis* enough to stagger down the stairs and out into the street, where the warm, wet air offered no respite from the heat of the club. We were wandering back up to the swingbridge to pick up a taxi when a mouth-watering smell hit my nostrils. Booze-hungry, I followed it on auto-pilot and at the end of the aroma I found a big, brightly-dressed Afro-Caribbean woman standing before a large open fire and two steaming pots. She greeted me with a beaming smile – the kind you just have to respond to.

'Hello, love,' I said. 'What's in the pots?'

She pointed. 'Rice and pea in dat one,' she said, 'an' chicken in dis one.'

It smelt and sounded like the answer to my prayers. She lifted one of the lids for me: pure fluffy white rice, shot through with sweet, bright green peas. I started fishing in my pockets for a fistful of crumpled Belizean dollars. Then she lifted the other lid. When the steam cleared, I peered in and saw a strange, bubbling grey fluid. It didn't look like there was any chicken in there, but then something broke the surface. It was a whole bird, complete with head, feet, half of its feathers and a neck like Deirdre Barlow's. 'Er,' I said. 'You know, I'm actually not all that hungry at the moment. But thanks a lot, anyway.'

Kate had been standing on the sidelines, and he was still laughing when we got in the cab.

'Don't worry, Eddy,' he said, eventually. 'I've done exactly the same thing before myself.'

The heat and the rhythm of the old cab – and, to be honest, the fact that I'd had enough drink to kill a family of elephants – sent me off to sleep. I was awoken by the jolt of the car pulling to a stop. I got out, fumbled for some money to pay and then turned to the guardroom to head back to my scratcher. But in front of me was not the entrance to camp but the floodlit mural wall of Raoul's Rose Garden.

EDDY NUGENT AND THE ROSE GARDEN OF RAOUL

AN OLD RASTA stood by the door, wearing nothing but a raggedy old pair of jeans, a big white beard and an expectant expression. Kate handed him a dollar, and suggested I did the same. 'It's out of bounds just now,' he said. 'We've got a new MO who's refusing to check the girls on moral grounds. If we look after the old boy on the door, he'll come in and let us know if the monkeys show up.'

I followed him inside, to the inevitable strains of *Me Donkey Want Water*. The place was divided in two by a 4ft high wall which ran down the middle of the room and led to a red door in the back wall. This led in turn to the rooms where the girls plied their trade – the only place where the military police weren't allowed. The door opened straight onto the dancefloor, but the bar was well over to the left of the building, and up a few steps; if you were drinking when the monkeys raided the place, there were lines of chairs and tables between you and the safety of the back rooms, which meant a desperate, running-and-jumping scramble for sanctuary known as 'The Grand National'. It was run on an irregular basis – basically, on nights when the authorities had nothing better to do than grip a few lads for having some fun. I had the good fortune to enter my first National that evening. I was drinking with Kate and Tony at the bar, and talking to a few girls, when the old Rasta poked his head into the room and shouted, 'RMP, RMP, RMP!'

Everyone dropped their drinks and did a bomb burst, like woodlice scattering after a rock's been lifted. Those guys fortunate enough to find themselves grooving on the dancefloor were in the back rooms before the monkeys could even de-bus from their Rover, but those of us pissing it up in the bar had it all to do. It was like a turkey shoot, and some of the lads were shit out of luck. One poor, stupid bastard I didn't know tried to make it straight past the entrance, but was hauled down by a couple of triumphant monkeys. The rest of us took to our heels and had it away over the tables. There was a faller at the first, and a few other blokes went down as we hurdled them three abreast. We didn't look back to check on their fate.

I was giggling insanely, like a kid getting chased after a game of Knock-Door-Run. Kate and Tony were the same, and we spurred each other on, focusing on the far door. Out of my peripheral vision, I saw a couple of monkeys running along the dance floor to our right, trying to outflank us. This just drove me on even harder – I was like a top-fuel dragster running on Appleton's Methanol, and I pulled ahead of Kate and leapt the dividing wall in a single bound. Then I was through the door, and holding it open for the herd of laughing, sweating drunkards who piled in after me. Once all the runners were through, I slammed it shut, leaving the monkeys hammering on it like nutters. We were all gasping for breath. 'Fucking hell, Eddy,' said Kate. 'I thought I'd had it at Becher's Brook.'

'What's Becher's Brook?'

'The last wall, mate. It can be a killer, but you were over the fucker like Spring-Heeled Jack.'

'Aye, well I could see the bastards coming around on the dancefloor. We were bang to rights.'

Our conversation was interrupted by a hand on my shoulder. I turned around and came face-to-chest with an enormous woman. She was well over six feet tall, with mahogany-brown breasts of epic proportions and a deep, husky voice. 'Hey, new bwoy!' she drawled.

'Er, hello.' I said, slightly intimidated, I shook her hand as if greeting another man.

She looked down quizzically at my hand, then up to my face and burst out laughing, and I couldn't help but laugh myself.

'Alright there, Flo,' said Kate. 'How you doing?'

They were obviously well-acquainted. 'Ha, ha,' she said. 'Katie, me bwoy! What ya doin' 'ere? Are ya wantin' some fun?'

'You know what, Flo? I think I do,' he grinned.

She turned to me and grabbed my packet in her large hand. 'An' what about ya likkle friend?' she chuckled.

'What do you reckon, Eddy,' said Kate. 'Two's up?'

I'd never had done anything like that, but it would be something to tell the grandkids so I agreed. Flo led us into her room, and, if I'm totally honest, I was shitting myself. I don't know if Flo sensed this, but just before we crossed the threshold she turned to us and said, 'Don't you be worryin', me likkle Eddy. I is gone give you me special wax treatment.'

We were in there for about an hour and she took us both to the cleaners. I think the 'wax treatment' referred to the wide variety of strange oils and sticky substances she employed to aid proceedings, but it might have been because when she finished you off the wax shot out of your ears.

When we left, I was walking like a 95-year-old with Parkinson's. It was a good job the monkeys had gone, because there's no way that I could have managed another Grand National.

It must have been about five in the morning when I eventually reached my scratcher. The walk from the guardroom to the block had been a nightmare: we'd made the mistake of taking the drunken shortcut directly across the cricket pitch, and had disturbed every sleeping mosquito and biting buzzy thing within a 400 metre radius. But even though I was munched to death, I still flaked out within seconds.

I woke up around lunchtime on the Saturday, and made painful tracks for The Sunspot. Most of the blokes were already in there and well underway. Kate nudged the drunken squaddie next to him. 'Fucking hell, Eddy,' he said. 'Look at the state of you. I was just telling Geordie about last night.'

'Oh, mate,' I said. 'It was like being in a fucking wrestling match. That Flo really did a number on us.'

Geordie burst out laughing. 'Fookan' hell, Kate. Ye never telt us ye went wi' Orinurkur Fleur last neet!'

'Don't listen to him, Eddy,' said Kate. 'Every time he goes to Raoul's, he wakes up in the morning and finds the girls have rolled him onto the floor with a sheet tied round him like a giant nappy because he's a bed lagger.'

'Haway and shite, ya bastad,' said Geordie.

'It's fucking true, though,' said Kate, laughing. 'Remember that lightweight civvie doss-bag liner you brought over?' Geordie was grinning ruefully and shaking his head. 'You used to wazz the bastard every night and make the dye run – you were blue all over when you got up, like one of them mad Scottish bastards from years ago.'

A few years later, I went to see *Braveheart* at the flicks, and I couldn't help imagining William Wallace as a medieval splashdown expert.

The bar only had Schlitz left, but I fired a few down as fast as I could by way of hair of the dog, and in short order I was in the swing of things again. One of telemechs, a lad called Dusty Miller, entertained us with his amazing 'stop the ceiling fans with his head' trick. He'd crouch on a table beneath a ceiling fan that was spinning at full speed, then stand up and insert his bonce gradually into the fan's arc. It took three or four good smacks to stop the blades, and each time the fan struck his skull a dull thud would echo around the bar. But he always pulled it out of the bag eventually, and he would stand there, arms aloft, with the electric motor whining away desperately.

After a few games of Mickey Mouse at the dartboard, we retired outside to the atap, and were met by a vile smell; the remnants of last night's gazome chilli had been left behind by the duty slop-jockey, and the bowls were teeming with insect life. Dusty joined us, still on an adulation-driven high from the fan stunt. He headed for the rancid food without a second's delay, scooping up a mouthful of the seething goo and grinning like a child who'd just licked the cake bowl clean, only with various grubs and other small animals dropping out of his mouth. Seasoned lunatics wretched at the sight and we all declared him to be a very bad man.

* * * * *

Before long, I was into the swing of things. Early PT was a bit unpleasant, particularly when conducted in a haze of rum fumes from the night before. We'd go circuit training on the cricket pitch or for a run outside camp, and each had its pros and cons. The downside to circuit training was the mozzies, but going for a run meant enduring the stench of the sweetwater canal on the return leg. The canal ran under the road in and out of camp. PT started early enough that the water was dormant on the way out, but by the time you got back the sun had started to gather some of its savage heat and the canal was radiating terrible gases. Running through a cloud of rotting eggs while ballbagged at the end of the session caused regular mass choking and vomming sessions. It was most unpleasant.

I spent the next month and a half in the Force HQ radio room. Life passed very quickly. Kate had sourced a buckshee mini grill, so the humdrum routine of sending messages and reading fraying copies of *Club* and *Men Only* was now broken up by making sausage sarnies. I had to make a conscious effort not to become a complete porker. Knocking up sandwiches was a great way to kill time during quiet night shifts: one was often faced with the dilemma of another butty or one's fifth thrap of the evening.

Captain Peterson-Smythe would put in the occasional appearance, but I'd got used to his teleprinter-knackering sausage fingers and kept a beady eye on him. His bullshitting stories usually concerned things that were off my radar, like Officers' Mess functions or university capers, but now and again he'd try and get a bit of street cred with the lads. Obviously, the modern Army is nothing like it was, when officers were permitted to use toms as pieces of furniture or for duelling pistol practice, but the fact remains that most officers have the benefit of a university education and most Signallers and Junior NCOs don't. It means that there are areas where the two sides aren't always on the same wavelength. Most officers learn to tread the fine line of cultural separation between them and the other ranks, but you'd get goons like Peterson-Smythe trying to engage on subjects they knew nothing about, in the vain hope that the lads would think they were good blokes.

He spent an hour of one evening trying to talk to me about football because he'd seen me reading the sports pages of an old paper. Whether you like football or not, its saturation coverage in the UK means that everyone can cuff it in a conversation on the subject.

Everyone except for Peterson-Smythe, that is.

'Which football squad do you follow then, Nugent?'

'Everpool or Liverton, sir.'

'Really, and are they any good?'

'They're OK, sir. Everpool need to get rid of their striker though, he's 62 next month.'

'Crikey, he must be a fit chap to keep going that long.'

'He is, but they stop the game every ten minutes so he can have a sit down.'

'How very considerate!'

We went on like that until I had him convinced that Johnny Weissmuller from the Tarzan films was England's goalie in the '66 World Cup and that Bernard Breslaw was the manager.

The shift pattern meant free weekends, and I would sometimes go out to the sandy cayes which make up Belize's barrier reef, the second largest in the world – they really were like the idyllic islands from the Bounty adverts I'd been sold at the recruitment office in Manchester all those years before. To get out to the cayes, we'd get the bus into BC and then hop onto a half-hour water taxi out to our destination. Caye Caulker was a favourite spot. It was split into two islands – one an unpopulated mangrove swamp and the other a sandy spit of land popular with tourists. The two islands were separated by a channel of water which narrowed to about 20 yards across where most people congregated. The narrowness of the channel created a very strong current, and sunburnt British soldiers under the influence of strong rum punch were forever being swept out to the shark-infested sea. They'd always make it back, but they tended to cover the final few metres of the return swim looking like bedraggled terriers frantically doggy-paddling to the edge of a canal.

When the day was coming to an end, we'd all pile back on board the water-taxis and speed back to BC. On the few occasions that I visited Caulker, every single return journey was delayed by some bloke or another diving off his boat at full lick and forcing it to turn back and pick him up. It looked spectacular, but the water was very shallow and almost all of the guys who performed the stunt said that bruised ribs and a 40 mph seawater enema were by no means the best way to end the day.

As Jim Dale had said, after a while I moved from the radio room to the stores up at the transmitter site, where all the radio traffic from Belize was transmitted back to the UK. It was the ultimate doss; in fact, if anything, it was *too* quiet. In the month and a half that I was in there, I painted one set of shelves, issued one backpack radio to the infantry lads, drank 200 stims, ate 90 sausage sandwiches and watched 60 pornographic videos. Additionally, to relieve the boredom, I had an average of one stone fight a week with the technicians.

Occasionally, we'd listen to BFBS or watch Belize TV.

BFBS had normal forces radio piped in, but sometimes they'd give one of resident infantry lads a slot and he would wreak havoc. I remember being riveted by one show concerning the fate of a particularly vicious parrot called Moriarty who lived at one of the Harrier sites, where all the plane crews hung out, maintaining and operating the aircraft. Moriarty had a penchant for biting visitors, and this particular infantry DJ was hosting a public vote over what should happen to the parrot; he crossed the line by suggesting it should be passed through a spinning Harrier turbine, with whatever came out of the exhausts being shoved up the Garrison Sergeant Major's arse.

Belize TV was equally entertaining. When they ran out of adverts and programmes, the screen would take on the appearance of Teletext, and then *The Death March* would start playing as they scrolled through local obituaries. Their trump card was a news presenter called Steve Lovell. Steve was a nice guy, but he constantly looked confused and this always gave an entertaining air to his shows. If he wasn't reading the headlines with a quizzical air upon his *mien*, he would be out and about doing features. I remember him broadcasting from the streets of the capital, Belmopan, where he was canvassing the views of residents after some recent floods. He knocked on one door, and – after about five minutes – a middle-aged rasta answered it, and just stood there in a pair of ragged denims.

Steve leapt into action. 'So tell me, what 'appen 'ere?'

The rasta gestured to the road. 'Well, me woke up dis mornin' and dere was water in de street.'

'So what did you do?'

The rasta looked at Steve as if he was stupid. Then he sucked his teeth and replied, 'Me went back to bed.'

I was supposed to be in the stores when Christmas came around, but Jim had pretty much closed shop for two weeks beforehand so I spent the whole period on the lash. On Christmas Day, I did nothing but drink and take part in a volleyball match which was conducted in a raging storm on a pitch which quickly churned up. As we stood out to wash off in the torrential, tepid rain, someone hurried over with news of some kind of accident. Apparently, an appeal had been broadcast on BFBS for all sober people of blood group O to report to the Med' Centre.

It turned out to involve The Snakecatcher.

This was the bloke whose job it was to catch any beasties which found their way into people's rooms and boots, and the poor guy had been bitten by the live fer-de-lance he kept caged in his office. The fer-de-lance is an aggressive and highly venomous pit viper, and Belize is basically crawling with the bastards. The idea was, he had one in his room so as you could go and check it out to know what to avoid while out and about. Personally, I worked on the basis that you should avoid everything, but I suppose the principle was sound. Anyway, Snakey had come bouncing into his office after a skin full of Bellyache, full of festive cheer, and his eye had fallen on the snake. For some reason, he'd suddenly felt all friendly towards it and, in a momentary and inexplicable lapse of sense, had lifted the lid to the cage and mumbled, 'Here you go, mate, get that down you!' before pouring beer all over the snake's head. I guess it didn't like Belikin, because it bit the guy several times and he had to be cas-evac-d to Miami.

EDDY NUGENT AND THE SHELLING OF PRONTO

BETWEEN CHRISTMAS and New Year, the Troop Staffy gripped me in the bar and informed me that I was going back to Holdfast. They'd finally found a replacement for the dipsomaniac whose departure from theatre had brought me over to APC. So it came to pass that, in the death throes of 1990, I found myself Holdfast-bound again on the Western Highway.

It was just after lunchtime when I got back in through the gates. Derek the Dalek was waiting for me, and he quickly brought me up to speed on what was happening round the camp. That took about 90 seconds, because what was happening was nothing, apart from the relentless drudgery of swimming, drinking, playing volleyball, sunbathing, drinking and more swimming.

It being New Year's Eve, the place was in a buzzing mood, with everyone completely neglecting their minuscule workloads. I ditched my bags, and Derek and I quickly joined the party in the NAAFI. The only real decision we had to make was where to be at midnight. We plumped for the Artillery Bar: 29 Commando had completed their tour in November and had been replaced by another Battery of equally deranged bomb-slingers. They'd decided to celebrate the British New Year at 6pm and then work their way across the time zones until midnight. It was very weird. In the five minutes preceding each hour, everyone would whip themselves up into a frenzy, before commencing the 10-second countdown with religious fervour. As the hours went by and we rang in the New Year for our friends in Iceland, South Georgia and Newfoundland, the enthusiasm was undiminished and each rendition of *Auld Lang Syne* grew louder than the last. Most of us were plastered by 11 o'clock, and some blokes actually got quite tearful whilst toasting the Puerto Ricans. I survived up until the Belizean New Year, but had to be carried to bed and missed the Mexican toast at 1am. Derek told me the next morning that, after celebrating the arrival of 1991 with the Pitcairn Islanders at 3am, a big brawl started when nobody could agree whether Hawaii was next. As with all squaddie fights, extreme drunkenness ensured that no real damage was done before it dissolved into a hug-fest of sobbing idiots.

On January 2nd, I got another surprise when I was asked to take out one of the jungle patrols. The Glosters lance corporal who was supposed to be the patrol leader had an eye infection and was confined to camp. The patrol would consist of myself and three privates from the Glosters, with a pair of NCOs from the BDF accompanying us to help with translation and local knowledge. The idea was that we'd spend seven days patrolling through the jungle, in the unlikely hope that we would encounter and apprehend drug smugglers from Guatemala. Along the way, we'd also talk to people in the villages we passed through to gather any useful information about criminal activity in the area. It sounded like proper soldiering, so I agreed immediately.

I was up bright and early and waiting with the other lads by the Helipad at 7am. The Puma dropped us at our pre-designated grid reference, and we set off. It was incredibly interesting and very enjoyable. Each night, we'd harbour up near one of the villages and go to sleep. The next day, we'd visit the village, and, through the BDF guys, speak to the Primero and Secundo of the settlement, effectively the mayor and his sidekick. They were always polite to a fault and very affable, and we'd chew the fat for an agreeable half hour. Then we'd dish out supplies from our big medkit, cleaning up parang cuts and dishing out antiseptic, and swap a bit of food with the local women, a couple of our tins for some of their tasty, floury tortillas. The kids in the villages would relieve us of most of our sweets and chocolate and then we'd move on and patrol for the rest of the day. My map reading was adequate so we didn't get lost, though one of the BDF guys, Miguel, knew the area like the back of his hand anyway. His oppo was a lad called Santos, and he was a proper bullshitter. He had himself down as a bit of a Central American Crocodile Dundee, and us as a load of gullibles. Any time I asked a question about an animal or a tree, he'd embark on a lengthy explanation, with Miguel chuckling to himself in the background. On the fourth day, as we moved along a small footpath, Santos – who was in front of me – stopped and dropped to one knee.

I moved forwards and squatted alongside him. 'Why have you stopped?' I asked, puzzled.

'Listen, can you hear?' He nodded to a clearing ahead of us.

I strained my ears and after a couple of seconds I picked out what sounded like an electric razor.

'What is it?' I said.

He thought for a few seconds, before nodding sagely to himself. 'Hummingbirds.'

I'd never seen one before, so I told him to proceed with me close behind. As we reached the cutting, I looked towards the source of the noise. Instead of a little family of hummingbirds, there was a fucking great bees' nest, about the size of a fridge freezer. Without hesitation, I did a quick 180 and legged it back about 50 metres, with the rest of the patrol following bemusedly.

When I stopped and confirmed that we weren't about to be stung to death, I confronted Santos angrily. 'You fucking dickhead. You said they were hummingbirds.'

Unconcerned, he simply replied in a wistful, man-of-the-wilderness tone. 'There were hummingbirds there, also.'

I didn't bother my arse to ask him anything else for the rest of the week.

On the seventh morning we made our RV point with four or five hours to spare. We gave away the rest of the rations to some more kids and waited for the pick-up which showed up bang on time to fly us back to camp. After getting scrubbed up, we handed in our radio and other bits and bobs and I got the anticipated bollocking for giving away all the medical supplies.

Derek was really pleased to have me around again, chiefly because his backbreaking workload would again be halved back into near-non-existence, enabling him to shoehorn even more leisure time into his schedule. But it didn't last long. After a week of the day-on, day-off routine, we got a call from 633. One of the lads on the Cooma Cairn rebroadcast station had to go home immediately on compassionate grounds as his father was gravely ill. One of us would need to replace him for a few weeks, and 633 had decided that it would be me as the departing lad was a lance jack.

* * * * *

Cooma Cairn was a hilltop site. It was resupped with essentials by helicopter, but once a week two of the Cairn-dwellers would descend the hill and stock up on general supplies at Holdfast. The plan was for them to pick me up and they showed up the next morning at 9am. After a quick trip to the NAAFI to stock up on beer, fags and any newspapers that were lying around, they came and gave me a shout and a hand with carrying my kit to their wheels. The REBRO re-sup wagon was ravaged and plastered in mud and all kinds of shit. The driver, 'Knocker' Door, was the power guy who maintained the generators up on the mountain. He looked like an aid worker, with his long hair and sidies. I suppose that was one of the benefits of being stuck on top of a hill in the middle of nowhere – there was no-one around to give you any shit.

Once we had loaded the Rover up with all the rations and my stuff, we were off. Before long, we turned off the highway and up a red clay road which was pot-holed to fuck. I hit my head repeatedly on the vehicle's roof as we bounced up the steep track through the thick jungle. Every so often, we'd catch sight of something truly stunning. At one point, a jaguar ran out in front of us. It was a majestic animal, but I still shat myself and locked the doors.

As he drove, Knocker gave me the low-down on life on the mountain. It seemed very relaxed indeed. There were three radio guys, myself included, who took it in turns to monitor the radios. There was him, and all he did was ensure that we had power. Finally, there were three blokes from a sneaky unit called JSSU. They were up there to earwig on the Guats, but we paid them no bide in the work stakes. We'd all take turns cooking, and the freezers were stocked with plenty of comestibles. It sounded OK.

Eventually, we crested the final ridge. The compound was in front of us: an old watchtower, two half-moon, tin accommodation huts, two concrete blockwork buildings – one for JSSU, and one for us – and a generator shed for the big machinery that Knocker looked after. All of this was surrounded by barbed wire, with just a gap in the fence for the vehicle to get through. To get into the perimeter, we drove across an open square of ground, which, it transpired, was the helipad. Bordering the pad, and next to the jungle itself, was a three-walled, wriggly-tin hole-in-the-ground toilet, with no door. So if you wanted to go in the night, you had to walk out to the undergrowth and brave the wildlife.

Once inside the compound, I noticed the masts for the radio links and two long, deep trenches for burning camp rubbish. The concrete generator sheds had ramps leading up to them, and at the base of these were about a dozen 44-gallon diesel drums. These would have to be humped up the ramp to keep the gennies topped up.

As soon as Knocker stopped the wagon, a little pack of short-haired mongrels ran over, yapping. There was a docile black thing called Ego and a fat ginger beast called Fergie, who developed an obsession with sniffing my plums. Trailing behind them was the most useless, savaged hound in all Belize. He was called Pronto, and he'd been on the REBRO for about 18 years. The poor bastard had really been through the mill in the name of entertaining bored soldiers, and rumours abounded that he'd even caught a dose off one of the lads. He had a bad limp, no bark to speak of and a bony skull which made him look like he had a horn. As he got close to me, Pronto sniffed the air and began growling in a savage manner.

'Fuck off, Pronto,' shouted Knocker, and Pronto obliged.

The view from up at the REBRO was breathtaking. I could see right down into the mist-clogged valleys of the Mayan mountains, and I stood staring for a moment, taking in the view and comparing it to the red brick and wet, grey skies of Manchester. If I never did anything else in my Army career, it had given me this. Then I wandered off to find the other Signals blokes. The full screw in charge was a guy called John Moore, and the tom was Aidy Holmes. Aidy cooked that night, knocking up a decent chilli, and afterwards John briefed me up, for what it was worth. If you weren't listening to the radios, which were remoted into the TV room, you could pretty much do whatever you wanted. Every so often, the rubbish had to be burned, and the guy on shift had to check the generators and re-fuel them at night. We each cooked once a week. If there was no rain for a while, someone had to drive down to a creek in one of the valleys and fill a trailer bowser with water. And that was it.

I'd been up on the REBRO for about a week when Rick, one of the JSSU guys, decided to take the dogs for a walk to a place called Baldy Beacon, another hilltop about a kilometre from camp. It was sometimes used for live-firing exercises. but because it was a Sunday there was no danger of anything happening. When Rick returned, he was minus Pronto. On questioning, he told us that Pronto had sat down two-thirds of the way up Baldy and had refused to go any further. Well, he was an old dog and it was a long walk. Rick had tried to coax him onto his feet to walk him back, but the cantankerous old git had just tried to bite him. This refusal to move was a stunt he'd pulled before, and he'd always come limping back the next morning, so it didn't seem like much of a drama.

The next day we were woken by engine noises and the sounds of equipment being unloaded reverberating from across the valley. By the time I had got my lazy arse out of bed to see what the noise was, I saw about four 105mm artillery pieces being set up and prepared for firing, with Dropshorts scampering all over the guns and making their final adjustments. I stood there, drinking in the sight of soldiers actually working for a living. Then it hit me. 'Fuck... isn't Pronto up by the impact area?'

Too late. The first gun bucked, let out a gout of smoke, and a second later the thunderous firing report hit me with a BOOM!

Almost instantly, the other guns did the same, and then the area where Pronto was last seen was turned over by four shells of high explosive.

He was never seen again, which was a shame, though I didn't miss being chased by the old bastard whenever he had one of his mental attacks. His remains were never found, so he was reported as 'missing in action', along with Chuck Norris's career.

Pronto's replacement was a young puppy called Rowdy, and when he came on board we constructed a miniature assault course and gym to get the little fella into shape. I don't think the dog understood what, 'Come on, you lazy bastard, you'd better start sparking and get over that shagging wall!' meant. But he certainly gave it his best shot, and by the time I left he was a mean little fucker.

My time up Cooma was to be limited, because I was going on R&R in mid-Feb. But it was by no means devoid of entertainment. The problem with having a really easy life is that you get bored very easily. And the problem with bored soldiers is that they start to do stupid things. Mix this with beer, and you're in a world of shit.

It started off with trying to dhobi the dogs. Ego and Rowdy took it in their stride, but Fergie went berserk and chased us all over the place for about five minutes until he was tired and had to lie down. We were still strapped for entertainment, so when Aidy went to the toilet on the other side of the helipad we grabbed a handful of rocks each and stoned the shithouse until our arms got tired. It certainly kept us entertained, although – judging by Aidy's swearing – he was not amused. The bog stoning was called off a few weeks later, after Aidy took a good-sized rock in the front of the napper.

After one particularly long drinking session, ostensibly to mark the passing of Pronto, we decided to burn the rubbish which was now filling one of the gash trenches. Boredom isn't the only thing that does not mix well with soldiers and drink; petrol is another. In our drunken state, we had no comprehension of how much fuel we were pouring over the rubbish pit, but it must have exceeded 40 litres. We used a further 20 litres to trail away from the trench as a fuse. Unfortunately, the majority of that 20 litres was dumped around where we were standing.

Aidy and I retired a bit, and John pulled out a box of matches. He shouted, 'TO PRONTO!', lit the entire box in a genie and tossed it onto the fuel-soaked ground. Instantly, he was engulfed by a terrible blast of heat and light, and a roaring flame then shot across the earth and erupted in the trench in the form of a fireball. This in turn sent rubbish flying high into the sky and raining back down on us. As John came steaming out of the flames, trailing fiery foot prints like something out of *Back To The Future*, a flying lump of metal which had been blown out of the rubbish pit came back to earth and smacked him on the head. He went down like a sack of shit. We raced over to him and beat the flames out in time to prevent any really serious burns.

A short while later I was on a resup run back to APC, so I went into the hospital to visit him. He was in a large ward kitted out for 12 patients, but there was only him and one other bloke in there. The other guy was in a right state. He had a broken jaw, and was missing his left arm. John's pit space was barren, other than a card from the troop composed of witty and compassionate 'get well' wishes, like, 'Fuck off you wanker! Love Jonah!' and 'You malingering cunt. Kate.'

I sat down with him for a bit. He said he was alright, despite having second degree burns to his lower legs and mild concussion. To lighten the tone, and also to take his mind off things, I pointed to the other patient, who was asleep. 'Still, mate,' I said. 'Could be worse. Look at that poor sod.'

'Yeah, that's Tommy,' said John. 'He's in the Glosters.'

'What happened?'

'He lost his arm in a car crash.'

'Fucking hell, that's a rough deal. He smashed his jaw up pretty badly as well, eh?'

'Yeah,' said John, 'but he didn't do that in the crash.'

'No?' I said.

'The other day he was up and about in the ward and we were talking about all the normal shit, you know, shagging, footy and all that. Then he sat down there.' John indicated a nearby table. 'He started to tell me about how weird it was, how he could still feel itches in his missing hand. As he was talking, he went to lean on his elbow. Of course, the fucking thing wasn't there so he just fell forward and cracked his face on the edge of the table. Honestly Eddy, he's the unluckiest bloke I ever met. If he fell into a barrel of tits, he'd come out sucking his thumb.'

We both had a laugh at that. No doubt Tommy would have joined in – had he been awake and had his jaw not been wired together.

Another reason for the run to APC was to pick up a replacement for John. The guy in question was new in theatre and on tour from 2 Div at York. Nick Bruce was another full screw, and therefore the big cheese up on the mountain. He'd only just landed in country and was very wary about going out into the J: I could imagine his dismay when, even as *Welcome To The Jungle* – played on BFBS to mark every flight in – was fading into the air, he was loading his kit onto the battered Cooma Rover and heading up into the unknown with me.

For the majority of the drive, he asked non-stop questions about the wildlife he might encounter whilst up on the REBRO.

'Are there spiders? I fuckin' hope not. I hate spiders, me. What about scorpions? They're even worse. If there's one thing I fuckin' hate, it's fuckin' scorpions. They're a right bunch of cunts, I tell you.'

Nick was a good corporal to have up there, a shit umbrella who found ways to stop most of the stupid ideas filtering down from the APC hierarchy. The father of an unfeasible number of children, the duty rumour was that he only had to wash his pants at the same time as his old lady's knickers to get her up the stick. He was a bit of a sporting type, too. He'd played cricket for the Corps, and had brought his bat with him; we ended up whiling away hours playing French cricket on the helipad, with the jungle valleys forming a spectacular backdrop. Every now and then, one of the dogs would run off with the ball in its gob and we'd end up chasing the bastard for half an hour. The wagging of tails made it obvious that the dogs thought the whole thing was a huge joke; the filthy language and threats coming from the human participants were quite lost on them.

The sun was hot, the beer was cold and the six of us just messing about… I suppose, looking back, that these were perhaps the last truly carefree times of my life, like a sort of echo of childhood, only with lashings of alcohol and lunacy.

All the fun came to an abrupt end on the morning of Nick's ninth day, when he awoke to his ultimate nightmare. He'd felt a strange scratching sensation on his chest, and found to his utter horror that it was caused by a large, black, jungle scorpion trudging slowly across his chest. His sudden movement caused the scorpion to stop in its tracks and ready itself to strike by raising its claws and tilting its sting forward. Jungle scorpions aren't actually very poisonous, but Nick didn't know that. There followed a Mexican stand-off which lasted several minutes as he debated with himself as to what to do. Eventually, he decided that the best course of action was to flick the beast off his chest as hard as possible. His theory was that if he struck it sweetly enough the scorpion wouldn't have time to sting him. Not a bad plan, but sadly it didn't survive contact with the enemy. The scorpion had lightning reflexes, and as soon as it felt the wind from Nick's approaching hand, it started stinging him for all it was worth. By the time he had got it off his chest it had hit him five times.

We heard his bellowing from outside the block, and then there was a brief silence followed by what sounded like a GPMG opening up in sustained fire mode. We all ran to the accommodation hut and when we opened the door, Nick was standing there, naked and breathless, frenziedly beating his bed with the cricket bat to the point where it had taken on the appearance of a rotating blur, like Billy Whizz's feet. The focus of the savage braying was the remains of the scorpion, which was now about two feet wide after being flattened out like a piece of filo pastry.

Eventually, he halted his attack and turned to face us. His chest was reddened, but since the jungle scorpion's venom is no more serious than that of a slightly supercharged bee, he'd live. His mental state was more of a concern, and we prescribed a course of beers rather than an emergency death race down to the medics in Holdfast. Sure enough, after getting a few brews down his neck he started to feel better, and was left merely with surface burning in his chest; he was never quite the same again, though.

* * * * *

After a month or so, my R&R rolled around. The night before I left, we had a little piss-up, having purchased a ruck-load of ale on the last ration run. Things were going swimmingly, and before long we'd polished off the better part of three slabs of Miller. Then Knocker disappeared for a few minutes and came back carrying a demijohn filled with a strange, milky fluid.

Nick let out an enormous burp that echoed down the valleys. 'What the fuck have you got there, Knocker? Have you been saving up all your wanks?'

'Fuck off, man,' said Knocker, looking fondly at the jar. 'This is me home brew. I've had the fucker bubbling away for ages now, just waiting for the right time to try the bastard out.'

'What's in it?' said Aidy.

'Everything, mate. There's potatoes – that's how you make moonshine. Rice – as in saki and all that. Sugar, compo fruit salad – for flavour. And the magic ingredient, a bottle of Appleton's 151, just to get it started, like.'

He held it up: it was minging. He'd obviously stored it amongst the diesel drums, because it reeked of fuel and was crusted with unidentifiable traces of animal faeces around its base. 'Get some fucking glasses then, gents, and let's give this little beauty a try,' he said, with a lot more enthusiasm than the rest of us felt. Still, Aidy went inside and returned with four glasses, a coffee mug and a soup ladle. I got the ladle, and also the dubious honour of the first taste of 'Knocker's Stevie Wonder Firewater', so-called because of its suspected potential to induce blindness.

It was fucking vile. However, it was also incredibly potent, and after only a few sips I could feel its toxins surging through my veins and giving me an uncomfortable hot flush. The other lads followed suit, and there was a mass choking fit, a few screwed-up faces and the odd comment of 'Fuck!' blown out through gritted teeth.

Before long the firewater had taken hold, to the point where we could no longer taste it. By the end of the night there were bodies strewn everywhere, and with the odd fire still burning away in the background the place looked like a post-airstrike Vietnamese village.

The next day, I crawled on board the wagon for my lift to Holdfast and on to APC and my R&R flight to New Orleans. I was in rags for the entire journey, and the side of the Rover was treated to a liberal coating of vomit on more than one occasion. Kate was going on R&R too, and we met up at the airport and started drinking. We soon struck up a conversation with a group of Wyoming Air National Guardsmen. We told them we were headed for the Big Easy.

'Say,' said one of them. 'Did you guys know that it's Mardi Gras this time of year?'

'No, mate,' I replied, 'What's that?'

The American got very excited. 'Shee-it!' he said, with a huge grin. 'It's only the biggest pardee in the fuckin' world, man!'

'Oh, right,' said Kate, nonchalantly. 'So there's a bit of drinking to be done, then?'

'Brother,' said the American, with a dramatic pause. 'You'd better prepare your liver.'

EDDY NUGENT AND THE WURZELS' FINEST HOUR

THE FLIGHT INTO Nawlins International took about an hour and half, in a rickety old aircraft operated by the TAC airline (I never found out what 'TAC' stood for, but prevailing opinion among the lads was that it was Take A Chance). I'd have liked to have got my head down for half an hour but I was up for a slash every five minutes due to the ale.

We were picked up by a portly old taxi driver called Zeke, who drove us to our hotel – The Economy Motor Lodge – while explaining how he dealt with 'good for nothin' freeloaders' with a Smith and Wesson snub-nose .38 which he brandished in our general direction. The hotel was the sort of joint where you could pay by the hour, though clean enough. Being a couple of skin-flints, Kate and I had booked a twin room – after all, it would only be a place to crash between boozing. (I know it sounds like that's all British soldiers do, but I was lucky enough to serve in the days before today's operational tours to hot and sandy places, and to be honest it is what most squaddies did back then, especially young, single ones.)

It was a five minute walk from The French Quarter, so in next-to-no-time we were staggering down the infamous Bourbon Street from one bar to the next. From then on, things soon fell into a predictable routine. We'd start boozing at about midday and finish at eight in the morning, before falling asleep and waking up three hours later with raging hangovers which could only be calmed by the intake of more drink. We ate wherever was closest to hand to assuage the munchies.

It was a great city, full of that famous southern hospitality, and everybody you met was all smiles and chirpy attitude. The atmosphere was buzzing non-stop, and the sounds of raucous jazz trumpets and haunting blues guitar filled the air morning, noon and night. And, as our airport American had predicted it would, the 'pardee' increased tenfold come Mardi Gras. I still don't know what it's all about, or where its cultural origins lie; the only thing I can say about it with any certainty is that it involves drunk women competing with each other to adorn themselves with the maximum number of cheap plastic necklaces which they earn by showing men their knockers. Even though I had become used to the antics of the girls at The Farm and Raoul's, I was still, at heart, an unworldly young lad from Manchester, and I was literally amazed by this. I suppose it was the thought of a normal girl on a night out being willing to get naked in front of me for 50 cents' worth of Chinese rubbish: it was, literally, tit for tat. Anyway, the first time I was treated to this colonial udder-fest I was left gawping and motionless, as though struck down by the gaze of Medusa, and I stayed in this position long after the flasher had strutted out of sight. Occasionally, a logjam would develop, with groups of a hundred or more inebriates gathering under the balcony of a given bar, chanting, 'Show us your tits!' After a few moments' pretence at coyness, several women would oblige, to the roaring approval of the crowd below.

The nudity was not confined to women. Every now and then, a drunken bloke would stagger past in the raw, completely unaware of everyone laughing at him. One night, I was drinking on the wrought-iron balcony of a bar called The Cat's Miaow, and regaling a ridiculously attractive college girl from Texas with anecdotes of jungle hardships and the single-handed taking-down of fearsome drug cartels, when my bullshit was interrupted by a shout from below. In the street was a fat, staggering youth of about 19, wearing baggy shorts and a back-to-front baseball cap. He was pointing to the girl next to me and hollering, 'WOOOOOOOOOOOOOO

HEY PRETTY MOMMA, SHOW ME THEM TITTIES BABY, HOOOOO-WEEE, DAMN THEY LOOK REAL FINE!'

I think he was expecting people to join in, but everyone in the street just gave him a wide berth. The girl just shouted down to him, 'Show me yours first.'

Without further a-do, he placed his beer on the ground, lifted his shirt over his head and began licking his nipples. As if that wasn't stomach-churning enough, he then dropped his kecks and started thrusting his hips back and forth, until his knob and plums started to slap against his gut whilst on the up-thrust, and against his arse/chin-rest on the back stroke. Soon he had forgotten all about the girl's tits, and was completely engrossed in his own performance. He clenched his eyes shut, bit his bottom lip, and held both hands aloft with his fingers in front-row-of-a-Megadeth-concert style – you had to give him his due, he was really going for it. So much so that he didn't notice the big police cruiser pull up behind him. He was snapped out of his trance when one of the cops gave him a minor night-sticking and bundled him into the back of the cruiser. My final memory of the fat guy was his white arse disappearing into the car, closely followed by his pleading voice calling out, 'Hey, man, it wasn't me!'

The festival finished the day before Kate and I flew back to Belize, so we spent the final day taking in The French Quarter properly. We checked out the odd voodoo shop, and bought a few 'I'm With Stupid'-type T-shirts. When we booked out from the hotel we had to spend a bit more money on damages to the room, after Kate had charged at an imaginary assailant during a gin-fuelled bout of psychosis and put a huge dent in the wall.

We landed at Belize International just before midday, and got the transport back to APC. I said cheers to Kate, loitered at the guardroom until the fortnightly Cooma re-sup run stopped off and jumped aboard and slept all the way back to Holdfast.

I got back at teatime and found Derek in the cookhouse, with a table to himself, no doubt down to his subhuman table manners: you know your eating behaviour is at rock bottom when even squaddies won't sit with you. I made my way over to him. 'Alright, mate. How's it going?' I said.

He was pleased to see me and grinned broadly, displaying a half-chewed mouthful of bread. I grimaced and sat down, steeling myself for the trial of watching The Dalek eat his tea. Swallowing a sausage in a manner strangely reminiscent of a pelican, he still found it possible to talk. 'Have a good time, then, Eddy?'

'Yeah, it was a top laugh, mate. I'm glad to get back here to give my internal organs a rest.'

Derek would be going on his R&R in two days and it would mean me being permanently on duty. The enforced lack of boozing didn't seem like too much of a drawback. My fitness had taken a real beating in the last couple of months, and it was gnawing away at me that we'd be back in Aldershot in a month and a half, running round the training area with Staff Herbert and the training wing Gestapo chasing us.

'Where are you going, anyway?'

'Just up to San Pedro, mate. I'm a bit too skint for America.'

I was mildly gobsmacked. I'd been living quite lavishly, but I'd still managed to box away just upwards of sixteen hundred quid in the last six months. I hadn't seen too much of Derek since the back end of September, but I had a good idea what he'd been blowing his cash on. 'Been down The Farm a lot?'

'Too fucking right, mate. I've been with every single one of 'em now.'

I chuckled. The girls down there must have been ticking off the days until Derek flew home.

He was soon gone. I waved him off by indicating, that, in my opinion, he was a wanker, and he responded by throwing an apple at me.

I spent the next two weeks trying to get myself into some sort of shape. I didn't touch a drop of booze and got out training on most afternoons. Not drinking had a bit of a novelty value, but mostly it highlighted what a dull place an Army camp is without its reassuring presence.

A couple of days before Derek got back, I was talking to one of the Glosters recce platoon in the NAAFI. I'd noticed a bit of activity on the grassed area near the front of the camp.

'What's going on out there, mate?'

'The CSE show's comin' on Saturday, bud.'

These words strike fear into the soul of anyone with an ounce of taste. The Combined Services Entertainment shows were noble enterprises. The poor bastards toured every little nook and cranny of the world where more than three British soldiers could be found and confined to camp. They would then try their hardest to entertain them. They scored high points for their effort; where they came unstuck was in quality. They were uniformly terrible. If you imagine the entertainment industry food chain, they're about fifteen links lower than a *nul point* entrant in the Eurovision Song Contest.

The shows always followed the same rigid format. A middle-aged, slightly rotund comedian would serve as compère for the evening, telling a few bad jokes, of the kind which had previously received telegrams from the Queen. Then he would introduce the 'entertainment', which generally comprised a singer, a dance troupe and a novelty act, like a magician. The singer would be someone that you vaguely remembered seeing on *Opportunity Knocks* in the '70s, and he always looked like he'd spent the interim years propping up a bar in his home town telling anybody who would listen how he'd been one point away from beating Keith Harris. The dancers always invited prosecution under the Trades Descriptions Act: a group of six women shaped like rugby players would clump, fully-clothed, around the stage, trying to communicate an eroticism that they were physically incapable of generating. The magician was always shit, but then magicians usually are, and the entire performance was usually conducted in opposition to deafening heckling which was generally much funnier than the CSE fare.

If it sounds ungrateful to lambast these honest troubadours, it's because I was ungrateful. The idea that somebody could go to all the trouble to produce such a feeble spectacle, never mind fly it half way round the world to punish innocent soldiers, always baffled me. I wasn't expecting anything different in Belize.

* * * * *

Derek got back on the morning prior to the show. We spent the day by the pool, with Derek filling me in on what he'd got up to. He was surprisingly downbeat, for a chap returning from R&R. But then, he'd spent the previous six months having unrestricted sex with a range of gorgeous and exotic women without even having to attempt so much as a chat-up line: San Pedro had turned out to be quite an upmarket holiday resort, and seven Belizean bucks did not get you laid. Derek had been left with no alternative but to fall back on his 'rough diamond' charm and, unfortunately, this had been completely lost on the affluent American birds.

He did have a few funny tales, mind. He'd visited a bar called the Tackle Box, where the owner was a jobbing actor whose finest moment was a five-second part in *Die Hard* which had involved him being blown away by Bruce Willis. Despite the diminutive size of the role, the interior of the bar was plastered with framed stills from the film, and of him and Bruce 'hanging out' 'on set'. Round the back of the bar was a big sea pool where the owner kept his own aquarium featuring a few green turtles and a couple of small sharks. Most people chose to gaze at them from the comfort of the bar, but enough pissed squaddies had decided to give it a whirl for the owner to have placed a sign above the back door:

SHARKS AND TURTLES ARE DANGEROUS ANIMALS
BRITISH SOLDIERS WILL PLEASE REFRAIN FROM
JUMPING IN THE SHARK POOL

Like most of the other lads, Derek had had his picture taken next to the sign. Its very existence was considered a great testament to the idiotic bravery of the tanked-up tommy.

I told him about the CSE show and his reaction was predictable. 'Awww, fucking hell, I thought we'd be out of their range.'

'No chance, mate. You'll never guess who they've got singing.'

'Give us a clue?'

'It's not worth the bother, you'll never get it.' I was beginning to smirk.

Derek persisted. 'Go on, you fucker, give us a clue.'

'It's a band.'

'Mud?'

'No.'

'Brotherhood of Man?'

'No.'

'Racey?'

'Not even close. They're from the same neck of the woods as the resident Infantry Battalion.'

That stumped him, but he had one more go at it. 'The Barron Knights.'

I waited for him to give up and then dropped the bombshell. 'It's The Wurzels.'

I was giggling as I told him and he flatly refused to believe me.

'Honestly, mate' I said. 'I couldn't believe it myself.'

He spent the rest of the day calling me a wind-up merchant, despite everyone he asked telling him the same thing. The show kicked off at 17.30hrs and Derek was still insisting that even the CSE organisers couldn't dish up The Wurzels. We'd have gone down town, but you were obliged to attend, with failure to turn up resulting in extras or a charge. It was the Army's way of being benevolent to us: You will enjoy yourselves, or you're in the shit.

The stage had been fashioned from two flat-bed four-tonners backed up to each other. All the officers and seniors were sat in chairs near the front, as befitted their rank and taste. Most of the rest of us formed a huge semi-circle to the rear of the seating and waited with wholly unbated breath; incredibly, a few of the older Glosters lads were actually getting excited about The Wurzels, and were trying to get find good vantage points.

The show went exactly as predicted. As soon as the PA whined into life, our compère, 'Diamond' Billy Haversham, sprang onto stage pretending that he'd been pushed. He was in his mid 50s and dressed in a Pearly King's blazer, and he had long, thinning hair which had been combed and hairsprayed to within an inch of its life. He wheeled through five or six medieval-era jokes in a broad Leeds accent, with the lads shouting out the punchlines for him, until he reached the end of his first slot.

'Now, fellas,' he said, with a broad grin and a series of theatrical winks. 'We've got a great treat for you all you randy lads. They're the girls you've all been waiting for. All the way from Burnley, please welcome The Foxy Six.'

We all cheered half-heartedly, as the aforementioned growlers lumbered on to stage and went through a five-minute aerobics routine during which they interpreted, through the medium of ropey dancing, the ska classic *My Boy Lollipop*. At each occurrence of the word 'lollipop' they would lick an imaginary ice-lolly suggestively. It was very sexy, if you find watching your gran eat an ice-cream sexy. Conceivably, it *might* have worked on sex-starved squaddies in the Outer Hebrides, where the only female flesh they'd seen in months was a crofter's missus in a woolsack dress, but the lads in Holdfast had done nothing but shag for months. They needed a far higher level of sexual titillation than this, and the only person remotely interested in the performance of The Foxy Six was the REME mechanic, who was concerned about the hammering that his four-tonners' suspensions were taking.

Mercifully, ska tunes are quite short, and the girls were off quickly, giving Diamond Billy his cue to stumble/walk back out. He wiped some comedy sweat from his brow. 'Whoooh, bloody hell, thanks girls. I don't know about you lads but I'm feeling a bit hot under the collar.'

'Lose some weight then, you fat cunt.' A huge peal of laughter followed the anonymous voice.

Diamond Billy ignored that, and rolled out a couple more steam-era jokes, even managing to reach the punchline of the second. This wasn't due to its originality, but because it was so bad that it had failed to register on the comedy radar of the joke-spoiling crowd at the back. He then moved on to his introduction for the next act. 'Is anyone in the mood for some magic?' he implored.

'Aye, let's see you if you can disappear, you fucking bloater.' The same, now slightly less anonymous voice retorted.

Once more, amidst roars of laughter, Billy ignored his tormentor and got on with the show. 'Here he is, boys... fresh from a sell-out residency in Great Yarmouth, bring your hands together for Mysterio Pendragon.'

Billy scuttled off the stage and the lights were turned down. A few seconds later, from behind the curtain, came a disembodied voice. It was Billy, trying to sound like that American bloke who does the cinema trailers but failing miserably. 'Be amazed, be amused, be convinced,' he exhorted hopefully.

In the absence of a smoke machine, one of the backstage crew set off a couple of dry fire extinguishers and Mysterio bounded on to the stage to the tune of *Pinball Wizard*, dressed in top hat and tails. He went through his entire repertoire without eliciting a single 'Ooh' or 'Aah' from the crowd. As multi-coloured handkerchiefs emerged from his sleeves and bunches of plastic flowers appeared as if from nowhere, people checked their watches and waited for him to wrap up. In the event, The Who finished before he did, so we spent a couple of minutes watching him do sleight-of-hand tricks in stony silence. Surprisingly, the hecklers left him alone. On the completion of his last trick, pulling a live chicken out of his top hat, he took a bow and walked off stage to weak applause, with the chicken under his arm.

Billy came back on, feigning astonishment and reverting to his original voice. 'Bloody hell, that was cracking, eh fellas? Let's have another big hand for Mysterio.'

A couple of people at the back had started chanting disinterestedly, 'We want The Wurzels, we want The Wurzels.'

We all joined in, but Billy didn't detect the sarcasm and tried to calm us all down. 'They'll be on in a minute, don't worry.' He tried another joke but was drowned out by the Wurzel chant. Eventually, with a quick look back stage, he grinned and announced, 'Gentlemen, for your delight, I bring you the chart-topping Wurrrrz*els*!'

As they took the stage, I waited for Derek's reaction. He was standing open-mouthed, slowly shaking his head. It really was The Wurzels. Not a tribute band, or a new line-up, but the original members, still wearing the same bumpkin-chic outfits they'd sported on *Top of the Pops* a couple of decades earlier. They took their places and the lead singer starting talking to us in his exaggerated Yokelese. 'Evening, laaads. How're you all doing?' Without waiting for an answer they launched into their set, kicking off with that old favourite *I've Got A Brand New Combine Harvester*.

They performed with unbridled enthusiasm and, against all the odds, they won the crowd over. There were even shouts for an encore of *Combine Harvester*, which they duly delivered, with loads of the lads joining in. At one point, Derek turned to me. 'I can't fucking believe it, Eddy,' he said. 'They're so shit I quite like them.'

They played for 40 minutes, ending with a little thing called *Blackbird, I'll 'Ave 'Ee*. By this time, everyone was up and joining in and they finished to rapturous applause, even stopping to sign a couple of autographs as they left the stage.

Diamond Billy was pleased as punch, but as soon as he walked back on the atmosphere that the Wurzels had generated evaporated. Ignoring a series of cat calls and groans, he wrapped up the show with an appalling version of *True* by Spandau Ballet, which he murdered in the coldest of blood. Try to imagine it sung in a broad Leeds accent by a man who sounds like he's got a throat full of greenies, and you're nearly there. His finest touch was to try and make the song more specific to his audience by chucking in a couple of spoken ad-libs:

'I've bought a ticket to the wor-hur-hurld (*Just like you fellas!*)'

'But now I've come back again (*On leave!*)'

He finished the song on his knees, totally lost in the genius of his performance and then, after a couple of tearful bows, he was gone.

As the lights went down, it was left to one of Diamond Billy's hecklers to summarise the evening succinctly.

'That was fucking shit. If that lot were playing at the bottom of me garden, I'd shut the bleeding curtains.'

EDDY NUGENT AND THE TROMBONE OF BELIZE

WE WERE NOW at the start of March, and Derek and I only had another month to push at Holdfast. For the last few weeks we made attempts to train, but we always derailed ourselves in San Ignacio at night. Well aware that time was running short, we really went for it at the weekends. Derek had as much financially-assisted sex as his bank account could stand, knowing he'd be back on a strict masturbation diet quite soon. I asked him about the imminent fanny drought, but he was philosophical. Making a vigorous gesture with his right hand, he said, 'There's nowt like the real thing, eh?'

On the penultimate night at The Farm, Mimi made The Dalek an offer he couldn't refuse. 'Shall I Trombone you, Derek?'

He had no idea what this entailed, but didn't want to appear naïve, so agreed immediately. He was back at the table within three minutes, with a faraway look in his eye. I had to know.

'So, what the fuck's a trombone, then?'

It was a full ten seconds before he replied. 'I'll tell you what, Eddy, I don't know what to think. I shouldn't have liked it, but I blew my beans in five seconds flat.'

'What did she do?'

'She made me stand there with me trolleys round me ankles. Then she knelt behind us and gave us a reacharound hand shandy.'

I was a bit puzzled. 'What's that got to do with a trombone?'

'While she was pulling the head off it, she gave me hoop a licking as well.'

Fucking hell. She deserved a Victoria Cross, never mind seven dollars.

A couple of weeks before we left, I rang home to let my folks know my leave dates. I'd done as dad had instructed, and kept in touch throughout the tour. Phone calls cost an absolute arm and a leg so it was mainly via blueys, but I'd managed to call them around Christmas and a couple of times since. As was usual in the Nugent household, dad answered the phone in his familiar brusque tone.

'Hello?'

'Dad?'

'Alright, son. How's it going?'

'Great. How's everything your end?'

'Champion, son. Are you back soon?'

'That's what I'm ringing about. I'm coming straight home from Brize Norton on the third of April. I've got three weeks' leave.'

'Great stuff, it'll be nice to have you back, son. I hope you're behaving yourself out there. Are you keeping it in your trousers?'

'Yeah, 'course I am. Listen, dad, I can't stay on long, it's nearly six dollars a minute on the phone.' It occurred to me that that was very nearly a trombone's-worth.

'Alright, just have a quick word with your mam. I'll see you soon. Stay safe.'

I heard the muffled scratching of the receiver changing hands before mum's voice crossed the Atlantic.

'Hiya, son. Are you having a good time?'

'Brilliant, mum. I was just telling dad, I'll be home on April the third. How are you?'

'Oh, you know, same as ever. We've missed having you around, son. Your nan's really excited about you coming home.'

'I'm looking forward to seeing you all. I've got you all presents.'

'Oh, you don't have to bother with all that. Just bring yourself back safe.'

'I will. Look, I'll have to go, mum, someone else is waiting for the phone, and it costs a bomb.'

'OK, son. See you soon.'

'Bye.'

As always, I felt a pang of homesickness after hearing my parents' voices. I'd had the absolute time of my life in Belize, but I was looking forward to getting home.

A week before we emplaned, our replacements arrived. Lance Corporal John Turner and Signalman Eric Burridge showed up, as we had, on the back of a four-tonner. Compared to me and Derek, they looked like they'd fallen in a vat of Tippex. I hadn't realised just how tanned and healthy-looking we'd got. The handover was a carbon copy of ours from Andy and Jase. We took great pleasure in introducing John and Eric to Mimi and, at Derek's insistence, they both applied to join her brass band. I signed over the det to John and we conducted the biennial opening of the battery shack ceremony. Suitably horrified by its writhing occupants, it was closed without any attempt to check voltage or electrolyte levels.

For our last night, we had a drink in each bar on camp to say goodbye to all the other units, and then headed down town. We had loads of accumulated Belizean shrapnel and blew the lot, mostly on drinks for lots of people in The Blue Angel. The Donkey trilogy was at completion now, and I enjoyed some dirty dancing with one of the local girls to *Shoot De Donkey*. Inevitably, we finished up at The Farm. In a spirit of camaraderie, Derek wanted us both to go in with Mimi. She was up for it, but the thought of having to watch Derek in action made me slightly queasy so I ended up playing topless pool with one of the other girls instead. Her breasts were quite pendulous and every time she bent over the table to take a shot they settled on the green baize like a couple of big, brown beanbags either side of the cue. It put me off my shots a bit.

When we left we said goodbye to all the girls, and they went through the motions of pretending they were arsed about us leaving. In the taxi on the way back to camp, Derek got all misty-eyed about the pleasures that would now be denied him, now that he'd said his last farewell to Mimi. To snap him out of it, I said, 'Listen, Derek. I don't know how to say this, but I think she might be seeing someone else.'

He shook his head in mock solemnity. 'They always let you down, eh?'

We burst into laughter as we swung through the camp gates for the last time.

We got all our gear together first thing in the morning and hopped on the mail run transport. As soon as we got in to APC we searched around for the rest of the group. They were in one of the NAAFI ataps, surrounded by rucksacks and sombreros and drinking stims. We had a lengthy debriefing session whilst we waited for the nod to get on the transport to the airport. It emerged from the conversation that Derek and I had had the best time. There wasn't as much to do at Salamanca or Rideau, and boredom had been a big feature. As the plane took off later that day, I watched the lush jungle of Belize disappear into the past with mixed feelings. I was glad to be getting back, but I knew I'd never pull another jolly like that again.

* * * * *

After another hefty couple of flights, we touched down in Brize at 9am the following morning. It was grim as fuck. The rain was chucking it down, and I'd made the classic British holidaymaker mistake of not wearing enough clothes. My teeth were rattling like castanets while we cleared customs, and I had to dig a fleece out of my bergan. As soon as we got out of the terminal, everybody legged it in different directions amidst a flurry of 'See-yas' and 'Fuck-offs'. Derek's dad was there to pick him up, and greeted him fondly with a big bear-hug. I was getting a train from Oxford and he offered me a lift, which I accepted gladly.

I'd have held my breath the whole way if possible. It wasn't hard to work out where Derek had picked up his dirty habits. His dad resembled a healthy tramp; I could see the BO coming off him like a wavy heat shimmer before catching at the back of my throat, and his shoulders and back were so covered in dandruff that he looked like he'd just climbed out of a snowdrift. Not wanting to give offence, I opened my window stealthily, bit-by-bit, until eventually my head was hanging out of it like the family dog. I gulped the fresh air greedily until we got in to Oxford station. Derek helped me with the bags then climbed back into the car. As it pulled away, he wound down his window and shouted, so that everyone on the concourse could hear, 'Now, Eddy, don't you be going with any more of those prosty-ma-tutes, you dirty dog.'

Caught without a retort, I just pretended I couldn't hear him and headed into the station, pausing to shrug my shoulders at an old dear who was glaring at me, and tutting loudly.

I rang dad when I changed at Crewe, and he was there to meet me. I hadn't realised just how pleased I'd be to see him until I actually did; he had a huge smile on his face and he hugged me like a long lost son, which I suppose I sort of was.

'It's bloody great to see you, son,' he said, in an atypically soft and emotional voice. He let me go after a couple of seconds and looked me up and down. 'You look really well, Eddy. You'll have the best tan in Manchester.'

We walked out of the station and into the car park. The sun was out now, but it was still cold and I had to have the heater on in the car on the way home.

My reunion with mum was a bit more tearful, but we were soon laughing. She wanted to know all about Belize, so I gave her the highlights, strictly edited to dwell on the flora and fauna but skirting over any mention of trombones or Orinoco Flo. This set the pattern for the entire three weeks. I was flush with money, so I set about blowing it as quickly as I could, going out almost every night. Following strict Army guidelines, my Central American adventure story grew more elaborate with each telling. By the end of my leave, I'd turned an uneventful jungle patrol into a cross between *Deliverance* and *Predator*, and all the girls at The Farm were retired Miss Worlds. My mates lapped it up anyway and ironically the only story they refused to believe was The Wurzels gig, which was completely true.

In my last week, I started to dread having to turn up back in Aldershot. I was well aware that my fitness was extremely lacking. I got out running in the afternoons but was quite far from my peak when the time came to go back.

I showed up on a Wednesday night and started to sort my bedspace out. Coming back to an Army camp after a big chunk of leave is always depressing. I suppose it's the realisation that you're currently at the furthest point possible from your next leave. I was sat on the end of my bed with my chin in my hands when Joey Donaldson came in.

'Heyyy, alright, Eddy. How's it going?'

'Fucking great, mate. It's good to be back.'

'Bit down in the dumps? I know how to cheer you up. We're doing the Horseshoe for PT tomorrow. Ha, ha, ha.'

'You're joking aren't you?' I knew he wasn't. If there's one thing that squaddies like more than giving good news to each other, it's giving each other bad news. The Horseshoe was a six-mile cross country run that went all round the training area and took in most of the big hills. It was a Pre-para staple and they used it to gauge what state the candidates were in. I averaged around the 40-minute mark on it but had gone round in 36 on my second Pre-para. I couldn't see myself breaking my personal record for a while.

I always slept badly on my first night back and now was no exception. I was tossing and turning all night, and I had nightmares that combined all my recent experiences with what was to come. It was awful. Staff Sergeant Herbert, dressed as a prostitute, was chasing me round the training area, holding a trombone, and I couldn't get away because I was only wearing flip-flops. Thankfully, I woke up before he caught me.

When I got down to Maida Gym, the squadron was assembled. Eighty or ninety blokes stood there, half asleep, in tracksuit bottoms and maroon t-shirts. Almost all of them had both hands plunged down the front of their Ron Hills, cupping their ballbags to keep warm: it was about as far from Belize as you could get. The only animated person there was Herbert. He'd decided that the run was best personal effort, not squadded. He set us all off, with the warning that no one should take longer than 42 minutes. I was absolutely chinstrapped from the moment I started out, and I suffered like fuck all the way through.

Out of all the Belize crowd, only Mark Smith put in a decent time. The rest of us went round like slugs, with Frankson running alongside us giving us a hard time. 'Not been training eh, lads? Don't fucking worry, we'll knock you back into shape.'

I sweated rum and sausage sandwiches, and felt like I was going to die. I got in in 45 minutes, with Derek spewing his way in a minute after me. We got a bollocking off Herbert, but I was too knackered to listen to him. I shuggied my way back to the block and got ready for work.

The troop hadn't changed a bit and I dropped into the routine immediately. Just before NAAFI break, Pete Allinson got hold of me. 'Eddy,' he said. 'Staff Jeans wants to see you.'

'What about?'

'He didn't say. He probably wants to give you a medal for working so hard in Belize.'

'I deserve one as well, just for having to watch The Dalek eating.'

Pete winced. 'Oooh, I know what you mean. Anyway, you'd better get up there or you'll miss NAAFI break.'

'Good point.' I legged it up the stairs and came to a halt outside the partly ajar door. I gave it a quick tap and Staff Jeans shouted, 'Come in, Corporal Nugent.'

I moved inside and stood near the door.

'You wanted me, Staff.'

'Yeah, we've had your new posting details in from Manning and Records.'

'Oh, right.' I hadn't really thought about it, but my four years would be up in August. I'd filled in a dreamsheet while I was in Belize, but I was expecting to hang round Aldershot for a couple of years more. If I was Para-trained I could apply to extend, but that wasn't going to happen now. The next Pre-Para was in September and I'd be gone by then.

'Want to know where you're going?' he said, picking up a sheet of paper from his desk.

'Is it somewhere nice, Staff?'

'Fucking lovely, son. You're going to the Sunny Seventh.'

7 Signals – Herford, BAOR. There were so many units in The Fatherland at the time that I was bound to cop it sooner or later. And, to be honest, Germany *per se* didn't bother me, since it provided an inexhaustible supply of the single man's dual essentials – cheap cars and high quality pornography. But 7 Sigs? What a pisser. The Big 7 was BAOR in microcosm – Panzers, continental lager and insane squadron bar antics – and it was considered by siggies and junior NCOs to be a penal regiment, performing the function of a

lower-tier pokey, a halfway-house to Colchester. 7 was where they sent all the mentalists that other units didn't want: the pad-shaggers, drunkards, sex offenders, bed-pissers, monkey-filler-inners, habitual brawlers and general all round flotsam and jetsam. I didn't consider myself any of the above – all I could think was that they must have a tossbag shortage.

'What date?' I said.

He looked down at the paper.

'You're due to start on Monday 15th July, but you'll get a couple of weeks' embarkation leave before then. By my reckoning, that means you've got a month to sort all your shit out before you leave. I was going to get you to sign for a det, but there's not much point now. It's a shame you didn't get yourself through P-Company, you could have done another five years here.'

'Yes, Staff.'

'Not to worry. You can always stick your name down again.' He checked his watch. 'You'd better fuck off, or you'll get no NAAFI break.'

'Cheers, Staff.'

That was that, then. I had conflicting feelings about my time in Aldershot. On the one hand, I knew that I'd find things a bit easier at another unit, particularly on the PT side. On the other, it rankled that I hadn't had what it took to pass P-Company and got to do all the parachuting and that. Most of the lads I'd turned up with had got through and were enjoying the opportunities it brought, like foreign jumps courses and more respect. I'd learnt the hard way that earning the 'blue badge of courage' took a bit more than a good time on the cross country runs, and I'd found myself wanting on the willpower and determination fronts. I didn't really think I'd be coming back. Once I'd been sucked into the BAOR vortex, I probably wouldn't get spat out again until I was married to a huge German woman and had grey hair and a couple of Boxhead sprogs.

I didn't get much work done in the last month. I MFO'ed all my gear to be sent on to Herford, and stored the boxes in my room for a couple of weeks. That was a bit of a mistake. Just like a skip outside someone's house, every time I left the boxes alone for a few minutes I'd come back to find them with some more rubbish in them. I was pulling out McDonalds bags and half-eaten apples every night. I finally got them filled up and nailed the lids on a few days before I left.

My last day at 216 was a Monday. In a hastily-assembled presentation in the Troop Stores, Staff Jeans gave me a copy of the recently-commissioned Airborne Signals painting, taking care to explain that it was the closest I'd ever get to actual parachuting. Although I was grateful to receive it, my first thought was that it was fucking massive and I was going to have to carry it all the way home.

I made a short speech which was constantly interrupted by industrial-strength heckling. After the abuse had finished, everyone wished me well and I was given a lift to the station in one of the spare Rovers. As expected, the train journey home was a bastard. I had to change at Waterloo and get my arse across to Euston carrying two rucksacks and the painting, whose dimensions were just big enough that I couldn't carry it under one arm. I managed to annoy almost everyone in London as I stumbled around numerous tube stations before finally emerging at Euston. By this time, I was trying to carry it between the thumb and forefinger of my left hand, a method which worked for approximately five seconds at a time before my hand cramped up and I had to rest. By the time I got to the train, I was ready to leave the fucker on the platform, but I eventually got it on board and sat down, sweating. I gonked for most of the journey, waking up for the last time as the train pulled into Stockport.

Dad, as ever, was waiting for me, and took one of the rucksacks off me when I got to him. 'What the fuck have you got there?' he said.

'A painting. It's me leaving present.'

'Is it big enough? I thought it was half a bloody door.'

When we got home I gave it pride of place in my Dad's shed, where it has remained ever since.

I enjoyed the unexpected leave. Best of all was a pep talk about the Germans from my nan. She wasn't what you'd call 'PC' about them, having worked in the heavily-bombed Trafford Park area during the war where she had lost quite a few friends in the air raids.

'Watch out for 'em, Eddy. They're bloody sly buggers.'

'Who, nan?'

'The Jerries, who d'you think? They'd bloody bomb you as soon as look at you.'

I chuckled into my dinner but she was quick to scold me.

'It's not funny, Eddy. My friend Ivy married a German and he was horrible. Always bloody shouting he was, about this, that or the other.'

Like grandmothers the world over, mine made no sense at all when talking about current affairs, and tended merely to spout out a stream of consciousness until it was time for another cup of tea.

'The war finished 46 years ago, nan,' I said. 'Things have changed.'

'Have they buggery. Look at *Auf Wiedersehen Pet*. That bloke in charge of the building site was horrible to them Geordie lads.'

Fair point, I thought. When I left, she gave me a big hug and kiss at the door, and ruffled my hair, as she'd done since I could remember.

'Bye then, nan. I'll be back in a couple of months.'

'You look after yourself, Eddy love, and don't trust a bloody one of 'em.'

My flight was leaving from Luton the next day. I had to get up early to catch my train down there, and dad was getting ready for work at the same time. We were heading in opposite directions, so I ordered a cab. Mum came down, rubbing sleep from her eyes as the taxi pulled up. We all hugged, and separated.

Dad went off to work, mum went back to bed and, running entirely contrary to my gran's Stanboardmanesque advice, I packed my kit and went to Germany.

EDDY NUGENT AND THE KICKED OUT PAD

AT LUTON AIRPORT, I had a quick look round for the military check-in for Gütersloh. It wasn't hard to spot, despite the advanced counter-terrorism skills which had been employed to confuse the Provos. The RCT had disguised it, optimistically, as belonging to a civilian airline called 'Smith Air', and the desk was manned by a spotty youth, straight out of training, with a regulation haircut and regimental tie. To complete the subterfuge, the only passengers milling around were young blokes with bone dome heads, dressed in Helly Hansen fleeces, jeans and desert wellies, and carrying green bergans. The winner of the IRA's 'Worst Recruit of 1991' would have clocked it in about two seconds flat.

'Alright mate,' I said, to the lad behind the desk. 'Is this the forces check-in?'

His eyes widened in horror. 'Sssssh,' he hissed, glancing over his shoulder. 'This is a covert operation!'

I had a sudden vision of him in Luton's hottest nightspot: 'Well love, I'd love to tell you what I do,' with a knowing tap of the nose and a wink. 'But it's better for both of us if I don't... Of course, I could've been in the Paras, but my shoulders were too wide to fit through the aircraft door etc etc.'

'Right, mate,' I said. 'Whatever. Anyway, here are my docs. I'm flying to Güt.'

The flight took just over an hour. In those days, most people flying into BAOR went through Gütersloh. After getting out of the airport I was confronted by 20 Army green bone-rattler buses, all going to different destinations. I found the one for Herford, loaded up my kit and got aboard. There was a group of very young lads sitting near the back, obviously fresh from training. But they knew each other, and their solidarity lent them a bit of boisterous volume. I listened to their conversation filling the bus, with all the usual bragging about what they had planned for the bars and brothels of Germany. It made my mind drift back to those first few days in Aldershot, straight out of training with Joey Donaldson, Scouse Marriott and Davey Bovan. Four years had passed since then, and I'd lost some of that 'first posting' greenness. They grew quieter as we approached 7 Sigs, perhaps reflecting – as I was – what a twat's throw of the dice it was that they'd landed Sunny 7 straight out of the factory.

I followed the usual new unit arrival routine by reporting to the guardroom and got directions to the squadron offices where I was met by the squadron clerk, Jim. He was the fattest bloke I'd ever seen in uniform, including the German from *Those Magnificent Men In Their Flying Machines*. Given half a chance, he'd attempt to convince you that he was a friend to the stars and an international *bon viveur*, but the mundane reality was that he was a sweaty desk jockey, so obese that you'd have had to skin three Idi Amins to make him a wetsuit.

After a smattering of Jim's bullshit, I had the usual brief off the SSM who was the typical sergeant major, all 'tache and shouting. Major Daniels, the OC Squadron, was something else, though. An old Aussie Major on an exchange visit, he'd gone up through the ranks – he was still 'tached-up, showing his SNCO roots – and had served in Vietnam. He was also sporting some SAS wings. Physically, he wasn't an intimidating man at all. He was as bald as a coot, whip-thin and only about 5ft 9in tall, and if you passed him in the street you wouldn't give him a second look – though in shirt sleeve order the muscles in his forearms were like knotted steel rope. But his soldiering credentials were second to none, and spoke for themselves; I made a mental note not to fuck up whilst he was in charge.

As it happened, he turned out to be just about the best officer I ever worked under – very fair, and without any of the usual officer/ bloke class distinction. Whether or not this was due to him being an Aussie, a ranker, SAS or a 'Nam vet, I'm not sure, but all four must've combined to have a profound effect on his personality. He was unlike any OC I'd had before and was very easy to talk to, with his loose Aussie drawl laced with a full swearing arsenal. On the rare occasions that we had bull nights in the block, an OC's inspection was always preferable to that of the sergeant major, or any other senior, for that matter. A guy who fought in Vietnam is probably not going to give two flying fucks about polished radiator handles, and this was certainly the case with the boss. So long as hygiene wasn't slipping, and there were no overtly slovenly cunts, he preferred to use his walk around to chat with the lads, find out how they were doing and maybe pick up the odd video of *Platoon* and give its owner a wry smile.

At times, it was easy to forget his standing within the regimental hierarchy, but that isn't to say that he didn't command respect. Quite the opposite: Major Daniels pulled off the supremely difficult task of simultaneously being both the best-liked and most-respected officer on camp. Sadly, save for the odd social function or Squadron-wide address, I didn't have a vast amount of interaction with him. That was a shame, because he was one of life's naturally intriguing characters, and I'd love to have had the chance to get to know him better.

Jim pointed me in the direction of the block so I went off to get my room sorted. The 7 Sigs accommodation was different to most other Army camps in Germany, in that it was all single-storey, single-man rooms, rather than the usual multi-storey affairs. (For example, 14 Sigs in Celle inhabited the largest red-brick building in Germany, described by the lads who lived there as a frigging nightmare. It was infested with a protected species of bat which dive-bombed the corridors of an evening, to the point where getting up for the toilet in the night was like walking into the opening credits of *Scooby Doo*.)

The single storey-ness of our accommodation was a major advantage, as I discovered some months later, while urinating out of my window one night. It may sound like social delinquency, but in BAOR if the journey to the toilets was more than five paces from the end of your bed, it was considered perfectly acceptable – not to say *de rigeur* – to make alternative arrangements. A lucky few had a sink in their rooms, commonly referred to as a 'hot and cold running toilet', with added cooling 'spud-shelf'. The rest of us used the window, and it was while enjoying a 2am wazz that I experienced a speed wobble and pitched head-first out onto the ground and into my own puddle. This was unpleasant enough, but better than falling three storeys into the bargain – a disaster which *had* happened to a mate of mine at 4 Armoured Division just down the road. 'Dog' Barker was a grade A maniac, given over to wickedness of outlandish proportions whenever he was drunk. One stormy night, after a drinking session considered extravagant even by his own standards, he found himself in his window pissing like a cow on to a flat rock. Unfortunately for Dog, it was that type of window which pivots through 360 degrees around centrally-mounted hinges on its vertical sides. As he stood there in mid-flow, already unsteady on his feet, a powerful gust of wind caught the window behind him. It spun round, hitting him on the backside and sending him arse-over-tit into the open air and plummeting the 20-odd feet to the wet ground below, where his elegant landing ensured that he broke both wrists and both ankles. Unable to move, he lay there in the pouring rain for a couple of hours before the prowler guard discovered him. They thought he was just a bag of rubbish lobbed out of the block until he started to moan, at which point they wandered lazily over and radioed the guardroom to say they'd located another Herforder Pils-and-Asbach Brandy casualty. Dog's only recollection of the whole event was his confusion at finding brickwork suddenly whistling past his face as he fell. He eventually recovered from his injuries, his recuperation being deemed complete a couple of months later when he saw fit to get so drunk that neat lager started fizzing from his Khyber, necessitating the insertion of a tampon.

* * * * *

My room was open, so I dropped my kit off and headed off to the stores. As always, it was a place of stygian gloom; it's my belief that they deliberately light them like Neapolitan knocking shops so that the storemen can deny having items in stock without having their integrity called into question. As I waited for my eyes to adjust to the darkness, the familiar waft of mothballs assailed my nostrils and caused me to let out an involuntary cough. The storeman appeared as if from nowhere, like a very angry Mr Ben. He'd obviously taken the cough as some sort of impertinent demand for service.

'All fucking right, you impatient cunt,' he shouted. 'I'm not fucking Linford fucking Christie, you know.'

Storemen (along with slop jockeys) make up a disproportionate percentage of the Army's disgruntled bastards, but this particular blanket-stacker took the biscuit. I peered at him in the dimness. He was leaning with both hands on the counter, staring at me; beneath his nose bristled an improbably large moustache.

I'd seen a few of these about the place, and I half-wondered whether 7 Sigs was some kind of John Holmes Memorial Residence for retired 1970s adult art performers. But then the moustache and the British Army have had a long and fruitful relationship since days of old. The popularity of facial topiary had dwindled in the population at large since its Victorian heyday, to the point where, by the time I joined the Army, very few individuals thus adorned themselves. These included the entire Liverpool Football Club squad, who – as you will recall – liked to accessorise the 'tache with perms of such furious curliness that their heads looked like hairy lightbulbs. As a result, it had come as a big surprise to me when I'd turned up at Harrogate and found that nearly all the permanent staff sported lip thatching, in varying styles and to varying degrees. I remember a couple in particular who had cleverly referenced their *Zulu*-era forebears, and had the sideys-and-moustache combo which were known as buggers' handgrips, made famous by Colour Sergeant Bourne in the eponymous film.

Moustaches do go well with the uniform, of course, and they had the added effect of making the wearer look a touch more experienced, so lots of younger soldiers tried to run before they could walk. Because shaving in the Army was obligatory, if you wanted to grow a 'tache, permission was needed from the Troop Staffy. After an abusive evaluation of the likelihood of success, a chit would be issued and a short period of grace allowed for the soldier to cultivate his instant maturity. When the time was up, the Staffy would have another look. If it was suitably bushy, the wearer got to be the newest member of the Wilf Lunn lookalike club. If not, he would suffer the ignominy of being told to go and wipe the fucking thing off with a flannel. (It's rumoured that the most cherished reason for passing SAS selection is not the beret or the wings or the feeling of joining that most elite of units, but the fact that the new trooper is allowed to sport the full-on gringo 'tache for the duration of his service.)

As the stores wallah looked at me, his eyes blazing with inexplicable contempt, I tried to lighten the mood. 'Hello, mate,' I said. 'I've just been posted into 3 Squadron and I've come for my bedding issue.'

My attempt at chirpiness entirely failed to break the ice.

'Oh for fuck's sake,' he said. 'Right, wait here.'

With that he hopped off... literally. I performed an involuntary double-take so over the top that Wile E. Coyote would have considered it implausible. The poor bastard only had one leg – no wonder he was so hacked off. Losing a limb is bad enough, but combining that with the naturally toxic temperament of a storeman had created a madly cantankerous hybrid of unique proportions. As he ferreted around for my blankets, I pondered, too, the psychological effects on a symmetry-maintenance-obsessed shelf-stacker of possessing one permanently redundant shoe. It must have put him in mental torment.

As he hopped back with my bedding, I leaned forward tentatively. 'Er, is the MFO store open, mate?'

He kept it brief. 'Get fucked. Come back tomorrow.'

I signed for my blankets on a 1033, resigned to collecting the rest of my kit the following day, and kept my gob shut. I'd developed a habit of accidentally saying the wrong thing, and I knew I'd start gabbing on about 'finding my feet' or 'getting a foot on the ladder', after which my MFO box would turn up six months later at the British Antarctic Survey. I grabbed up my stuff and fucked off to my room, pronto.

My scratcher was the classical inherited pit space, with a wall covered in bits of Blu-Tack, a ravaged jazz mag of ambiguous pedigree in the locker and a stain of unclear origin and impressive proportions located in the centre of the off-brown carpet. Still, I was pretty chuffed with it. Although quite small, it had a couple of lockers and – most importantly – only one bed. Stretching ahead of me for the next few years was a vista of undisturbed, 24/7 masturbation. In Aldershot, I'd had to develop counter-surveillance skills to prevent being rumbled, mid-thrap. Those 'danger-thraps', though enjoyable in their own way, had you twitching about like a meercat as you tried to concentrate simultaneously on the room door and the pleasures of Linda Lusardi. I was looking forward to a spot of privacy.

My posters were in my MFO box, so the walls would have to wait. Poster choice in the Army was very revealing of character, and a quick blimp round a lad's bedspace told you quite a bit about him. The 'serious relationship' guy would have hundreds of pictures of his girlfriend dotted around, and wouldn't welcome anyone lingering too long over any particular shot. The less-committed were more than happy to stick up more risqué photos and saw no moral dilemma in having them next to a picture of Jo Guest with legs thoroughly akimbo. The complete singlies would have their spaces wallpapered with floor-to-ceiling grot, punctuated by the occasional band or motorbike poster.

The room also needed some furniture other than the standard plastic orange laundry bin, bed, table and wastepaper bin. Over time, I knew, it would accrue a little additional comfort. There were always bits of non-issue furniture – 'corner sofas' and the like – floating around. These tended to be inherited when their owner moved on to pastures new. Some of the better pieces would be referred to by their original owner's name – 'Dusty Miller's table', say, or 'Fat Frank's Fridge' – but in generic terms they were 'Gizzits', as in, 'Fucking hell, mate, that's a nice chair… Gizzit, will ya?'

One particularly famous Gizzit, fondly recalled by an old mate of mine who'd been posted to Germany ahead of me, was 'The Chair of Death', so-named because of its preternatural comfortableness. To sit on it was to fall asleep; not such a bad thing you may think, but a five minute sit-down after lunch could rapidly turn into a three-hour kip, with the kipper waking in a pool of his own dribble, with a sleep-creased face that looked like an AA road map and facing Jankers for missing a parade. Even worse, testing the wrath of the chair with a little sit-down after work, ahead of an evening piss-up, was bound to lead to the foolhardy soldier staggering into the bar at closing time, still in uniform and rubbing the sleep from his eyes after missing all the action.

I made it my mission to get my grubby mits on such an item. But I'd have plenty of time for all of that later. I decided to head up to the troop offices to introduce myself and get some NAAFI break scoff with the chaps.

* * * * *

If the accommodation was different, the vehicle parks and garages were the same as everywhere else – the generic set-up of large, old, corrugated sheds with various wire cages for each vehicle's equipment and multitudes of tins of grease and oil cans and God knows what other toxic substances lying around the place. The air was heavy with lingering diesel fumes, and I spotted a group of lads in greasy green overalls standing around a trailer, bullshitting wildly. It warmed the cockles of my heart. The 'trailer of knowledge' is an age-old institution, and the single most important debating chamber of the working soldier. The senior privates and junior NCOs will congregate around a vehicle trailer for the majority of the working day and, over lukewarm brews and pilfered fags, discuss the pressing issues of the moment. Worldly wisdom and half-baked nonsense will be liberally dispensed, and solutions to many international problems, none of which would ever work, thrashed out. A recurrent theme is the 'Cunts-squash-ladder', a rigorous analysis of who in the regimental hierarchy has been seen to be fucking the lads about the most. To be a regular around the trailer was a sign that you were in the upper echelons of the troop and had the respect of your peers; its pecking order went beyond the imposed military rank structure, with experience and capacity for talking shite being more desirous than a tape or two. Sessions ended informally, as soon as a senior or rodney showed up. Cigs would be flicked away and everyone would move off simultaneously, whilst pretending to be busy. Knowing my place, I gave the trailers a wide berth and made a beeline for the troop offices.

I had a sneaky look through the open door. There were desks for the OC Troop, the Troop Staffy and the Troop Sergeant. Each was tidy except for brown ring marks from years of spilt coffee. Their mugs highlighted their previous service: the OC's was a Sandhurst official-type affair, whilst the other two were from different units where the seniors had served. The walls were adorned with the photos from the two SNCOs' past units. If you worked your way back, you could watch them getting younger and using less notches on their webbing belts; the wall behind the OC Troop was conspicuously bare which, when combined with his youthful demeanour and his brand-new mug, pointed towards The Big 7 being his first unit.

Off to the left I could see a small brew-making room, about the size of a fortune teller's booth. Inside there was the traditional proffed cookhouse table with all the paraphernalia required for continuous hot beverage production. A battered old fridge lurked under it, containing milk of various vintages, some approaching the consistency of a ripe brie. A spoon stuck out of a crumpled Tate and Lyle bag, and I didn't need to look at it to know that it would be rendered almost useless by a thick crust of old sugar; despite the fact that it would take 40 dips into the bag to get the equivalent of a level spoonful, no-one would ever rinse it off. This was primarily because of the fundamental truth, that all blokes are arseholes and can wait indefinitely for someone else to do things.

I knocked on.

'Who the fuck are you?' came the welcome from the sergeant.

'Lance Corporal Nugent, sarnt.'

After knocking up a quick salute to the OC, a Lt Chesterton, I got the usual grilling off the Seniors. Staff Martin and Sgt Brown seemed like alright blokes, as far as they could be to a junior, and it was relatively informal. Whilst the OC Troop was talking, he swilled his brew round like a fine cognac and once or twice he seemed to thrash his thigh with an imaginary riding crop, which was a bit odd. But then, OC Troops were always a bit odd: a *lack* of idiosyncratic behaviour would have been more worrying.

Eventually, Staff Martin wrapped up the briefing. 'Anyway, Corporal N,' he said, 'let's get you issued some webbing and all the usual bumf. I'll get one of the toms to show you around.'

At that, he got up and walked out of the office, I followed him out to the vehicle park and he summoned one of the lads who'd been skulking round the back of a Land Rover. 'Pissy,' he said. 'Get over here and get your covvies off.'

The guy in question wandered over and took off his coveralls, handing them to me. 'Lance Corporal Nugent,' said Staff Martin. 'Sig Dickinson.' With that, he left.

'Alright, mate,' I said, venturing an outstretched hand.

Dickinson shook it and returned the greeting. 'Alright. So where've you come from?'

'216.'

'Right.'

Formalities done with, we headed off to the Diana Dors, where Pissy introduced me to the squadron storeman, Pete 'Ronnie' McDonald. He was the classic 7 Sigs monster posted in from another unit after doing 28 days in nick for drunk and disorderly. I discovered later that his 'drunk and disorderly' was another man's minor mental meltdown. He had started by getting olympically lashed on Korn in the block, climbing into his issued PT kit and fixing his only campaign medal (NI GSM) to the shirt. Then he had begun knocking out press-ups whilst shouting abuse at himself in the manner of a PTI, as his bemused mates cheered him on.

'COME ON, PUSH IT OUT YOU LAZY BASTARD!'

Why he had decided to do this, no-one knew, but after his little upper-body workout Ronnie had gone outside to do a self-inflicted BFT. This is where he was happened upon by the orderly officer. The officer observed Ronnie, cross-legged drunk, staggering the full width of the road and shouting to himself, 'Right, gents! Form up on the startline! TOO SLOW! Drop and give me 20 squat-thrusts.'

At this, Ronnie had adopted the squat thrust position and begun the exercises, each successful movement being punctuated by a fart with a potentially risky outcome. After watching him for a moment or two, the orderly officer had intervened. 'OK, McDonald, I think you should go to bed.'

Ronnie had completely ignored him, carrying on regardless until he had reached the required amount of repetitions, after which he had taken two minutes to clamber to his feet – all of this accompanied by grunts and mutterings only intelligible to Ronnie. Once upright, he swayed to attention and continued commanding his imaginary troops. 'Remember… any failures and you'll be on remedials! Blooooaaargh!'

The final part of the sentence was cut off by an all-too-predictable honk from both nostrils. The orderly officer had seen as much as he needed to. 'Right McDonald, you've had enough. Hello Zero, this is Alpha-One-Zero, send prowler to 2 Squadron accommodation block main entrance. Out.'

The 2IC of the guard's report made for an interesting read. 'Sir, on arriving at the incident reported by the Orderly Officer, I witnessed Signalman McDonald staggering in a puddle of vomit (his), dressed in PT kit and wearing a General Service Medal (Northern Ireland). I informed Sig McDonald that I was taking him to the guardroom to calm down. He shouted back at me, "Right, son, you're on a fucking fizzer!" He then threw a large haymaker at the Orderly Officer. Said punch bypassed the Orderly Officer by approximately 18 inches and caused the accused (Sig McDonald) to perform a pirouette and fall to the ground into the previously described puddle. He then became acquiescent due to near-unconsciousness, though he managed to make the occasional threat to someone called "Mocksy" as we carried him back to the guardroom.'

An incident like this was bound to lead to a bit of stir. A posting to 7 became inevitable after Ronnie's release from nick when the OC came across him and asked, 'Ah, Sig McDonald... how was jail?'

'Fine thank you, sir,' he replied. 'It was the best sex I've ever had.'

To speak to Ronnie, you wouldn't have thought there was a drunken maniac lurking below the surface. Although quite a big chap, he was relatively baby-faced and had a soft Scots accent. Unfortunately, he was an instant-social-hand-grenade-just-add-alcohol type of guy. Still, in the sober light of day he was thoroughly amiable and for a squadron storeman he was very helpful indeed. I chatted with him for quite a while as we drank a brew and he gave me the low down on the Regimental players.

'The CO's a cunt,' he said, with some vehemence. 'And the RSM is a wanker. But the OC Squadron and your OC Troop are good blokes, and the SSM is into piss sex.'

I spat my tea across the stores. 'I'm sorry, mate, say that again.'

'Aye, the badge is into toilet sex.'

'Sorry Ronnie, call me cynical but how the fuck could you know something like that?'

'A while ago I acquired a new bit of audio visual entertainment...'

'You mean a video?'

'That's the bastard. Anyway, it was a top-class title called *Pissing Party, Volume 3*. I'd had it for a couple of weeks and it had done the rounds and then one Saturday morning there's a knock at the door and it was the fucking SSM in his civvies. I shat meself because my room was in rag order but he just stood in the corridor, checked the coast was clear and says, "Here, Ronnie, Lend us your pissing vid." That was it, I haven't seen the fucking thing since, which is a shame. But then, I haven't had any guard duties either, so it's no' all bad.'

We shot the breeze for a while longer and then I took my newly-issued kit back to the block, where I could spend the next couple of years trying to keep it from being nicked. As I walked in, I saw another guy trying to manoeuvre an enormous shrank into the room next to mine. (A 'shrank', for the uninitiated, is a long, low-level, wall-length cupboard, with space for your videos, somewhere to stick your telly and a couple of drawers for stuff.) I stopped and watched him, my heart sinking.

He was a nondescript sort of bloke – late 20s, around 5ft 9in tall, with the sort of tan you get from working outdoors and a sandy-coloured 'what's under the beret is mine' hairstyle – short at the sides but embryonically mop-toppish. I've always been crap at guessing someone's heft, but he looked like an 8 min 30 sec BFT kind of guy – the unofficial unit of how fit/be-pisstanked a soldier was. This gave me some hope – certainly he was no buffet-slayer, and he showed no signs of the wok smuggler gut that seemed to befall a good percentage of the married blokes.

But despite his relative slimness, the shrank and the boxes of belongings littering the corridor told their own stories. The scenario before me could mean only one thing: he was a pad who'd been ejected from his house by the old lady.

I sighed.

When a married guy moves back into the block, his behaviour follows a pre-set pattern.

Stage one: freedom. He behaves as though he was 18 and unattached again. It's a heady mix of binge-drinking, smashing up his room and the NAAFI vending machines and trawling the other lads' rooms on the scrounge for any decent filth, because his missus has forbidden jazz mags and thrapping since the day he mistakenly placed a ring on her claw. This behaviour is a backlash against years of perceived repression.

Stage two: depression. Although still fully on the booze, the rejected pad retreats to his darkened room and listens to weepy music, interspersing each song with the occasional wail of, 'Ooooh, why did you leave me, Julie?' At this point, he is at his lowest point and should be avoided at all costs. If you don't shun him, he'll collar you in the corridor and regale you with stories of how happy he was, and how he and his Julie had such a great time at that barbeque last year. Then *Lady in Red* will start emanating from his room, and his eyes will mist over. With a quivering lip, and full glass of Johnnie Walker, he will gesture to the stereo and whimper, 'That were me and our Julie's song.'

Stage three: resignation. After a couple of weeks of blowing all his cash in the squadron bar and on fines for damage to the accommodation, the once-married, now-single soldier turns *into* his wife, only in the block. He hoovers at ridiculous hours, begins walking around in 'His' share of a 'His-and-Hers' dressing gown/ slippers set, and starts complaining about the state of the place. Worst of all, if there is any noise caused by drunken singlies at any time, he's straight out into the corridor toting an oversized coffee mug from Ikea, and saying things like, 'Do you know what time it is?' and, 'Keep the noise down, we're not all drunken idiots you know!' This from a man who, two weeks before, got so inebriated that he fell off the toilet in mid-turd and, in the process of trying to clamber back on his feet, smeared cack on the walls to such an extent that the chaps in the block thought a poltergeist was trying to pass on messages.

After watching him struggle with half the contents of a fair-sized MFI for a minute or two, I wandered over.

'Alright mate?' I asked, adopting a cheerful demeanour.

He just muttered under his breath and continued doing battle with the huge shrank.

Yep, definitely a kicked-out pad.

As I started to unpack my uniform, my fears were confirmed by an almighty crash followed by him shouting at the top of his voice, in a strong southern accent, 'FACKING FACK! FACKING FACK YOU, YOU FACKING BITCH! THIS IS *ALL* YOUR FACKING FAULT!'

My admiration for his expletive skills was blurred by the knowledge that I was in for a good few weeks of night time disruption from a weeping, burbling wreck. I decided to take the bull by the horns, and go and offer him a hand. I went out into the corridor and poked my head into his room to survey the damage. The first thing I saw was the remnants of the wall cupboard strewn across the floor. It had obviously toppled forward and broken up on impact and the poor, downtrodden bastard was standing amidst the wreckage, shaking his fist at the gods. On seeing me, his shoulders slumped and he bent down to gather up what was left of his furniture and started muttering that he hoped her tits fell off.

'Hello, mate,' I said. 'I'm Eddy Nugent. I've just been posted in from 216. Sounds like you're having a bit of jip here. I thought you might need a bit of help?'

'No thanks, I'll get it sorted,' he replied, face to the ground like a sullen teenager.

'Right then, well... anyway, if you do need any help, I'll be next door. By the way, what's your name?'

He stood up and seemed to relax a bit. 'Yeah, sorry, mate,' he said. 'My name's Vic – Vic Kerr. The lads either call me "Wan" or "The Padre". Or sometimes "The Wanking Padre".'

Wan Kerr. I had to chuckle. The inventiveness of nicknames, so easily earned but impossible to disown, was one of the things I liked about the Army. Often, you never found out lads' first names – they went through their service careers with a pseudonym based on their surname or some weird physical characteristic, even to the point where their made-up moniker would get used on the charge sheet when they were put on a fizzer. Luckily, you couldn't do much with 'Nugent' – unlike Shufflebottom, say, or Cummings – and I was fairly normal in appearance and habits, so I never moved past 'Eddy'. Others weren't so fortunate. Terry Sharpe from basic training was the only bloke I ever saw enjoy the deathpack sandwiches, which he devoured with relish. For this he was known as 'Tapeworm'. If he lives to 80, and becomes the Prime Minister, or the Archbishop of Canterbury – both quite unlikely, to be fair – he'll always be 'Tapeworm' to his ex-Army mates, whether he likes it or not.

'No worries, pal,' I said. 'Ronnie McDonald tells me there's a do in the squadron bar tonight. I'll maybe catch you there?'

Vic had been grinning with me, but now his jaw set and his face darkened, giving him an almost demonic look. 'Oh, I'll be facking there alright,' he said.

'Right,' I said, slightly unnerved. 'Well, give us a shout if you need a hand?'

I got on with sorting my stuff out, pressing my kit and brushing my boots. I'd occasionally hear Vic angrily addressing another inanimate object with shouts of, 'Gertcha, you facking bitch!' before reducing it to its constituent parts. At one point, I walked past his open room and saw him on all fours with a boot in his hand, smashing a laundry basket to pieces for getting in his way, with a cry of 'That'll facking learn ya!'

At one point, a young lad meandered up our corridor and stuck his head in my room. 'Sounds like he's trying to roar one up a rhino's shitter next door,' he said, in a broad West Country accent.

I laughed and we shook hands. 'Alright, mate? Eddy Nugent.'

'Jango,' he said. 'A bit fuckin' weird I know, but me old man was into his spaghetti westerns. Where you posted in from, then?'

'216.'

'Fuckin' 'ell, that's a bit wank, comin' 'ere. What did you do? Kill your OC's dog?'

I replied as deadpan as I could, 'Kind of. I bummed it, then killed it, then dug it up and bummed it again.'

This got Jango laughing and he walked off. Eventually, with everything squared away in my room, I lay down on my bed, closed my eyes and tried to block out the sound of the ranting next door.

EDDY NUGENT AND THE DANCE OF THE FLAMING ARSEHOLES

I MUST HAVE dozed off, because the next thing I knew Vic Kerr was leaning over me, shaking my shoulder.

'Hey, Eddy,' he said, as I opened my eyes. 'You want to get some scran before the piss up, mate.'

I'd made the mistake of sleeping for just the wrong amount of time and in the wrong position. I had fifty percent of a 'Flock of Seagulls' haircut and my left hand was dead. I propped myself up and tried to blink myself awake.

Vic seemed to have cheered up a bit and despite having known me for only a couple of hours, was being quite the pal. 'Shake a leg, you facking mong,' he said. 'Let's get some scoff from the Colonel Gaddafi, I'm facking Hank Marvin, you wanker.'

It was impossible to take offence. Squaddies address each other in the most abusive manner possible; being called a 'cunt' is among the highest terms of affection.

I gave myself a quick squaddie shower – a squirt of Insignia under each arm – straightened my hair a bit and followed him.

The NAAFI was right across the road, directly opposite the gym. It was open to debate whether this was a coincidence of camp planning or to remind fat knackers stocking up on pies and stickies that there was always a beasting around the corner. We sat down in the vending machine area, which was an absolute Ginsters paradise. I snagged a pasty and a carton of pre-piss up, stomach-settling Danish milk. As it went down, I surveyed the surroundings. The floor was an unappetising combination of chocolate- and caramel-coloured lino squares, bonded together with old cheese and spilt beer. The walls were brown and stained with an infinite number of unidentifiable substances. There were a couple of phone booths at the end of the room and a brace of standard metal microwaves had been installed into the wall, each plastered with crumbs and dried-on ketchup. Scattered round the room were the reliably boring circular tables with moulded red plastic seats affixed to them. It was the sort of set up you might find in an American lockdown facility.

The vending machines were half empty, the remaining items only still available because they were complete shite. A lone Double Decker leant against the inside of the glass on one of the machines, having failed to make the drop to the collection tray, no doubt causing a minor 'Hulk' episode on the part of the seen-off buyer. Army vending machines are always dented and cracked, the damage wreaked by pissed-up squaddies raiding the food machine area when suffering an attack of the drunken munchies. You'd see them, armed with hands full of ten pfennig pieces after emptying their coin jars (all bank accounts being dry since the first weekend of the month), bouncing off the walls for about two hours before they could insert the small and fiddly coins into the slot – with at least an hour of this spent dropping the coinage and snuffling around like a French truffle-pig to retrieve it. The decidedly worse-for-wear soldier would often then press the wrong button and would be presented with an empty compartment or a packet of out-of-date fig rolls, instead of the food he wanted. This provocation would be met by immediate counter-attack, during which the disappointed lad would spend several minutes trying to kick-box the machine into submission. When this proved unproductive, his dipsomaniacal thoughts would eventually turn back to the food still stored within. He'd try to manoeuvre his arm into the serving hatch, like a chimp using a stick to catch ants, until, with impeccable sitcom timing, it would get stuck. The following morning, on opening the premises, an entirely unsurprised NAAFI manager would discover the offender asleep on the floor, with his arm still elbow deep in the ruined vending machine, like a narcoleptic vet who'd dozed off with his hand up a cow's Gary Glitter.

We finished our pasties and went back to the block. It was starting to fill up with bods who'd knocked off from work early, which meant that the usual 'Battle of the Stereos' had begun. Life in the block wouldn't have been the same without it, but six blokes with stereos the size of church organs in a confined space, playing different music, at full volume, was a discordant pain in the arse. Every stereo in the block was living on borrowed time. Young lads would make their way to the NAAFI shop at the start of the month buying ever larger and flashier systems in a bid to have the loudest set-up on camp. After a few months, the money they needed to keep up with the NAAFI re-payments would end up squirting up the side of a kebab shop or leaking into their mattress at 03:00 hrs. When all other forms of cadging and scrounging had been exhausted, they would flog it to one of the other lads at a ridiculous, knockdown price, somewhere between five and ten percent of the original layout, regardless of age. This would be just enough to get them out of the red, and stop the powers that be from charging them for being in debt.

That was a bit of Army logic that I could never figure out. If a guy bounced a cheque or got in debt, the OC would fine you. I'm still baffled by this method of discipline: it's like sentencing a kid to 120 hours' community service in a sweet shop.

As we parted at the door to my room, Vic turned to me, his face suddenly serious. 'Cheers for knocking on for me, Eddy,' he said. 'I was getting a bit lairy in there. The problem is the facking rooms are too small for any decent furniture. I've just moved out of my pad you see.'

'Don't you worry about that, fella,' I said, hoping to steer the chat away from all mention of his married life. 'You just have a few drinks and a bit of a fall over tonight and you'll be as good as new.'

'Yeah, fack it!'

* * * * *

We wandered down to the 3 Squadron bar with Jango and a couple of other lads. It was housed in a single-storey, pebble-dashed building next to the western perimeter fence on South Camp, and was just one watering hole in a block complex that also housed booze emporiums for 1 Squadron and The Rugby Club. All three were on the same, seedily-lit corridor, which was crossed by several pipes, fitted just low enough to be reached with a jump. They were purpose-built for drunken gymnastics or pull-up competitions and as we walked though several lads were already thus engaged. As per the norm, they were the types of lads least suited to feats of strength or fitness, and their attempts to impress their mates already looked to be resulting in the usual low repetitions, muscular injury and derision all round.

In a big Regiment like 7 Sigs, each Squadron tries to engineer a reputation as the hardest drinking and working, and for indulging in the wildest antics. Like empires, these reputations rise and fall. At the time I went there, 3 Squadron's star was in the ascendant and they were current holders of the most-out-of-control-gobshites-on-camp title.

The bar's general décor and state of disrepair lent credence to the award. It was a real spit and sawdust kind of place, and the combination of aromas that hit my nostrils was complex and layered enough to interest a skilled perfumier. The top note was of stale beer, but it harmonised with the nuanced, almost undetectable and yet cloying bouquet of dried urine. The infusion was rounded off by a B and H musk, and the whole thing stuck to my clothes like marine grease.

There were no pictures on the walls, the furniture was a slack handful of old Officers' mess soft chairs which were so heavily discoloured that they looked like they'd been used as sacrificial altars, and the walls and ceiling were heavily scarred with beer can indentations and what looked, to my untrained eye, like blood. Several of the windows were cracked, and some had been broken completely and replaced with pieces of cardboard, thus allowing a cold draft to blast through. The carpet might once have been red but was now a greyish brown: its stains were a poor man's Rorschach test, and walking on it was like trying to fight your way along the Bristol Channel mudflats at low tide.

I turned to Jango. 'Fucking hell, Jango, is it normally like this?'

'No, mate,' he said. 'It's normally in rag order.'

Apparently, the squadron barman, one Chopper Harris, had been in all afternoon tidying up. It looked to me as if Chopper had spent his time smashing the place up and spraying it with cowshit, and I hoped his skills as a barman were inversely proportionate to his cleaning abilities. 'Who's this Chopper bloke, then?' I said.

Jango provided the answer with considerable gusto, 'Chopper's a monster. He was the youngest ever guy sent to P wing at Woolwich to dry out. How cool is that?'

I had to admit that being the youngest bloke in the Army to be officially certified an alcoholic was by no means a small accomplishment.

'He's a top bloke, Eddy,' said Vic. 'He's a lance jack in Bravo Troop and since he's been in charge of the bar it's always mental.'

A squadron's reputation is often attributable to the bloke in charge of its bar, and how he runs the show. As things stood, it sounded like Chopper was the ringmaster behind 3 Squadron's title.

'Well, he's not here, so what do we do?'

In answer to my question, the door opened and in walked a guy of about six feet with blond hair of slightly longer than regulation length. He was walking stiff-legged, feet wide apart and bent forward at the waist, like a giraffe having a drink. He was also holding his arse and grimacing in pain and disgust. 'Fuckin' hell,' he said, in Glaswegian tones through gritted teeth. 'What a fuckin' horrible shite that was. I tell ya, I dinnae remember drinkin' fifteen pints of gravy last night. Ach, ma fuckin' arse is like the Jap flag.'

Jango started laughing, 'I'm not surprised mate, you were drinking shots of neat Tabasco in Willy's.'

Chopper's grimace deepened, and he clutched his ring a touch harder. 'Oh fuck aye, that's right, it's all coming back now.'

Jango introduced us and I shook his hand, ensuring it was not the one with which he'd been soothing his savaged hoop. Then he clapped his hands and, with them still clamped together, his eyes wide and in a voice of insane glee, he said, 'Right lads, let's get fuckin' pissed!'

With surprising speed for a man with third degree ring sting and concurrent chafing, he rounded the bar and within a couple of seconds was rooting large bottles of Grolsch out of a sizeable beer fridge.

He lined up five bottles on the bar, popped the fliptops and raised his drink. We all picked up our own bottles and Chopper made the toast. 'Up ya fuckin' arse!'

After a couple of seconds of chugging, he lowered his drink and breathed out.

'Aaah, ya fucker that's better. So Eddy, what do you think of 7 Sigs so far?'

'Not too bad, mate. I like the single man rooms.'

Chopper put one finger on his left nostril, closed his eyes and blew out an enormous stream of snot onto the floor. He casually rubbed the nasal emission into the carpet with his foot. 'Aye mate, I ken what you mean. I almost wanked myself to death when I got posted intae this place. I was thrapping that much, I fuckin' swear my knob was glowing in the dark like a fuckin' cylume.'

I'd only meant that it made a pleasant change to the normal four-man rooms that I was used to, but when I looked round at the other lads they were all miles away, digesting Chopper's pearls of masturbatory wisdom and nodding sagely to themselves as if to say, 'Hmmm, yes, I too have suffered the trial of a thousand J Arthurs.'

The door kept banging, and within a few minutes the place was full of blokes dressed in a mixture of working dress, coveralls, civvies and combats. Chopper was soon working like a madman, almost becoming a blur as he moved between the beer fridge and the bar. His voice could be heard loudest of all as it broke clear from the ambient noise of the social crowd. 'Fuckin' alright, you cunt, I'll serve y'in a minute! What the fuck do you think ah am, a fuckin' octopus? I've only got one pair of fuckin' arms you know!'

It was a pleasure to watch him in action, his relentless activity broken only by the occasional stop to wince, cup his ravaged balloon-knot and mutter, 'Oooh, ya fucker.'

The place quickly became a sea of green clothes and bad language. I could pick out snippets of conversations drifting through the air, their originators' volume switches gradually turning up as they consumed more alcohol. As I always will, I marvelled at my comrades capacity for jamming expletives into conversations, rendering them almost unintelligible. One disgruntled lad was explaining, with accompanying vivid hand gestures, how he had remonstrated with a colleague recently about a damaged vehicle. 'Aye, I fuckin' tell ya, I fuckin' said to the bloke, I said, "Fuck the fucking fucker, the fuckin' fucker's fucked", and he just fuckin' fucked off, the fucker!'

Because I didn't really know any of the other guys in the unit, I stayed with the blokes I'd already met. When any acquaintances of Jango or Vic turned up, I was introduced to them and they all asked the same question. 'Where you posted in from then, mate?'

I could feel my senses starting to numb, not from the repetitive conversation but from the relentless intake of strong continental lager. I'd switched to Herforder Pils, and on about my fifth pint I caught sight of one of the young lads who'd been on the bus from Güt. He was a wretch of a thing, even thinner than myself when I went through Sutton Coldfield – his uniform hung off him like a trailer canopy. He was swaying slightly as the bloke next to him shouted something into his ear about brothels.

Just then, the loud banging of a bottle on the bar cut through the melee, quickly followed by the OC Squadron's Aussie tones. 'Alright you fackun' cants, fackun' siddown!' he said, semi-slurring, a half-drunk bottle in his hand. The whole bar went quiet – in itself a testament to Major Daniels' mettle and the admiration in which he was held.

'Right, gents, you all know why we're fackun' here today – promotions. Today's promotions are for siggies to lance jacks. It's an old saying but a true one, "Your first tape is the hardest to get, but the easiest to lose". So any of you blokes getting made up today, I don't want to see your fackun' ugly mugs with your heels together in my office in the next couple of months for getting pissed up and chinning some fackun' German downtown!'

A ripple of laughter flowed through the crowd and a few of the guys looked quite sheepish. I had a bit of an internal chuckle to myself as I had visions of a cement mixer falling into a hole in the ground. That had been the only real time that I'd dropped myself in the shit in Aldershot: the seven days' Restriction of Privileges and loss of an impending promotion had had a powerful effect, and I'd kept my nose comparatively clean since.

'Right, I won't waste any more drinking time, so first up is Sig Dooley. Get up here, mate, and congratulations!'

Dooley stood up. He was a big chap, about six-four, and built like a brick shithouse. His nose was fucked up and his cauliflowered ears – which looked like Dalepak grillsteaks – suggested he was a member of the rugby team. 7 Sigs was known as the Corps rugby regiment, and the decent players were posted in so they could all train together. Units specialising in sport tend to promote their Regimental team players as soon as possible, sometimes to the detriment of guys who are very good professional soldiers. It always led to some super-strength moaning when the promotion boards came out, particularly since the sportsmen got to swan around in tracksuits all day and take extended NAAFI breaks, whilst everyone else grafted. Of course, the moaning was confined to the trailer of knowledge or other small gatherings, and nobody would actually say anything – especially to a bloke like Dooley, seeing as he was a such a big cunt and could easily knock you into next week for gobbing off.

Dooley sauntered up to the OC, and was handed his tape, 'There you go you big ugly fackun' brute!' They shook hands, Dooley muttered his thanks and the OC took a big swig of beer before continuing with the next promotion. 'Right, gents. Just the one more. Johnson, congratulations.'

Johnson was obviously a very popular bloke, because the bar went bonkers, as if England had just scored the winning goal in the World Cup. He stood up, his face a picture of complete amazement, and received a devastating volley of dead legs, dead arms, camel bites, monkey scrubs and crow pecks from his mates. Some of the people on the peripheries of the group fizzed up their bottles of lager and sprayed it over the mob in the style of a Poundstretcher Grand Prix.

Johnson managed to break free from the congratulatory melee and limped towards the OC. He was about my age and height but with jet black hair and big ears, which were now glowing bright red after being pulled by his friends. The cheers segued into a chant of, 'Swampy, Swampy, Swampy', which, in turn, became Dionne Warwick's classic *Heartbreaker*, with the lyrics wittily changed to 'Why did you have to be a bed-pisser?'

Obviously the new lance corporal had a reputation as a bedwetter – and to have acquired such a rep in the company of drunken soldiers, where such behaviour is almost to be expected, was no mean feat. No doubt tonight's celebration would see him waking up tomorrow with a raging hangover and that familiar cold, wet sensation around the midriff. I leant over to Jango and shouted in his ear in order to be heard above the cheering. 'I take it he hoses up his scratcher, then?'

'Ah, he's a rum bugger is old Swampy. Last week he woke up with his bed bone dry from the waist down, but soaking from the waist up, including his pillows. The dirty bastard had only splashed down with a panhandle and swamped over his own face.'

The OC was shaking his hand and Swampy grinned from ear to massive ear. Another round of rapturous applause lit up the bar and the two exchanged friendly words before Swampy walked back to his place in the crowd through another gauntlet of back-slapping. I was just about to make a move to the bar for some more ale when the OC addressed the squadron again. 'Right, gents. Last, but by no means least, we have two new arrivals in the squadron today. First up is Lance Corporal Nugent.'

Without missing a beat, I strode up to the front of the crowd and turned to face them. In times like these, a show of weakness is a terrible error – another hard-earned lesson from life as a junior soldier. The OC spoke again, 'Right Corporal N. Introduce yourself and then let's see what you're made of.' He brandished a two pint clay stein that was frothing with beer.

I took the large, heavy container and looked ahead of me, but at no individual in particular. 'Alright fellas, I'm Eddy Nugent, just in from 216.'

Without a second's pause or build up, I immediately started drinking as fast as I could from the mug of doom. The first couple of gulps were quite refreshing, and was relieved to find that it was only beer. I was half expecting a piece of cack to be floating around in it, or for the fluid itself to be suspiciously warm, thus indicating possible urinary contamination. But by about five good-sized chugs, I was almost wishing that it *was* piss, as my stomach swelled under the fizzy assault. Knowing how much shit I'd get if I biffed out, I carried on regardless.

It's a horrible feeling, necking booze under pressure, but the stein got lighter and I could feel it coming to an end. With eyes tight shut, I put in a final spurt and finished the remnants as fast as I could, capping it all in the traditional manner by putting the upturned pot on my head and burping like the foghorn on a Saudi oil tanker. The blokes cheered and clapped with enthusiasm and, as I looked around the Toms and seniors, I was met with approving looks: another test passed.

The OC took the stein off my head and shook my hand, 'Good man, Corporal N. Fackun' good man!'

I turned around and weaved my way back to where I had been standing. Once back to my drinking partners, I received a few hearty slaps and propped myself up against the wall. I wiped my eyes and nose and spent the next few minutes continually burping up and re-swallowing frothy beer sick.

Meanwhile, the OC had drained his bottle and clapped his hands together. 'Right, gents. I promise this is the last one of the evening. Our final new arrival, Sig Tomkins.'

It was my mate from the Gütersloh bus, and the poor bastard made the fatal error, borne, no doubt out of inexperience, of staying where he was. Immediately, all eyes were on him. The OC spoke up to snap him out of his trance-like stare. 'Fackun' come on, Tomkins ya flamin' gallah. You're delayun' fackun' drinkun' time, here!'

That, and the murmurs of disapproval from the crowd, forced him to stutter forward to face the music. Once up there, the OC handed him the big clay jug. 'Right, young fella,' he said. 'Say your bit and give this a go.'

Tomkins was so scrawny that he had to use both hands to support the stein, and I had flashbacks to the Gurner at Sutton Coldfield – he'd been doing the pull-ups with me when we were completing our physical tests to get into the Army. We only had to do three of them, but the Gurner had looked like he was trying to pass a kidney stone the size of a cricket ball.

Eventually, he spoke. 'Er, hello, er...'

There came a sudden interruption from the crowd, 'SPEAK UP YOU FUCKING POOF!' followed by a roar of laughter.

'Er, yeah, I'm Sig Dave Tomkins.'

Another interruption followed, but this time by someone picking up on Tomkins' scrawny appearance. 'Fucking hell, it's Dachau Dave!'

This time everyone collapsed with laughter. It was the most horrible, un-PC nickname I'd ever heard and, looking back, I cringe at it for obvious reasons; unfortunately, teenage soldiers don't tend to exhibit too many sensibilities as regards anything, up to and including the Holocaust. Anyway, Dave was going to be stuck with it for life. In all fairness to him, he carried on regardless. Although he could hardly be heard above the laughter, he said, 'Well, er, anyway, my name's Sig Dave Tomkins and I'm just out of 8 Sigs.'

Then he raised the stein to his lips, looked around as the crowd went silent and took the plunge. At first, he went great guns, and I thought he was going to take me to the cleaners. But to my relief, after about 20 seconds he slowed his pace and beer started spilling from the sides of his mouth. Desperate gasping noises escaped from the stein, and young Dave was obviously in a world of hurt – his gut was becoming visibly distended in relation to the rest of his skinny body.

The occasional shouts of encouragement started to come from the audience.

'Come on, Dachau. Push it out, you skinny fucker!'

'Drink up, tinribs. Chop, chop!'

'Jeldi, jeldi Skeletor!'

But he was spent. He pulled the stein away from his mouth with both hands, his bottom lip drooping with a long length of spit hanging from it almost down to his waist. His eyes were half-closed, as mine had been, and he looked like he had just been administered morphine. Then came another shout: 'What you don't drink goes on your head!'

Dave did nothing at first until the chant grew, 'On your head! On your head!'

He eventually gave in to the pressure and inverted the stein over his bonce. What appeared from the mug looked like its entire contents – he must have been drinking like a cat, the big gulps just for show. As he stood there, soaked through, the crowd picked up on this immediately. 'YOU FUCKING WANKER!' started echoing around the bar.

Before it got too ugly, the OC stepped into the breach. 'Alright, keep the fackun' noise down, gents. The bloke gave it his best shot and, like you lot said, what doesn't get drunk went over the head.' He turned to Tomkins and shook his hand, 'Well done, mate.'

Dave was absolutely fucked, and pinballed back into the crowd as the bar returned to normal activity, with the Stranglers' *Peaches* on at full blast.

* * * * *

As the night wore went on, I got speaking to more bods from the squadron. There was the odd cock and bullshitter, but most of them seemed like good lads. Half of them were still ingrained with black in every crease of their skin from working on Panzers all week. Someone once told me that you only had to look at a tank and you'd get blackheads. Another summed armour up in one neat sentence: 'Panzers are 18 tonnes of dermatitis.'

Around elevenish, I found myself talking to Chopper and a big lance jack called Steve 'Hooch' Turner who I'd later go on exercise with.

Our conversation was cut short by a huge cheer, followed by the chanting of, 'Swampy, Swampy.' I turned just in time to glimpse the new Lance Corporal Johnson, naked and running over the soft chairs with about three feet of flaming toilet roll trailing from his arse, like a surreal, post nine o'clock watershed advert for Andrex.

The Dance of the Flaming Arseholes is a tri-service tradition and the epitome of sophistication. The aim is to complete an obstacle course in the raw with a length of burning trap paper hanging from your arse before the paper burns away and frazzles your butt hairs. The secret to a successful fire dance is speed. Too slow, and the paper burns away before you finish the course and you end up in A&E with a poached ball bag. Too fast, and the paper burns too quickly and again it's off down to the med centre trying to explain how your knackers and tea towel holder got scorched. Swampy had it just right, and was clearly a master of the fire dance, an X-rated Michael Flatley.

That said, his performance was not faultless. On the final hurdle of the chair assault course, his left foot slipped and forced him into an involuntary display of the splits. This compressed his pods against the chair arm and forced the remnants of the burning paper onto his arse cheeks, extinguishing the flames. The onlookers went quiet for a second as Swampy bit his bottom lip and sat, wide-eyed and motionless, his legs either side of the chair arm. The silence was finally broken by Ronnie McDonald blowing out through pursed lips, shaking his head and saying, 'Oooh, you fucker, that had to hurt.' Then, 'Come on Swampy, you big knacker, there's still plenty of drinking to be done. Schnell! Schnell!'

Ronnie placed a beer in Swampy's motionless hand, took his own bottle and clinked the two together in salute. Johnson didn't move for fully five minutes. Then he raised his beer to his lips and began drinking. No other part of his body moved, his eyes staring straight ahead, and he didn't stop until he'd drained the bottle. Then he slowly rose to his feet and walked to the bar to order another round, looking as if he'd just ridden a camel round Aintree. He spent the rest of the night drinking in the buff, as if it was the most natural thing in the world, running the occupational hazard of people slapping his arse or trying to burn his ring with a lighter.

Eventually, we hit the point where some of the pads had to start thinking about getting home. To emphasise the point, I could hear a bloke shouting, 'Bollocks! I fucking tell you, just you watch. *I'll* show you who wears the fucking strides in *my* fucking house. I'll tell her to fuck off and pick me up whenever I want, and if she doesn't fucking like it, she can fucking *lump* it. *I* call the shots at our gaff.'

Over the general hubbub, I heard the reply: 'Frosty, you say that every time we have a piss up, and you always end up doing as exactly as you're fucking told.'

I looked over. A bloke of about 35, hair greying at the temples, had exploded in drunken anger, to the extent that he couldn't even swear properly.

'FUCKING... FUCK OUT! *Right*! Give me that... that... that fucking... that fucking phone.' He was nodding furiously to himself as he spoke, and pointing at the landline behind the bar. 'I'll tell the bitch now, you just watch me!'

I had to laugh. For reasons best known to themselves, some of the pads felt it necessary to assure all the singlies that they were the men of their houses, even though nobody gave two fucks about their domestic set up. He started dialling his home number, all the time burbling under his breath, 'No bird's going to tell me when *I* can fucking drink and when I can't.'

His face set in a stern scowl, he nodded his head to *Since You've Been Gone* by Rainbow as he waited for her to answer. As soon as she picked up, he snapped out of his trance and his hard man exterior melted away. Occasional attempts to assert his authority ended with him meekly saying, 'Yes, love', or, 'I'll only be five more minutes'.

All around him, blokes were making 'hock-tsschh' whip sounds, throwing empty cans at him or trying to snatch the phone. He wore a look of deep misery, nodding occasionally as his missus gave him the good news. Finally, he hung up gently and turned to the other blokes. 'Sorry lads,' he said, shamefacedly. 'I've got to go… one of the kids isn't too well.'

'Fuck off, Frosty,' someone jeered. 'You just got gripped and you know it. Just admit it!'

'Er, well anyway, does anyone else want a lift back to the quarters?'

With that, half of the guys who had been berating Frosty drank up quickly and scuttled off as slyly as possible, avoiding the haranguing that had befallen him. I couldn't help grinning. Forces wives were a special breed – unsurprisingly, considering how much they had to put up with. Most of the married guys had great home lives, but a few seemed to find it a bit emasculating that their missuses could get on perfectly well without them. As I've said before, blokes can be knobs.

I turned to the still naked but even drunker Swampy and asked, 'So, Swampy, who's that Frosty bloke?'

'That's Frosty Winterbottom,' he said. 'He's a full screw in Alpha Troop. A nice enough geezer but, fuck me, his wife's a monster. He picked her up from the Sin Bin in BATUS. I swear she's just a badly-shaven gorilla.'

This was no surprise. Along with Belize, BATUS in Canada was renowned for single guys heading off on a six month tour, only to return married to something that wouldn't look out of place in the Mos Eisley cantina from *Star Wars*. These wives were only one step down from Big Grace, the chief hooker in Kenya where exercise Grand Prix happened every year.

'Aye,' said Swampy. 'And another thing, I heard she's got a knob an' all.'

'You're shitting me?' I said.

'Well, yeah. But it's a great rumour to start, isn't it?'

Jango had sauntered over and caught the tail end of the conversation. 'What's this?'

Swampy took another long pull on his beer. Then he lowered his can and pointed to Jango. 'You're not going to believe this, but apparently Frosty's old lady's got a cock.'

'No fucking way!'

'Yes way.'

Jango needed no further persuasion and he disappeared into the crowd, saying to himself, 'Fucking hell... wait till I tell the lads about this.'

It was a perfect demonstration of the rumour machine in full flow: by the next morning, it would be common knowledge in the cookhouse, the NAAFI and on the tank-park that Frosty Winterbottom's wife had a schlong. By NAAFI break, it would have been embellished to the point that the she-male regularly cleaned out poor old Frosty's cack pipe with her yoghurt slinger.

The rest of the night was punctuated by eruptions of laughter and sporadic comments like, 'Fuck me, poor old Frosty. Mind you,

I always thought there was something strange about that thing he married,' and, 'Fucking hell. Hang on, doesn't that make Frosty technically gay and in contravention of Queen's Regs?'

Some of the lads were planning on going down town, but, after a day's travelling and a good seven hours on the lash, I was absolutely fucked. Despite their protestations I hit the sack. As I walked out of the door a bottle shattered on the wall immediately to my left, only missing me by a couple of feet. I turned round to see Jango grinning, the obvious culprit: 'Don't say goodnight then, you ignorant cunt!'

EDDY NUGENT AND THE GOLDEN BLANKET

I WOKE WITH a surprisingly clear head – relatively speaking, I mean.

By any normal standards, I was in a terrible state – I felt like I'd been expertly beaten up by the Spetznaz during the night. But compared with the average BAOR soldier the morning after a piss up, I was raring to go. I counted my lucky stars. Had I stayed on the lash then fuck knows where I would've ended up. No doubt we'd have swung by the Jungle – the main Pigs Bar on camp, which was, like all NAAFI establishments, one step down from a Wild West saloon – and followed that with the joys of Herford's squaddie bars. I blanched at the mere thought.

As I headed through the block to the washrooms, I could hear a strange, whirring noise coming from one of the rooms. Inside, I could see Swampy, naked except for flip flops, waving a noisy hairdryer over a mattress which was propped up against the wall. It was adorned with a piss stain the size of Uzbekistan, and the hairdryer didn't seem to be making much of an inroad.

'Alright, Swampy?' I said.

He turned and shook his head. 'Don't, mate.'

'Have you pissed the bed?' I ventured, sarcastically.

'Not really, no.'

My eyes widened with surprise, 'Are you sure, mate? Did someone accidentally spill a bowser of Sugar Puff water on to your maggot, then?'

'No, mate.' He paused, gathered his thoughts and then continued. 'What I mean is, I didn't actually *piss* my bed.'

'Sorry, mate, call me a thick twat and all that, but you're going to have to explain.'

'I don't fuckin' know,' he said. 'I went into town last night and brought some bird back. She was a bit of a horror, but she let me drop the A bomb on her.' He winked and pointed to his arse to emphasise his point. 'Then she got her fat square head down next to me in me scratcher, and I wobbed out behind her, up against the wall. I was worried that I was going to swamp, like usual, but I thought I'd be clever. My brother's in the Marines and he's got the same problem. He told me to stick a johnny on the end of it and it would catch the first batch and give me a bit of a warning. I thought I'd give it a go.' Given that a packet of johnnies was ten bob and mattresses were fourteen quid in the stores, that made sense. He paused and shook his head. 'Fucking hell, Eddy. I woke up this morning, and the johnny had done the trick alright. It was still on me cock, but I swear there must've been 10 pints of piss in the bastard. It was fucking enormous... it looked like I was getting a nosh off a baby seal.' He shrugged his shoulders as I laughed at the horrific analogy. 'Well, what the fuck could I do? I tried not to wake her up, but I had to climb over her to get to the bog. It wasn't easy, mate, it took two hands just to support the fucking johnny. I almost made it an' all. I had one leg either side of her when she woke up. Fuck knows what she must've thought, mate, opening her eyes to see me straddling her with a 3ft, piss-filled condom hanging off me rod.'

'I suppose you're right,' I said. 'What did she say?'

'Nothing, she didn't get a fucking chance. The bastard johnny burst just as she opened her gob. I tell you what, mate, for a fat boxhead she was pretty fast. She made it from here to the guardroom in about 30 seconds. And in wet PT kit an' all! That's pretty good going.'

I creased up, and left him to his ineffectual evaporation technique. He'd struck another blow for the British Army's standing in Herford: I could just imagine the fräulein recounting the horrific tale to her mates and them all swearing off the schweinhund Tommies for life.

As I got near the wash area I was hit for the first time by a tremendous sensation known as the 'Herfy Squits'. Herforder Pils, it seemed, had a magic ingredient that turned your hoop into a cross between Victoria Falls in the rainy season and a blast furnace. I got to the toilet just in time. As soon as my cheeks touched the seat, what felt like four gallons of red hot rice pudding and a couple of dead water voles made a sharp exit. I let out an involuntary wail and sat there with my face in my hands. Over the next few years, it was a position I was to find myself in with depressing frequency.

Someone had carelessly left a European jazz mag on the floor, and as I waited for my internal gurgling to subside I leant over and scooped it up. Perusing the garishly-coloured pages, showing a variety of orange women being thoroughly serviced by be-mulleted boxheads, my eye was drawn to the odd, German-to-English captions helpfully explaining the action. The bizarre phraseology and mangled syntax employed in this attempt at porn-across-the-borders sadly removed any eroticism from the attached pictures. 'Lars shoots his sting through her rosette and a rich sauce spoils her mothers' cushions!' said one. Another read, 'When one has a dirty goat such as Sophia, the only option is to put her in your pipe and smoke it!'

I mean, what the fuck? Of course, the British soldier is every bit as guilty of contorting foreign languages as any ponytailed European filth flogger. Squaddies speak a language unto themselves anyway, and our vocabulary has been greatly enriched over the centuries by eager linguistic poaching. When I joined in '85, I encountered words seldom heard on the streets of Manchester, like 'dhobi', 'jeldi' and 'buckshee'. Along with a few more common terms – 'khaki' and 'char' spring to mind – they'd been picked up by my military ancestors during the days of the Raj, and handed down with each generation until they lost any exoticism and were just absorbed into common speech. I have no doubt that the men and women now in

Afghanistan will be speaking bits of Pashtun to bewildered relatives every time they go on leave. In our day, of course, it was a tour in Der Vaterland which added to our already odd vocabulary with all manner of quasi-German lingo.

The problem with squaddie German is that it never used the Deutsche equivalent of a British phrase. Like verbal Lego, it just took various German words and reassembled a given expression literally. For instance, the phrase 'All over the place' became, 'Alles über die platz.' 'Fuck that for a game of soldiers' came out as, 'Fik das für ein spiel of soldats'. When taken aback, the British soldier of the Rhine was likely to shout 'Fik mein alte stiefeln!', its British translation being, very approximately, 'Fuck my old boots!'

It worked perfectly on camp, where 'Fancy another pint, mate?' would be met with 'Nicht-halb-bergermeister!' ('Not half, squire!'). The problem came when we attempted to interact with Mister Herman T. German and his Frau. Pads would turn up at local furniture stores and insist on buying a 'Drei-stück-bonbon', leaving a confused shop assistant wondering what the hell a 'Three-piece-sweet' was. In extreme examples, lads would resort to phonetics. There is no German word for 'khaki' so squaddies changed it to 'car key', with 'khaki trousers' becoming 'auto-schlüssel-hosen'. I can't imagine a more useless phrase, though it stayed in vogue, purely for its humorous connotations. I heard tell of one young thruster who, on arrival in the Fatherland, tried out his skills on one local prozzie with merely an Army Basic German language course under his belt. His attempts at fractured Deutsche whilst negotiating price scales led him to asking her for a 'luft arbeiter', literally translated as an 'air work'.

Anyway, after a desultory scan through the weird bongo publication, I staggered off the bog and back out into the washing area. I cleaned my railings and shaved, getting a good gander at my face in the process. I looked like I'd had a Domestos and absinthe eyewash, but I had a shower and the hot water freshened me up.

As I was drying off, Jango came in. He didn't look up for much conversation, greeting me with a grimace. 'You OK, mate?' I ventured.

'I need to fart, mate, but I'm pushing my fucking pulheems. There's a shit stagging-on at the exit of my arse, and I just know it'll come out when I'm least expecting it, the cunt.' He paused. 'Fucking hell, Eddy, what a night.'

I gave him a double thumbs-up and a smile then headed off to get changed. Just before the door to the washroom closed behind me I heard him fart. It started like a Bangkok tuk tuk pulling away from the lights then built in fury to a Panzer with a blown exhaust. It was swiftly followed by Jango laughing his head off whilst shouting, 'GAS! GAS! GAS!' His tone soon changed when it hit his nostrils though, his last comment being, 'Oh, Jesus... I can *see* it. Visible shit particles! What the ...?'

* * * * *

The walk to the troop took me up the main road in camp, past the accommodation blocks and the various squadron bars. The road was covered with dried splash marks and zigzag water trails along its full length. I had seen this before and knew it was from drunken blokes staggering out of camp either honking or urinating as they strolled. Pissing on the move was thought of as great time-management and hugely manly. Within the strange protocols existent in that odd subculture, having to break your stride to take a leak could see you tagged as a little bit too 'prim and proper' for forces life.

The unit was split into two camps, North and South. They were separated by the civilian road that went from Herford to Bad Salzuflen and conjoined by a metal footbridge called Barnes Bridge. The occasional foolhardy daredevil would use the bridge as a makeshift launch pad to dive on to one of the grass verges that ran either side of it, presumably to make the walk home a bit more exciting.

North camp was bordered predominantly by woods and South camp by a road and, of all things, a zoo known as The Tier Park, which was a great source of urban myths. There were stories about llamas being tethered to the front door of RHQ, of regimental parades where the CO insisted on the return of a valuable eagle as the zoo's manager stood behind him, crying, and of chimps working in the MT. (I think the latter may have had some basis in fact.)

The other main feature of the camp was Willy's, a German bar built into the camp perimeter. It did a pretty good trade all week from the camp, with some guys even eating up there, and was always packed to the rafters on weekend nights, being the first stop for pissed-up blokes on their way into town after leaving the squadron bar or the NAAFI. It was a small place with seating for about ten people at the bar, wooden booths along the frontage and several high, circular tables, plus some weird gaming machine that seemed a compulsory fixture in German pubs, the hang of which I would never get during the entire three years of my posting.

Unsurprisingly, the owner was called Willy. I think his wife's name was Ingrid, but she was always affectionately referred to as 'Rocket Tits'. Her udders were the size of those which adorned Les Dawson in his best Panto Dame outfit, and that wasn't where the physical similarities ended. Years of OD'ing on Wiener Schnitzels and Bratwurst had grown Rocket Tits to an ample size all over. To make matters worse, she had a pair of oversized lips, a flat nose and frizzy hair which gave her the air of an electrocuted Worzel Gummidge. Willy was the archetypal innkeeper – balding melon, dark 'tache and a pisstank that not even Richard Branson would attempt to circumnavigate. Both always dressed scruffy-casual and opted for the ever popular socks and sandals look.

But they were a nice, welcoming couple, for all their physical unattractiveness, and I think everyone from camp treated Willy, Rocket Tits and their pub with more respect than other establishments. Rocket Tits' female presence, for all its ambiguity, provided a calming air and kept hot heads in check, and even at its busiest I never saw any trouble there, just the odd session of rowdy-ish high spirits. Because of that, locals of all ages and both genders also felt able to use it without fear of a gang of drunken toms deciding to re-enact the Sword Beach landing on them.

Life on camp was similar to Aldershot, or, indeed, anywhere else in the mob.

Every day started with a parade – not the sort civilians might imagine, with brass bands, pageantry and shiny boots, but just a quick form-up to confirm that everyone was still alive and out of bed. There'd be guard duties or fire picquets for some, and the rest of us toms, lance jacks and full screws would spent our time grafting on radio dets.

I say 'grafting', but that's perhaps that's not the right term. We'd roll out the 20-year-old Land Rovers from their wartime, half-moon, metal garages and go through their daily first works – an inspection which involved giving them the once-over to make sure they were as roadworthy as when we'd parked them up 16 hours previously. The idea was that if the Commies ever changed their minds and piled across the border we would be able to meet them head on in good time, to allow them to kill us with maximum efficiency. Actually, it could be quite sobering if you looked at our shagged-out vehicles and allowed your mind to wander onto the millions of tonnes of gleaming Soviet armour which was massed a few hours' charge away, poised to give it to us decadent western imperialists. As it turned out, their vehicles were even more shagged out than ours, but we weren't to know that then.

After going through the motions with a modicum of industry, by NAAFI break blokes would be starting to doss around, trying to sleep off hangovers in the backs of lockable vehicles or under stinking old cam nets. The more creative types would go so far as to lie underneath the wagons while tying their hands to the rear diffs, to give the impression that they were working under them while they were, in fact, having a crafty snooze. This was a fine ploy unless someone failed to spot them, and took the vehicle for a cabbie round camp.

The German version of the Sally Bash would turn up at 10:30am. It was known as Frau Miggins' Pie Van, but was actually the YWCA from 4 Div Hammersmith Barracks down the road. The lads would normally buy a slack handful of rolls and stickies, and there'd always be a few copies of *The Sun* floating around. Vic Kerr had a bizarre theory that if Lynn from the *George and Lynn* cartoon didn't have her tits out then the crossword was going to be a bastard; a few of the other fellas were deeply involved with *Deirdre's Photo Casebook* and would go ballistic if disturbed whilst reading it.

NAAFI break lasted half an hour, and from then until lunch it was prime, standing-around-the-trailer bullshitting territory. Those lucky enough to have a lockable wagon would spend their time wisely by drinking brews and reading porn. The less fortunate would have to make to do by sitting around with a shovel and some wire wool, primed to start scrubbing as soon as anyone of authority rocked up.

Lunch would be pie, chips and beans, then a bomb-burst back to the block to catch *Neighbours* or, for the more adventurous, an all-out, full bollocky-bufters, sub-duvet, iron-man, half-hour gonk.

The afternoon would involve even more exotic skives, like bimbling around camp with a clipboard, or doing a fabricated driving detail where the reason for the journey would state, 'Pick up of jerry cans from 4 Div', but should actually have said 'Cabbie round Herford looking at fanny and maybe stopping for a schnelly'.

The clipboard skive was great. As long as you walked around purposefully enough, you always looked like you were on your way to, or back from, something important, so nobody ever stopped you to ask you what you were doing. Sometimes, all the clipboards were being used so the slyer operators quickly improvised; one of the lads managed to spin an entire week of skiving out of one bolt. He just walked around with it in his hand, and whenever a senior asked him politely what the fuck he was doing he'd hold it up and say, 'I've got to get the nut for this, sarnt', and he'd be left alone.

On my first working day, being a lance jack, I was given a detachment to take over. I signed for a ravaged old Land Rover with an HF installation in the back. It looked in shit order, but to my surprise it was in good nick, having been well-maintained by my new crewman, a tom called Phil Ash. Phil was from Newcastle and was known as 'Tsetse' because he liked his sleep so much. He was a good egg and worked his plums off, despite his reputation as a golden blanket. I had to sign for the wagon off Tsetse, and we deliberately dragged it out for most of the day, which gave me time to get up to speed on his Geordie-German. He explained how he got his nickname by saying, 'Eeeh, I fuckin' love schlafing, me.'

Any genuine work on the dets was normally some sort of prep for either exercise or an inspection. The LAD, a Light Aid Detachment staffed by the REME, would check the vehicle and the Radio Technicians would do the det.

I needed a pair of coveralls to keep my working dress from getting too shitted up so I nipped down to the stores and signed for some covvies from Ronnie. He complained bitterly that my arrival had put the kybosh on the wank that he'd been planning to clear his head, but he was kind enough to offer me a brew, which I declined. I'd quickly learned that Ronnie was a beast: any Saturday or Sunday morning would find him stumbling around the corridor in the raw, sporting a panhandle and a Stan Laurel hairdo, with his room lined with piss-filled bottles. The happiest I ever saw him was when camp security fitted blast curtains in the rooms due to the terrorist threat. Each curtain hung into a tray that secured its weights; on seeing this, Ronnie said, 'It's about fucking time they fitted some decent piss troughs. I'm fed up of wazzing on me floor.' Drinking from one of his cups wasn't to be advised.

When I got back to the troop I bumped into a few of the blokes I had been drinking with the night before. They were all loitering around a trailer of knowledge, and all had 'T Birds' written on the backs of their covvies in black vehicle paint. We reminisced about the previous evening's action, and there was much joviality. I passed a pleasurable enough half hour, chewing the fat and getting to know the lads a bit better, and then returned to my wagon. Tsetse was going great guns and I mucked in. We decided to get everything wrapped up ASAP, because duty rumour (along with the one about Frosty's old lady having a wanger) was that there would be a spot of PT in the PM. It panned out to be true and we ended up on a troop run in the wooded hills that surrounded North camp.

There was a definite scale down in the amount of phys you were expected to do, compared to Aldershot, but after four years of failing pre-paras and P Companys, I didn't mind that so much. And I had no problem with the run itself, either, although there was one evil hill called 'Heartbreak' which was a bit of a bastard, with four demoralising false peaks. A lot of the lads were still feeling the sting from the night before and there was a shitload of shuggying going on. Some of the guys who'd been at the unit a year or two had obviously not been keeping on top of their fitness and dregged their way round at the back, alternatively being sick and getting shouted at by the PTIs.

Once we got back to camp we had a brief parade where we were warned off for an exercise in the forthcoming weeks, then we fell out, checked Squadron/Regimental orders and knocked off for the weekend.

End of work was pretty simple, with tea followed by dossing round the block, hitting the squadron bar or flicking through the German TV channels in the hope of catching a 70s soft porn flick.

I took the opportunity to take to my bed and spend half an hour girding my loins for the ordeal to come. I knew the weekend was going to be apeshit. While Germany was the same as the rest of the Army in most respects, one thing that was different was the dynamic amongst the lads. Given that we were all in a foreign country, without the chance of fucking off home every weekend, there was more camaraderie, and we all socialised together more. A lot of the blokes in Aldershot made their way home at the weekends, and there was only ever a small nucleus of guys, The Aldershot Orphans, who were there all weekend, every weekend.

Here, there was no escape.

EDDY NUGENT AND THE CONNOISSEUR'S KEBAB

MY FIRST FRIDA... night in Germany was always going to test my liver almost to ...uction – in which respect, I suppose, it was not very different ... ny other Friday night in Germany.

We kicked off ... Jungle, and it was still going strong when we left to head d... wn at around 11pm. Half of 4 Squadron were drinking in ...f, but whereas nudist boozing in civvie life would raise an ... y or two, it barely warranted a comment. It's a popular p... with British soldiers, and is dazzling in its simplicity. Mid-... someone casually calls 'NAKED BAR' and protocol dictate... eryone present immediately removes every stitch of clothin... en carries on as normal. If you fail to join in straight awa... ll be given vigorous assistance in disrobing by your helpf... Initially, of course, most people feel a bit self-conscious... is quickly tempered by the fact that you're not on your o... only consistent worry I had was what to do with the hand... 't holding a beer. I'd normally stick it in my pocket, but n... prevented this affectation. I tended to rest it on my hip ... one starting singing 'I'm a little teapot', at which point I'... the bar.

There was ... ueue of taxis waiting outside camp, so we didn't bother ... Willy's and just hopped into the first set of wheels we saw... c Kerr instructing the driver to head to the Café Vichtig. ... about this place and was looking forward to seeing it. E... son town has its squaddie bars, where only soldiers and ... lubious moral pedigree drink. Some 'belong' to a given uni... off-limits to all other servicemen, but there's usually one ... ere everyone congregates at the end of the evening. In Aldershot, for instance, there was the Pegasus and the Trafalgar; in Herford there was the 'Tig, and it was an unapologetic shithole.

When the cab pulled up outside, to be honest I assumed we'd been dropped off at the wrong place – it just looked like a large, private house with shutters on the windows. I was just about to start giving the driver some jip when Chopper clapped me on the shoulder and propelled me towards the front door. There were other lads milling around, and we joined the back of the line and waited to be let in. I could just make out the muffled bass of dance music and the drunken shouts of the revellers inside.

The queue moved quickly and before long we were handing over our five Deutsche Marks and walking into the darkened interior. There was a small bar area three-deep with guys waiting to be served, most of them soldiers. I had a butcher's around the room as my eyes adjusted. There were a few local girls in, but they weren't exactly stunners. Most of them were pear-shaped and spotty, and they had all adopted a uniform style: way too many earrings, overdone eye make-up and short, spiky, peroxide mullets. It wasn't an intoxicating mix, but I suppose the lack of any really attractive women served to confirm that belligerent, balding, drunken men who shout a lot and drop piss-filled condoms on you in the morning aren't much of a catch.

Dead ahead was a well-lit doorway that led to the toilets – there wasn't any sign, I could tell by the smell – and off to the left was an open archway which led to a dance floor/disco area about the size of a Muslim prayer mat. Someone had made a half-hearted attempt to make the disco look like a cave, with papier-mâché being used to smooth off the join between the ceiling and the walls and create a rounded look. The furthest wall from the door was mirrored in a hopeless attempt to make the place look bigger. It might have worked once, but now most of the mirror panes were broken from years of British military heads being smashed vigorously against them.

If all you had to go on was the DJ's enthusiasm, you might have been forgiven for thinking he was headlining Ministry of Sound. In fact, there was no one on the dance floor and he was, essentially, talking to himself – fading the music up and down whilst adding what he must have thought were cool comments in a strange, American-tinged, half-German, half-English lingo.

I watched as he pulled the volume down and introduced *I've Got The Power*. 'OK Guys, here we go, es ist die number von hit von Schnap!'

It was a routine he repeated every three minutes or so.

'For sure, kommt next ist Ace Of Base, mit *All Dat She Vants Is Anazzer Baby*. You know it.' *Music.*

'Ok, und später we got Doctor Alban mit die neue hit, *It's My Life*. Crazy! Vas ist in der house Herr Doctor!?' *Music.*

'She has die cool beat, ya?' *Music.*

'Techno! Techno! Techno! Techno!' *Music.*

'Let's paaardy mit Rozalla, ya?!' *Music.*

Meanwhile, everyone was just standing around with bottles of beer in each hand, occasionally tilting their heads to shout into the ear of the blokes next to them.

The only exception was two young lads at the far end of the room from me who were rolling around fighting in a puddle of spilt beer. God knows what had started it – it couldn't have been over any of the Kraut growlers, surely – but it was quite entertaining to watch. The stroboscopic effect from the disco lights made it look like they were brawling in slow motion, and it was actually the best entertainment in the place. When the bouncer ran in to break them up, he was jeered and canned by the disgruntled crowd.

Perhaps sensing that the mood might turn ugly, or just to stop people loitering on the peripheries, the DJ gave up his policy of 'Die

Funky Beats' and resorted to playing some *Blues Brothers* classics in an effort to populate the dance floor. As soon as *Everybody Needs Somebody To Love* started blasting out of the speakers, 80 percent of the blokes charged the floor and started dancing the Squaddie Two-Step, which involves bouncing up and down like you're running on the spot. The Blues Brothers were closely followed by *Woolly Bully*, and *Town Called Malice*, and then a procession of other hits familiar to anyone who's ever attended a wedding reception in a British working men's club.

It was a shrewd move by the DJ. Once the dancing ice had been broken, the floor would be full for the rest of the night, with the dance moves resolutely unvarying no matter the tempo or the tune.

For the next few hours, myself and the chaps I'd turned up with stuck together and took it in turns to go to the bar, bringing back two bottles of beer per man. We shot the breeze and marvelled at the crap dancing and low quality women. When enough alcohol had taken hold, Chopper and a few other guys hit the floor in a blistering display of drunken granddad grooving.

Around 2am, Dachau Dave turned up with some of his young oppos from out of training. He announced himself by tapping me on the shoulder, we chatted for a bit and then he introduced me to his mates, who'd all been put into different Squadrons. Dave was visibly very drunk and he started trying to pester me into escorting him to Valentino's, a local knocking shop of some repute.

'I haven't got a scooby where it is, mate,' I shouted, at around 140 decibels. 'You'd be better off asking Chopper.' I knew the Scottish barman was bound to have a mental map of every den of iniquity in town.

Dave started trying to get Chopper's attention, not an easy task since he was concentrating on dancing like an epileptic stick-insect. Eventually, his eye was caught and he weaved his way over to us, heavily out of breath and sweating profusely. Dave started firing out questions about the proximity and standards of the brothels in the Herford area; he was like an excited kid, barely stopping to catch his breath. Eventually, Chopper held up both hands to quieten him. 'Don't you worry about that, young Dachau,' he yelled back. 'You just stick with your Uncle Chopper and everything will be fine. I tell you what, we'll leave here in a bit and do a tour of the knockers so you can make up your own mind?'

Dave grinned from ear to ear. Before he could say anything in reply, Chopper put his arm around him. 'Before we go though, fella, I'm dying for a wazz,' he shouted. 'And there's a fucking massive queue for the traps. Do us a favour and hold out your coat so I can piss in a glass wi'out anyone seeing?'

Dave did as he was bid, holding out the right side of his coat to act as a shield. Chopper shuffled forward and ruffled Dave's hair. I read his lips over the sound of Blondie's *Call Me*: 'Cheers, Dachau, you're a real pal.'

Then he produced a tiny shot glass, whipped out his knob and immediately began a giant horse piss. His eyes were closed with pleasurable wazz-relief, but Dave's were out on horrified stalks. As soon as the heavy stream of urine hit the bottom of the glass, it fired straight back out in a huge arc, with the young tom in the immediate firing line. Straight away, he tried to dodge the spray, but Chopper's eyes snapped open. 'For fuck's sake,' he yelled. 'Stand still Dave, you stupid cunt… are you trying to get me caught or something?'

So Dave just resigned himself to his fate and stood there with his coat held out and a dejected look on his face, gradually getting wetter and wetter. It seemed like Chopper was pissing for ten minutes but, fair play, Dave took it like a man. And Chopper was a man of his word. After 20 minutes of further drinking and drying off, they set off on a trawl of Herford's brothels.

At around the same time, myself and an incredibly drunk Vic Kerr made tracks for food. After enacting lots of eating gestures to a taxi driver, we ended up outside a grotty-looking joint with a sign saying, 'Gyros Konig'. I tapped the taxi driver on the shoulder, held up my hand with all five fingers visible and said, 'Fünf minuten.'

He seemed to understand, so I dragged the burbling Vic from the car and we entered the food emporium. Being a stranger to German cuisine, I asked him for his recommendation. All I got was, 'Ooooh... f...f...f...fackin' g...g...g...gyros mate... mit Suzuki sauce!'

Armed only with this dodgy advice, I turned to the bloke behind the counter. 'Two Gyros,' I said, holding up two fingers and scanning the menu for 'Suzuki'. I couldn't find that, but I happened upon 'tzatziki' and added that to my order. I also made a sweeping gesture to all the salad that was on display. I had no idea what I'd just ordered – it could have been a plate of pickled dog's cocks, for all I knew – but as it transpired 'Gyros' is just a particularly tasty kebab. In fact, imagine, if you will, a kebab that is so nice that you would actually eat it sober: I realise this sounds impossible, but that's how nice Gyros is.

Vic had fallen asleep on a small plastic chair in the takeaway, so when the scoff was ready I woke him up, helped him back to the cab and we set off back to camp.

I got him squared away in his room, and then went to my own where I devoured my kebab like a pig and promptly fell asleep. I was awoken a few minutes later by a feverish beating on my door. Outside was a semi-naked Vic, propping himself up in my doorframe with both arms and one leg, the other leg was roaming around the floor in a losing battle for stability. He was looking down at the ground as the drink had sapped his ability to hold his head upright, and he spoke in a rambling mumble which was not easy to decipher.

'Heeargh, ooh Eddy m... m... mate, come on mate... have you got any p... p... p...p... porn 'ave ya? Go on fella, you m... m... must 'ave. G... g... g... gertcha ya bazza, you're not a fackin' singlie unless you've got porn!'

'Wait here Vic,' I said, and dug out the old copy of *Fiesta* that I'd found screwed up in the locker when I'd moved in. 'There you go mate.'

At this, he got all sentimental, and his voice began to quiver with alcohol-induced emotion. 'Cheers Eddy, I tell you what, you're f... f... fackin' a top mate, a fackin' *TOP* mate, you are. I tell you what...'

Seeing the big red flashing danger sign above his head, I quickly interrupted him. 'Yeah, it's alright, Vic, no dramas. Anyway, you get your head down mate and I'll see you in the morning, eh?'

I didn't want to be too curt, but if I allowed a conversation to develop I knew I'd be there all night, and I was too tired to fuck around. The last thing I wanted was to get bezzered.

As in most predominately male environments, the military world is extremely straight and conservative, and revealing compassion for a comrade if not comprehensively roostered will result, at best, in an embarrassed shrug of the recipient's shoulders; at worst, the two will never speak to each other again during the remainder of their 22-year service careers.

This stiff-upper-lip reaction is good for the maintenance of military discipline, but prevents the necessary release of emotional steam: this is where the bezzer comes into its own. When a bloke is drunk, the rules are inverted and outward displays of affection for his fellow man are accepted and reciprocated, in direct proportion to the amount of beer necked.

Bezzering can be witnessed at around half past twelve on most Friday nights in any garrison town. The SOP is to grapple your target in an affectionate headlock, while simultaneously monkey-scrubbing his hair, and offer a non-existent sister's hand in marriage or inform him that, if you won the lottery, you'd give him half.

If the bezzeree is at a similar level of lubrication, the headlock is soon reversed and a compliment such as, 'You're a fucking smasher, mate!' is offered. Low-level bezzering like this creates a general feeling of well-being in the group, the price to pay being merely mild embarrassment at the next day's NAAFI break.

Inevitably, some lads get it wrong. One of the classic errors is to be out of lager-sync. The standard time to hit the pub was half-past eight. Nobody ever made that rule, it just seemed natural, and it provided you with enough time to sink a few in the bar *and* make it to a club *and* last until closing. But if a man had snuck out of the gate early, perhaps on a flimsy 'bank-related' pretext, he would find himself having already drunk an evening's-worth of beer when his sober mates turned up. In the hour and a half that it takes to establish lager-equilibrium, he can then be relied upon to subject his buddies to the excruciating experience of unrequited bezzering. I remember Joey Donaldson and me turning up in the George in Aldershot one Friday night to celebrate Frankie Tarbert's promotion. By the time we arrived, he was hovering over his eleventh pint in a corner. Before I could say a word, he spotted us and shouted, loud enough to be heard in Guildford, 'I told you me fuckin' mates were coming!'

Then he burst into joyful tears, and delivered vertebrae-demolishing bear hugs to both of us. I'd only known Frankie for a couple of months, but that didn't stop him from declaring to anyone who would listen that I was like a brother to him. He insisted on buying us both a top-shelf concoction that we had no intention of drinking before slamming a few pound coins in to the jukebox.

'Pick whatever you like, lads,' he said, with an expansive wave. '*That's* how much I fucking love you!'

Joey had the temerity to stick on Rick Astley's *She Wants To Dance With Me*. Rick's sub-standard, blue-eyed soul brought out in Frankie another aspect of bezzering-gone-wrong. Within the delicately-balanced protocols of the bezzer there lurks the danger of an over-the-top declaration of love turning suddenly belligerent. Bezzerers can be confused and suspicious individuals, and sometimes discern an insult in the most innocuous of actions. Under these circumstances, it's possible for the bezzerer to go from inappropriate bonhomie to declarations of war within the space of a couple of sentences.

'Who put this fucker on?' screamed Frankie.

'Me, mate. It's fucking boss,' replied Joey, grinning inanely, and failing to spot the warning signs.

'You fucking *cunt*. I love you Joey, you're a great lad. But I've just give you four quid and you've stuck that shitehawk on. I could do better me fucking self.'

As a placatory gesture, Joey offered Frankie a quid. Frankie knocked it out of his hand and pointed a finger at him. I say 'at him', but Frankie was waveringly indicating a spot some four feet above and left of Joey's shoulder. 'You keep your fucking quid. Are you trying to say I'm a fucking tramp?'

Unsure of how to respond, Joey just gave a palms-out shrug. Instantly, the fight went out of Frankie. He stopped pointing and gurning, and adopted a shit-eating grin, before doing a quick shadow box in front of us. 'I'm only kidding, Joey,' he slurred. 'What would I fucking do without you, eh? You're the salt of the earth, you are. Eddy an' all.'

He then peeled away and danced to the rest of the tune, exhibiting levels of rhythmic coordination not dissimilar to those of the artist himself, and managing to knock over eight pints on four separate tables in three minutes.

The other key to the successful bezzer is its venue and circumstances. Clubs are too loud, and feature other distractions; in taxi queues, everyone is too focused on the business of queue-monitoring. The perfect spot is the late-night takeaway, especially if it is within walking distance of camp. By the time a bunch of lads have reached this point of the evening, sleep is near. As long as the usual perils have been avoided along the way, then an all-round feeling of optimism and good humour descends on the group, whilst they wait to collect the ridiculous amount of food they've ordered – much of which will soon form a Hansel and Gretel-like trail to help weary travellers home from 'Kebabbington Jones' to the front gate.

I once witnessed a classic bezzer in a Catterick takeaway, between four infantrymen waiting for their bin-lid sized pizzas to materialise. As I hung around for my three pieces of Chernobyl Chicken and chips, I listened in as they tried, in the style of the Four Yorkshiremen, to outdo each other in their professions of brotherly love. The first soldier, visibly more paggered than the others, informed them that if *he* won the lottery, he would disperse it equally amongst them, before even considering his immediate family. One of his mates then claimed that if *he* won the lottery, he would give the entire amount to the other three, leaving himself nothing in the process, his love for them ran that deep. Instead of this eliciting a burst of laughter, it produced a short period of almost prayer-like reflection before the next man had his go. My food had arrived, but I was spellbound as he laid out his plan: his winnings would be spent on forming the quartet into a squaddie version of *Summer Holiday*. They would jack in the Army and travel the world on a converted London bus, spending freely on anything their imagination allowed, including but not limited to Booze Bin vouchers, high-class hookers and subscriptions to bongo mags from around the globe. They warmed to the theme of the bus conversion, but despite there being a nominal pot of eight million pounds on the table, the best that they could come up with was a set of optics where the luggage normally goes and a disco ball on the top deck. The whole conversation took place at a decibel range more commonly found at a Motörhead gig, with hugs all round and occasional jabs to the breadbasket.

The fourth man had no chance of topping the bus idea, so took a different tack, suggesting in a voice thick with emotion that he would simply hand the cheque back to the Lottery people, because he was already content with his life as long as the other three were in it.

This lent a new solemnity to their discussion and their subsequent power hug was only interrupted by the announcement of the arrival of their scoff. At that point, they went from being millionaires to realising that they only had enough money for three of the pizzas, even if they clubbed all their money together. The bosom companionship of seconds before was instantly forgotten, and as I walked off with my scoff I could still hear them arguing and telling each other to fuck off a lot.

Luckily, Vic just took the mag, said cheers and pinballed off down the corridor.

* * * * *

In the morning Vic and I grabbed a bit of brunch from the cookhouse and then I mentioned that I could do with checking out the pad's NAAFI for some dhobi dust. He said he needed a haircut so we decided to hit the barbers on the way round to the Colonel. All the places we wanted to go were in town, but fortunately Vic had a car, a red XR3i.

We got in and hit the road, and as we headed to our requisite destinations, Vic gave me the guided tour of Herford. Situated in Nord Rhine Westfahlen, north of Bielefeld and south of Hannover, it was a nice, picturesque town that had survived the war quite well, to the point where new blokes posted in would ask in consternation, ''Ere, did we bomb this place or what?' It was straight out of *How To Fit In With The Locals, 101*.

Even so, among the stunning examples of the medieval and gothic architecture, there were enough new buildings in the normally very traditional Alt Stadt, or Old Town, to suggest that it had taken a bit of shoeing during 1939-45.

Our route on the main road around the centre took us past the Kreissparkasse bank, a big glass-and-steel building set stark against the old yellow stone church nearby – a real architectural yin-and-yang of perceived modern German efficiency clashing with its historic past. Most soldiers in Germany got their wages paid into a local bank account, and the 'Sparky' was the main one used. I noticed a few lads milling around outside, and in the months and years ahead I'd witness the most surreal scenes imaginable inside that bank. On deploying into the field on exercise, lads on free-running dets would park outside the Sparky to get their 'Schnelly money' for exercise. The problem was that a lot of blokes didn't have cashpoint cards (usually confiscated for a litany of financial misdemeanours), so to get some dough out they'd have to go inside, queue up, and make a withdrawal at the counter. Not a problem for the average working man, you might think, but bear in mind that most of these lads would be stood in line sporting a loaded SA80 rifle. I imagine they do it differently these days.

Up the main road from the Sparky was the Herford hauptbahn-hof railway station. A few blokes (those who didn't actually own a car or have a friend with wheels) would train it in to Bielefeld on a Saturday morning to catch the big shops before they closed at mid-day. But in all my time in Herford I don't think I ever travelled by rail – despite their admirable punctuality, I just didn't want to get on the wrong train and end up disembarking at Colditz. I realise that this was hugely irrational, but maybe nan's lunacy was rubbing off on me in some subtle way.

Vic pointed out a club called the Go Parc across the drag from the station. 'That's the biggest nightclub in Germany, Eddy,' he said. 'Only one problem – they won't fackin' let us in.'

Over the years, the place had achieved almost mythological status, not least due to the lengthy queues of fräuleins outside, and whenever you happened past you'd find a slack handful of boneheads hanging around saying things like, 'Aaah fuck off then, ya big German boxhead cunt! I didn't want to get in anyway, it's fuckin' shit!' At which point, a big Jerry biker-looking bouncer with long hair and a beard would step forward to move the troublemaker on, generally eliciting the response, 'Alright, Catweazle, keep your fuckin' rug on. I'm fucking going, aren't I, Adolf?' (If the soldier in question was up on his history, the swearing might be punctuated by references to annexing the Sudetenland.)

The doormen seemed to have a squaddie-detecting device that was 100% reliable; even lads who spoke fluent Deutsche, or tried to get in with their German wives, got fucked off at the high-port. Nevertheless, hope sprung eternal and I'd soon be giving it a crack myself once or twice a month, and failing like everyone else. I even thought about purchasing a mustard-coloured shirt with metal-tipped collars, a shoulder-padded purple suit with the trousers tucked into cowboy boots and a packet of Lucky Strike oder Camel cigarettes, but nobody made blonde mullet wigs at the time so I'd still have been knocked back after all that. Even if I'd made it inside, one of them would probably have said, 'Good luck, Herr Bartlett!' as I sauntered past.

We sped on, past the verboten territory and then past Dimitri's gyros palace a few hundred metres away, with Vic still burbling away about the place. I remember him pointing out what a useful posting Herford was for the seasoned bullshitter, in that it sounded almost exactly like 'Hereford', home of the SAS. By simply employing a slightly different inflection in pronunciation, lads could lead their unwitting families to believe that they were off to plan the next embassy siege, instead of churning up German B roads in an armoured vehicle.

As he chatted, I people-watched. It was obvious that – despite the language barrier, obvious cultural differences and love for David Hasselhof power ballads – folk in Germany were pretty similar to their UK counterparts. All the usual characters were there – the geriatric couple, where the fella was just bimbling along letting his missus do all the talking, the ridiculously young-and-in-lust teenage couples, and the mid-30s mums and dads trying to round up their unruly kinder. I noticed, too, the groups of lads hanging around, with their first cars all decked in spoilers and garish colours. The only difference here was that the British gopping-vehicle-*du-jour* was a Vauxhall Nova, and its German equivalent was the Tiger Tank Mark II of boy racer wheels, the Opel Manta.

Vic took about an hour to show me around the strange new sights which would become more than familiar in the forthcoming years until, at about half past eleven, we broke off the tourism gig for him to get his haircut.

The main barber used by soldiers in Herford was called Salon Buba, named after the proprietor Dirk Buba. Dirk looked like an older version of Dustin Hoffman, he had a very deep voice and the only English he spoke was, 'Square neck oder taper?'

Saturdays were his busiest day and guaranteed, no matter what time you arrived, there would be a queue of hungover soldiers in the waiting room, with Dirk ploughing through them like an Australian sheep sheerer. It was hilarious to watch some of the young trendy lads, with their sunbed tans and highlighted hair like George Michael circa 1984, sitting down in Dirk's chair and saying. 'Take a little bit off the sides, don't touch the burns and a bit more volume on top, bitte?' At which point Dirk would brandish his clippers, welded permanently on to No3, and gouge a big trench through their precious locks and then, completely oblivious to the look of shock on the young lad's face, say his famous line: 'Square neck oder taper?'

I didn't need a haircut, so I waited for Vic outside in the fresh air, trying to quell the delayed reaction nausea I was going through from the night before. After 20 minutes or so he came out, and was rubbing the back of his neck with the piece of white tissue that Dirk had given him. I noted that he had gone for the No3-all-over-with-tapered-neck option. It must have been all the rage at the time, because I seem to remember that everyone else who came out had had one, too.

We got back in the car and headed to the main NAAFI, me making mental notes of the routes for future reference. It was just off a main four-lane drag which led up to the barracks that housed 16th/5th Lancers, and it actually looked like a proper supermarket. Due to the security situation at the time, there was an oldish guy in a security guard uniform controlling traffic going into the car park. 'There's one of the fackin' NAAFI Republican Guard,' said Vic, with a smirk.

The aisles were full of pregnant women dragging around screaming broods of children with chocolate smeared around their faces. Every now and then, a shrill voice would cut through the wailing with 'I'll give you something to cry about in a minute!' or 'No, you bloody can't!'

In the far corner of the NAAFI was an area that sold military kit made by a civilian company called Survival Aids. This stuff always sold well because, not to put too fine a point on it, the issued kit in a normal unit was (in those days) completely shit – all of the issue combat clothing that you wore on exercise trebled in weight as soon as it came into contact with any water. Wan pointed out the area of camouflage clothing and referred to it as 'bullet corner', which made me smile. I grabbed myself a packet of Daz or Persil, and we took off back to camp.

During the cabbie back, Vic took a detour off the main road and into the pad's quarters. He knew where the SSM lived and he wanted to wake him up by screeching past his house and leaning on the horn. The route took us through a residential area, and I noticed that all the houses had wheelie bins outside featuring a sticker of

Grover from *Sesame Strasse* saying, 'Herford ist groovy!' – one of the stranger allocations of taxpayers' money that I've seen.

As we drove, I asked Vic about the best places to buy some 'adult reading material'.

'If you want some quality art,' he said, sagely, 'you don't need to bother buying it, mate. We'll go and see Terry Waite when we get back in the block.'

Terry was another of those blokes who fell into the category of 'unknown real Christian name', and the lads had lately taken to vexing him by singing *Love To Hate You* by Erasure, with the lyrics altered to something along the lines of, 'I love to hate you, I Terry Waite you.' This would send Terry apoplectic with rage, and would elicit shouts of, 'Stop singing that fucking woodclanger shit!' with him tapping his two index fingers together to symbolise a couple of angry penises clashing in the throes of manlove.

When Vic knocked on his door, he answered quickly and ushered us in to a dark and uncomfortably warm room, with the curtains shut.

I recognised him from the vehicle park, but hadn't really seen much of him as he was in another troop. I presumed he was another kicked-out pad, because a massive shrank completely dominated one side of his bunk. It was absolutely jammed with porn. Don't get me wrong, like most other blokes I like a bit of pornography – I believe that statistic that 95% of men have used it, and the other 5% are just fucking liars. But Terry was clearly obsessed.

I introduced myself, but instead of replying with the traditional pleasantries he launched into a tour of his collection. It was not only stored alphabetically, he explained, but alphabetically within different genres. For example, had the sergeant major been seeking the latest release of *Piss Slaves*, there'd have been no need to flick through all the Ps – he could simply locate the pissing section and go through that in alphabetical order, thus saving valuable wanking time. He moved on to his latest cinematic acquisitions and recommendations, but when he'd finished describing the pros and cons of *Sodomania 6*, and was beginning the preamble of his critique on *Dwarves Just Wanna Have Fun*, I stopped him.

'Er, that's great Terry,' I said. 'And I appreciate you recommending these to me. But haven't you got anything... normal?'

'How about *Schindler's Fist*?' he said, eager to help.

'Well, actually, mate... I was just thinking of some normal, consenting adult, man-on-woman, straight sexual intercourse knob-in-fanny stuff.'

Terry recoiled slightly and furrowed his brow, as if alarmed at my strange tastes. Then he rubbed his chin and said, 'We*ellll*, I don't normally get much call for stuff like that, but I've just got in this new one, it's starring Peter North and it's called *The North Pole*.' He dug it out and handed it over, circling his thumb and index finger and nodding to himself. 'Great money shots.'

I examined the box. It didn't look particularly vile or illegal. 'Cheers Terry,' I said. 'Is it alright if I borrow this, then?'

'Certainly,' he replied. 'Just sign here!'

At which point he produced and opened a huge book, the size of a King James Bible. The pages were populated with lines of names, signatures, borrowed film titles and dates the movies were taken out and brought back. Clearly, he had almost industrial quantities of filth on the go. Jokingly, I asked him if he offered memberships. To my surprise, he reached into a draw and pulled out a stack of cards. 'Certainly, my good man,' he said. 'You can join if you want.'

'Fucking hell, I was only kidding!'

'Suit yourself. Right, when you bring back the film, make sure you sign it in and also that it's rewound. If it's not, then I'll just play it to see where you finished off, and if it's on a knob close-up then I'll tell everyone you're a bender. Oh, and by the way, should you require a more discreet service then I can provide a plain cover for the video box, just in case you don't want to walk around with the hardcore cover on display.' He pulled out an opened-up video box cover with a picture of Frankie Vaughan on the front. The guy was fucking nuts.

As devoid of morals as Terry may have been, he was part of an almost generic cast in any single soldiers' living accommodation. There will always be the sex pest, the racing snake-keen blokes, the scruffy bastard, the golden-blanket-schlaf-monster and those like me, on top of their admin but seeking the path of least resistance.

I spent the rest of morning and early afternoon fannying around in my room getting everything in good order and sorting out my kit for RSM's parade on Monday morning. Later on, a few of us made our way to the squadron bar, where we found Chopper asleep in one of the comfortable chairs. He'd clearly had a good time the night before, because he was still in the same clothes. I woke him up to get some drink for everyone, and he gave me a run-down on proceedings.

He'd taken young Dave around as many brothels and boozers as possible, and once the young signaller had slaked his thirst for flesh they'd stayed in the last establishment, drinking until it had closed at 8am. They'd then headed to the train station, as the café there had just opened, and it sold beer. So Chopper and Dachau had been on the pop until midday. Well, strictly speaking, Chopper had been on the pop and had just carried the unconscious Dave around with him like a combination of an issued sausage bag and a mobile cashpoint.

I asked him where Dave was. 'Och, don't you worry about him Eddy, he's helping me.' This was accompanied by a dismissive wave of the hand in the general direction of the bar. Concerned for Dave's health, I went looking for him and eventually came across his comatose body in the rear storage area. He was lying on four crates of Grolsch that were acting as a makeshift bed, and he looked as rough as arseholes. Not one of his hairs was pointing in the same direction as the next, his shirt was open, there was dried Gyros and tzatziki all over his clothes and head, and he was barefoot.

I was just about to try and wake him up when Chopper staggered into the room next to me. 'Fucking hell, look at him go! I think he's no' too healthy there, Eddy. He needs waking up!'

Chopper then shuffled over to Dave's body and started undoing his flies to give him a 'continental shower'. Before he could carry it out, I stepped in. 'Whoah, Chopper,' I said. 'If you do that you'll ruin the beer he's gonking on.'

'Aye, you're right,' he said. He bimbled off and came back with a jug of cold water which he poured all over Dave. It worked a treat: he came to life in a spluttering blur of fists and obscenities and once he got his bearings, we sent him off to his room to square himself away and with orders to get back down to the bar, pronto.

When I went back through, there were considerably more people in the bar than before, all crowding in to watch a big footie match on the telly.

The day turned into night, and the night into weeks and subsequently months.

The repetitious nature of drinking in Germany became a pleasantly foggy sort of *Groundhog Day*, with variety or interruption only being provided by exercise and leave.

EDDY NUGENT AND THE BIRDMAN OF OSNATRAZ

VIC 'WAN' KERR was becoming a good mate, and I couldn't help but notice he was plummeting headlong into advanced, stage-one, kicked out paddery. I'd catch him shadow-boxing in his room, lurching forward behind a lacklustre jab, and crashing into his shrank. Or I'd hear him leaving in the wee small hours, via the windows, his heavy, uneven footsteps disappearing into the night, the morning light revealing muddy footprints around his room, like those of a troubled werewolf. He even got away with the occasional bit of unwarranted property destruction, but that was purely by chance. Vic wasn't your normal lairy kind of bloke, and had it not have been for his marital breakdown he would've bumbled through life without a blemish to his behaviour. But the finality of the loss of the woman who he clearly still had feelings for turned him into a proper loon for a while.

It took him two months before he hit stage two, and the slight reduction in his chemical intake allowed me to catch him during the odd lucid moment. Sundays in the block were always terminally boring, especially when there was virtually nothing on the box, and one quiet morning, as I headed off to the ablutions, I noticed his door was open. He was sat on his bed, clearly sober and just looking at his feet. I knocked on. 'Are you alright, mate?' I said.

'Yeah,' he said. Then he paused. 'Actually, no.'

I took a tentative step into his room. In the Army, blokes will jip you over anything – I've done it myself loads of times – but just occasionally the wall of insensitivity is breached, and empathy is allowed. I was acutely aware that there was a time and a place for pisstaking, and this was neither.

'What's up?' I asked.

Vic looked up. 'I dunno, Eddy. Facking everything, mate.' He checked his feet out again. 'Facking everything...' He trailed off.

'Anything I can help with?' I had no idea what I could offer. If he was having trouble passing a BFT or bulling his boots, I might have been some help, but for any kind of seriously effective relationship advice, he'd have been just as well off talking to Doctor Crippen.

As with most people, though, all he needed was an ear for five minutes. He basically started talking, and within a few sentences it all came out with audible relief. 'I still love her, Eddy.' He looked back at me. He wasn't crying, but given a stiff breeze, he would've had rollers. 'I really do. Ah, for fack's facking sake, I've been such a cunt, mate. She only wanted kids! What woman doesn't, eh? Facking kids.' He looked up at the ceiling, gathering himself. 'Fack, mate. I didn't want them though, I thought she was just facking up our nice little world. We had a nice place, a nice car, we went out. Nippers would just fack all that up, wouldn't they?'

He seemed to want a bit of moral backing, but the best I could muster was a buckshee shoulder shrug and a quick, 'Dunno, fella. I've not got any.'

'You're right.' He stood up. 'I've been such a dick, mate. The more I think about it, the more I realise, how hard could it have been? There's all sorts of strokers have youths all the time, and those cunts cope, don't they? I spoke to some of the other lads with nippers, and they love it, too. I dunno what to do, mate.'

'Tell her about it,' I ventured. 'Let her know how much you care.'

I couldn't resist a spot of Billy Joel, but Vic didn't notice.

'I facking tried, mate,' he said, sighing in utter resignation. 'I told her the lot, but it's too late. She's facked off back to the UK and reckons she's found some other cunt already.' He shook his head and turned away. 'Fack! The thing is, mate. I've done so much thinking about kids and what might've been recently that it feels like I've lost more than just her, and it's made things even worse!'

I don't know where I got it from, probably a spot of lunchtime *Neighbours* on SSVC, but I said, 'Well, mate, if you told her you'd give it a try and she's still said no, then it's just not meant to be.'

Vic thought for an unnervingly long period of time, and then just shook his head. 'You're right,' he said, sitting down again. 'You're facking right, but it's facking killing me, Eddy. It really is. Every facking day, I can't put it out of my mind.'

'You're gonna have to, mate.' I surprised myself with this sudden pearl of wisdom. 'No one can sort it out for you. If I could I would.'

Had the situation been even the tiniest bit less serious I would've added, 'You big silly cunt,' followed by a dead arm, but Vic was really laying it on the line and it might been moderately counter-productive.

'Yeah, you're right. Thanks, Eddy,' he replied and we consoled ourselves with a post-dhobi brew and bacon sarnie in the cookhouse.

I don't know if it was our conversation that did it, but Wan only stayed in stage 2 depression for a couple of weeks, and mercifully seemed to bypass stage 3. He seemingly came to terms with the fact that he had to make a completely new start and opted instead to become a born-again singlie.

* * * * *

Not long after that, I went on my first German exercise. Back in Aldershot, these had been quite tough – we'd worked hard on comms, or focused on individual soldiering skills, honing our big hole-digging and laughing-whilst-piss-wet-through abilities until they were quite sharp. But this one was an unbelievably easy number.

For a start, it was completely non-tactical – we were only on rent-a-det out to 1 Div in Verden, and would only be doing the umpire networks. And to top it all off, I wasn't even the Det commander this time, leaving me in a position which is the envy of every soldier – possessing rank, with zero responsibility. We were only taking Rebros up north, so I tagged along as the two ice-cream on a three-man det, with young Dave as the tom and a semi-waster full screw called Dicky Bird running the show. Dicky wasn't a bad bloke, but he was a bit of porker and constantly shimfed about his piles. He had overly-long blond hair and huge eyebrows, and his predominant idiosyncrasy was his insistence on comparing everything he did to how it used to be done back in the 'Traz'. His last two postings had seen him stay in Osnabruck, and he fucking loved the place, never hesitating to bore the arses off us with tales of its superiority to the rest of BAOR. I thought this a bit odd, because most lads who'd been there thought it was like a nick, one up from a stint in Colly. It wasn't known throughout the Army as Osnatraz – or The 'Traz – for nothing.

With his penchant for all things 'Traz shining through, Dicky became known as 'The Birdman of Osnatraz'.

The wagons we were taking on eccers were old one-tonne Land Rovers, or 'Tonnies' as we called them. The Tonnies were packing a big, noisy V8, looked like a military version of The Mystery Machine from *Scooby Doo* and handled like jelly on stilts. Although technically I suppose this last was a failing, some of the guys enjoyed it tremendously, and would often indulge in 'Death Rallies' on exercise. It goes without saying that crashes often ensued: the excuse of, 'A dog ran out in front of me', became so utterly ubiquitous on the FMT3 crash report forms that there was talk of having it placed on them permanently.

The cab was a bit crap, with a huge transmission tunnel splitting it in half and a weird gearstick that came up to the driver's armpit, but for all their bad points Tonnies were peerless when it came to revving the tits off them at 4am in a sleepy German village. They generated huge backfires, tailor-made to wake the snoozing Hun in terror that the USSR's Third Shock Army had just arrived over the hill.

The morning of the exercise was like an average work day. The wagons were already prepped and POL'd, so we just turned up in our combats, loaded up the bergans and hit the road free-running. All crypto and rations were to be provided by 1 Div and being non-tac meant we didn't even need to sign out weapons.

The drive to Verden took a couple of hours. We stopped at a Schnelly at around NAAFI break time for currywurst and chips, and arrived at 1 Div in the early afternoon. But my dreams of the easy life were promptly shattered by the vision of an entire Armoured Division preparing to deploy on exercise.

People were running around frantically, waving and shouting over the racket from dozens of madly-revving Panzers which were billowing out huge gouts of black smoke and chewing up the tarmac as they trundled forwards and backwards to form up. I suppose there must have been some sanity to the chaos I was watching, but I remember thanking fuck I had no part in its organisation. I could imagine rodneys and yeomen wandering all round the camp with their hair falling out in clumps as they tried to get the Div on the road.

We pulled up just past the guardroom and Dicky and I jumped out, with Dicky eagerly seizing the chance to bend double and clutch at his arse. 'Ooooh,' he moaned, shooting an evil look at the one tonner. 'The fucking bastard who designed the driver's seat for that bastard didn't have any consideration for people of my delicate condition.' I had to smile; whining about his Emma Freuds was just about the only thing that kept him off the wonderful world of Osnabruck. Eventually, after much groaning and grunting, he staggered upright and we wandered over to report to the guard commander and get ourselves pointed in the right direction. There was a brief tête-à-tête through the guardroom window and we headed off to get round all the relevant bods to sort out our rations, crypto and POL.

One of Dave's mates collared us near the ration wagon. 'Youse lot wanna get the fuck out of Dodge,' he said, with a wary eye on a nearby NCO who was furiously ticking things off on a clipboard. 'If you hang round here you'll get yourselves noticed.'

He was right: with all that stress and rank floating around, it was only a matter of time until we got gripped, regardless of how well we were conducting ourselves. We managed to look busy enough to avoid attention, and then slipped away quietly to our first exercise location as soon as we got the chance.

With me reading the map, Dave driving and Dicky moaning, we found our way to a wooded knoll in the middle of the oo-loo. One-tonnie det set-ups followed a generic pattern in BAOR. There were normally three 12-metre masts deployed for the rebro and the generator put way out into the bondoo. The 9x9 tent, where you cooked and slept, was placed at right angles onto the side of the vehicle, with the open end placed over the side doors to the radio compartment to prevent any light from escaping at night. At any given time, there would always be a guy on radio watch. From his position in the vehicle, if he looked to his right, he could see immediately into the tent. A fundamental part of the furniture was a kerosene space heater, which was ideal for four things:

1. Spitting greenies onto when you were bored, so you could watch your dockyard oyster bubble and dry out.

2. Making kero heater toast. This was great once you got over the fact that the toast tasted of oven cleaner.

3. Standing over until your trousers got so hot that they burnt your inner thighs if they touched your skin. (This was more difficult

than it sounds. The British Army combat trousers of the time were of a unique design. The day you deployed on exercise, they were figure-hugging. Within two days, they began to wilt at the gusset. After a week, they were hanging down to such an alarming degree that you looked like one of MC Hammer's dancers.)

4. Making washbowl curries. The washbowl – or 'compo all-in' – curry, made in non-tactical locations where you could expect to be static for a couple of days, offered a culinary delight almost beyond compare. You lobbed the entire contents of several ration packs into the wagon's metal washbowl, and whacked in loads of curry powder and/or chilli sauce. It was then left to simmer on the kero heater for several days, like some sort of witch's cauldron. Everyone ate directly from the bowl with a racing spoon, and, as the level went down, more compo was introduced to the mix. People weren't particular about what foodstuffs went in there, working on the digestive principle that, at some point, everything eventually turned to shit. This allowed for the unique experience of dipping your spoon into a large curry pot and coming out with a catch comprising a teabag, a lump of un-dissolved powdered milk, a half-melted piece of cheese possessed and a boiled sweet.

Unfortunately, the curry was not to rear its head on that exercise. We had a lot of fresh rations, so once the network was up and running we sparked up the gas cooker and it was egg banjos a-go-go.

Life soon fell into the normal routine of sleeping, eating, stagging-on and checking the generator every six hours for fuel and oil. Any requirements for the toilet were met with a good walk away from the area for a piss, or an even longer walk for a shovel recce. The strange thing about shitting in the field is that no matter how remote or well-hidden you were, as soon as you squatted down and started a nice German family was guaranteed to appear from nowhere and catch you mid-log. It was always an awkward situation. Saying, 'Guten tag!' to someone whilst squatting with a shit hanging out of your arse didn't really smooth things over, and my German was never good enough to permit me to convince them that I was just actually sitting on a stick, and not dunging up their glorious countryside.

On the second morning of the exercise I added another image to my album of the visually horrific, when Dicky unzipped his sleeping bag and proceeded to rollover in full view of us, before shoving a suppository up his hoop. He then turned to Dave and me in his martyrdom and said, 'I tell you lads, much more of this and I'm going to take a soldering iron to my grapes!' The thought still makes me gag, not so much at the level of pain involved but at exactly what the smoke would smell like.

On the third night, the peace was broken by a minor first aid casualty. Dicky and I were kipping whilst Dave was on radio stag. Fuck knows what time it was when Dave woke me up, but he was obviously in a bit of a panic.

'Oh God, Eddy,' he hissed, shaking me violently. 'Eddy, wake up!'

'Alright Dave,' I said, rubbing my eyes. 'Calm down. What's wrong?'

'Well, I was on stag and some animal was trying to get into the tent, mate. I thought it was a wild boar or something. It kept pushing against the sides and when it got near the entrance flap, I hit the fucker as hard as I could with a shovel to get it to fuck off.'

'OK... so what's the problem?'

'Er... that was an hour or so ago, and I've just been outside to check the generator. And the fucking re-supply sergeant is spark out on the floor.'

Dave pointed towards the entrance. I could just make out a lone boot sticking out from under the tent flap.

'Oh fuck!' I said, and in that moment – even though the incident had happened some time before – I swear I could still hear the shovel singing like a tuning fork. I scrambled out of my sleeping bag and over to the sergeant. Dave was only a little bloke, but he'd obviously swung the shovel with all his might; the NCO had a lump like a boiled egg on his swede and a sizeable triangular bruise. Thank fuck it had hit him flat side on. We dragged him into the tent and started shaking him and talking in his ear, and I was on the verge of sending for proper help when he started to come round. He was as shaky as fuck but, after a shitload of pain killers, several brews and a lie down, he said he was feeling well enough to at least drive back to Exercise HQ where he could get himself checked out. He was pretty understanding, really – he could have had Dave bounced for assault, but he acknowledged that he should have shouted to let Dave know he was coming, thus avoiding his accidental braying.

He was later diagnosed as having mild to severe shovel rash; like every ailment treated by the Royal Army Medical Corps, including cancer and AIDS, this could be sorted out easily enough by two Brufen and a bit of Tubigrip. They were a great bunch, the medics. Right from the start, in Harrogate, if you ever went sick it was instantly assumed by all military medical staff, from surgeons to reception clerks, that you were bluffing your case. You'd turn up at the MRS with the flu, snot pissing out of your face, only to be given a suspicious dead-eye from the guy on reception. A fair few remained unconvinced by cuts or even broken limbs, despite the visual evidence on offer.

Mind you, the only thing worse than being fucked off was managing by some miracle to win them over. If you were on the sick you didn't parade with the troop properly – you formed a 'supernumerary rank' at the back of the squad, 'supernumerary rank' being defined as 'lazy, skiving, fucking malingerers'. As the Troop sergeant formed the lads up, he'd casually say, 'Sick, lame and lazy to the rear,' and even your mates joined in with the marginalising of the infirm. If you were excused boots for a foot injury, you'd have to wear the dreaded 'trainers and lightweights' combo. This all but certified that you were pickpocketing the British taxpayer whilst everyone else carried your useless carcass. You had to carry a 'sick chit' with you, detailing your illness or injury and the extent of your capabilities, and had to be ready to produce this for a higher rank. They'd hold it like it was used bog roll and give it back to you with a look that said, 'I know you're lying, I just can't prove it.'

If you managed to jump through enough hoops to convince the doctor that you were ill enough to be bedded down, your oppos had to go and get food for you from the cookhouse at mealtimes, it being a chargeable offence to be seen up and about if you were confined to your scratcher. They would always retrieve the shittest items available from the hotplate, spilling a good portion of it on the way back to the block, and if you deigned to ask for anything extravagant – like a piece of bread, say – you'd get a big roll of the eyes and a reply on the lines of, 'Yes, your fucking majesty!' The biggest tossers would lull you into a false sense of security by asking you what you wanted, only to return with a big grin, an inedible plate of fish fingers and custard, and an excuse of, 'Sorry, mate… that's all they had!' The only people who were exempt from this opprobrium were Victoria Cross winners, and even they would have to wear their VC for the entire duration of their illness to demonstrate their immunity from suspicion.

After the shovel rash incident it was plain sailing until day five when we received notice to move. We were to head up to Soltau and RV with one of the other 7 Sigs callsigns, then set the wagons up in a cluster. The lads we were meeting were from another troop, callsign Foxtrot 22, and the RV point was, as always, at a Schnelly. Looking back, if the USSR had staged a synchronised series of one kiloton hits on the fast food outlets and pubs of Western

Europe, they could have taken out half the British Army on any given day. Once again, we stocked up on chips and all manner of cooked swine, Germany having an astonishing plethora of pork products from which to choose, before heading off to our location. This time, being co-located, we arranged the vehicles in such a way that the tent entrances were facing each other with six feet of separation.

The other Det commander was Hooch Turner, a quiet, good-natured bloke. That was a good job, because he was built like a brick shithouse and rumour had it that he was extremely tasty with his hands. He was the kind of bloke that country and western singers wrote songs about; dead quiet but, when pushed to action by a great injustice, capable of wreaking terrible havoc with a ten-knuckle boarding party. Weirdly, he was completely and utterly shit-scared of the dark. This wasn't the normal natural trepidation that everybody who's seen *Salem's Lot* gets, he was almost phobic about it. He used to say that if we ever went to war he hoped it was during the day or in the Arctic circle in summer. The other blokes on Hooch's wagon were a lance corporal called Gordon 'Stung' Sumner and Signalman Colin 'Bearskin' Smith. Bearskin had acquired his nickname due to his enormous melon and its covering of very dark, thick hair, which made him look like he was permanently wearing the famed Guards head-dress. If he shaved it all off down to a number two, the lads just used to call him Basketball Head instead.

Hooch had a couple of crates of Warsteiner on his Det and he was quite forthcoming in dishing out the 'Wobblies'. Drinking on exercise was new to me, so I only had six cans on the first night. To be honest, field locations and boozing don't really complement each other very well, and not just because they inhibit your ability to secure West Germany in the event of a surprise Soviet attack. More to the point, I spent the evening garrotting myself on mast guy ropes every time I went for a piss.

The following morning was a gloriously clear day. I got out of my sleeping bag and took a quick walk round the masts, checking everything and clearing my head of the thickness caused by the Wobbly fumes. I stuck my face in the washbowl and then, following the agreed protocol of detachment living, cleaned it out thoroughly for the next man, Dicky stayed in his wanking chariot for a few minutes scratching his plums, and when he did get up his maggot let out a wave of hot air that exhibited similar thermal characteristics to the initial blast of a medium-yield nuclear device. I tried to turn away, but my nostrils had been mugged; his doss bag smelt like a pair of tramps had spent the last three months fucking in it, while suffering from dysentery.

He took the washbowl outside, stripped off and stood in the bowl to douse himself down. Most squaddies are fairly comfortable about being in the buff around other men – the close proximity you're forced to live in make privacy a bit of a luxury. But blokes like Dicky took it to another level – even when discretion *was* an option, they preferred to soap up their knackers in full view of the nearest German B road.

When he was finished washing, he braced himself against the frame of the tent and fired another suppository up his arse, like the loader on some sort of obscene artillery piece; despite my disgust, it was hard not to watch. The crowning glory of the whole spectacle came when he'd completed his alfresco ablutions. He handed the bowl to Dave, complete with a magnificently pube-infested scum ring and said, 'There you go, Dachau, she's all yours.'

The young squaddie's face was a picture of disbelief. A minute before he'd been watching Dicky give himself a haemorrhoid-antagonising ring dhobi in that very same vessel: now he was supposed to get a shave out of it. He took the bowl, and I reckon he washed it out 30 times before he used it. When he finally mustered the courage, he was very tentative – watching him psyche himself up to stick his face in the water was like watching a bush tucker trial from *I'm A Celebrity*.

That night, I had the 'Death Stag' from ten till six on our wagon whilst Hooch manned the other. We couldn't really leave our respective installations to talk to each other and pass the time, so it was utterly boring. However, Dicky was a wily old sweat so he had a multitude of home comforts on the vehicle, including a nifty portable radio that picked up BFBS a treat. So with the headset on, but only covering one ear so as the comms were still audible, I settled in for the night.

I checked the generator at midnight as per the timetable and carried out frequency changes. Come half-past one it started getting fucking icers, and my breath was visible inside the wagon, even with the kero heater on. I was faced with the eternal night-stag dilemma of, 'Do I get into my maggot?' It probably sounds like a no-brainer: if you're cold, what could be better than warming up in your sleeping bag? As long as you don't fall asleep, nobody's to know, are they?

Like a lot of things in life, it isn't that easy. It's a bit like getting into drugs – you start with just a little taster, you think you're alright and you've a got a lid on it, and the next thing you know you're selling your granny's telly for a fiver. The way it worked with the 'doss bag on stag' routine is you started by convincing yourself that if your feet were warm then the rest of you would be alright. So you put your feet into the warm schlaf sack and zipped it up to your ankles. And it was fucking great and it did the trick for about ten minutes, but then, because your feet were warm, you noticed that the tops of your legs were cold. Again you'd tell yourself that it wouldn't do any harm to just raise the zip a bit and cover your knees. A quarter of an hour later, it would be up by your hips and your hands would be jammed down into your combat trouser map pockets for additional comfort. It would go on like that until, two hours later, you'd find yourself sitting there with just your nose and eyes visible from a fully-closed sleeping bag, looking like a rat peering out of a bear's arse. And suddenly it was eight in the morning, there was a big dribble patch on your sleeping bag, the generator had seized because it had run out of oil and the OC was screaming your callsign down the Division command net. You'd just experienced the radio watch equivalent of a massive overdose.

I went for the to-the-knees option and settled down to BFBS. Things got considerably more serious at 2am, when the calming voice of 'Whispering' Bob Harris entered my ear. Don't get me wrong, I don't mind a spot of easy listening if the time is right, and Bob Harris seemed a decent enough bloke. But soothing melodies with softly-spoken 'hepcat' links have a time and a place, and this wasn't it. What the fuck were the programme organisers at BFBS thinking of?

I imagined a brain-storming session: 'OK, guys, we've got a four hour show of music that helps you doze off... when shall we stick it on air?'

'I know!' says some young go-getter, clicking his fingers. 'How about between two and six in the morning, when the only people listening to forces' radio will be bods on guard or radio stag who are fighting to stay awake? They'll really thank us for it!'

'That's it! Nice work, Julian. I'll get Miles on it right away. OK, guys... if there's no other business, it's a wrap.'

To avoid the Bob/Bag combo, I reluctantly took my legs out of the maggot. In an attempt to prevent my plums from freezing off, I dug out an extra fleece from my bergan and took the remaining cold on the chin. The rest of the night wasn't too bad, although at one point Bob stuck on a bit of Clannad which almost did me in on the spot: I quickly made a brew and went outside to get some fresh air into my lungs.

The days blended into each other, as they often do, and not much of interest happened. Actually, I tell a lie – there was Wolfy's cameo appearance.

Despite being non-tactical, we were still in a fairly remote, well-hidden location. Nevertheless, a few days in to our stay the half-light of dusk was broken by glaring headlights and the revving of an old diesel engine. Before long, a shitty-white Mercedes van came thrashing up the track and screeched to a halt in a cloud of dust and gravel. Out clambered a fat Jerry with ruddy cheeks and a wide grin.

Wolfy was a legend on Soltau. He was widely believed to possess the best Schnelly wagon in the whole of BAOR, and his van was a common sight on the training area. So common, in fact, that all sorts of stories abounded as to his superhuman troop-locating abilities: the theory was that he would bribe the monkeys into spilling the beans on unit locations, with just a portion of Pommes mit Mayo and a frickadela. I'd even heard about him helping REME recce mechs pull out a bogged-in Chieftain.

He was a jovial kind of bloke, and it must've raised his spirits to see us pegging it over with such speed to get some novel scran – I remember Hooch gave Stung a dead leg and neck-chopped Bearskin to get to the front of the queue in the stampede. We ordered a couple of meals-worth each, and a ruck load of stims. We didn't eat all the food straight away. but even a cold schnelly was better than compo.

The great thing about Wolfy was that he was into a bit of quid-pro-quo. If you were a bit strapped on the Deutsche Mark front he'd let you pay for your scoff with some diesel off the wagon. I'm not sure what the official Sausage/Fuel exchange rate was, but we weren't paying for it and therefore gave not a flying fuck, quickly amending the fuel cards to absorb the loss.

Not long after Wolfy's visit, Endex was called. We returned our crypto and jerry cans to 1 Div and had a bit of a one-tonnie death race back to Herford, where we turned the dets around and sorted our personal admin out.

Back in the block, all the talk was of an impending über-disco in Rheindahlen that lasted a life-threatening 52 hours. It appeared that the post-exercise weekend had already been planned for me.

I spent a good hour in the shower trying to remove the accumulated shite from under my fingernails with a pink nailbrush. I was still scrubbing up when Vic Kerr scared the life out of me by banging on the cubicle and informing me that our 'Limo' was about to leave.

EDDY NUGENT AND THE FIFTY TWO HOUR DICKSHOW

IT TURNED OUT that the 'limo' for the ride down was actually The Padre's XR3i. It was an ugly little red beast, with a massive – and entirely superfluous – black spoiler and more lights than would have been strictly necessary on an aircraft carrier. But it was all that was left of Vic's torpedoed marriage, and was obviously his pride and joy, so I kept my opinions to myself.

In the Army, owning anything other than a money-and-porn tree is a double-edged sword, and nowhere was this more apparent than having a set of wheels in BAOR. On the one hand, it offered escape from the block at the turn of a key. On the other, it also brought with it perpetual lift-scroungers. Blokes would plague the driver with endless requests for everything from short cabbies to Fat Sam's Gyros platz down the road to lifts back home to Blighty on leave, when promises of going halfers on the benz would vanish like a midsummer frost when it came to filling up at Wankum services on the border.

For some reason, the local journeys drew the most cadging. One time, when Vic was posted to the Falklands, he asked me to look after his wheels. I remember a stout northern lad called Ken 'The Stroker' Coaker pleading with me for ages to give him a lift down to Valentino's brothel on the outskirts of town. I gave in, and as we approached the place Ken suddenly went a bit sheepish. Then he blurted it out. 'Listen, Eddy, will you wait fer us? I'll only be 15 minutes and I've not got enough gelt fu' t'pay fu' t'taxi as well as t'shag. Go on, mate. Don't be a jack bastard.'

He went on in like fashion for several minutes, without even giving me a chance to respond. Eventually, when I pulled up, I said, 'Alright, Ken. But don't take the piss, eh.'

He was over the moon. Just as he was about to close the car door, he poked his head back in and said, "Ere, Eduardo... when you think of me in there wi' t'prozzies, you'll affut play wi' ya widgie.'

Cleverly inverting the jack-bastardness of the situation, he then left me sat out there for two hours. He wasn't a bad bloke, Ken, but he was prone to flights of fancy every now and again. The last I heard from him he had his sights set on America, where he planned to go 'Affut joining t'LAPD.'

Chopper and Hooch filled Vic's motor up, and we headed off, starting on the drink with undue haste. The first cans were broached as we passed the junction for Bielefeld Ost and by the time we got to Rhein D we'd opened the second lot. We parked in a good-sized car park opposite a pub called The Queen's Arms, quickly de-bussed and headed up the road, following several other revellers, to the Queensway Club.

It was early, only about 19:00hrs, but there was already a queue to get in. The sheer number of guys who had turned up from 7 Sigs meant that it wasn't feasible to go in one big round, so the blokes from our car stuck together for the drinks. Soon the night had entered the drunken groove I'd become familiar with, and as one song blended into the next, so another beer followed the last. It got to the point that I had no idea how many I'd drank but the training I'd been putting in since posting from Aldershot began to reap dividends. I found myself able to hover around a particular plateau of inebriation; I responded to conversational prompts as and when they came, and the rest of the time I'd focus on something in the middle distance and stare at it with one eye shut. I probably looked like Columbo.

I remember chuckling at Chopper dancing like a chicken on a hot tin roof while also indulging in the moderately dangerous pastime of minesweeping anything he could get his hands on. It's a weird one, minesweeping. Technically, it's the theft of someone else's property. But there was, nevertheless, a bit of grudging respect for the more gifted exponents of the art. Chopper always selected his prey carefully – the perfect target being a leathered young tom buying more than two handfuls of drinks. As the lad carried the first batch from the bar, Chopper would wander past, whistling like the Artful Dodger, before rendering the round one pint light. He wasn't just running the risk of a good filling-in – some people made the working assumption that their pint would be snaffled at some point during the evening and elected to inject a shot of their own piss into the glass or bottle before leaving it to go to the toilet. If it did get stolen, they'd got their revenge in early.

At about four in the morning I went outside for some fresh air – which hit me like a hammer, considering I'd spent the last nine hours in the baking atmosphere of the club. I leant against the wall with both hands and breathed in deeply whilst waiting for the oxygen to do its thing and wake me up. Over to my right, I heard an argument break out between two blokes, one of whom sounded like Phil 'Tsetse' Ash from my det.

'Listen you fucker,' said the first voice. 'You just stay away from my girl, alright?'

'Ah fuck off, man,' said Tsetse, in a drunken slur. 'I was awnly talking to the lass, what's the fuckin' problem, like?'

It sounded like it was just about to turn nasty, so I started to walk over with the intention of providing back up to Tsetse in the form of clumsy diplomacy. As I got closer, it became apparent that the person who was arguing with him was in fact a large girl with a skinhead haircut. I quickly sussed out that she was one of the legendary 'Man-WRACs' of 16 Tank Transporter Regiment – a rock-hard bunch of warrior women who were always duffing up unsuspecting blokes brave enough to chat up their other halves.

I could see her moving on Tsetse in a threatening manner. 'I won't fucking tell you again, pal,' she said, poking him in the chest.

Tsetse reacted in an entirely blasé way, clearly having no appreciation of the pickle in which he found himself. 'Ah fuck off, ya big fuckin' bull dyke,' he slurred, weaving slightly as he did so. 'See if I give a fuck. I was awnly talking to her, anyways, an' if she's a fuckin' flicker like yee, then what are yee fuckin' worried about, eh?'

His logical assumptions about the WRAC's girlfriend's sexuality failed to soothe the situation, and she immediately began to ball a pair of fists more suited to wrestling with an HGV steering wheel. Before the situation got any worse I stepped in between them and ushered Tsetse away. He wasn't a big lad, and all the beer had made him very loose; one punch from the lezzer RCT Amazon would have killed him. I suppose some sort of residual survival gene must have kicked in, because he didn't protest much as I pushed him towards the door.

As soon as I got him inside I went back to the still-seething skinhead to diffuse matters and, hopefully, head off any future unpleasantness. 'Sorry about that, love,' I said. 'He's a bit drunk.'

She stared at me. 'Who the fuck are you calling "love" you little cunt? Do you want a fucking smack?'

I immediately became George to her Mildred, inadvertently using the word that had made her angrier. 'Calm down, love, for fuck's sake. He was just a bit pissed up, that's all.'

She told me to fuck off again, but did at least drop her mitts, excusing me the indignity of a good panelling. I probably wasn't worth it, her sumo wrestler proportions being designed more for fighting large primates than slightly pot-bellied Mancunians. I watched as she stalked off in search of her missus.

The adrenaline release had woken me up a bit so, riding on the crest of a second wind, I returned to the bar with renewed gusto and got back into the swing of things.

* * * * *

At seven in the morning, they kicked everybody out for the first of the hosing-downs. This was a sight to see: the manager and bar staff just unravelled the fire hoses and blasted the walls and floors, sending all the cans, fags, beer and God knows what out of the front door in a tsunami of shit. They'd then give the floors an hour to dry before reopening, at which point everyone would immediately pick up where they'd left off. It was truly marvellous.

Of course, some of the guys were utterly spent after a dozen solid hours of piss. Vic was included in this list, and he staggered off to his car to get his napper down. Chopper and Hooch were still going strong and as soon as the doors re-opened, we went back in and ordered three beers.

To tell you the truth, I don't really know what happened between then and midday. I just sort of came to and realised that I'd lost the other two blokes, and was in total rag order myself. There was no other option left but to get my own head down for a bit. Feeling the maternal pull of Vic's motor, I went looking for Chopper or Hooch to let them know I was going. I couldn't find them anywhere. As a last option, I checked the toilets. As soon as I went in I skidded and fell flat on my back in a urine lake. Though exceptionally honking, the cold liquid sticking the t-shirt to my back woke me up a bit. After steadying myself I shouted their names. After a few seconds I was met with a pathetic wailing noise coming from one of the shitters. It sounded like Chopper, so I called again.

'Chopper, mate! Is that you in there?'

'Oooooh, don't worry, it's under control, it's all going to be alright.'

'What the fuck are you on about?'

'It's all under control.'

His voice was weak and fluctuating. To make sure he was OK, I booted the door to his cubicle open and was presented with the personification of the drunkard. The normally robust Chopper was slumped on the toilet seat with his head lolled to one side. His eyes were closed, and he was rambling incoherently. His strides and undies were round his ankles and he had been sick onto them. Every now and then, his knob would release a squirt of urine down his leg, like a knackered sprinkler. Along with the rest of the free world, I crossed my fingers and hoped that the Russians wouldn't choose now to launch World War III. I filled a glass with cold water and threw it on him.

'Grooogh!' he yelped. 'Splooough!'

But after that brief episode of coughing and spluttering, he quickly sank back into whatever drunken dream he'd been having. Breathing hard, I pulled him to his feet, shook him enough to get him to pull his puke-encrusted trousers half up and then used the battle PT skills I'd learnt in Aldershot to fireman's lift him out of the bar and back to the car. All the space was taken. Vic was gonking in the fully-reclined driver's seat and Hooch was snoring loudly, fully-stretched across the back seat, giving no consideration for late arrivals. I placed Chopper down on the floor, where he passed out immediately, but then he was so ballbagged he could have slept on a chicken's lip. The sun was high and warm in the sky so I decided to join him on the grass. I crashed out and within seconds I was out for the count.

I came to what felt like a couple of minutes later, but the sun's position in the reddening sky – and the fact that I was freezing my tits off – confirmed that we'd all been schlafing for some time, lying there like a freeze-framed car crash.

We all looked, felt and smelt like the public toilet outside the Rumbelows in Mogadishu. But in the absence of washrooms there was no other reasonable course of action than to immediately get back on the razz.

Instead of going straight back to the Queensway, we headed across the road to the Queen's Arms and got some scran down our necks, washed down with a pint that took a bit of manly grimacing to swallow. Once stoked up again, we returned to the disco. There was no change to the stifling atmosphere. It was just as hectic as it had been the night before and you could hardly move or breathe.

To get a bit of respite from the crowd, some of us hung from the metal window bars. As well as giving us some much-needed space, the lofty position also allowed us the opportunity to look down girls' tops. It was most gratifying. As I get older, I often wonder when my libido will wane: indeed, I'm quite looking forward to it. George Melly said it was 'like getting off a runaway horse you didn't realise you were riding', but there's no sign of it yet. From the age of around 12 onwards, I have spent what I regard as an inordinate amount of time trying to catch a glimpse of uncovered female flesh. Had I set aside those hours to more serious-minded pursuits, I might have learned five or six new languages, or developed and patented a new form of motor propulsion. Instead, I have nothing to show for it but a confusing jumble of odd and fleeting memories of random knocker-glimpse, the owners long forgotten. I'm 40 now and, despite love, marriage, children and cherished monogamy, I still keep my hand in, figuratively-speaking. To tell the truth, I suspect that so long as women continue to wear slightly ill-fitting blouses exhibiting the 'gap-of-plenty' between the second and third buttons, I'll be unable to resist the occasional crafty blimp.

In the early hours of Sunday morning, Hooch got involved in an ironman competition with some big wedgehead from 21 Engineer Regiment, based in Neumburg. It had been quite nip and tuck, but Hooch clinched the title by eating one of the pineapple chunk bleach blocks out of the urinals. To make it easier to eat, he first sucked all the liquid out of it forcefully, like a kid getting all the flavour out of an ice pop. It was an outstanding touch that, rightfully, vanquished his foe, who accepted defeat with good grace. The phenomenon of 'gross out' competitions was commonplace, despite the fact that there was no reward other than notoriety, the admiration of one's peers and the disgust of anyone not involved, and it did bring out the best in a man. But despite feeling good after his victory, Hooch soon fell victim to his unusual meal and began vomiting in a fashion that would have put the shits up the most hardened exorcist. I was quite concerned about the amount of chemicals that he had digested. The main NAAFI wasn't far away, so I shepherded him over there and got him sat down in the vending machine area, where I filled him with two cartons of milk. As he chugged it, I encouraged him by shouting, 'The power of Christ compels you! The power of Christ compels you!' I'm not sure if it was my quasi-religious exhortations, or the milk, or just that his body was physically unable to vomit further, but it appeared to settle his guts quite quickly. After a 20 minute 'no honking' convalescence, we returned to the other chaps.

Towards the end of the night, I noticed that everyone's jeans were black from the knees down, presumably because of all the ghastly fluids on the dance floor accumulating over the weekend. I dread to think what the stains were comprised of, but I had to throw my jeans away after.

I hit my second brick wall at five in the morning and can't really remember much after that. I managed to find a side room in the Queensway with an open door. It was a very posh lounge, obviously off limits to the likes of us, but there were several other blokes asleep in there, one of whom I presumed had been the perpetrator of the break in. At the time, I took it as read that it was a designated crash out room and I only found out about it being forbidden to sleep there the next day.

Whilst trying to tiptoe around the collapsed bodies, I accidentally trod on someone's foot and started receiving abuse accordingly. 'Howay and shite man, ya fucker! Worra ya deein' like! You've brerk me fuckin' ters.'

It was Tsetse. I calmed him down so as not to wake the other sleepers and as he massaged his foot he continued. 'Ah Eddy man, Ah'm ackshally glad yer've werk us up, like, mate. Ah'm dyin' forra piss an' that.' He climbed unsteadily to his feet, hoiked his knob out of his zip and bent his knees a few times in readiness to take a whizz on the floor. But just before he started, he looked around and, with guilt in his voice, said, 'How, Eddy man! Ah cannat lag all erver this floor, like. Look at the place, man, it's geet fuckin' snooty! Ah tell ye wot, like, ah'll hev a slash in a glass. That'll dee the trick!'

He rustled up a nearby pint glass and began relieving himself into it. His bladder being fairly full, the glass soon started filling to the top. He looked around for a replacement, but there were none to be found. So when the pint was full he just poured it onto the carpet and began filling the glass all over again. He repeated this process four times, and every time he poured the contents onto the floor he didn't even stop his stream of hose. It made no sense to me, but Tsetse seemed to be abiding by some sort of internal protocol.

I managed to get some kip in one of the soft chairs for a couple of hours, then made my way to the car. The three blokes were already in there and we decided to get back to camp to sort our shit out for razzer's, after a quick visit to the vendors for a growler frenzy. In the vending area there was a young lad of about 18 or 19. He had no trousers on, and was doing the one-footed stagger almost as if the other foot was stuck to the floor. He was waiting by a microwave that was whirring away and making strange crackling noises. I assumed he'd soon remove a chicken and mushroom pie, or something equally mouth watering, but when it eventually pinged he reached inside and pulled out his jeans. He'd evidently been drying them off after suffering an 'accident' that necessitated emergency cleaning. Within ten seconds, the place smelt like the chimp-enclosure at Chester Zoo. But – amazingly, now I think back – it didn't put us off our scran. We started cramming food into our necks while he treated us to an hilarious floor show, hopping around on one foot whilst trying to get his leaden, drunken limbs into his red-hot trousers without burning himself. After bouncing off every table, chair and wall in the place, he eventually flashed. 'CUNT OFF!' he shouted, at the top of his voice, and threw his strides in the bin, before storming away in his underpants, shirt and shoes. We never saw him again.

The conversation on the drive back took the form of the eternal triangle facing all squaddies on a Sunday night: what a great weekend we'd had, how shit we were feeling and how meticulous was the RSM's inspection likely to be the next day.

At one end of the scale, you might just get a quick once-over from a Troop Staffy who wasn't a bullshit merchant. In these circumstances, only something massively incompetent, like forgetting to put one of your boots on, would get you a rifting.

At the other end, if the RSM was in a bad mood for any one of a hundred reasons, we'd get placed in open order and he'd get his magnifying glass out on every one of us. If you ever called it wrong and took it easy on your kit when 'the Badge' was inspecting you may as well have started making your way to the guardroom before he got to you. One bit of fluff on a beret or shit on a toecap could see you copping for Christmas guard duty.

I was once picked up by him for my laces not sitting straight on my boots. He justified the five extras I got by eyeballing me manically and saying, 'Twisted laces, twisted mind, Nugent!' They always liked to imply that a badly-polished pair of boots was the thin end of a wedge leading inexorably to the complete breakdown of society. My favourite story in this genre was told to me by a Marine I knew. His RSM had picked him up for having one of his combat jacket buttons undone, which led him to make the extraordinary claim that, 'It's buttons today, but it'll be fucking submarine hatches tomorrow!'

Getting insider info from Squadron HQ was invaluable, but it couldn't always be relied upon. The RSM might have no plans for an inspection on Sunday night, but his mind could be changed by something as simple as one of his kids taping over *Who Dares Wins* with Friday night's *Coronation Street*.

The block was quiet that night, with a few lads still down at the 52, chancing it – blokes always hated the idea of sweating on something unnecessary. Those who'd taken a more sensible approach and had returned early to do their kit were in shit state. All over the place, lads were using trembling hands to try and iron straight lines into jumpers and lightweights, coughing back nausea caused by boot polish and starch fumes and sweating heavily from the heat produced by tiny little irons.

The whole thing reminded me of Sunday nights as a kid, when I'd be dreading the week ahead at school. Downstairs, mum and dad would be watching *Last Of The Summer Wine*, which only ever seemed to have one episode, and up in my room I'd be trying to box off a week's homework before bedtime.

It was the same in the mob in Germany, the dual effects of self-inflicted skintness and the prospect of another week on the Job Creation Scheme always combined to bring the mood down: it was at times like these, when I was physically wilting, that I'd have niggling thoughts about sorting my life out, and wondering where – or indeed if – my future lay within the Army.

Luckily, a small act of generosity could alleviate this malaise and, on that particular evening, Vic Kerr provided it. He knocked on my door and waggled two videos at me. One was *Highlander*, and the other a little thing called *Girls That Eat Red Snapper*. They formed an interesting combination, so I stopped what I was doing and accompanied him to his room.

EDDY NUGENT AND THE DEADMAN'S WEE

I'D BEEN IN Germany a few months by the time I went back on my first leave.

It was Christmas 1991, and there was the usual silly season run-up to knocking off for the festive period, with some sort of do every couple of days. PT sessions got that bit dossier, and the volleyballs put in their annual appearance. The walls and ceilings in the gym were covered in Arctic camnets and white parachutes for the Squadron dos, and the cookhouse aroma of lasagne and chicken curry could be smelt wafting through the air.

Traditionally, the Christmas dos also provided opportunities for scores and grudges to be settled without worrying too much about Queen's Regulations or the rank structure. Any senior who'd been a particular knob in that year would be careful about trips to the toilet, which could often result in a 'nasty fall' or some heavy chest poking from an irate tom whose respect for military authority had been eroded by too much Wobbly.

As much as I was enjoying life in the Fatherland, I was looking forward to getting home, especially for Crimbo, and when I walked in through the door, I was delighted to find a full house. Mum and dad were both in, and nan was there with Alfie, her new beau. I'd only seen him once or twice since he'd attended my graduation, but I was really chuffed that they'd forged a friendship. It was good for my nan – she always blossomed in male company – and I felt a strong forces bond with Alfie myself. These bonds have always transcended the generations: the wars and equipment differ, but a soldier's life remains the same. I have no doubt that members of Cromwell's New Model Army shimfed like fuck at the thought of another dose of area-cleaning on Marston Moor. Some infantry regiments refer to this as the 'golden thread', an intangible line that runs through and ties together the careers and memories of generations of British professional soldiers. Although Alfie often displayed Olympic-level cantankery, I looked upon him with awe given his row of gongs from World War II.

Mum and nan went over the top, ruffling my hair and hugging and kissing me as if I was seven, which I loved, while the men hovered conspicuously in the background. Eventually, dad stepped forward and shook my hand before pulling me into a bear hug. 'Welcome home, son. Welcome home.' He said it stoically but, as he looked at me, I could detect traces of emotion. I just smiled and said, 'Alright, dad?' the classic answer of a young lad who's never understood a father's pride.

Alfie was wearing his regimental tie and blazer and his immaculate white hair was combed into a side parting which looked like it had been done with a slide rule. He gave me a strong handshake, clasping my hand in both of his fists. 'Good to see you young, Eddy,' he said. 'How're you doing?'

He was an easy man to talk to. Although, like many of his generation, he was quite reserved, we'd soon end up swapping anecdotes. Of course, his always blew mine out of the water. The hook always went in at the beginning, with a tantalising opening sentence like, 'So, young Eddy. There were me and Lofty Scrivens and we were in The Palestine on this bloody BSA Bantam...'

I had a whale of a time, of course. I slept all day, didn't shave and hassled my civvie mates into going on the lash whenever I could. Unfortunately, most of the lads I used to knock around with were either still students or on the rock-and-roll. Subsidised by their parents, they were the classic 'Bedroom Millionaires' – dressed from head to toe in Paul Smith clobber, but lacking the funds to buy a round. They couldn't afford to piss it up for the two weeks straight that suited me, and this caused a bit of resentment on my part. I'd started to develop an independent streak, and it led me to rip the piss out of their rent-free existences. Rightly, they didn't give a fuck what I thought and were not slow to remind me that they were able to enjoy life to the full while I spent my days running everywhere in ill-fitting green clothing.

This was most apparent whenever I chatted to Jimmy Connolly. Jimmy had been with me on the day I'd first entered the recruiting office, way back in 1985. He'd got as far as the door and had turned back. Six years on, he'd got himself a degree in history and was now spending his days trying to find out how much weed one man could smoke. The munchies that accompanied his habit saw him putting quite a bit of beef on, but he seemed happy enough. Like a lot of lads in Manchester around that time, his accent had undergone a bit of a metamorphosis as a result of the worldwide 'Madchester' boom, with everyone desperate to emulate Shaun Ryder's *laissez-faire* attitudes to speech and life. A simple 'Alright?' now came out of Jimmy's mouth as 'Alriiiiiiiiiiiiiiiiite!' and this was accompanied by a 'have you just shit yourself' walk and a bowl haircut like Clint Boon's out of the Inspiral Carpets. Variations on this theme were the general uniform for all my civvie pals, so I sometimes stood out a bit, in particular because of the regulation haircut. No one was wearing it that short back then.

I managed to get down to the British Legion with Alfie a few times, and we'd get absolutely falling over drunk along with some of his old oppos. Some of the old boys would get so pissed they'd start dredging up arguments from 1942, their animation offering me a glimpse of them as young men. On rare occasions, once the drink had broken down enough barriers, Alfie or one of the others would let his guard down and start relating something more sombre. These stories always had the effect of pulling me up short.

I remember him telling me a funny story about himself, a mate called Vic Tanner and a goat. The goat, a large and vicious animal, was another regiment's mascot. The upshot of the story was that Vic and Alfie had kidnapped the goat and it had ended up served to its own CO in a Gurkha curry. I was in stitches. As my laughter began to subside, Alfie gathered his thoughts. 'Aye, nineteen forty three that happened,' he said, his voice now gentle and reflective. 'I were 20, and Vic were a year younger. A real country lad, he were. A good lad. My *best* mate.' Alfie straightened up. 'He... er.... he copped it the year after that. Blown to bits on Gold Beach. Poor bugger. A better man than me.'

He quickly stood up and headed to the bar for another round, leaving me sat with my thoughts. It was the first time I really thought about what those old boys had been through. I'd always had immense respect for the veterans, but for the briefest of moments I'd got a proper glimpse of their reality.

* * * * *

Nan of course, was as mad as ever, asking me all sorts of crazy shit about being in Germany and ever keen to impress upon me the essential untrustworthiness of the Boche. ''Ere, our Eddy,' she'd suddenly say, leaning over and tugging at my sleeve. 'Have you seen many of them Germans over there? Sly buggers, you mark my words.' While I tried to formulate an answer, she'd shift gear and launch into something I was utterly oblivious to. 'I see Ivy got a new cat, then? Well, ever since her last one died she's been ever so lonely. It was probably her new hairdo that did it. You know, the one she got from them new queer fellas at the salon. Such a waste that, good-looking lads getting up to all sorts. I blame their mums.'

Inevitably, as with most nans and mums, she was forever hassling me about my single status. 'So are you courting, Eddy? Don't you go seeing any of them bloody German girls, mind. Oh no. Shoulders on 'em like Geoff bloody Capes.' Then a mischievous glint would enter her eye, and the mild insanity would clear the decks for a lucid moment. 'There's a new family moved in round here... they've got a lovely daughter, only a year or so younger than you. A pretty little thing she is, called Jenny.'

I feigned indifference, but kept the comment logged. I thought it might be worth a run past her house one morning – a bit of impromptu leave PT. Nothing too obvious, like press-ups or star jumps on the pavement outside the front door, that would've been too cockish, even for me. No, just a manly, chest-out, ostentatious jog to demonstrate my physical superiority over my peers. That would be the ticket.

The fact that I even *thought* of this as a sensible strategy demonstrates how shit I was at hitting it off with lasses, especially when sober. My wooing skills lacked subtlety to such an extent that, horrifyingly, I'd even looked to my BAOR compadres for guidance.

In the end, I decided to let fate take the lead, and spent my leave getting sozzled in all the local pubs, hoping I'd just bump into Jenny and work my ham-fisted verbal magic on her. As it happened, fate's 'fixing Eddy up with the new girl' admin was in rag order, so the day before I flew back I resorted to the 'last day of leave guilt run' and took a route past her house. This is a traditional run performed by all squaddies just before going back to camp, but particularly by those who've been drinking like George Best and smoking like beagles, leading them to dread their next PT session. Physically, I was in bits: my few months in Germany had led me to developing the first signs of a piss-tank which slowed me right up and left me sweating all sorts of crap out of my system. The days of my blistering Swastika runs round Aldershot already seemed distant. But as I approached her place, I smartened up and adopted a Seb Coe-like stride – and it bloody worked!

She was at her front door saying goodbye to her mum as I made my approach. I nodded to her and she said a quick hello with a mildly flirtatious smile. Amazingly, despite her bonkers worldview, nan had actually given me a good steer: she really was a good-looking girl, not too thin but no horrific porker, either. She had long, straight, mousey hair, wore no make-up and was casually dressed. Had it not been so cold, I might have had to nurse a semi-panhandle for the remainder of my run.

That afternoon I popped out to the shops for mum and saw Jenny down there. I broke the ice with another 'Hello' and she came out with the usual 'I saw you running earlier, you must be mad!'

Me, being a bit of knobber, tried to pull the troubled hardman bit. I was wincing internally, but it seemed like the right thing to do at the time. Unfortunately, I was going back to Germany the next day, but I threw that in to add to the mystique and eventually got her name and address to write to. I'm actually cringing whilst I write this, but when she said that her name was Jenny, I replied, 'I'll have to check you for oil and petrol every four hours, then.'

She was monumentally dumbfounded. Instead of glossing over it, I went into a lengthy explanation about how we called generators 'Gennies' and needed to constantly monitor them to prevent them running dry. It had to be the shittest bit of patter she'd ever heard, but she seemed to let me off. In our quick conversation, I found out that she was 18 and at college. Up close, she was even more attractive than I'd first thought, blue eyes and just the right smile. It was a shame I'd left it so late to meet her, but for the time being I had to make do with filing her in my memory bank.

* * * * *

I got some right shit when I got back to the block. I'd put on more weight than intended over Christmas and I was just in the middle of writing Jenny a quick letter, with the aim of meeting her again the next time I got back on leave, when Vic stuck his head round my door.

'Facking hell, Eddy,' he said. 'What did you do over Crimbo? Eat Santa?'

As a form of atonement, we took it easy on the lash the first weekend back, and hit the flicks instead. The cinema for Herford Garrison was on one of the 4 Div barracks and every so often they'd show a film worth going to see. It was in much better order than the flicks in Belize, and you didn't get bitten to death by mozzies, either.

As it happened, they were showing *The Silence of the Lambs*. A decent film in itself, for us it served a higher purpose in that it ushered in a new era of squadron bar nudity. When enough of the chaps had seen the film, the days of a normal naked bar were gone. No longer would bollocky buff antics be restricted to just getting in the raw and drinking with your hand on your hip: now we re-enacted the moment in the film where the murderer dons his outfit of human skin and parades lasciviously in front of his mirror. Called 'The Buffalo Bill', it required you to get starkers and tuck your meat and two veg between your legs. Hey Presto! You are a woman. Eventually, it became known as 'Billing' or 'Doing a Bill', and a really good quality Bill went beyond just the knob-between-the-legs gag: to pull it off properly, you brought your elbows into your sides, held your forearms up with wrists cocked and teetered around on the balls of your feet shouting, 'PUT THE FUCKING LOTION IN THE BASKET!' in a distressed manner.

If you happened to wander into the bar quite late on, it wasn't uncommon to find seven or eight guys hobbling around in this fashion. If you were unlucky enough that they had their backs to you, their hidden tackle provided a horror show all of its own, like a series of semi-inflated pink marigold gloves. In the office where I now work, I'll occasionally get called about invoices that need paying. The girl who rings up always says, 'Hi, Eddy, it's Janice… from billing.' I always have to compose myself before replying.

The introduction of Billing led, in turn, to a multitude of other exotic and ever-more inventive nude antics. One, the Bulldog, involved tucking just the ball bag between your legs and getting on all fours to strut around the bar while barking. It was so-named because it caused your sack to go all tight and protrude from behind you like a Bulldog's knackers.

Sometimes, probably in direct relation to a the moon cycle, we would partake in a game of Deadman's Wee. This would see the majority of the squadron lying naked on their backs, seeing who could piss the highest, like a budget version of the famous Barcelona fountains.

The pinnacle of drunken naked bar lunacy was reached in the spring of 1993, after Steve 'Huggy' Bairstow had been to see an old school friend who was serving with the Royal Engineers in Hameln. On his return, Huggy brought two things back. One was an earth-shattering hangover, and the other was the rudimentary details of a game called 'Naked Powerlifting' which he'd been playing with the wedgeheads.

It has to be said that the Royal Engineers were a brilliant bunch of lads, awesome on the piss, hard chargers in the field and a cracking laugh, but they were crazy motherfuckers, to a man.

As a game, it's not too far removed from what you might see in some mad Japanese gameshow. Two chairs are placed approximately a foot apart to form the base for a lifting platform. In between the chairs is a 20 litre jerry can of water, and attached to the top handle of the can is a six-inch bootlace or piece of para-cord, with a slip knot for tying onto your old chap. The lifter has to get naked, with one foot on each chair and the can directly below him. He then crouches down so that his arse cheeks touch the arms of the chairs, and the cord attached to the can is tied to the end of his knob. The name of the game then is to stand up fully, with both knees locked out. The short length of the cord ensures that, regardless of the athlete's height or the size of his schlong, the can will always clear the deck, transferring the jerry can's entire weight to the knob end. A 'good lift' is only called when both knees are fully locked out. There was a judge for each knee to oversee proceedings and to be a judge at these contests was an extremely high calling, as it called for rigorous impartiality.

Back then, the entry weight was two litres (5kg with the can), increasing in increments of two litres. Each competitor got two attempts at a weight. and once the lifts started getting up into the 14 litre ballpark, blokes started dropping like flies – not surprising, as having 15kg hanging off your cock is very painful. Whilst in mid-lift, the average penis took on the appearance of Stretch Armstrong caught in a tug of war between two dogs, and if you made the full 20 litres the following morning your dick would look like a banana that had been left out in the sun for too long.

I remember the night that Huggy first broke the 20 kilos mark. Just as he locked out, he bellowed and flexed his biceps, King-Kong style; at that very moment, the Orderly Officer walked into the bar to close it for the night. I'm sure the rodney thought he'd opened the door on one of Dante's more deranged visions, but before he could speak, one of the naked judges turned to him with a beer in hand, lifted his glass in a 'cheers' motion and said, 'Don't worry about us, sir, we're just doing a bit of power-lifting.'

Without a word, the officer departed the bar and let it be for the rest of the night. By the time I came to leave the Army, the record for power-lifting had been set in Bosnia, with two sappers going head-to-head in Kiseljak. They had tied for the championship on a full jerry can and an SA80 with SUSAT and a 20-round mag fitted. When the second guy locked out on this weight, he roared at one of his mates, who quickly draped a full set of wet, 58-pattern webbing over the whole arrangement. This increased the weight by another fifteen pounds, causing everyone present to cheer and wince simultaneously. Witnesses described seeing the winner's cock stretch to well past its breaking point. It took him 45 minutes to get the bootlace unhooked from his bellend, whilst he basked in the glory that such an achievement warranted. I'm not sure it's ever been bettered.

EDDY NUGENT AND THE WORST LAGER IN THE WORLD

I GOT HOME every few months, practising my pidgin German on a resolutely unimpressed family. Nan used to say, with utter solemnity, 'People died so you wouldn't have to speak like that.'

I saw plenty of Jenny during my leaves. Our physical relationship had moved on quickly, because of the rare times we actually got to be together. I was too immature to be anything but a drinking companion and occasional shagging partner to her, but the arrangement seemed to suit us well. Because I was earning and had literally zero outgoings, I was able to treat her well during the couple of weeks I'd have at home, and I was more than happy to sub her for the pleasure of her company.

After that first Christmas, we'd written to each other a lot, and I'd tried to phone her once or twice a week. The phone calls were never stilted, we always seemed to talk easily, though to be honest I preferred her blueys. She was a good wordsmith, and always managed to put in a few things that would make me laugh and think fondly of home. My replies were rather more brief, given that most of what went on at 7 was best not committed to a permanent written record. I did try to stick in anything cultural I'd been engaged in – usually nothing more than that I'd happened to catch sight of the Münsterkirche, say – to showcase my non-existent hidden depths, because I was conscious that she was already more edu-macated than I was.

She'd started her English degree, and was planning to become a teacher, while I was spending most of my time learning the arcane intricacies of BAOR life. The only time we didn't quite see eye-to-eye was when we went out with her mates. They were a generally nice bunch from all over the country, and they liked to hook up on Fridays and get leathered in the Students Union bar on Oxford Road, where the price of beer was nothing short of extraordinary – it was as though there'd been no inflation since the 1920s. It was a great place to get pissed with lots of exotic-looking boys and girls using it as a cheap staging post before they moved on to gigs and nightclubs.

It wasn't that I felt intellectually out of my depth, I really enjoyed hearing about life from different angles, but a couple of them were classic student bell-ends, or 'three year socialists' as my dad liked to call them. I've always admired anyone who has the courage of their convictions, regardless of political persuasion, and even if I don't agree with them I'll usually respect their adherence to their principles. But one thing I struggled with was Northern Ireland. The British Army was still heavily involved in Operation Banner, and the Troops Out movement had a lot of support at the universities. Two of Jenny's mates, Mark and Patricia, were always giving me jip on the subject. Latterly, I can understand some of the more nuanced arguments for and against the Operation, but at the time I was a simple, apolitical being who just liked a pint and didn't want a row. Mark, in particular, would never leave me alone about it. There did seem to be a bit of an ulterior motive, as I think he quite fancied Jenny and wanted to make me look like a dick to impress her.

I'd have taken him more seriously if he hadn't been an obvious trustafarian, who was going to ditch his strongly-held views on the day of his first accountancy interview in Leighton Buzzard. The only time I'd really bite was if something had happened in the Province shortly before one of his broadsides. He didn't know anyone in Northern Ireland, but I did and it would fuck me off a bit.

One night, when I'd had a bit too much to drink, I followed him into the bogs after he'd spent half an hour telling me that all my mates were murderers and that the IRA was staffed by cheeky young scamps with a song in their hearts who used Robin Hood as a role model. I threatened to use all my military skills to stuff him into a wheelie bin and roll him down the road. Little did he know that those skills were principally in morse code and typing, both generally non-transferable to acts of violence. Predictably, he described my outburst as 'the Army in microcosm', hot-footing it back to the table, to tell Jenny all about it.

'Is this true, Eddy?' she said. 'Did you threaten Mark?'

Not seeing this as an obvious opportunity to diffuse the situation, I told the truth. 'Yes, he's a cunt and he knows fuck all about anything, the fucking mummy's boy.'

I'd forgotten that the word 'cunt' – though ubiquitous in Army circles – was still ever so slightly taboo in the real world, and I could actually hear the sharp intake of breath around the table on the execution of the 't'.

Jenny was horrified to be shown up in front of her mates. 'I think you'd better leave, Eddy,' she said, quietly.

It took me a couple of days to bring her round. I surprised myself at how disappointed I felt about pissing her off. I still felt bang on about Mark, but she was right to try and highlight that I was living in two different worlds. We agreed that I'd minimise the cunt count and we moved on.

* * * * *

Back in Herford, life consisted of excessive RSM's parades, a bit of guard duty now and then, area cleaning, painting the undersides of Land Rovers with kero and oil, and ruck-loads of exercises. It was a bit of a bind, but you adapt and after five or six years in, it felt normal to me.

I remember having to stag-on the gate once, as there weren't enough toms available to fill the guard roster. It turned out I was on with Terry Waite, the Porn King of Herford. Apart from the occasional rental of some of his more normal filth, our paths didn't cross that often, and it was a salutary reminder of just how lecherous he was – it was alarming even by 7 Sigs standards. It was a warm old day, and his sap was certainly rising – it was almost impossible to hold a conversation with him, as all roads led to stories of his sexual endeavours, which generally involved him performing anal sex with his latest conquest, or 'Doing The Big One', as he liked to call it. It was accorded this sort of status because, as Terry so eloquently put it, 'There's nothing bigger than going stage three in a bird's stench trench by first light.' Eventually this descriptor caught on, with blokes placing the thumbs and forefingers of each hand together to make a letter 'A' to lend additional emphasis.

Terry only broke off from his sex chat to leer at the pads' wives as they drove on to camp. He'd engineer some excuse to keep them talking whilst checking out their cleavage and legs, and once they'd driven through the gate he'd turn and say something like, 'Ooooh, fuckin' hell, Eddy. Did you see that? She was hot!' He would re-adjust his semi-on, and continue, 'I've got the fucking tide coming in here! I'm going to need to go for a little milk in the bogs when we knock off. If I had my way with her, my cock would end up three shades suspiciously darker.'

Area cleaning was an unavoidable feature of Army life. Visit any camp and you'll be impressed at how spotless the place is. This isn't due to the lads forming a responsible community and endeavouring never to drop litter – it's forced on you by the full screws. Every weekday morning, us toms and lance jacks would work our way round a given area on the camp and pick up all the shite. It was a horrible job. If you were doing a bit of camp that didn't get visited much, you'd end up finding all sorts of gopping rubbish, like used johnnies or crisp bags full of slugs. Everyone used to shimf their way round the entire circuit. The biggest gripe was from the non-smokers who resented having to pick up cigarette butts. Occasionally, they'd attempt to insert some sort of fairness or democracy into the process – always a mistake in the Army. In Aldershot, I witnessed a short conversation on the subject, which took place near a set of wheelie bins.

Signalman Bluebottle: 'Why've I got to pick up fag-ends? I don't even smoke.'

Corporal Capbadge: 'Who the fuck are you? The unit shop-fucking-steward? Get 'em picked up, or I'll fucking flatten you.'

Sig Bluebottle: 'No problem, corporal.'

Corp Capbadge: 'I should fucking say so, Trotsky!'

Use of over-the-top Communist terminology like that was commonplace throughout the Corps. Accusations of left-leanery were always done in a slightly tongue-in-cheek manner, but they usually left their mark. Rodneys and seniors going round the lads' bedspaces on inspections were the worst offenders. A discarded copy of the *Daily Mirror* could see its owner being accused of flagrant Bolshevism. Woe betide anyone who made a suggestion like 'Why don't we just share the job out equally?' This automatically meant that you were a fierce supporter of collectivisation and the Glorious Five Year plan.

You'd start off cleaning with all the toms, but the numbers soon dwindled. The lads were brilliant at sloping off whilst the corporal's back was turned. Always making sure to split one at a time, so nothing was suspected until too late, they'd hide behind blades of grass or traffic cones and then disappear back up the block. The toms were self-regulating in this respect, 'Right, I've picked up three Ginsters wrappers and a Newky fuckin' Brown bottle, my work here is done,' being the tone. After 10 minutes or so, the corporal would be on his own save one or two lads who were oddly diligent/terrible creeps.

The monotony of camp life was often broken by someone going to nick. Despite there being an element of 'There but for the grace of God, go I', it was always piss funny watching them getting beasted around camp, marching at record speeds whilst we bimbled down to the cookhouse.

Whilst in training and at Harrogate, getting banged up was a day-to-day occurrence, with the guardroom cells resembling Piccadilly Circus. Getting jailed there was no big thing – you could easily get locked up for not marching properly, or having fluff on your beret, and quite often it'd only be for an hour or two, just so as you learned your lesson. If anyone did actually get properly banged up, their youth and immaturity meant they didn't get an indelible stain on their military records. A bit of stir at a working unit, however, was a more serious matter. If you got a stay over in the grey bar hotel, then you'd fucked up big time. If you happened to be a junior NCO or a pad, the implications of demotion or financial loss made it all the worse.

Once someone was inside, there would always be a bit of gossip flying around as to the origins of their crime, and it was routinely exaggerated. A bit of high jinks fisticuffs could come out of the other end of the rumour mill as an attempted murder.

Different camps had different standards of prison beastings. Aldershot was a fucking killer, with days and days of running around with bulled artillery shells. 7 Sigs was a bit of a middle ground, with a healthy helping of PT where the prisoner would be assigned his own log to lovingly care for and carry everywhere. There was also a shed-load of bullshit. The RPs had a list of shitty jobs that were left undone until the next internee showed up. You could always tell when someone was in pokey because all the guardroom brass paraphernalia was gleaming and the kerb stones had a new coat of paint.

Exercises were still the big thing in Germany in the early '90s. The massive Cold War stand-off which had defined the last four decades was only just coming to an end, so we still found ourselves out and about somewhere most months. Sometimes we'd be spread out as individual dets, others we'd set up in some horrific Corps headquarters, which was a nightmare. There were so many Officers, Warrant Officers and SNCOs in a Corps HQ that bullshit and grippings were an inevitability. You were always guaranteed to have your day spoilt by an unreasonable request from one of the rodneys like, 'Could you answer your radio checks?' or 'Could you stop spitting on that kero heater, it's making me gag?'

There was one advantage of exercise at HQs – you got your scran laid on by the slop jockeys, and most of the time there was no pan bash to do because they'd got in a load of mojos. Mojos were a weird bunch of near-unemployable Turkish Germans who were paid to do all the gash jobs. They dressed them in a strange mix of Army and RAF uniform – blue RAF shirt, green Army jumper, combat jacket, coveralls and RAF shoes. Fuck knows what their selection course was like.

Mid-1992, I went on my first exercise with armour, and it was a gas.

By the time it came around, I'd been on many other manoeuvres including 'Exercise Flying Falcon' and 'Exercise Summer Sales' which were standard fixtures in the calendar.

I was attached to Alpha 5 Troop, the armoured boys in our squadron – they were down a few chaps through leave or illness, so I was drafted in. The old 1960s-built AFV432 was the armoured workhorse of the Signals and many other Corps, and to some, working on them was a pain in the ring. I was in two minds; they did require a lot of maintenance, but they looked pretty cool driving through towns and they were lockable from the inside, making them great for getting your noodle down when you were supposed to be working.

I went across to Alpha 5 about a week before the exercise began and got roped into all of the det prep. I was put back onto a rebro with two other guys, 'Peculiar' Pete Theakston and Wilf Cornwall.

Pete, the det commander, was an oddly-shaped bloke of the type commonly referred to as a 'Storeman's nightmare'. He was quite short, and as wide as he was tall, a characteristic which extended to his extremities – he had a pair of feet like the Incredible Hulk's, and would have been better off wearing the boxes his shoes came in than the shoes themselves. He was an amusing bloke and we got on well, but he was a classic bean-stealing pad, always trying to get some free scran from the singlies cookhouse, despite being married. Because they weren't paying food and accommodation, pads weren't meant to come in our cookhouse, but some of the neckier chancers like Pete would risk it. He'd just turn his hearing off when he was spotted, and ignore the shouts of, 'STOP! THIEF!' coming from all sides.

Married personnel obviously had more to worry about in terms of dependants than the rest of us, and this issue always manifested itself in terrible stinginess and blatant petty theft. If the bog rolls were missing from the troop trap, you could be certain that one of the pads was walking home with them in his pocket. If you ever found yourself doing guard round the quarters area, you'd see loads of kids covered in cam cream, eating compo boiled sweets and riding around on MFO box go-karts. Pete himself was so tight that, after doing a day at the ranges in Sennelager, he would take home all the food that the lads didn't want from their death packs and SELL IT to his own kids. He tried to justify it by saying that at least he knew where their pocket money was going, but his protestations were always drowned out by shouts of, 'You fucking tight cunt!'

Wilf was an 18-year-old lad labouring under a handle that made him sound like he'd fought at Passchendaele. He didn't help matters by opting for a rather severe short-back-and-sides and always having a rollie on the go. I tried chatting with him, but he was hard work, always complaining about something, like the Bully Beef rations not getting through or the perils of trench foot.

The build-up to deployment was more hectic than I was used to because of all the prep that the 432s needed. It was non-stop maintenance, like pumping up the tracks and generally getting covered in strange chemical lubricants. I also discovered 'Panzer Rash', a condition symptomised by a row of permanent lumps and bruises on your swede which is experienced by all who are new to working in the confined spaces of an armoured personnel carrier.

The exercise was similar in content to the one I'd enjoyed with the Birdman of Osnatraz. We were by ourselves or co-located with one other wagon for the entire duration, although this time it was tactical and we had several more location changes. This wasn't too much of a ballache because we were free running and didn't have to dick around with convoy drills.

When we were on the move during the day, I'd be inside the main compartment of the 432, with Pete in the commander's hatch and Wilf at the tillers. This would change slightly at night. Wilf would still drive again, but I'd be in the commander's hatch whilst Pete would be on the louvres that were just to the left of the commander's seat. The louvres were metal slats that ventilated the hot air from the engine and they were redders, making them an ideal spot for keeping warm at night.

On one move, Pete got bored and, as we were thrapping down an A road, he wiped his finger around his ring piece and leaned forward and dragged it under Wilf's nose in a movement known as a 'skiff'. When practiced on the more gullible, skiffing was often preceded by the skiffer walking up to the skiffee whilst holding an empty jerry can. He would then extend the skiff finger and enquire, 'Is this benz or kero?' If the fall guy took the bait, he would go in for a sniff and then be assaulted with great vigour.

It was considered universally hilarious and there was never any sympathy for the victim. A particularly persistent skiff could see its recipient having to shave off his moustache the next day. Wilf almost honked but was unable to stop or take his hands off the tillers as there was traffic everywhere; he had to drive for a further 45 minutes whilst breathing in dung fumes until he found a place to pull over. During that time, Pete treated us to his theory that a human being can get used to any smell after two minutes, but that the nether-regional butter used in a skiff had the ability to genetically modify itself slightly every one minute 50 seconds, rendering the smell impossible to cope with. This was all delivered in a convincing and quasi-scientific style, punctuated by the sound of Wilf swearing like a docker.

As ever, the exercise was a pretty hum-drum experience – except for the last night, just after Endex had been called. We were on Sennelager training area and we'd torn down everything, packed up and were free running up the autobahn at about two in the morning, heading back to Herford. I'd been in the commander's hatch, but went back into the belly of the wagon to get my noggin down for a bit. I nodded off and the next thing I knew I was waking up, because the wagon had stopped and the back doors were wide open. Silhouetted by car headlights and flashing blues were Pete, Wilf and a couple of German coppers who were jabbering at them. I hopped out of the back and asked Pete what was going on. He looked at me, shamefacedly. 'Well, what it is, Eddy,' he said, 'is I was getting a bit bored, so I plugged in the searchlight. Every time a car tried to pass, I gave them some full force death rays with it.'

I should point out that the searchlight to which Pete referred was about a foot in diameter and plugged into the 'dash' of the panzer via a two-pin connector. It was incredibly powerful: the Fritzes Pete had been shining it at must have thought they were following a lighthouse.

I blew out air. 'Fucking hell, Pete,' I said, under my breath. 'Are you on crack?'

'Well, anyway mate, this went on for a bit and there was a big queue of cars behind us. When another car tried to overtake, he got the same treatment. The only problem is that it was the fucking fuzz, and here we are.'

At that, he shrugged and spread his arms out, as if to imply that our current plight was entirely unrelated to him, and had been somehow unavoidable.

Interrupting our conversation, the Boche copper tapped Pete on the shoulder. 'You mast tell me, vhere ist ze light zat you ver uzink?'

'OK, OK,' said Pete, impatiently. 'Wait here and I'll get it for you.' He disappeared into the back of the panzer. There was a lot of banging and clattering and a couple of minutes later he emerged carrying a four-inch-long, right angle torch with a red filter attached to the lens. 'Here you go, mate,' he said, with exaggerated glee.

He turned it on. It gave off the same amount of light as a clown's nose, and after three seconds it spluttered and died like Arnie's eye at the end of *Terminator*.

The German copper went absolutely rhino. 'You mast not lie to me! Zis ist nicht ze light zat you use!'

Pete looked at him as though hurt by the suggestion that he was being untruthful. 'What you talking about... it's a torch isn't it?'

The policeman pushed his way between us and went into the back of the wagon. 'Oi!' shouted Wilf, a cigarette dangling from his mouth. 'There's crypto in there!' Then, just out of the hearing range of the enraged polizei, he added, 'Ya fucking Nazi!'

A couple seconds later, the copper re-appeared holding the still-warm searchlight. His anger vindicated, he adopted the sort of sarcastic tone apparently taught in Police School the world over. 'Unt vas ist zis?'

'It's *broken* is what it is,' replied Pete, pointing at the exposed connector. 'That fucker hasn't worked for months.'

The two policemen spent the next five minutes attempting to get it to work. It was like watching two chimps trying to open a can of lager, and their fruitless efforts only wound them up even more. Eventually, the one who'd been doing all the talking handed it to Pete. 'You vill make it vork!' he barked. By now he was starting to sound a lot like Sturmbannführer Ludwig Kessler out of *Secret Army*.

Pete kept his cool admirably. 'Sorry, mate,' he said. 'I can't. Like I said, it's fucked.'

The two rozzers had a conflab in German. As usual, my Deutsch let me down, but I imagine it was something along the lines of, 'Gott in Himmel! Once more these ingenious Tommie schweinhunds have foiled us and our plans for some sort of unspecified global domination.'

Eventually, they finished their discussion and levied us with an on-the-spot fine of 50 Deutsche Marks. Pete didn't seem bothered, but Wilf exploded from behind his cloud of Old Holborn smoke. 'Fifty Deez!? Fifty fucking Deez! You're 'aving a fucking Turkish, pal! That's my fucking beer money for tomorrow night!'

Myself and Pete calmed him down. If we didn't take it on the chin and get on our way, they'd only call the monkeys and then we'd be in a world of shit. Ten minutes later, and lighter in pocket, we were on the move again, getting back to camp just in time for breakfast. On Pete's instruction, and mainly because he was the dick who'd caused it, we kept news of the incident under our hats.

* * * * *

Every now and then, a juicy roulement tour for the death trap prairies of Canada or the super-weight-gain mountaintop rebros of the Falklands would come up but, unlike with my Belize posting, I was always in the wrong place at the wrong time to get the swan. I did, however, get on to several 'Snowqueen' exercises. If ever there was an über-skive masquerading as some form of constructive work, this was it. Snowqueens were a two-week trip to the Bavarian Alps where you were taught downhill ski-ing during the week and Langlaufing – cross-country ski-ing – at the weekends. Mind you, I say 'über-skive' – the downhill was a great laugh, but the cross-country stuff was fucking murder, like a PT beasting in Narnia. The problem is that you need to put the right wax on your skis. It's dictated by the snow conditions and temperature, and if you stick the wrong wax on your planks, you're fucked. If the snow was cold and you put warm snow wax on, you ended up with clumps of the stuff the size of dead dogs stuck to your skis which made them a knackering bastard to use. On the other hand, if you used cold wax in warm, wet snow, the skis got no traction and you ended up on your fucking arse all day, like Bambi after a big night in the squadron bar.

Luckily, the downhill side of things was much more attuned to the natural, devil-may-care attitude of the British soldier. While all the other learners were tottering around on the nursery slopes, the equally inexperienced squaddies would take carelessly to the lifts, heading straight to the tops of the red runs. Once there, they'd don their Union Jack hats and head full-tilt in a straight line down the run, regardless of obstacles. This was normally done in the 'egg' position, with the eyes tight shut and screams of 'BANZAI!' It always culminated in an explosion of snow and ski debris that looked a lot like the opening credits of *The Six Million Dollar Man*, where Steve Austin stacks his space capsule.

Although we were always chin-strapped after a full day on the slopes, there was always enough residual energy for a night on the beer. The local piss in Bavaria was a strange brew called 'Weisen Bier'. We knew it as 'Banana Beer' due to its fruity taste; it wasn't a bad drop, but it generated brain-splitting mongovers.

The Snowqueens were a highlight of my time in Germany, but to be honest I enjoyed pretty much all of it. So it crept up on me a bit when my time came to an end at 7 Sigs. One morning in the autumn of 1994, I received warning orders that I'd been posted to 30 Signal Regiment. They'd just moved *en masse* from Blandford in Dorset to the entertainment capital of the Midlands, Nuneaton.

I didn't know much about the unit, but when I asked around I found out that it wasn't considered a bad posting at all. There was the opportunity to do UN work with them, which was particularly good for the singlies as you could get in a ruck-load of tours.

In a way, though, I'd miss 7. It had been a good posting, even if I had, like so many lads, pretty much pissed it up against the wall.

Actually, that fact occurred to me, for the briefest of moments, when I got my posting orders through. I had that slightly grown-up feeling – that it was about time I started to look at doing something more constructive with my time in the Army, or life generally, other than being a screeched-up knobber. Mind, like I say, it was only for the briefest of moments.

The Army had obviously been thinking the same thing, though. They'd seen fit to advance my career by sending me on my Class One trade course in Catterick before taking up my post at 30 Sigs. It was a three-monther, and everyone who'd been on it before me said that it was a good laugh with the odd hard-ish exam. Before going on the Class One, we had to sit a week's crammer course at our unit, with an exam at the end. It was a good job we did, because I hadn't touched loads of the stuff since Harrogate – morse code and typing, to name two. I felt like a right biff not knowing half of the things that we covered, but I suppose that's what the course was there for.

Around the time I left 7, a lot of the lads who'd been there when I arrived were in the process of moving on, too, some back to the UK and others staying within Der Iron Triangle of Germany and its Divs. Because we were posted around as individuals, there was a constant troop movement in and out of the Squadron. So there were lots of leaving dos, with weapons-grade bezzering, and more often than not, the departee would be gone by the time you'd woken up and old times with old friends would be saved for Herfy-fuelled reminiscing.

Chopper was the first to go – he left in a January, posted to 249 Signal Squadron, just in time to get on his Arctic course. Pre-leaving, he'd done a stint in Colchester six months earlier for chinning a driver from 4 Div outside the 'Tig, and Collie had rejuvenated his inner green machine. From there he fairly flew up the ranks. I heard he did his 22 years, finishing as an RSM, but diffy his Long Service and Good Conduct medal.

Hooch went in the March – to 216 where he passed P Company in a oner. I can't say I was surprised. He was strong as an ox and always stayed on top of his phys, not to mention that he was pretty unflappable. I'd've hated to have been the poor sod who drew him in the milling. The last news on him was that he got out after his nine years and moved down to Oz.

Dicky Bird got posted the week after Hooch, although his leaving do was a sedate affair. That didn't bother Dicky, because he was delirious with happiness as the top choice on his dream sheet had come through and he was off back to his beloved Osnatraz. Such was his joy that, for the briefest of moments, even his roid pain didn't get a look in.

Dachau Dave was still there when I left, and still as emaciated as he'd been went he posted in. He'd become very much the senior siggie, having served an apprenticeship as Chopper's pre-incarceration wingman, and it was now he who was taking the sprogs on tours of Valentino's.

Vic Kerr got posted in the May – on May 8th, in fact, VE Day. Following his spell of post break-up depression, he'd turned out to be the life and soul of any party – not an over-the-top dick, just a really fun bloke to be with. He still had the odd pang for his ex, but they'd reconciled any bad feelings and got on with their own lives and he was a pretty chilled bloke. To everyone's undisguised jealousy, he managed to wangle a posting to Cyprus, a three-year holiday which you even got a gong for, the jammie sod. As befitting his single status, he got himself on the Cypriot 'ride round the block' motorbike course and then bought a nice Suzuki GSXR750.

He was killed three months later by a drunk driver. I found out whilst scanning a copy of the Corps magazine, *The Wire*, and the news hit me really hard. Vic was the first mate I'd known die, and for a short while I had a strong sense of my own mortality. I spent a lot of time wondering how his life would have turned out had he given his wife the kids she'd wanted.

I had two weeks' leave booked before the course start date, so it was with mixed feelings that I turned left out of South Camp gates and past Willy's for the last time. There was a dried up vom patch on the steps, and Rocket Tits was outside with a mop and bucket, looking threaders and surveying a broken window.

It was all strangely comforting: some things would never change.

EDDY NUGENT AND THE GOING DOWN OF THE SUN

SINCE I WAS staying in the country after my leave finished, I was really looking forward to chilling out without the long haul back to Herford facing me at the end of it. My dad was mildly horrified at how little I'd managed to accumulate in the way of material goods during my German posting. He'd emptied out the boot of his car in preparation for picking me up at Piccadilly station, so there was plenty of room for my two holdalls and CD player with fucked pause button.

'Jesus, son,' he said. 'I thought we'd need a removal van. What have you been spending all your money on? In fact, don't tell me, I can guess.'

His comments induced a short period of navel-gazing in me as we headed over the Mancunian Way. He was right – I really didn't have much to show for my eight and a half years in the colours. I'd met a few sensible lads down the years, who'd talked to me of a strange phenomenon they called 'savings', where you placed a small portion of your wages into a separate account each month. That way, it seemed, you accrued money, which enabled you to buy things without having to get a Burton's store card with an APR that even Tony Soprano would think unreasonable. These ultra-sensibles had saved enough to buy and subsequently rent out houses, earning a 'secondary income', another phrase that was met with astonishment by the majority of the singlies block. In the upside-down mind of the typical British soldier, being fiscally prudent indicated deviance of one sort or another. Soldiers liked everyone to be in the same boat: millionaires for the first weekend of a month, and skint for the rest of it. Men who managed their funds carefully were thought to have something of the night about them. Ever the sheep, I'd sought to embrace the ethos of the crowd, crossing my fingers and hoping if I found myself at a cashpoint after the 15th of the month. (The only time this changed was if the 'food and accommodation' rumour went up. When you went on exercise, the Army continued to charge you for the shit food you weren't eating and for the concrete favela that you weren't staying in. At some point shortly afterwards, though, the money would be refunded, providing a lifeline during times of hardship. It was paid in in haphazard fashion, and rumours of its imminence were always sweeping the block. Someone would say, 'I've heard there's 63 quid food and accom in from Purple Warrior,' and there'd be a stampede down to local banks, with everyone determined to extract the cash and keep their accounts firmly in the red.) As we headed into Manchester, I wondered if perhaps the sensible savers might not be onto something.

All those thoughts were forgotten when I got home. I'd only been in for ten minutes when the phone rang. I answered it, assuming it was one of my old school mates or Jenny, desperate for my interesting company, but it was nan.

'Hiya, nan. It's me, Eddy.'

'Hiya Eddy. Nice to hear you're home. Can you put your mam on love?'

Ordinarily, I'd have been a bit put out by the lukewarm greeting, but the fact that she was obviously close to tears meant that I grabbed mum quickly, then stayed close to the phone as they spoke. After a couple of minutes, mum hung up quietly and told us what we'd suspected. Alfie Silver had made it to the end of his colourful life. His 72 year journey had drawn to a close in exactly the fashion he would have wanted. 'Your nan's really cut up, Eddy,' said mum. 'They'd got so close.' I could see my mum was sad herself. She moaned about nan from time to time – she said she was like a crafty, wrinkly kid – but she'd watched their companionship develop with real delight, seeing a more youthful side to her mum that she'd forgotten about.

'What happened, mum?' I said.

'He was at his grandson's sports day. He'd took your nan along for company. She said he spent the whole day complaining about how fat the kids were.'

That sounded like Alfie – in common with many of his generation, it was one of his pet themes. They had a point. I'd even noticed it myself – kids were getting noticeably plumper as the playing fields disappeared and school time got eaten up with things deemed far more important than sport. Alfie had spent long hours pointing out to me that a short period of National Service, preferably conducted in uncomfortable surroundings with lots of 'character building' verbal abuse, would soon cure it. It sounded scarily familiar, and not something I'd wish on sedentary ten-year-olds, but I got the point.

'Go on,' I said.

'Well, he was sat watching the egg and spoon race, in a deckchair. Your nan said he was saying the whole thing would have been easier in his day, because the kids would have been fitter and they'd have been using powdered egg.'

I laughed despite the solemnity of the moment. I had the greatest respect for Alfie and his ilk, but they could be relied upon for a regular output of half-baked nonsense. Mum chuckled as well. 'You've got to laugh, I suppose. So mum ignored him and carried on chatting to a lady she knew from bingo. The next time she turned around... he'd died.'

I was shocked. 'That quick?'

'Not a sound out of him. He'd just fallen into a bigger sleep than he was expecting.'

'Did they try and save him?'

'No. Your nan just gave him a little kiss and said ta' ra.'

We sat in silence for a few moments. Of course, I was sad, but it sounded like no bad way to go. Surrounded by laughing kids, sat in a deckchair on a sunny day, moaning away without fear of criticism. Given the choice, it would be high on my own list of ways to peg out.

Mum laughed, half to herself.

'What?' I said.

'Your nan said she thinks his last words were, "That lad's arse is like a barrage balloon".'

Though lacking the historic resonance of 'Kiss me, Hardy', it would have looked great on a headstone in a particularly liberal churchyard.

* * * * *

The funeral was the following Tuesday at St Kentigern's church in Fallowfield, where Alfie had sought confessional forgiveness during a lifetime of minor religious misdemeanours. He'd somehow managed to reconcile his love of foul language and beer with a reasonably devout Catholicism, mutually exclusive pastimes to some folk. But Alfie's God wasn't particularly vengeful and, in his opinion, was quite prepared to turn a heavenly blind eye to the occasional pub fight or bit of cheating at dominoes.

At nan's insistence, I dusted off my two's dress and sat with her throughout the service. The church was packed. Relatives of all generations filled up the first three rows, but there must have been another two hundred people stood shoulder to shoulder all the way to the back of the church and spilling outside. Old boys from various branches of the British Legion, bedecked in blue blazers and straight-backed despite their age, shared pews with men in their forties who'd played in the boys' football teams Alfie had taken charge of in the 1960s and girls from the youth club he'd helped out. The odd cough or sniffle apart, you could have heard the proverbial pin drop as the priest, Father Fallon, addressed Alfie's coffin, placed front and centre of the church with his beret atop it.

'He was a great bloke, Alfie,' said Fr Fallon in a broad, Irish brogue. 'It's my job to say he swore a bit too much, but I got the feeling he was doing my share for me. I only have to look round at the faces in this church today to know that he had friends in many places. He was a great lover of life. Like many who fought in the war, he was determined after it was over to take pleasure in what life had to offer, and to ignore the minor indignities that age brings. It's fair to say that he could have single-handedly kept the social club going with his bar bill. It's also fair to say that, when he'd had a few, he could argue with his own hand.

'When I first started in the parish, he talked to me outside the church one day, after mass. I'd given, by my own admission, a bit of a dull sermon on the fiscal pinch we'd found ourselves in. It went on a bit, and I could see people in the congregation flagging towards the end. I asked Alfie what he thought. I've removed some of his more colourful adjectives but I think you'll get the gist. He put on his hat and said "Well, Father. You can shout at me and call me a bluebeard. You could hit me over the head with that bible of yours. You could tell me once a day that I'm going to hell but, for God's sake, don't bore me. Life's too short for being bored." I got the message and I've abridged them ever since. If nothing else, that's a great legacy he leaves you with.'

His words had set the tone for the day. It was a time to be sad at the passing of another bit of local history, but that didn't mean we couldn't have a laugh at a dead man's expense.

The Legion lads had arranged for a trumpeter to play the Last Post as they lowered Alfie into his new home at Southern Cemetery. It's a short tune, but it has the power to catch you by the throat and make the hairs on the back of your neck stand up whenever it's played. I got that tell-tale tingle in my eyes by the end of the second note and put my arm round Gran's shoulders as she cried into a snotty hankie.

At the end of the interral, we walked back to the cars. Though the tone was still respectful, I could feel the mood change, as the real goodbye approached.

Alfie's best mate, 'Ack-Ack' Mulgrew, was working his way round the crowd, repeating the mantra, 'See you in St Kent's, there's a few bob behind the bar.'

And the wake was brilliant. For me, it's like weddings: the church bits are essential, but to all but the holiest of rollers they're really a preamble to the actual business of the day. They bring out the best in people, too – they're forgiving, considerate and eager to reconnect with folks they haven't seen for a while, and many of the normal conventions and formalities are swept away with the emotion of the occasion.

The St Kentigern's Irish Club, a low, brick affair built in the 1970s, was next door to the church on Wilbraham Road. It had a couple of function rooms, and one of them was already buzzing with lots of people of all ages, the craic and the Guinness both starting to flow nicely. I got mum and nan sat down at a table and made my way to the bar, which was being propped up by half a dozen of the blazered old guys, all with pints in hands. It was impossible not to eavesdrop on their conversation, punctuated as it was with staccato bursts of raucous laughter. As I got my change and gathered up my pint of Harp and two gin and bitter lemons, one of their number leaned back and made the universal 'ka-ka-ka-ka-ka-ka-ka' kids' machine gun noise as he approached the crux of his anecdote. I couldn't help chuckling as the tale's completion was greeted with hoots of derision and disbelief from his mates, who'd obviously heard it hundreds of times before and had charted its evolution from something fairly innocuous to a war-winning exploit. Ack-Ack spotted me as I made my way past, and grabbed my sleeve.

'Here he is, boys,' he said. 'A real soldier.'

In the company of war veterans, I was uncomfortable with his description, until I realised he was taking the piss. I moved over sheepishly. 'Alright, Mr Mulgrew?'

'I'm well, Eddy,' he said. 'It's sad to see another of the old and bold disappearing over the hill, but we're getting used to it.' A murmur of assent went round the group. 'I'll tell you what though, son. He'd have been chuffed to bits to know you were here, in your uniform.'

'Those trousers need a better pressing though, eh lads?' muttered one of the group, laughing.

'What would you fucking know, Hampy?' answered Ack-Ack. 'When did a bloke with seven fingers become an ironing expert?'

Hampy immediately saluted with his two-fingered right hand. 'You have a point, sir!' he shouted. 'John Hampson, Eddy. Ignore me, I'm pissed already.'

They all roared at that one. It was good to be in their company: they were all in their 70s, but you could see the decades dropping away from their faces as the minutes passed and they relived a youth far more adventurous than anything I'd experienced.

I took the drinks over to mum and nan, who was already surrounded by friends and was working her way through all the local gossip. It was a testament to her character that she'd refused to let Alfie's death get in the way of this all-important community function. Seeing that she was being looked after, I put their drinks down and made my way back to Ack-Ack and Hampy's group.

I knew Alfie well enough, but only through what he chose to tell me, and I'd guessed he must have gilded the lily from time to time. It's only human – there's always that temptation to paint ourselves positively when telling stories. I once served with a lad who told me about a fight he'd had in a pub in Aldershot. The way he told it, he'd sorted out three blokes in the South Western who'd given him a bit of lip, and then made a quick escape before the monkeys turned up. It was a great tale, but he'd forgotten that I was actually there when it happened, and its truth-to-bullshit ratio was almost off the scale.

But it's an old soldier's privilege to embroider a bit, and everyone gives it tacit acceptance, enjoying the stories for what they are, rather that the specific events they describe. Part of saying goodbye to Alfie was to let people know that he hadn't always been an old man with a great line in cantankery.

Ack-Ack greeted me. 'Hey, Eddy, you're just in time. Hampy was just going to tell us about Alfie's career as a Sino-British diplomat.'

Hampy took a swig out of his pint.

'About ten years ago, a young Chinese family moved in next door to me. They were a lovely couple with two little lads. Couldn't speak a word of English, like. We used to say hello in the morning and smile at each other and that, but no proper communication, so to speak. Anyway, they bought a dog. It was nice, but it kept coming in to my garden to shit. Big shits, as well – they looked like one of the donkeys from Blackpool had made a break for it. I used to clean it up, but I was a bit fucking sick of it after a while. But I wasn't sure how to bring it up.'

He stopped for another slurp, allowing Ack-Ack to chip in, with a wink, 'That's when High Commissioner Silver stepped in.'

'Aye,' said Hampy. 'Alfie was round my house having a brew and I told him about it. "Don't worry," he says, "I'll go round and have a word." He said he'd picked up a bit of Chinese on his travels. So we goes round next door, and Alfie knocks on. The littlest lad answers, he was only about five then. Alfie bends over at the waist and says to him really slowly, "Eeeessss you mavvver in?"'

There was a massive burst of laughter. 'The fucking idiot,' said Hampy, chuckling away. 'He must have done all his studying by watching Charlie Chan films and Bert Kwouk, the daft bastard.'

I watched as they doubled up with chortling, beer slopping everywhere, their laughter turning into wheezy coughs. It's easy to look right through old people – to see them as part of the furniture – but I got a great buzz out of listening to these guys talk about their pasts. I'll sit in my car, watching a brace of old blokes taking three hours to dodder over a zebra crossing, but it doesn't wind me up: I'll sit there, thinking, 'They might have been Spitfire pilots 50 years ago.' They could well have been complete tossbags as well, of course, but I like to give them the benefit of the doubt.

Eventually, Ack-Ack recovered his breath and looked over at another of the old boys, Joey Maloney. 'Tell Eddy about your escapades in France, Joey,' he said.

Joey took a long pull on his Guinness, wiped away the froth clinging to his grey 'tache and started relating a story straight out of those old *Commando* comics. It was in France,1940, and he and Alfie were part of a unit which was rushing headlong for the coast, trying to escape the massive German advance. They found themselves pinned down in a roadside ditch, with the Germans firing at them from what felt like all sides.

'So anyway,' said Joey. 'I'm lying there with Alfie in that fucking ditch, and we're trying to dig a bit deeper in with our bloody eyebrows. I really thought we'd had it – bits of soil kept jumping up around us, so the Jerries knew exactly where we were. I started doing the one thing you shouldn't in that situation: I got to thinking how maybe it wouldn't be that bad to die. Our lass was bound to find another bloke. I was from a big family and the kids would be well looked after. All those stupid, wistful things that go through your mind when you feel death tapping you on your shoulder.'

He stopped for a moment as the weight of those feelings settled on him. Tears filled his eyes, and the group was unusually silent for a few moments, everyone pointedly watching their old mate's face as they waited for him to go on.

He shook himself loose. 'So, as I'm saying, we were in a right friggin' pinch, Eddy. Then Alfie says, "How many rounds have you got left, Joe?" I had a quick look. Seven, I says. "Bloody hell. That's not much good, we've got 20 between us. Give us 'em here, I've got a plan." I didn't have much faith, but anything was better than nothing. I gave him the bullets and he stuck them in his pocket. He made himself ready to move, but I thought that he'd be certain to be killed. He could see the fear in my face and gave me a crazy smile and a wink. "Don't worry about a thing, Joe," he says. "I'll be back in ten minutes." And with that he scarpered out of the ditch, he was off like a bleeding greyhound. I didn't even get the chance to say ta'ra.'

We were all riveted, even those who'd heard the story scores of times. 'So, what happened Mr Maloney?' I said.

'Well, I didn't hear him die straight away, Eddy, so I took the chance to peek over the ditch. He was still running. He'd have given Jesse Owens a good go. And before I had the chance to get back down again, I got shot in me neck. Look 'ere.' He pulled his collar down to expose a still bright scar. 'I thought I was *proper* fucked. I lay there crying me eyes out, with me hand over the wound, cursing my luck. A handful of Jerries arrived and started prodding me, with their boots. I must have caught them on a good day, 'cos they didn't shoot me.'

He stopped to take a drink and I waited for the next instalment. In the vacuum created by the pause, I imagined Alfie jumping back down into the ditch, gun blazing, to save his old pal. He'd have sorted out the Germans and run off with Joe over his shoulder. I couldn't wait. 'Is that when Alfie came back, then?' I asked, excitedly.

To a huge roar of laughter he shouted, 'Is it fuck as like, Eddy! The next time I saw Alfie was in the Red Lion in Didsbury in 1946, the wanker.'

Once again, everyone was bent double. I goggled. 'You what?'

'They took me prisoner, and that was me for the duration. Alfie said he'd planned to come back, but when he saw how many there were, he just fucking scarpered. I don't blame him, son. We can't all win the Victoria Cross. I made him buy all my beer that night though, I can tell you.'

I learned an interesting lesson that day. The vision of the soldier as hero is more of a civilian and media construct than a reflection of how men in uniform see themselves; one of the British soldier's most admirable qualities is his modesty. I've watched gallantry medal winners squirm with embarrassment at having to describe the situations which led to their being decorated. It's not that they're not proud of their achievement, just that they're thinking of the other guys who were there with them, who may have been wounded or killed. Crowing about yourself is just not the British style, and it's hugely admirable. To some people – mostly people with no experience of the sharp end of war – Hampy's tale might sound like one of cowardice. But who knows how he'd react in a situation like that until it happens? The fact that Alfie's decision to leg it and leave Hampy to an uncertain immediate future was squared away with a few beers illustrated the point perfectly.

The stories kept coming from the old blokes, and I had a great day. Alfie's send-off was exactly what he'd have wanted; by the end of the night, Hampy had my twat hat on and was marching up and down the bar doing impressions of Blakey from *On The Buses*. It was quite apparent that generational differences counted for nothing as soon as ex and serving soldiers got together.

Understandably, nan was pretty fragile for a while. She was from a background that insisted on stoicism in times of crisis, but she'd obviously been knocked for six. Between me, mum and dad, we made sure to get round and see her every day, to make sure she was coping. It was my duty to take round her nightly copy of the

Manchester Evening News and make her a brew while she perused the columns and interpreted all the stories into her own form of gobbledygook, taking care to point out regularly that the country was going to the dogs.

Looking after nan meant I didn't get to see quite as much of Jenny as I'd have liked. Now that I was back in country on a permanent basis, I'd wondered if this was a chance to push things along further, maybe get to a point where we were actually considered boyfriend and girlfriend. We got out to the flicks and pubs quite a bit, but we were always strapped for a place to be alone. Her house was always manic – she had two younger sisters and her mum never seemed to leave the place, so that was a waste of time. My place was even worse as nan had taken to stagging-on there. Alfie's absence had left an intelligence hole for her, and I think she was hoping to give Jenny the third degree.

But the brief times we snatched together alone were a great laugh, not least because our musical preferences were in parallel. There was some stellar quality shite in the charts in those days, with Jimmy Nail and Right Said Fred becoming increasingly harder to avoid. Jenny was a real hometown girl and her musical tastes reflected her civic pride. She liked flying the flag for James and The Durutti Column, and was always dragging me along to gigs at The Hop and Grape on the top floor of the Union. In the Army, I'd got used to sharing musical space with fans of bands as diverse as the Proclaimers and Pink Floyd. I'd kept myself going quietly on a diet of The Smiths and A Certain Ratio, so me and Jenny gelled quite well on that all-important relationship point. We were pretty much on the same wavelength about most things, and having stuff in common like that was a good thing, mostly because it allowed me to keep conversations going without having to break the ice with Army tales, like about the time that Vic Kerr pissed in his own gob for a 20 Deutsche Mark bet.

We did manage to get a bit of time alone on the Friday before I disappeared on my Class One, when mum and dad went out and left us alone for the evening. I was particularly keen to accost Jenny, but managed to watch 15 minutes of *The Fresh Prince of Bel-Air* before making my move. We spent the evening in various forms of undress and then settled down to enjoy a bit of post-coital Vic and Bob, with one eye on the clock for mum and dad's return. Jenny had obviously been giving the boyfriend/girlfriend thing a bit of thought. She took a drag on her cigarette, and said, 'So, Eddy. Where do we go from here?'

Fucking Haircut One Hundred. It was a pivotal moment in my life and all I could think was, 'Is it down to the lake I fear?' It's my reaction to this day: I've done it in meetings, and when people are asking for directions. In the right company, I won't just think it, I'll fucking sing it.

But that wouldn't have been at all appropriate, with Jenny looking in to my eyes, almost beseeching me not to confirm myself as a dildo.

'Dunno really, Jen. I'd love to see more of you and it should be easier now I'm in the Midlands. What do you reckon?'

She held my face with both her hands, 'I'd like that, Eddy. My dad told me to watch out for soldiers, but I think you might be the exception.'

I smiled and kissed her back, thinking, 'In all but a very small minority of cases, your dad is abso-fucking-lutely spot on.'

After the sadness of Alfie's death, my deeper romantic entanglement put a real spring in my step and I headed up to Catterick with visions of domestic bliss and sex on tap.

EDDY NUGENT AND THE CATTERICK SCHOOL OF DANCING

THE JOINING INSTRUCTIONS for the Class 1 had come through at just the right time.

The relentless kicking I'd been giving my system, via the twin assaults of a gallon of beer a day and a vast array of German processed meat products, had seen me developing the very early stages of a BAOR belly. I'd always hovered around 11 stone, regardless of what I put in, which had been handy – especially during my time with the Airborne Brigade. Soldiers are never meant to be fat, but gutbuckets were particularly unwelcome in Aldershot, and anybody who did slide a bit was quickly encouraged to mend their slovenly ways. This was usually done using subtle peer pressure, and extensive use of the phrase 'fat cunt'.

I remember one guy, a big old unit who was posted in to the Squadron MT down there. The MTWO, a parsimonious chap with one eye on a BEM, had threatened to have him charged for burning more diesel than the skinnier drivers on four tonner details, and I'd taken great delight in joining in with the ridicule of a more portly colleague. Healthy doses of remedial PT and 'harsh but fair' verbal encouragement saw him drop a few dress sizes in a matter of weeks. Now I'd started tipping the scales at just over the 12st mark myself, I was suddenly starting to get concerned. Still, attending the Catterick course was bound to provide me with a brief respite from the pop, and allow me to get sorted out physically while concentrating on becoming a better tradesman?

Sadly, and not for the first time, I would be proved wrong.

Any thoughts of a period of zen-like technical contemplation and intense study were quickly dispelled. After our initial trade tests, where our morse and typing skills were recorded, we fell into a pattern of cheating and skiving our way to the end date. Once the skills tests were out of the way, it almost became an 'attendance course' – two words guaranteed to bring gladness to the heart of the instinctively lazy. Army attendance courses were great: you showed up, got your name ticked off and that was it – unless you managed to blow up the camp, you received a pass. The 'Unit Projectionist Course' was a perfect example of this sort of dick job. The instructors on a course like that would be at pains to remind attendees that 'This is isn't just a fucking attendance course, you know', but the only purpose that really served was to puff up their flagging egos, bruised at having found themselves teaching disinterested young men how to show three-reel films, usually starring Chuck Norris or Patrick Swayze, to other optionless NAAFI-dwellers in places like Belize.

Of course, ours wasn't *actually* an attendance course, and within the modules of the Class 1 we were regularly monitored and tested to ensure that taxpayers' money was being wisely spent on our progression. I say 'monitored and tested', but the truth was that the assessment processes had long since fallen victim to the low cunning of young men intent on drinking instead of revising. Multiple choice exams were particularly easy to bypass. Because the test papers generally consisted of 20 questions with options A to E, it was quite easy to pass round a 20-letter mnemonic consisting only of the first five letters of the alphabet. Although 'BABCEBABDABBABCABBEB' may sound to you like a late night attempt at procuring food from a takeaway, or the refrain from a minor Showaddywaddy hit, it was actually the condensed answers to a 'Jamming and Deception' paper – good for a 30-second chuckle over a few pints in The Fleece in Richmond.

You had to play the game, though. I remember one instructor getting a bit disgruntled when he was dealing out papers and he noticed that a couple of the lads at the front had already filled in their answers on the piece of paper provided by the time he sat down.

'For fuck's sake, lads,' he said. 'At least make it *look* decent. This one's supposed to take three quarters of a fucking hour, not five seconds.'

Protocol was generally observed from then on. And to be fair, some of the lessons were actually very interesting. As with most jobs, I guess, the majority of what I'd been taught in training had been forgotten once I started work proper, so having another look at all the antenna principles we'd originally learned and going out on exercise to reacquaint ourselves with forgotten disciplines was good stuff. As long as you took care to do the work set, and not to annoy anybody too much, the three months of the course were like a working holiday.

I did at least try and work on my fitness. Though, as ever, we seemed to spend an inordinate amount of time in the pub – of the 14 blokes on my course, the three from the Gurkha Signal Squadron were the only ones who weren't hungover during the entire period – most of us were self-motivated enough to get out and do a bit of running. In my case, rather than go to scoff straight after trade had finished for the day, I'd get my kit on and go and do a few miles before I had a chance to think better of it. I was a bit too easily distracted, otherwise; if you're sharing a room with seven other lads with the same bullshitting credentials as yourself, it's lethal to sit at the table for 'a couple of minutes' before getting yourself out for some phys. Before you know it, that couple of minutes has turned into three hours, with the topics of the day being batted back and forth as the clock ticks down. Eventually, after working your way through Kim Wilde's yo-yoing weight, the thorny issue of who owned the most Captain Kirk-like lightweights, and whether or not having a haircut other than a short-back-and-sides or skinhead was a graphic indicator of sexual deviance, all thoughts of pounding the pavements would have retreated, and a couple of pints in the Corporals' Mess would replace physical exercise as the leisure pursuit of choice.

In fact, some of my best laughs in the Army happened whilst sat round the table in an eight-man room having conversations about pretty much fuck all. If you had a good combination of regional accents and a couple of natural comedians present, the potential for hilarity was limitless. Anything could be offered up for dissection and abuse from the gathered party. It was at these tables that soldiers would inform their mates that the letter that they were reading contained news of the death of a granny, a pregnancy announcement or their marching orders from their latest girlfriend. The default reaction was either incredulity or outright hostility.

Anyone suggesting that he'd had his heart broken would be counselled to get a fucking grip and get himself down town to remove the memory of his lost love courtesy of a hearty blowjob in some car park. A death in the family was treated with a little bit more reverence, but not much. 'Hard luck, mate. Have a Benny Hedgehog,' was about the closest we got to empathy. A man who ventured to inform the chaps that his girlfriend was pregnant would be rounded on with accusations that he was infertile or otherwise incapable of siring offspring, and suggestions that the newborn child would turn out to bear a close resemblance to a local MOD Plod.

Another common tactic was to reinterpret a given statement in order that it might be cleverly turned back on its originator. For instance, remarking in passing that you'd recently attended a Bad Company gig would rapidly see you accused of claiming to have passed P Company. This would be compounded if anyone walked in without hearing the initial statement. Whilst the victim pleaded innocence, the rest of the room would call him a 'walting fucking cunt', until someone else said something better, like they'd recently used SAS airlines to fly to Norway.

* * * * *

It was an interesting place, Catterick – or would have been for Desmond Morris and a documentary TV crew. For the rest of us, it was a bit shit. It's utterly synonymous with the British Army, so it won't surprise you to learn that it isn't the greatest place on earth in which to wind up. I'd only been there the once before, for my Detachment Commanders' Course, but that had been for four weeks, with barely enough time to fart, never mind get settled in. Now I had 12 weeks to get properly acquainted.

Unlike most garrison towns, which had existed long before the Army ever set up shop on their doorsteps, it was pretty much purpose-built from scratch after the mob first arrived in 1923. Having started out as a windswept backwater somewhere up near Richmond and Darlington in north Yorkshire, by the end of WWII it had turned into a sprawling maze of camps named after various battles. It was as though the Brass had scoured the entire country for the bleakest location possible and thought, 'Right, this'll increase their sense of isolation and get the fuckers working,' before throwing up a multitude of large barracks and other associated shite.

The overwhelming majority of houses in the town were pads' quarters, and pretty much everything else was either camps, stores or civvie boozers, takeaways and shops. Even these had all acquired a NAAFI feel: the pubs were all decked out in regimental plaques, and every shop assistant was instantly identifiable as a pad's wife. A glimpse of what lurked beneath that Spar serving tabard would usually reveal the unofficial uniform of the soldier's spouse – a pair of white stilettos, complete with matching heel plasters, and a set of Ron Hill running trousers designed more for marathon *runners* than Marathon *eaters*. It was strange; there was the odd svelte racing-snake among them, but most were behemoths of dramatic proportions. The larger the ladies, the more attached they were to their skin-tight running bottoms, when clearly the only running they ever did was across the kitchen floor to stop the fridge from closing. I used to wince at the sight of those ample behinds bound in by a single micron's thickness of cloth stretched so tight over their cellulite that it looked like they were wearing wicker knickers. If only there'd been the slightest hint of irony in their sporting of such unflattering trouserings; but I fear that, for some, Ron Hills were a bit of an identity badge, to the point where it became a source of great amusement to the toms.

Despite their penchant for ill-fitting clobber and always fucking off for a brew just as you got to the till, I was actually a big fan. It must have been a poisoned chalice, being a pad's wife. Girls married to squaddies have always had to put up with mountains of shit – often away from their own familial support network, with husbands always away on exercise or operations, they'd be stuck with three or four bin-lids and jammed into houses that were one step up from a FIBUA village. It wasn't a job for the weak-willed, that's for sure.

The aforementioned Spar was nestled in among a small row of stores and eateries called 'The White Shops' on the main drag through the garrison, which made them a decent yardstick as to how far you'd done/had yet to do on a run. As well as the Spar, there was a pub and a pizza/kebab joint – on my first orientation walk around, I noted with pleasure that it was just about pin-balling distance from 8 Sigs Barracks, so that eternal, end-of-the-night decision between food and taxi looked to be in the bag for the next three months.

There was also a shop that sold ruck-loads of military paraphernalia, where lads could purchase their own snazzy bergans, boots and dossbags etc. A really decent bit of kit was often referred to as being 'Gucci', which may seem slightly bizarre to the casual civilian observer. After all, surely the British Army provides its soldiers with all the best equipment available? Why on earth would a squaddie need anything other than that which the MOD has seen fit to issue them? I mean, the MOD is the government, right, so they must know what a soldier needs?

Unfortunately, whilst issued kit was OK, it was by no means the best on the market. A warning above the exit door in one of the SF bases in Northern Ireland summed up the problem for soldiers just going out on patrol. 'REMEMBER', it stated simply, 'ALL YOUR EQUIPMENT WAS MADE BY THE LOWEST BIDDER.'

Most of us bought at least one or two bits of our own kit because it made our lives a little easier in the field, and it looked flash. In fact, an individual who turned up on eccers dressed in MOD combats with issue webbing and a largepack might be thought of as a dreg. But, as ever, there was a fine line to be walked. The idea was to have just the right amount to confirm you as 'one of the lads'. If you had no kit, you were a 'mong'; if you went over the top, you risked straying into the unwanted territory of the 'warry bastard'.

This was another weird phenomenon of Army life. Depending on the unit you were in, sometimes even apparently insignificant idiosyncrasies could lead to accusations of being 'keen', 'warry' or 'Green'. In these circumstances, being an enthusiastic soldier was valid cause for derision. Even if you've never served, you'll know by now that soldiers love giving each other shit more than almost anything else, and will do so in the most inappropriate of situations, where sympathy or pity would normally be expected. For instance, I knew a guy in Harrogate who'd suffered from alopecia. As his hair fell out in clumps, his mates competed to come up with the most offensive nicknames for him.

Admittedly there were times when such allegations were well-founded. Blokes making impromptu para-smocks by sewing green woolly sock tops or jumper cuffs on to the sleeves of their combat jackets would certainly earn the title of being too green, for instance. And I once bimbled into the room of a notable lover of all things green called Steve Jones. Steve was sat on his scratcher, engrossed in a book. I asked him what he was reading, and he held it up for me to see. It was, almost unbelievably, called *Eastern Bloc Anti-personnel Mines, Recognition*.

Quite rightly, I just laughed and said, 'Fucking hell, Steve. You're a warry bastard.'

Steve's military diligence did pay dividends once, though. Ever ready to take on an unspecified/non-existent enemy, his webbing was always immaculately packed to deploy at a moment's notice. Among the many items in his kit was a survival tin containing everything he'd need to stay alive, should he find himself out in the oo-loo on his todd. One lucky Saturday night, he happened to meet the only woman in the world who cared to know the difference between the T-64 and T-80 main battle tanks, and she accompanied him back to his bunk. In a fit of social responsibility, and much to Steve's frustration, the young lady would not let Steve make the beast with two backs unless he had a condom. As none were to hand, a downcast Steve prepared for disappointment. But he suddenly remembered: just such an item was stored away in his survival tin. A flurry of activity saw his webbing dismantled and the johnny retrieved, in an explosion of scalpel blades, wire saws, Potassium Permanganate, fish hooks and hunting knives.

That nodder had been in there for years, waiting patiently to carry water in the jungles of Borneo, and the rubber would have been close to perishing. But Steve later confided that it had been worth having to re-pack his entire Active Edge kit to get a new coat of varnish on his old man.

Whilst Steve was definitely at the far end of the green spectrum, the situation was relative; in a room full of layabouts, you could be accused of being keen for almost nothing. I once got jip for using starch on my jumper. This shouldn't have been a big deal, but to the extra-lazy bastards I was bunking with it meant that they'd have to do theirs as well, or risk getting picked up on the next inspection. I was made to feel like a monumentally jack bastard for a whole afternoon.

Another offence that would bring a slating was if any of the toms had the temerity to have a compass on a lanyard in his pocket. 'What the fuck's that for?' his peers would ask in incredulous wonder. 'A fucking *compass*? What do you want one of them for, you warry bastard? Some cunt'll tell you which way to point.'

Even tying your boots in a slightly different way from everyone else could leave you on dodgy ground. One particular method of tying them meant that the boots were easier to cut off following a lower leg injury. This technique was useful to infanteers, where every second might count on the battlefield. It seemed less important when applied to certain elements of the Signals, where the most likely foot injury to occur was a twisted ankle from jumping off a Land Rover tail gate too quickly in a bid to remove a burning toastie from the kero heater.

Anyway, that military shop in Catterick did a roaring trade. I bought a brilliant set of boots from there which I still use to this day, and I also splashed out on a decent sleeping bag that ended up in flames on exercise a few years later.

* * * * *

Because so many people were there on courses, everyone but the orphans would bomb-burst home as soon as the CO's run finished on Friday afternoon, which left Thursday as the big night out in

Catterick. Anyone who had any dough left might treat themselves to a cab ride over to Richmond, where the nightlife was plentiful and the young ladies were reasonably easy on the eye. But most of us were almost permanently skint, so we tended to end up at a nightclub on the outskirts of town. From the outside, it looked like something from a Lowry painting, but it was the jewel in Catterick's crown. Over the years, it had been christened and re-christened with various formal names, like 'Stax' or 'The Scorpion', but to everyone who ever served there it was just 'Scabs', with 'Scabby Doos' and the 'Catterick School of Dancing' offered as occasional variations. In the immortal words of New Jersey's ex-hairdressing, big-bouffanted, tight-clobber-wearing, former king of dire '80s American stadium rock, and general all-round shagger of super-fit women, Jon Bon Jovi, 'It's all the same. Only the names will change.'

Every Thursday night, hordes of semi-skint soldiers who'd found themselves marooned in the Colburn Lodge, nursing a thirst for a slightly later drink, would head up there for some end-of-week male bonding. Like most historical revisionists, I'd like to say that I gave Scabs a wide berth, but I found myself gawking around in there on all but two of the weeks I was in town. It was a strange old place, particularly in retrospect – more of an anthropological study than a night out, in many ways. It seemed to exert a strange tractor beam which pulled in women from a far bigger catchment area than it had any right to. Girls from as far afield as Middlesbrough and Penrith would find themselves sampling the pleasures of frozen pies from the kiosk near the front door, gnawing on them like savoury Calypsos. Most of my memories of the place are fond, if hazy; it was there, for instance, that I spent five minutes gazing, as if mesmerised, at the prodigious back of a dancing Hartlepool princess. The large butterfly tattoo at the nape of her neck looked like it had been self-inflicted with a blunt crayon.

My recent monogamy prevented me from getting led astray, but people would cop off in there left, right and centre. There were booths and secluded seating areas all round, where groups of Bishop Auckland's finest womenfolk would accost sleeping soldiers and force them to the bar for a round of pink drinks. I remember waiting in the queue to go in late one night, and watching in awe as two Leviathans in mini-skirts went toe-to-toe in the carpark to compete for the affections of a Combat Lineman. Despite having been on operational tours, and having spent what must add up to years in some of the world's roughest nightspots, I've never seen a fight which matched it for ferocity. No quarter was expected or given as they rolled round the place, so locked together that they nearly became one, like Siamese twins joined at the hair. Every now and then, a flash of knicker at the top of a sturdy leg would bring a cheer from the queue. After a few minutes of this mortal combat, one lad made as though to separate them and was immediately restrained by a bouncer who suggested, with a concerned expression, that death lay in wait along that path. I forget which girl won – it was either Shaz or Tray – but her victory was pyrrhic. Whilst they were scrapping, the liney had taken the opportunity to lie down and go to sleep in a load of thigh-high nettles.

When we weren't skiving, boozing or bullshitting, we were engaging in other traditional Army pastimes, such as shaking our heads at the young recruits and informing them that the fucking Army was in shit state now it was letting in the likes of them. That was one of the odd things about 8 Signal Regiment – it was slightly imbalanced, in that upgrading personnel like myself mixed with lads who were undergoing initial trade training. This could create friction: some of the training staff took themselves a bit seriously, and often failed to differentiate between sprogs and trained soldiers. Since most of us had already had our fair share of being shouted at and fucked about gratuitously, we strongly objected if we felt we were on the end of an unnecessary injustice.

Of course, that didn't stop us having a go at the recruits. Although we weren't in charge of anyone, we at least outranked them and we were quite free with comments of our own if we saw anyone acting the twat or looking slobbish or scruffy. This is nothing new. Since the British Army came into existence, it's been almost mandatory for soldiers to belittle those who follow them into the colours. When I was in training, we were regularly told by sergeants who'd joined in the '60s that the Army was going to rack and ruin because someone had seen fit to let tossbags like us get past the Careers Office door. They'd been told exactly the same thing by the Second World War veterans who'd trained them, who in turn had come in for all sorts of abuse from men who'd survived the austere years of the 1920s. I'm sure it continues to this day, with guys returning from Iraq and Afghanistan shaking their heads in disappointment at the calibre of the blokes being sent to replace them. We certainly weren't going to miss our turn at unfairly looking down on people with 'what's the world coming to?' expressions plastered across our faces.

Pretty much the only other thing we did was mooch around drinking tea. Rather than buy a brew in the NAAFI after scoff, we clubbed together to buy some brew kit. One of the lads was duly despatched to the White Shops to procure the cheapest kettle on sale, a big jar of coffee, some shit teabags and a bag of sugar. The idea was that we'd take it in turns to knock up the brews, saving ourselves a bit of gelt and acting like grown-ups. It was a great idea in principle, but it immediately fell at the first practical hurdle. From the start, nobody could agree whose turn it was to make the brews. It was perverse, but the lads seemed to prefer having an argument to sipping a hot beverage. Lofty, chest-poking phrases like, 'I think you'll find it's your turn, you fat cunt', would provoke ripostes of which Oscar Wilde would have been proud, such as, 'Get fucked, you dick-chomper. I made 'em last week.'

It went on like that for the whole course, and got to the point where the rows provided far more entertainment than any mug of coffee ever could. If anyone got sick of the whole affair and attempted to make a brew for themselves, he was literally rugby-tackled on his way to the kettle and forced to take part in the dispute.

It might not sound like it from all of the foregoing, but I was actually starting to grow up. I was keen to pass the course, because it would mean a decent increase in my wages and probably my second tape. This is a significant point in any soldier's career, heralding the moment at which he might start to become less of a dickhead as he begins the gradual move up the Army's non-commissioned, middle-management strata.

Obviously Jenny had played a part in my new thinking. Although she never pointedly discussed our respective careers, I had deduced from the general tenor of our conversations that she'd soon get tired of me being a drunken bell end. She was quite focused on a career in teaching and her sense of purpose had rubbed off on me, if only slightly.

Eventually, the end of the course rolled around and I found I'd passed: I was now Lance Corporal Edward Nugent, Radio Telegraphist Class 1. This meant a small bump up in money terms and a bit of kudos at a working unit, but there was no badge to accompany the award. Unlike marksmen, divers or P-company graduates, whose achievements were plain to see on their jumpers, successful candidates on the Class 1 could only boast about their proficiency to anyone unwise enough to allow themselves to be cornered in the NAAFI.

It had definitely matured me, comparatively, and I was ready for the next posting. We said our goodbyes and went our separate ways: in my case, for a long weekend before I had to make my way down to Nuneaton.

EDDY NUGENT AND THE LIPSTICK OF ENOCH

I WAS ON A BIT of a timetable when I got home. I'd arranged to go with my dad to buy myself a car on the Saturday morning, and Jenny's folks had invited me over to a barbecue at their place in the afternoon. I was a bit worried about the barbecue – Jenny said her dad had warned her off about the dubious moral hygiene of squaddies, so I could see me getting more of a grilling than the sausages – but I put that to the back of my mind as I went shopping for a motor.

Getting myself some wheels would give me some real freedom at the weekends, now that I was going to be based in the Midlands. I'd be able to get up and down from Warwickshire in a couple of hours, which would really open up my social life. It wasn't just about Jenny and my folks. Some of the friendships I'd had with lads from school had started drifting a bit while I was in Germany, and I wanted to reconnect with Manchester.

I knew absolutely nothing about cars and without the old man I'd have been a car salesman's dream – I could easily have bought a Reliant Robin with a missing front wheel. Dad was no mechanic, but like most men of his generation he'd learnt to be canny with money and was quick to spot anyone trying to make a monkey out of him. There was a second-hand car place a couple of miles down the road from our house, so we drove over there in his car whilst he gave me a pep talk which mostly consisted of letting him doing all the talking and keeping shtum as to how much money we had.

He'd already scoped out a few motors for me while I'd been on the Class 1, so we were able to eliminate some of the fannying about that normally goes hand-in-hand with the process. He'd decided on an ugly-looking brute of a vehicle, and I have to admit I wasn't keen when he pointed it out to me on the forecourt. It was a flat red, D-reg Volvo 340 DL, and it looked a bit boxier than the Ferrari I'd been dreaming of buying with my 800 quid budget.

'What's up with you?' he said, seeing my face fall. 'That's a lovely car, that is.'

'I know, dad, it's just a bit... well, it's a bit of a funny shape.'

'Don't talk shite. It's a bloody *car*. A to B, lad, that's all you want it for. You can't go wrong with a Volvo. If you want to do a 200 mile round trip in it every week, you get something reliable. If you go getting something daft like an XR3i, you'll end up wrapping it round a fucking lamppost the first time you drive it.'

I was dubious, but he was right: that motor never let me down for the two years I owned it, not least because it was built like something out of the Henschel & Sohn tank works at Kassel. I always felt safe in it as I trundled up the A5 on my way home.

Dad got the keys from the office and we took it for a quick spin round the block. It was a good feeling, driving something I was about to own, and even dad's constant correction of every single thing I did failed to dent my pleasure. I even got cocky enough to stick the radio on as we drove down Princess Parkway, but quickly switched it back off, dad's moaning being preferable to Robson and Jerome's musical homicide.

After the test drive, dad did the business with the salesman, managing to get a few quid off the marked price. We'd got a cover note earlier in anticipation, so I was good to go as the driver. He nipped off home and left me to make my own way back. I stopped off at nan's to show it off and see how she was doing; she seemed a lot perkier than when I'd last seen her, and had obviously started to bounce back from the loss of Alfie. Mum had bought her a dog, which had helped. She had it under her arm when she came to the door, and it crossed my mind that mum had got it from a WRVS surplus store: it was one of those generic little Yorkies that seem to go with the territory of old age, like trousers up to your armpits and tartan shopping trolleys. Personally, I can't stand them, they're like little fucking werewolves, but she seemed pretty happy with it. Not being troubled by political correctness, she'd named him Enoch. Unsettlingly, the whole time I was there, his lipstick was on full display. Maybe he had a thing about Volvos. It turned out nan did, too, since she entirely failed to make any distinction between Sweden and Germany. 'You go careful in it, Eddy,' she said. 'They'll have made it so that the steering wheel comes off in your hands and kills you.'

I was glad dad had come with me to buy it instead of her.

* * * * *

The barbecue was much more enjoyable than I'd expected. Jenny had a Saturday morning job, and I'd picked her up and taken her for a spin before driving back to my house. She was extremely impressed with the car and didn't have my misgivings about its aesthetic value, though she did call me a knob when I over-revved the engine at a set of lights.

As we walked from mine to hers we linked arms. It felt a bit weird, and she laughed at my self-consciousness. 'You're alright, Eddy. There's none of your big, tough mates around to take the mickey out of you.'

'S'pose not.'

'Hey... that's some spot you've got on your nose, there!'

I'd been hoping she wouldn't notice, but it was a difficult one to miss. I don't know if I'm just unlucky, but whenever I've needed to be on display as a younger bloke, my body conspired against me. If I needed a passport photograph, or was going to a christening, some sort of chemical reaction used to take place and a spot would appear, front and centre, to spoil any pictures. I never had many of the bastards, but they were always big fuckers when they showed up, and the one Jenny was gawking at was one of those big, red, slow-burning swines that take days to come to a head. They hurt if your finger brushes within two feet of them and they're almost impossible to squeeze, sandwiched in that tricky hollow just above the nostril.

Her family lived in a small, terraced house with a yard, and when we got there several members of the Warner clan were there to meet me. Jenny did a quick set of introductions, nervously.

'This is Eddy, everyone,' she said, working her way round the room as I hovered near the doorway. 'Eddy, this is mum, dad, Uncle Pete, granddad, Aunty Karen and these two are my sisters, Ella and Jayne.'

Everyone nodded hello, and then Jenny's dad stepped forward with his hand extended. 'Nice to meet you, Eddy. I'm Kev.'

I shook his hand as firmly as seemed necessary and said, 'Thanks for inviting me, Mr Warner, Mrs Warner.'

'Call me Kev, and this is Rose,' he said, his hand sweeping towards Jenny's mum. She stepped forward. 'It's lovely to meet you, Eddy,' she said. 'Jenny talks about you a lot.'

We both blushed, and out of the corner of my eye I could see Kev eyeballing the plook on my hooter. I assumed he'd just keep quiet about it, but he immediately pointed straight at it. 'Who's your mate, Eddy?' he said.

'Dad!' Jenny shouted, but I burst out laughing. It was the perfect icebreaker, and I had a great afternoon. Her folks were nice. I could feel the inquisitorial nature behind the seemingly innocuous questions that her dad ran by me, but I was scoring big for having enough sense to own and run a car, in spite of the fact that I'd be paying the bank back for four years. His suspicion of soldiers was entirely sensible, but I could tell that I was doing alright. As the afternoon wore on, and the beer lubricated everyone, it all got more jocular. Rose didn't talk to me much and busied herself with making sure everyone had all they needed.

Jenny's granddad Arthur was a grumpy twat. He only spoke once or twice, and when we went into the backyard to fire up the barbecue, he just stood there shaking his head. Rose asked him what was wrong. 'The world's gone fuckin' mad, I tell ya,' he said. 'When I was a lad, you ate in the house and shat in the yard.'

Rose stuck him a corner with a paper plate and a couple of chicken drumsticks, and that was the last we heard from him for the day.

Her Uncle Pete was a bit of a frustrated soldier. You met a lot of guys like that on leave – as soon as they found out you were in the Army, they had to bore you with the reasons they didn't join, as if your presence alone stood as some sort of accusation of cowardice. It was always some feeble excuse, like the Careers Office was closed the afternoon they went, or they wanted to join the Household Cavalry but they had piles, and Pete was no different. It turned out he'd been absolutely determined to join the Green Howards, but being a caring son (and inveterate bullshitter) he'd decided against it because he didn't want his mum to worry about him going to Northern Ireland. I stood and nodded along, out of good manners. Personally, I couldn't care two tits whether he'd wanted to join the Army or not – I didn't mind what people did for a living, as long as they seemed alright.

As he polished off another hamburger, Pete also produced the other classic: 'Do you know Dave Smith? He's in the Army an' all.'

At that time of my service, there were more than 100,000 of us, but that never seemed to stop people asking this inane question. I usually played along, and on one occasion, against all the odds, I actually knew the chap and had to spend ten minutes trying to avoid telling his mum that I thought he was a fucking stroker.

'Dave Smith?' I said. 'No, can't say I do, Pete.'

'Tall bloke?' he said, wiping sausage off his grid. 'Short hair and a moustache. He usually wears jeans and a t-shirt and one of them Jelly-Jonsson fleeces?'

'Yeah?' I said. 'No.'

After the barbie, Jenny and I escaped for a walk. She congratulated me on my performance; I'd managed to have swear-free conversations for the entire afternoon. This is a skill which has served me well since leaving the Army. At work these days I'm quite happy to function and converse with no recourse to foul language, but as soon as I get put with a few old mates that I've served with, it never takes long for it to get post-watershed fairly quickly.

On the Sunday, before I headed south, we took the opportunity to christen the car in a layby near Northwich.

The generous interior of the Volvo wasn't something I'd particularly considered, but I came to recognise it as one of the model's best features.

EDDY NUGENT AND THE RETURN OF THE DALEK

IT WAS A BRIGHT warm day when I turned up at 30 Sigs in accordance with my posting instructions.

They were based on a former WW2 air base at Bramcote, four miles south east of the cosmopolitan and sophisticated Warwickshire town of Nuneaton. Having been built for aircraft, the camp was spread out over a large area, with several hangars now housing Signal Squadrons instead of bombers. The unmistakeable 1930s RAF accommodation H blocks were dotted liberally about the place, and the modern Army naturally hadn't seen fit to re-furbish them. Like our vehicles, they were held together by paint and zip ties: it was generally held that the brass believed that all a soldier needed to get by was a tub of Brylcreem, a short-back-and-sides and a roll-up ciggie, a list of requirements that hadn't changed since the days of *The Goons* and Norman Wisdom.

The guardroom was directly opposite RHQ, just inside the gates, with a large tarmac area immediately outside. I parked the car up and went in to get a car pass and present myself formally to my new unit. As I pushed the door, I heard a loud sneeze from inside and froze as I heard a familiar, high-pitched, clipped Yorkshire accent. 'Oooh, fuckin' lovely. Come 'ere, ya beauty!'

It couldn't be!

But it was.

As I entered the guardroom, stood there licking away two post-sneeze snot candles was Derek The Dalek.

'Fuckin' 'ell!' he said, forgetting his supper for a moment. 'Fuckin' Eddy! 'Ow do, ya cunt?'

He seemed genuinely happy to see me.

'Jesus, Derek. Alright, mate? How long have you been here?'

'A fuckin' year or so. But never mind that. Check this cunt out!' He pointed to a spot just below his parachute wings where a single white chevron nestled proudly. Good God. Derek was now a lance jack. His ceaseless devotion to bogey-eating and all round depravity must have been misinterpreted wildly enough on his confidential report to have deemed him worthy of promotion.

'Fucking nora, mate.' I said. 'Congratulations.'

He grinned. 'So are you posted in then, fella?'

'Aye, mate.'

'Fuckin' nice one Eddy!' he said. 'We'll 'ave some fuckin' fun, mate. It's alright here. There's a great fuckin' place in town. The Crazy Horse, it's fuckin' magic. We call it 'The Donk'.'

I knew that any establishment that came with Derek's stamp of approval had to be pretty gopping, and probably on a par with Scabs and The Farm. He carried on. 'This is fuckin' great, Eddy. I'd make you a brew,' he said gesturing towards the back of the guardroom, 'but I've just domed all the mugs and me cock's itching like buggery at the moment so I won't bother.'

The 'doming' of mugs was one of many forms of playfully grotesque tomfoolery used as a form of revenge when the rank structure prevented more immediate action. In a similar fashion to a waiter adding 'special sauce' to the dish of a customer who's fucking him about, quite a few seniors and officers became unwitting recipients of junior rank DNA if they crossed the line. Had anyone else have said it I'd have taken it as a joke, but this was the Dalek and he took being a gopper very seriously. I was quite certain that the next cup of tea that the Duty Officer drank would have the dubious distinction of being 'non-specific-urethritis' flavoured.

I cackled. 'Fucking hell, Derek,' I said. 'Hey, did I ever tell you about that sergeant from 216 and his pipe?'

Some years earlier, I'd gone on an adventure training course. One of the seniors had messed us all about, insisting we all met up at 7am to go rock-climbing instead of having a bit of a lie-in. He smoked a pipe, and when he carelessly left it lying around one day as he went to get himself a brew, one of the lads had managed to jam most of its stem into his urethra. Extracting it with a wince, the lad had contented himself with a quick, 'That'll teach the cunt!' and we'd all watched in horrified glee as the sergeant had spent the next 20 minutes having a satisfied chomp on the pipe.

Showing up at a new unit was pretty much old hat to me now, so I went through the normal rigmarole of sorting out my room and kit and then tootled over to my squadron – 256 – to touch bases with the powers that be. The squadron clerk was drinking coffee and playing solitaire on the computer when I entered the office, and he wasn't best pleased when I spoke.

'Fuck me,' he said, under his breath, like *I* was the idle cunt doing fuck all but interrupting him and his vital work. He swilled some coffee down and sucked his teeth, which were so bad they looked like they'd been painted in NATO pattern. But once I explained my situation, he was cool. We had a bit of chit-chat about this and that, and then he pointed me in the direction of the stores. 'When you get your bedding, ask to see the Mattlas,' he said, with a grin and another slurp of coffee.

Fearing a wind up, and being a little too long in the tooth to fall for a fool's errand, I asked for an explanation.

'The stores wallah's got this collection of mattresses with lag stains on which look like countries,' he said. 'It's a bit of a regimental talking point – he's always on the lookout for new ones. He's got a stack of Ukraines and Bulgarias, and three maps of Africa, but he's desperate for an Italy. Technically very hard to produce. It's his holy grail.'

(Later, I would see for myself this odd geographical collection, and it was actually very impressive. The storeman had them all filed alphabetically, and Italy was, indeed, regarded as the ACME of the art. In his expert opinion, the swamper would need to begin his wazz with a lob on which would recede during the process. If the erection waned too slowly, be believed, Mexico would be the outcome; if it disappeared too *quickly*, Chile or Argentina beckoned. 'It's a bastard,' he said, shaking his head. 'But one day… One day.')

The clerk took me into the YoS and then the Sgt Major, both of whom were decent eggs. I'd seen the YoS way back, floating around APC in Belize when he was a full screw, and a herb monster of some note, I might add. Not to mention the fact that, although married back then, he was also quite partial to, as Derek would've said 'Them there prost-y-matutes.'

To this day, I still can't make my mind up about the OC. Sometimes he could be a total rod, and others he would go out of his way to help you out. Love him or hate him though, Major Daniels had the biggest 'tache I'd ever seen. Ridiculously thick, and so long it almost obscured his gob, the boss was a walking caricature of the Victorian Officer. He also had a couple of old scabby lurchers which would often appear, as if from nowhere, leading to speculation amongst the lads that they lived in his muzzy.

* * * * *

One thing that struck me about 30 Sigs was the lack of people floating around on camp. Half of the regiment must've been on ops in one corner of the world or another; even the cookhouse was pretty thin at lunchtime. It was known as the 'Juniper restaurant', and by cookhouse standards – admittedly, not all that high – it was a definite winner, mainly because there was a Gurkha squadron on camp. It meant that half the hotplate was given over to Nepalese cuisine, which knocked spots off the spam fritters and jacket spuds on offer in the 'British' section.

The accommodation at Bramcote was a different matter, though. It was in rag order. Virtually everyone was in eight-man rooms, with just a single electric plug socket at one end to run all the TVs and videos for everyone. As I was going to be a room NCO, I got the pit space nearest the plug socket. At first sight this sounded like a privilege, but the cluster of dodgy plugs hanging out of it always worried me.

Luckily, the block was inadvertently improved within my first month.

A Senior NCO in our squadron – a grade one throbber with apparent domestic sex issues – had just got his Unit Fire Officer qualification and wanted everyone to know. He was one of those blokes who walked around with a big bunch of keys on his belt; occasionally, he'd point to them and say, 'That's responsibility, that is.' As I said, a tool of epic proportions. He'd been giving us all kinds of fire practices of a night time, which would normally entail a roll call on the square with everyone freezing their pods off in their undercrackers and just a *Razzle*-induced one-bar radiator to keep them warm. As a general rule, we'd be stood around for an hour or so while everyone was accounted for to the satisfaction of our tormentor.

One night I'd just got back to my room after a shower, and was in the process of swinging one leg over my towel to dry my plums with a lacklustre sawing motion, when I heard the familiar cry of 'FIRE, EVERYONE OUTSIDE, FIRE!'

Not willing to endure another stint on the square dressed in nowt but a wet towel, I took my time getting dried and dressed in a load of warm kit, chuntering about the injustice the whole time. As I ambled out of my room, I walked into a wall of thick smoke with a backdrop of flames.

'FUCK ME! IT'S A REAL FUCKING FIRE!' I shouted.

Suddenly, lots of doors flew open and blokes in various states of dress and undress came tanking out of their rooms. Once outside, we had a grandstand view of the action. One of the upstairs rooms was well ablaze and had already blown out its windows, and as we stood there the fire piquet turned up, thrapping up the road in a clapped-out Land Rover with its trailer full of perished hoses and archaic equipment. They screeched to a halt on the verge and piled out like the Ant Hill Mob.

Almost immediately a joker from the audience shouted, 'Oi! Get off the fucking grass!'

This was met by raucous laughter by the blokes, who were safe in the knowledge that their mates were out of the building. He then screamed in mock distress, 'Please! You must save my baby.'

That couple of jokes set the scene, and a full-on comedy show ensued as the piquet tried every last hose connector in the trailer before finding the correct one. Each failed attempt brought calls of, 'Come on you lazy cunts! I've got a taxi booked in half an hour!'

When the hose was finally connected to the hydrant there was a huge cheer followed by a round of applause. Unfortunately, the hydrant didn't work, but by this time the local fire brigade were pulling up and they got things squared away in about two minutes.

A couple of the now redundant piquet tried to chat to the firemen as if they were on the same professional footing and for about a month afterwards they got beasted with about three drills each night. But on the positive site, it did kickstart the hierarchy into sorting out the blocks.

* * * * *

The lads in my room were a nice enough bunch, despite the odd character flaw here and there. Most of them were on their first posting and were keen as mustard. There was one senior siggie on a second posting, Paul 'Stretch' Armstrong, who had done four years in BAOR before coming to 30 and had the clearest 'didn't give a fuck' attitude I'd seen in a long time. Some people thought he was either just a dreg or a lazy cunt, but I liked him. He did his job well when required, but during normal everyday camp life he simply couldn't be persuaded to give two shits about anything. His reaction to being given two weeks off or two weeks' guard was exactly the same: a small shrug of the shoulders and a laconic blink.

As a general rule, Stretch would just mooch around the block in the nuddy, or sometimes in a knackered old towelling dressing gown that he seemed attached to. I'm not sure which was worse: whenever he wore the dressing gown, he'd never tie the fucker up so his springs were always on display.

Returning to multi-occupancy rooms after so long spent in single bunks in Germany was a real shock to my wanking system. Gone were the days of blatantly lying on my scratcher, fully bollocky, in a birthing-stirrup position, whilst watching dwarf porn and having a super-aggressive Chinese burn milk. I was left with either stealth-wanking in my pit at night or a more open approach, as favoured by many of the lads. Some of them employed a 'bear bells' method, making enough noise to scare off anybody in the area. If you suspended any self-consciousness, common decency and shame for the period of the thrap, you could almost guarantee that you wouldn't be disturbed.

I'd palled up with a guy called John Hunt, and he was a big fan of the *laissez faire* approach. He'd bimble into the room with a copy of *Fiesta* in one hand and a wad of Andrex in the other – though he'd only ever go down the Andrex route when all of his catching socks had become so over-used that they'd taken on the physical properties of a wobble board, and the idea of using soft civvie bog roll for its intended purpose was anathema to him. 'It just ain't the wiping kind,' he'd say. 'One minute, you're getting used to soft bog roll around your arse, and the next, if you're not careful, it'll be cocks, and then you can just fuck right off.'

I found his logic skewed and worrying, but John stood firm.

Talking of Andrex... apart from the constant to-ing and fro-ing on operations, 30 Sigs wasn't all that different from most units, but it distinguished itself from the competition by the sheer length and severity of its bog roll famines. I don't know if someone was stockpiling them, or the MOD was cutting back so that they could buy another submarine, but there were long periods of time during my posting to Nuneaton where it was impossible to get hold of any. A simple trip to the NAAFI to buy your own trap roll might appear to be an obvious way around the problem, but many of the blokes treated the shortfall in issued toilet paper as a test of their initiative and resourcefulness, as well as their mental and physical endurance. John Hunt almost relished them, though he was the kind of fella who would take cold baths just to see if he still 'had it'.

During one particularly drawn-out shortage, I walked into the room to find him teetering on his tip toes and sort of walking on the spot – imagine a ballerina marking time, and you have the picture.

'What are you doing, John?' I enquired.

'SD-ing!' came a clipped response between short breaths.

'What the fuck's that?' I asked.

'Shit dance... got to keep... it up my arse...'

'Have you tried 20 knees-to-the-chest reps?' I said.

'Can't... too far gone... prairie dogging...'

'Sorry, mate,' was about the best I could offer. 'Why not use the NAAFI bogs? They've got bog roll.'

'Can't... cheating...'

So I left him to his shit dance. Although John tended to take things to extremes, his behaviour wasn't considered particularly unusual amongst the blokes. During hard times, you could use anything in the block to wipe your arse. The first things to go were the inners from the empty rolls, followed by newspapers and other peoples' pillowcases and, eventually, bits of wood. The unwritten rule was that you couldn't buy any bog roll or shit outside of the block, including the NAAFI or work. That was odd because, in normal 'non-famine' seasons, you could shit anywhere you liked, apart from the left hand trap in 256's hangar, the one marked 'SCENE BLOKES' in scrawled biro. You would often see lads queuing up outside the right hand bog 'SD-ing' or doing knees-to-chest to keep a turd at bay, but refusing to use the 'SCENE BLOKES' bog in case their actions were misconstrued.

During a shortage, the theft of toilet roll was actively encouraged and a good snatch earned the admiration of your peers. Anywhere supplied by the same QM would be under similar drought conditions, so the NAAFI and work bogs would be quickly cleaned out and the other blocks would offer very slim pickings. This would leave a desperate shit paper thief one final option: the WRAC block. For some reason, the female personnel on camp had no qualms about buying their own bog roll and leaving it in their block toilets. In our block, people even nicked the bath plugs to have for themselves, leaving everyone else to make do with the lid off a polish tin which you'd need to keep your foot on for the duration of the bath. The women were far more civilised: in their accommodation, so the story went, you could leave something down and it would still be there five minutes later. Apart from chocolate, that is.

Inevitably, a prolonged famine would drive a bloke to carry out a late night recce on the girls' block. Bearing in mind that it was a chargeable offence to be found there, such raids were not without risk. There would normally be a two- to three-man raiding party, invariably screeched up on Dutch courage and doing those horrible pre-crap farts that have visible shit particles in them.

Some guys would just make off with the bog roll, whilst others would be complete cunts. My first such ablution-orientated hunter-gatherer patrol was on a Saturday morning at about 3am when all the girls were in bed. Myself, Derek and John Hunt were pissed up in the block, and had just polished off a large kebab each with extra chilli sauce. Derek was trying to instigate a game of 'Knob or Bollocks', where you drop your trousers and pull a tiny amount of genital skin from a hole in your undercrackers, leaving the other competitors to guess whether the skin is scrotal or penile – hence, 'knob or bollocks'. He went first, even though the rest of us didn't want to play, and fished out what looked like the dried brain of a medium-sized rodent. I was completely stumped. It looked bollock-like, but it wasn't hairy. Then again, this was The Dalek's tackle, so anything was possible. I was thinking about giving up when I noticed John's mind was not on the problem. It had dawned on him that he'd have nothing to clean up with when the inevitable post-kebab trauma hit him the following day.

'Fucking bollocks,' he muttered. 'My fucking bum's going to be ravaged without any decent trap paper, and no cunt's got a stash left to borrow.'

'There's only one thing left to do!' boomed Derek, in a surprisingly authoritative manner – hard to pull off, for a man with his trousers around his ankles and an off-pink growth still protruding from his shreddies. He waved a finger in the air to emphasise his rhetoric. 'Times are 'ard,' he continued, 'and such situations call for men to do what must be done, to seize what is needed for the good of his fellow man!' With a flourish of his arm towards the door, and carried away on the emotion of his own speech, he shouted, 'TO THE CHICKS' BLOCK, YOU CUNTS!'

We tiptoed in to the darkened hall of the girls' block and split up to try and find sheets of that soft, downy gold. I headed for a door off the main corridor. The place was totally silent, but this was soon broken by a loud hissing noise. I headed back, and in the gloom I could just make out Derek and John giggling as they let down the tyres on several of the girls' mountain bikes. In the loudest whisper possible, I said, 'Knock it on the head, you cunts! Stop cocking around! We only need bog paper!'

They gave a little thumbs up and pinballed off to some other doors in search of the traps. I found them first, and gathered up four rolls – I didn't want to kick the arse out of it, so I left some for the girls – and headed back to the hall. John was mooching around, but Derek was nowhere to be seen. Pointing John in the direction of the toilets, I went off to find The Dalek so we could scarper. The first door I tried was the dhobi room. To the left was a row of top-loading tumble dryers lined up along the wall, and opposite them were four front-loading washing machines. The room was lit only by the streetlight filtering in from a window. I took a step forward in the dimness and stood on a pile of clothes. Picking them up, I realised they were Derek's jeans and t-shirt. Nervously, I took another step forward and that's when I saw it: an image that was instantly and permanently scorched onto my retinas. An unsteady Dalek was squatting above one of the open dryers, in a wide-knee crouch, like some pissed-up sumo wrestler.

At first I thought he was naked, but on closer examination I saw that the weird fucker was wearing a stolen bra and a pair of knickers which he'd pulled to one side. Then the smell hit me and before I could get a word out, I realised that there was a vintage turd leaving his hoop. As the crowning glory, and whilst the shit still hung from his ricker, Derek began to piss, a long, lazy arc across the room straight through an open washer door. It crossed my mind, in the horror of it all, that he was simultaneously contaminating both appliances for all eternity: they'd have to be sealed in concrete and dumped in the middle of the Atlantic.

Eventually, the shit broke off and there was an agonisingly long pause before it hit the bottom of the dryer. It sounded like someone throwing a bag of cement into an empty skip. I expected it to wake up half the camp, but amazingly, no-one stirred.

'You fucking *dreg*!' I said. 'We only came for bog roll. What are you fucking playing at?'

Derek looked at me. 'Can you get DNA from shit?' he said.

I gave up and went to fetch John, hoping he'd've grabbed his stash and would be ready to get going. Was he bollocks. Like Derek, the nervous excitement generated by the thievery had speeded up his requirement to pump some mud. I walked in and found him in trap one, door open, wobbed out on the can. He was facing the wrong way, like some obscene version of Liza Minnelli straddling the chair in *Cabaret*. I nudged him with my foot and he startled awake with an involuntary cry of, 'No more fannies!' Fuck knows what he'd been dreaming about.

'What are you doing, mate?' I said.

He stood up and pointed down at the toilet. He'd left skiddies on the front of the pan, stark against the white porcelain like the blood from a butchered pig in the snow.

'Anyone can dung up the traps,' he said, with a smile. 'But this is the only way to be sure.'

I gave up at that point, and just did a runner with my four pristine rolls. Derek and John followed behind, John shuffling along empty handed with his strides round his ankles like a startled penguin, and Derek like an amateur tranny in his new found underwear, carrying nothing but his own clothes and a mountain of ladies' smalls.

As we hustled back to the block, The Dalek started giggling. It turned out he'd also pissed in a few irons: the girls were about to discover that Lenor had started a new line of Sugar Puff-scented conditioners.

I punished the pair of them in the following week by a strict rationing of my stash. It was strangely empowering, and I wallowed in my short-lived status as the trap roll kingpin of block two. I was fully expecting a big enquiry and lots of chest-poking until they found the culprits, but we never heard a word. The girls didn't seem to mind: perhaps swamping in the washers and facing the wrong way on the can was *de rigeur* in their accommodation.

EDDY NUGENT AND THE EYE OF JAPAN

EVERY GARRISON TOWN has its share of infamous local ladies who, for reasons which escape the more sound-of-mind female, have developed a penchant for random military cock-a-leekie.

Down the years, they will acquire nicknames which mock their physical characteristics or idiosyncrasies – Fat Shaz, Big Petra, Odd Job, Splashplates and The Black Widow were a few of the more memorable ones from my day. They sound offensive, but in the topsy-turvy world of British Army etiquette, they were actually meant to be moderately affectionate. Their main source of carnal prey were toms straight out of training, who were over the moon to find someone who wasn't shouting at them or jiffing them for guard. It was a rite of passage for the young siggies and when they'd get back to camp after a night grappling with Big Petra, they'd have to endure the additional horror of having a 38-year-old full screw comparing notes about the first night he'd spent with the same woman, and asking if there'd been any sign of the underpants he'd left behind in 1983.

Of course, the thought of bucketloads of derision from their oppos did nothing to stop many a young soldier from taking the lonely walk up the stairs to Petra's flat. One problem with these levels of promiscuity was that as soon as a dose of blobby knob appeared, it spread like wildfire. And when you added Derek The Dalek, and his love of jiggery-pokery in all its forms to the mix, you had a major problem. Every Thursday, Friday and Saturday night was like the wheel of fanny-fortune for The Dalek. He seemed to have a Boddingtons-powered slash detector that helped him to isolate only those women most likely to give him an STD. His short

251

time in the regiment had already seen him build up a harem of regular shags, and they were, in turn, getting roared by someone else when The Dalek wasn't 'on the nest'.

Not long after I arrived, Derek came back from leave with a dose. Being the predictable horror that he was, he knew he had gonorrhoea right from the off, but didn't go sick with it for a good couple of weeks. During this time he'd been up to his normal shagging down town, figuring that spraying his bell end with Old Spice before going out would clear things right up. It wasn't until he was having to peel his cock off the sheets every morning that he thought to seek medical advice on his condition. By the time he did go sick, half the blokes in the MRS were lining up sheepishly to get their doses squared away, too. Derek later confided in me that he believed the MO to be a Napoleonic war re-enactor, given his zealous, musket-loading-style approach to swabbing the guilty penis. A month or so later, he infested the guardroom beds with crabs; that was the point at which the MO, worried about the sexual and moral health of the regiment, called in the Dick Doctor to scare the shit out of us with mutated schlong movies.

After this news did the rounds, I caught up with The Dalek in the NAAFI. 'You're a filthy cunt, Derek,' I said, pointed the finger squarely at him. 'This is all your fault. If you'd have sorted your dose and crabs out straight away, we wouldn't have to watch these fucking films.'

'Don't you fuckin' worry about that, Eduardo, old chap,' he said, subconsciously clutching his knackers. 'Those VD videos give me a twitch. Besides, you should try catching a few Sandy McNabs yourself. That cream makes a great wanking lube.'

I'll never be able fully to articulate the levels of The Dalek's degeneracy and moral ambiguity. He'd eat snot, ear wax, scabs, toe-jam and even the sleep from his eyes but he even shocked himself one night. While in the bath, he noticed a small scab in his pubes and, as ever, he picked it out and had a nibble. Curious as to its unusual texture, he found another. As he examined it, a series of legs popped out and it scuttled down his hand. Telling the tale later, he'd shudder and say, 'That would've killed a straight man.'

Eventually, the Sexual Health police showed up at camp to inform us of the potential side effects associated with too much shagging, a concept most of us believed to be a literal impossibility. The gym had been set up as a large lecture theatre. With the prospect of sexual titillation, however deviant, in the air, it took a while to get everyone sat down, as all the usual jokes had to be performed first. There was lots of dry air humping, wanking gestures and blowjob mimes being acted out amongst the ranks; some of the lads had clearly got it into their heads that they were getting a day off work watching porn at the tax payers' expense.

All the noise and tomfoolery ceased in a oner when the RSM walked in and shouted, 'SIT UP!'

Everyone braced up. 'Right, you filthy fuckers,' shouted the Badge. 'You're having this lecture 'cos half of you cunts can't keep your dicks in your fucking pants. So pay attention, because the next horrible bastard who reports to the MRS with a snotty cock will be on a fucking fizzer.'

The gym stayed quiet, apart from a few muffled chuckles. The RSM then turned and saluted a bloke in a tatty uniform before marching out of the gym. The scruffy bloke carried all the military authority of Charles Hawtrey's 'Private Widdle' from *Carry On Up the Khyber*, and I half expected him to open his address with a large 'Ooh, *hellllooooo!*'

But in fact he was a Colonel Morris, and a doctor, and a supremely boring bloke – the human equivalent of a viewfoil projector. The old fucker could have talked a glass eye to sleep had it not been for the subject matter, and, more importantly, his 'instructional videos'. They'd have captured the attention of even the most hardened 'look awake but actually be asleep' lecture slumberers. Morris would mutter, 'Here we can clearly see the effects of untreated herpes on the female genitalia,' and there'd be a clattering noise as the relevant slide slotted into place. A close up of a strange, red-pinkish mass would appear on the screen, looking like someone had chainsawed a wolf in half, and everyone's heads would tilt gradually left, then right, as they attempted to find some kind of vaginally-orientated reference point to get their bearings. Every now and then you'd hear a muttered, 'What the fuck is that?' or 'Is that a clitoris or a boil?'

After a while, the Colonel's ramblings just became part of the ambient noise in the background, as one horrific picture followed another, focusing our attention in the manner intended. From huge pink cauliflowers to something you could dip your bread in, each slide was worse than the last. At one point Morris managed to raise a laugh when he warned us, 'Gentlemen, you are about to witness the most be-barnacled penis in the history of the British Army.'

Cue the slide of an identifiable set of knackers and a knob shaft, but attached to the end of said shaft was a bell end the likes of which you've never seen. It looked like one of the cannons off the Mary Rose, or as though the guy had smeared the end of his cock in golden syrup and dipped it in a huge bag of pick 'n' mix. He had warts of every size, colour and shape that the human body can create.

I had Derek on one side and John Hunt on the other. John was making squelching noises with his tongue and doing porn voiceovers like, 'Go on, John. Be a real gen'leman and lick the fucking slash.' The Dalek was worse: at one point, he pulled his cock out of his lightweights and began examining it, with the occasional wank burst thrown in for good measure. 'What the fuck is wrong with you, Derek?' I hissed. 'Put that fucking thing away.'

The Dalek just waggled it at me. 'Go on, Eddy,' he said. 'Just give us a little wank. With your arse.'

He'd definitely got worse since Belize.

After the horrible slide show came a video dramatisation which followed a young soldier who got a dose and failed to go sick with it. Eventually, his whole unit was bedded down, leaving all of Germany open to attack by Ivan the Terrible and his mates. After the graphic nature of the pictures, this outdated 1960s film, with its exaggerated Dick Van Dyke (two innuendos for the price of one) Cockney accents, was good for nothing except playing 'spot the now-famous actor when he was down on his luck'. It was a great bit of sport, and you could often see strange combinations that fucked with your mind a bit, like a young Mike Baldwin getting marched to jail by Doctor Legge from *Eastenders*, or David Jason trying not to get hypothermia in the Brecons. I could have done without the image of Tosh from *The Bill* advancing to contact, but at least they hadn't used actual soldiers. Every year, we were forced to watch a 'Law Of Armed Conflict' video which dealt with the rules of war. Its gravity was seriously undermined by the decision to employ genuine Bill Oddies to illustrate the points. In one scene, a medic is seen treating an enemy combatant whose injuries are greater than the British soldier lying on the adjacent stretcher. Another squaddie enters the tent to object, failing miserably to project any feeling or anger, as he shouts, 'What ya treatin' enemy for? That bastard shot Schofield.' In another scene, two soldiers are seen hassling a young woman in a barn, in direct contravention of the Geneva Conventions concerning the treatment of civilians. Had they used actors, the tableau might have been full of menace, with the actress conveying fear for her life. Because they used a couple of toms from the nearest guardroom, the 'menace' consisted of them standing next to her and looking embarrassed, as one of them tries to relieve her of the oldest Walkman you've ever seen. My personal favourite was always the guy making dum-dum rounds by filing down some conventional ammo. This practice was outlawed, because dum-

dums really hurt whereas, as everyone knows, normal bullets merely sting a bit. It's funny not so much for the bad acting, but because the villainous private uses a word that everyone in the Army actually stopped using decades before. When an eagle-eyed full screw spies his antics and challenges him, the soldier winks and replies, 'Got to get the bastards first time, Corp!'

* * * * *

Itchy todgers notwithstanding, time waits for no soldier and he must do as he's bid. After a short period, which saw half the lads drinking orange juice on nights out, the warning orders and build up for the regimental Battle Camp began. Given that most Royal Signals soldiers spend the majority of their exercises and operations in the role of communicators, annual Battle Camps are put in place to serve as a refresher course for their pure soldiering skills: ambushes, section attacks, platoon harbour areas, recce patrols, using four tonners as Chinook simulators, all the usual guff.

While there's no doubt that it was important to stay on top of your field admin, if you boiled things down to their bare essentials, you were basically going to be diffy shed-loads of gonk over a two-week period.

No-one in his right mind seeks to be cold, tired, hungry and generally fucked, but what such experiences *are* good for – and this is something that only occurred to me in later life – is helping you get on with the job in hand, in the knowledge that you've been colder/wetter/more tired than this before, and are therefore not about to expire.

If approached with the right mindset, Battle Camp could be a great laugh, though some lads would just grumble their tits off for the entire duration of the exercise. All power to them. It's the soldier's God-given right to moan about anything and everything –

'For fuck's sake, this compo's fucking shit!' etc etc – and I loved the way the proper moaner would resist all attempts to cheer him up with a dismissive, '…and you can fuck off, as well!'

Although I liked to join in from time to time, I'd learnt to adopt a slightly more upbeat attitude. I'd been in a few years, now, and generally knew what was coming, so there was less trepidation and subsequent shimfing at being caught out for being unprepared. I was safe in the knowledge that any Battle Camp would offer up a rich selection of hilarity. People falling off walls and into piles of sheep shit, or completely losing the plot and blowing up on inanimate objects like their bergans for not containing sufficient space for all their equipment: 'YOU CUNT! JUST LET ME PUT MY FUCKING DOSSBAG IN! IT'S NOT FUCKING ROCKET SCIENCE!' they'd yell, at an object incapable of reply, before getting gripped for having poor noise discipline.

With Battle Camp being a regimental exercise, it was run by the training wing.

There were two types of instructors. The first kind were good blokes who'd done their bit at places like 216 or 264, or on attachment to infantry units, and who'd therefore gained a good appreciation of how to get the best out of the guys. The other kind were the strokers who'd spent most of their time in training regiments, and they tended towards knobbishness because they'd lost the ability to distinguish between recruits in training and experienced soldiers in a working unit. It was pot luck as to what kind you'd get, but 30 wasn't too bad. The operational nature of the unit meant that custom webbing rigs, smocks, shemaghs and exotic boots were allowed a bit of slack, whereas too much of that kind of clobber in a big German Regiment would get you rock all off the instructors – you'd soon find yourself running round a field with your rifle above your head whilst your personally-acquired kit got thrown into the nearest river.

My first Battle Camp in 30 was to be on sunny Sennybridge – or 'Sennyfridge', as it was affectionately known – on the edge of the Brecon Beacons. You were guaranteed to return with every item of your kit wet and caked in sheep shit, but at least a relatively arduous stint in the field would keep the pisstank at bay for a while.

Being a senior lance jack, I got rumbled to be a section commander (or 'sexual banana' as it's sometimes called) for the exercise.

I had a good section, and even some of the lads who cocked around on camp were normally Johnny-on-the-spot when out in the field. Battle Camps reminded a lot of the blokes why they'd joined up in the first place, and there would be a noticeable transformation in their attitude. After all, when you go to a recruiting office there are no pictures of blokes picking their noses in the backs of Land Rovers – it's all glitzy snaps of fully cammed-up soldiers with shooters and tough expressions that bring people through the door.

John Hunt and Stretch were the only lads from the room in my section. The rest were buckshee toms from the troop, except for the section two icecream, who was a lance jack Tech called Dave 'Shady' Lane. Shady had been in a few years but kept getting busted and sent to Colchester for 'not-quite-kick-outable' offences like affray, drunk-and-disorderly and fighting. They used to say that Collie either made you or broke you, but it seemed to have fuck all impact on Shady – he stayed exactly the same despite his occasional visits to jail, and could be a good lad if the fancy took him.

In the greatest of Army traditions, we had to sign our weapons out of the armoury at 05:00. Had the brass cut us some slack and made it 09:00 it wouldn't have made any difference to the day's proceedings and I often suspected that they did it for comedy value. I liked to imagine the CO leaning against the mantelpiece in the mess with a brandy in his paw and a roaring fire behind him. 'Do you know,' he'd say, with a fond stare into the middle distance. 'I recall getting the chaps up at 04:00 one morning, and they were still as bright as buttons, the rascals.'

The reality was blokes with comedy hair-dos and blatant lag marks on their boxers would shuffle round the ablutions like zombies, sleepily horrified at the knowledge that the rest of the country would be kipping for another couple of hours.

Once all the kit was loaded onto the four tonners, they'd set off with the avowed intention of causing as many traffic jams as they could, while the rest of us piled on to coaches for the drive in to Wales.

I'd been in the Beacons a few times before, and I'd always thought that if I'd been there of my own volition, and not getting bugged out of my maggot, then I'd have loved the place. Unfortunately, on exercise you had other things on your mind. The scenery took a back seat against priorities like getting your hexi lit and ramming some hot scoff down your grinner in preparation for a night ambush.

Our first night was spent billeted in 30-man wooden huts in Sennybridge camp itself before deploying in to the field. As usual, with all the stereos and tellies stuck back in Nuneaton, the blokes just mooched around and had arguments to pass the time. The main debate was as to the best-looking women within a given environment or profession: women on camp, female news readers, pop singers and athletes... all were rigorously arranged into pointless Top Tens. Blokes with faces like a can of smashed arseholes would insist in the most graphic and deluded manner that the Scandinavian princess of pop, Whigfield, 'needed' a brand of luvvin' that only they could supply.

I always had trouble getting my head down the night before an early deployment in to the field, and this was no exception. A snore or a sleep-loosened trump would drift across the billet just at the right time to wake me prior to drifting off, or someone would utter an unsettling sentence from a dream that I had no desire to dwell on. I must've got about two hours proper gonk, tops, before reveille – not a good start. But judging by the state of half the people in the cookhouse, I wasn't the only one; that ushered in a strange but not unpleasant feeling, the squaddie's primeval urge to blend in and be in the same boat as his oppos.

Scoff scoffed, we loaded up in the backs of the four tonners and set off. Before long, the wagons stopped and we debussed. After the requisite milling about, it was webbing and bergans on, rifles in hands and a two-hour tab to the first platoon harbour area.

The first few days of the exercise were static, just bashering out and doing practical first aid, NBC, fieldcraft etc. After that, we'd be fully tactical and putting everything to the test as we got bumped by the jammy cunts who'd managed to wangle playing enemy for the period.

But it was over the initial instructional period that the best laugh was to be had, most notably in the first aid practical.

The first aid simulation, especially 'battle shock casualty', offered *carte blanche* to the regiment's budding actors to showcase their immense repertoire to an audience who couldn't have cared less. Such performances included the harrowing 'open sucking chest wound' and the infinitely touching portrayal entitled simply 'burns'. Regardless of how well the 'victim' could act, how realistic the make up was, or how obvious the injury was, the inherent, corner-cutting cunning of the British soldier would come in to play. When you arrived at the stand, the first aid instructor would tell you that you were about to come across some casualties and you were to treat them appropriately for their wounds and in order of severity. The first thing the would-be medics would do was to check the instructor wasn't looking. Then they'd kneel next to the patient and whisper, 'What's wrong with you, mate? Go, on, tell us what's wrong with you. Don't be a fucking jack cunt!'

Victims who steadfastly refused to let us in on their injury details were cared for properly, with a combination of sideburn-pulling, nose-twisting and threats of Nuneaton-based violence in the near future.

There were arms missing and gunshot wounds, but the military thesp regarded 'Battle Shock Casualty' as the highlight of his week. Without the aid of make-up, the budding Larry Olivier was forced to fall back on his innate talents to simulate the loss of his marbles. This led to some stellar performances which varied wildly in their interpretation. Some went for the more overt Ministry Of Funny Walks, while others would just sit there listlessly and sob, 'All me mates are dead,' by way of response to any question asked of them. (Which was, invariably, 'Don't be a cunt, tell us what's wrong with you, will ya?')

I saw a lesson once where the instructor was giving advice on treating a battle shock casualty, followed by a practical demonstration.

'The idea,' he said, 'is to be sympathetic and reassuring. This will help prevent further deterioration of the casualty.'

In this particular case, the condition had manifested itself in the form of disorientation and constantly bimbling off aimlessly, and the instructor was getting more and more threaders as he kept on having to break away from the lesson to retrieve his charge from a distant bush or from behind a tree.

The end of the lesson went something like this.

Instructor: 'Right, Gents. To conclude, you can see that victims of battle shock casualty can behave in many irrational ways, and need constant reassurance until they can receive the correct professional treatment.'

Pupil: 'Staff?'

Instructor: 'Yes, Sig Plughole?'

Sig Plughole, pointing to ambling casualty disappearing over the field behind the instructor: 'He's off again.'

Instructor: 'RIGHT! THAT'S IT, YOU CUNT! IF YOU'RE NOT BACK IN THREE FUCKING SECONDS, I'M GOING TO FILL YOU FUCKING IN! COME ON, OLIVIER, CHOP FUCKING CHOP!'

Along with first aid, NBC was another staple of battle camp training. We'd have multiple lessons, get gassed and get used to living in the field in Three Romeo (while this may sound like an R'n'B group, it actually meant wearing all of your protective equipment, including respirator, at the same time). Part of the acclimatisation for this always involved going for a run. Running and trying to catch your breath in a respirator was never fun, but it did allow you to trip your mates over as you went round without being too easily identified.

The repository of all NBC learning was the instructional book *Survive to Fight*. This publication covered step-by-step techniques, or 'tasks', which were numbered and accompanied by simple drawings to illustrate how to avoid a horrific death in the apocalyptic world that would be the result of Nuclear, Biological or Chemical warfare. It was a document that should have caused sober reflection on the realities of life for anyone who read it. But this was the British Army, and like most hugely important works, it was used instead for low amusement. As at school, where the main purpose of a dictionary is to look up dirty words, everyone in possession of *Survive To Fight* quickly turned to the page showing the soldier carrying out his defecation drills. The amount of mirth the picture generated was out of all proportion. It was always noted that, during the entire task, the soldier had failed to produce the requisite log. This was usually drawn in by the book's owner, with traditional flies and wavy lines.

Whilst brewing up by my basha, John Hunt was sat next to me on his webbing, leafing through his *Survive To Fight*. After a couple of minutes, he cast it to one side with a look of disgust. 'What a load of useless fucking shit,' he said.

'What are you on about, John?' I said.

'That fucking thing,' he continued. 'It's supposed to be about surviving in a world where the bomb's gone off, right? But it says fuck all about how to fight off cyber-punk mohicans wearing American football padding and chasing you through the desert on big motocross rat bikes, does it? No use to man nor fucking beast.'

John was a bit of a loon at times.

* * * * *

The final part of training was FIBUA – Fighting In Built Up Areas. Sennybridge, like most large training areas, had its own FIBUA village where we were taken through training for storming houses and so on. (I did an exercise on one area whose FIBUA village consisted of one house – its open location meant that it could have been defended against a company attack by one man with a 9mm pistol. It was laughingly referred to as FIBUHITMON – Fighting In a Built Up House In The Middle Of Nowhere.)

It was also where the final part of the tactical exercise would take place. Whilst many parts of FIBUA made sense, like grenading rooms before entry, others seemed to me like basic lunacy. At some point in the past, it had been decided that one method of gaining entry to the upper floors of an occupied house was for the entire section to hold onto a ladder and run at the building as if holding a medieval battering ram. When about six feet away from the external wall, the feet of the ladder were jammed into the floor and the top was forced up and forwards into the air, in an Iwo Jima flag-raising stylee. Where this process becomes a bit nuts is that the section sprog would be clinging to the top of the ladder, holding on for grim death. If he didn't have his head pulled off by getting it jammed between the top two rungs, he'd be thrown into the room. Fuck knows what he was supposed to do when he got there, other than die at the hands of an enemy well-prepared for the attack by listening to us arguing about it for ten minutes beforehand. It was a feat of mad military gymnastics which must've been dreamed up by a training wing OC somewhere after watching *The Crimson Pirate* on a Sunday orderly officer duty. Only Burt Lancaster and his mate Nick Cravat, the one who looked like an athletic Rolf Harris, could have feasibly carried out the manoeuvre.

The close quarters nature of practical FIBUA training meant that whilst clearing buildings you would be in the same room as 'The Enemy' and this would lead to plenty of larking around. Most of the guys in the mob in the early '90s had been brought up as kids on a diet of comic reading material like *Battle*, *Victor*, *Warlord* and *Commando* magazines. Charley's War, Johnny Red, Union Jack Jackson and D-Day Dawson were the mainstay of our youthful reading, and we loved every word and picture that they had to offer. As such, even as adult soldiers, the effect of their stirring Second World War prose came to the fore as we stormed the enemy-filled structures.

There was a lot of shouting in FIBUA fighting: 'ROOM CLEAR!' 'FLOOR CLEAR!' 'TRIP WIRE!' 'ENEMY FRONT!' were all being yelled in full voice as the lads moved round a building to ensure everyone in it was killed and none of the attacking party was injured. Pyrotechnics were also used to add to the noise and excitement. If the DS weren't watching properly, some unofficial orders and warnings started to be heard. You'd hear someone shout 'GRENADE!' and the mock grenade would be lobbed into a room. On its detonation, three soldiers would charge the room and empty a mag of blanks into one of the enemy, with the less conventional cry of 'Eat hot lead, Fritz!'

The enemy would respond in kind with blood curdling yells of, 'Aaargh, Gott in himmel! Scwheinhund Englander!' or 'Nein! Kamaraden! For me, zer var is ofer!'

There was a very strict death cry protocol to be observed on behalf of the enemy, as dictated by the comics. When a German soldier died, they always passed on with an 'Aaaaaaarrrgghhhh!' or an 'Urrrrggghhh!' Japanese soldiers were more prone to the higher-pitched 'Aiiieeeeeeee!' and would regularly shout philosophical or eulogising statements in the last moments of their lives. I remember one particularly aggressive room clearance, where one of the enemy, a bloke from 258 Sqn called Paul 'Bing' Crosby, wailed, 'Aiiieeeeee! By Shinto... the mad Britisher, he fights like a thousand tigers!'

The actual chances of fighting Japanese Imperial troops on a Dortmund housing estate were slim to non-existent, but strangely nobody ever pretended to be Russian. That said, I suppose the whole practice made no sense whatsoever, other than a means of garnering laughs aplenty.

EDDY NUGENT AND THE JACKSON FIVE

AFTER BATTLE CAMP, I cracked on with buckshee life, squaring the wagons away, trying to stay on top of my phys and getting blootered in The Donk on most Thursday nights. The odd afternoon saw us squared away in the George Vortex – a pub officially known as the 'George Eliot', after Nuneaton's most famous citizen, but renamed by us due to the place's uncanny ability to make entire afternoons disappear.

The Germans had bombed the fuck out of the town in 1942, leaving the planners free to inflict their own brand of architectural vandalism after the war; it was OK, I suppose, but the 'Welcome to Nuneaton' sign looked a lot better in the rear view mirror than it did through the windscreen, and I did my level best to get home every weekend. That was never a given. Every Friday afternoon we'd watch the clock tick down, knowing that if we made it to four o'clock without getting jiffed for anything, it was bomb-burst time. Without fail, some time around three o'clock, some sort of edict or requirement for manpower over the weekend would emerge from Regimental HQ, and the chase was on. It'd usually be something like working on a camp car boot sale or beefing up the guard, but whatever it was it had the capacity to completely torpedo your plans and the jiffers would end up having to look under trailer canopies or in top boxes to find their men.

About a month after the Camp had finished, in April '95, I was ironing out my Monday blues in the NAAFI bar with a couple of pints. John Hunt was on guard at the time and he bimbled into the bar, making a bee-line straight for me.

'Alright, John. What's up, mate?' I asked.

'Believe it or not Eduardo, I've been looking for you.'

'Oh aye,' I replied. I tried to sound as nonchalant as possible, but I had an initial stab of worry in my guts. The guard don't come looking for you unless you're in the shit or something has happened at home. Since Alfie had pegged it, I really didn't fancy any more bad news.

'A signal's just come in from the Commcen, mate. You're deploying out to Bos tomorrow.'

Bosnia? Fuck.

'Tomorrow? Piss off, John. You're having me on, aren't you?'

'Sorry, mate. It's straight up. It's a six-monther. They said you've got to get as much of your room boxed up as soon as possible, get your kit sorted and the duty clutch will take you to Brize in the morning.'

'Fuckin' hell. The cunts could've given us a bit more warning,' I said.

'Aye. Well, good luck, fella.'

That was it. By the time John came off stag, I'd probably be in the air, heading for my first war zone.

All those years of training and dossing were coming to a head: everything that you joined up for, the action, this was it.

As it sank in, I was a mixed bag of feelings. There was the natural worried anticipation at the prospect of going on an Op, but that started playing second fiddle to the excitement. I felt an overwhelming urge to tell my folks and Jenny what was going on before I did anything else. I was on Spearhead standby anyway, so most of my kit was packed – all I'd need was the odd luxury item to make my six months in the Balkans that little bit more comfortable, and there was more than enough room in my bergan for a copy of the prized *Color Climax Volume 6* that currently lurked under my mattress.

Most lads deployed as an entire unit, especially the infantry and artillery. As a general rule, for ongoing roulement tours like Bos, lads from 30 would go out by themselves, but they would at least have a month or so heads up. At least I'd forego all the usual preparation and lectures that normally preceded an operational tour. The fast-ball nature of the deployment meant that there would be no time for training camps, there'd be no PT beastings, riot control lessons or well-meaning but slightly unnecessary lectures on the geo-political causes of the conflict. However, the lack of explanation about the hazy and convoluted nature of Yugoslavia's recent past would lead to some confusion amongst the lads as to the reason for our deployment. A lot of them read the broadsheets and were well up to speed with what was going on, but there was a significant minority who thought 'The Balkans' was just a *Carry On* film joke specifically created as a testicle substitute to avoid censorship in the 1960s. The Dardanelles performed a similar function, and mention of Tito's death only made things worse: quite how a tragedy in the Jackson Five could create such a bloody conflict thousands of miles away would be unfathomable to them.

Joking aside, it was the first time since WW2 that the spectres of concentration camps, mass graves and ethnic cleansing had visited Europe, leaping straight out of the history pages and onto *News At 10*. When the former Yugoslavia had broken up at the end of the '80s, the political instability it had generated in the region allowed factions to start carving up the area along racial and religious lines. Things had really kicked off in March '92, and the fighting would go on for another three and a half years spreading with a domino effect through the various countries of the old federation.

Working under the UN banner, the British Army had been involved since the start, providing an armed presence on the ground – ostensibly to deter the opposing sides from attacking each other, and thus enabling the safe delivery of immediate requirements like humanitarian aid. There was, of course, an eventual long term aim of providing enough stability for the people to become peacefully self governing.

It wasn't Afghanistan 2009, obviously, but by the standards of the day it was pretty hairy at times. Like any other conflict, only really major events made the news, but the guys who'd been out there were clear that places like Goražde were on a war footing. Our guys out there were always getting bumped, and it barely got a whiff of media coverage.

* * * * *

Whilst still in the NAAFI I dug out a ruck load of shrapnel to make the necessary calls home. As I was picking up the receiver of the pay phone in the foyer, it occurred to me that, basically, I'd been dicked for a job. In essence it was no different to the instantaneous 'Pick that fucking fag butt up' from a troop sergeant. This particular dickjob had a six month time-frame and life-changing potential, but the principle remained the same.

Mum was both worried sick and angry in equal measures. She flitted from concern, 'Oh please be careful, sweetheart. Come home safe, for the love of God!' to 'No leave? No chance to say goodbye? That's not right! They can't do that!'

I reassured her as much as possible, but not being a parent myself at the time I suppose I couldn't even begin to understand the worry that she'd be going through.

Dad maintained his usual stiff upper lip approach, but I could tell he knew this wouldn't be Belize.

Then I had to phone Jenny. This was going to be the hardest. We'd been going out since Christmas '91. For the first couple of years it'd been an easy going thing but since getting back to England I'd started to feel more serious about her. I really didn't want to see her upset, especially considering she was just about to do her finals, but unfortunately the somewhat inflexible rules of the Army meant that I couldn't just fuck The Brass off at the high-port because my girlfriend didn't want me to go away. Playing into this was a bit of selfishness on my part. I really wanted to get on an Op. This is what young blokes who joined the mob wanted to do. Whether or not they wanted to keep doing it after six months was up to the individual.

It was as bad as I expected. Jenny cried, the sudden realisation that I actually might be in harm's way (however unlikely that was) bringing her feelings to a head. But amongst all the worry she had an immense pride in me. The large scale deployment of British forces on UN Ops has seen a subtle change in how they're perceived by the public. For many years, the most common vision of the televised British soldier was on the streets in Northern Ireland, a situation which had polarised opinions. Getting involved in humanitarian ops was seen as a more benevolent use of our skills. I can't be sure, but I think it was during that phone call that we both first dropped 'The L Bomb'.

Once all my phoning home admin was done, I got up to the block and started stuffing as much kit away as possible. It was mostly civvie clobber that got stowed – I'd need a lot of my issued stuff for the six months out there. I didn't see there being a huge requirement for any 'getting into clubs' shoes or Chinos, and my Global Hypercolor T-shirt would have to wait for me to get back.

I'd only been packing for two minutes when the first scavenger appeared.

It was always astonishing to me how quickly the Army rumour mill kicked in. If there was any bad news, or you needed to be somewhere, the lads would always tell you even before the orders had been issued. One time, Derek had done a night in nick for a filthiness-based crime and when the guard woke him in the morning, his walls looked like they'd been subjected to a sustained dirty protest. Two days later, Stretch got back from Bos. I happened to be near the camp gates, and he saw me before he'd even walked back in. He bimbled straight over and collared me. 'Fucking hell, Eddy,' he said. 'I heard about Derek the other day. The dirty bast.'

'How the fuck did you know about that, mate?' I said. 'You've only just got back in country!'

'Oh,' he said, completely unflustered. 'One of the lads sent us a message from Rwanda.'

Un-fucking-believable.

The lads in the block had obviously heard that I was being sent out on an Op and they immediately started jostling for position, offering to 'look after' any nifty bits of kit that I'd be leaving behind. The less ambitious would be after a buckshee bit of furniture, whereas the real high-rollers had designs on my car. Their enquiries followed a set pattern – mock concern, quickly followed by blatant avarice. They'd mooch into my doorway, hands down the front of their Ron Hills.

'Alright, Eddy? You been fast-balled? That's a bit of a pisser, mate. No leave? The tight *cunts*. So, what you gonna do about your motor? I had a mate who worked in the LAD at 1 Div. He reckoned that if you don't drive your car every week, the oil turns to sludge and it fucks up your head gasket...'

I placed smaller bits of kit into safe hands, but they could all fuck off if they thought they were getting my car keys. I'd heard horror stories about trusting blokes who'd left their motors with lifelong friends, only to come back from a tour to find nine points on their licence and a summons from the Belgian police.

Despite their self-serving motives, the lads taking things off my hands made packing a bit easier. But you always had to be careful. Memories had a funny way of getting vague in the Army. You'd come back off a tour and go to get your bike off its temporary caretaker, only to find he'd fallen victim to a strange amnesia. Not only had he forgotten it was yours, but he might also fabricate a realistic back story about purchasing it a couple of years ago. Fist-waving and expletives generally brought about a satisfactory conclusion.

I gonked on a bare mattress in my maggot that night. All my bedding was stashed, and I may as well get myself re-acquainted with the old dossbag as it would be my sole form of bedding for the next 165 days (give or take). I really didn't sleep well at all. Admin worries about transport and stuff did battle with what might await me in theatre. I sweated my knackers off too. The frigging heating in the block was stuck on max: no doubt they'd get it turned down just in time for winter.

I was up in time for an early breakfast, and then I got my kit, picked up my weapon from the armoury and went down to the guardroom.

It was a lonely departure. I didn't really know anyone on guard – there were some young guys from 258 Squadron and a few Gurkha lads, and one of them said, 'See ya, mate,' as he walked in off a front gate stag. And that was it. Mind you, I don't know what I was expecting – maybe something along the lines of the *Canberra*'s send off to the Falklands, or the whole camp applauding as they lined the route from the guardroom to the waiting Land Rover? As I'd often had to, I reminded myself that I wasn't in an American film, threw my kit in the back and we left camp.

That was it, Eddy off to sort out the Balkans conflict, no ceremony, mum, dad, nan and Jenny a hundred or so miles away, and all my lazy cunt mates still gonking.

We drove down to Brize on the Fosse Way. The Cotswolds were as glorious as ever, with their welcoming yellow stone walls and posh houses, and my mind drifted like buggery. Before long, we were at RAF Brize Norton and the driver was getting directions for check-in from a Snowdrop on the gate. I'm sure the bastard was eyeing us up for some form of grippable offence, regardless of how flimsy; as bad as the monkeys could be, there were still a fair share of good lads in their ranks, but the RAF police really took the biscuit. I was once pulled over on an RAF camp for the heinous crime of doing 12mph in a 10mph area. I'd had sloths on methadone overtaking me and shaking their fists angrily, but the copper dealt with me as if he'd finally nabbed Jack The Ripper.

Outside check-in I got all my kit out of the wagon. The driver wished me luck then fucked off back to 30 via a long stop at Heartburn Harry's butty wagon.

Check-in was a doddle and pretty soon I was at Gateway House waiting to be called forward for the 14:30 to Split. Fair play to the lads and lasses in movements, they seemed to know their onions. They had an unfortunate unit abbreviation though. UKMAMS stood for United Kingdom Mobile Air Movements Squadron, but to most of us it sounded like some sort of society for the adoration of British breasts.

Gateway was awash with every cap badge imaginable. There were all sorts of people going out to Bosnia, from morbidly obese mechanics to gringo-tached Hereford Gun Club members in their civvies.

I took the time to make a last-minute call home. Jenny was at mum and dad's, which was a nice surprise. The thought of her being accepted by my family was really comforting. But saying goodbye this time, as we were getting ready to emplane, was even worse, and I actually got a bit tearful. After I hung up, I whiled away the time by drinking a shed-load of brews and reading a snaffled copy of *The Currant Bun*. Not renowned for its in-depth news articles, I contented myself with the important knowledge that Boyzone appeared to making a few dents in Take That's fanbase.

I didn't have to wait long. The call came over the Tannoy for everyone on the Split flight to move to a holding area. Loads of bods stood up and we filtered through. Someone must've been gonking somewhere as multiple calls went out for a missing goon.

It was one of the greatest announcements I've ever heard: 'Would Lance Corporal Nutter please report for flight...' The rest was lost amidst roars of laughter.

The final trip was out to the pan in a bus. In the distance was an aircraft that just kept getting bigger and bigger. It was a C5 Galaxy, and it was huge. I'd been on jumbo jets before but this thing was ridiculous. Climbing up the steps to the door in the aircraft's side, I turned around for a last look at England. I don't know what I was expecting – rolling hills, maybe, castles, or the holy lamb of God. But whatever it should've been, all I saw was a ruck load of tarmac and an RAF bloke who needed a haircut. Either way, it was a lovely day so I smiled to myself and walked through the door without looking back.

Inside the Galaxy, trucks, Land Rovers and trailers were lined up as far back as you could see. Overhead was a gantry that you accessed via a ladder, and a USAF loadie, probably fresh from a homoerotic volleyball game, directed us up it, along the upper walkway and to the passenger compartment. I just followed the lad in front of me, and we ended up in an area just like a normal airliner cabin, except with no windows. This made it feel like night time, and because it was no longer available I had a terrible pang to look outside one last time. But, like everyone else, I didn't let it show. I just sat down, buckled up and waited.

The United States Air Force don't have to worry about dwindling passenger numbers, so we were left to our own devices without any announcements. Some of the guys in the compartment knew each other and bantered, but I closed my eyes. Eventually, the big engines started to whine and we felt the odd movement of the aircraft, so we must've been taxiing.

Everything had happened so quickly that I'd not had time properly to think about what was going on. I wasn't being sent out to Bosnia because there was a shortage of people with Manchester accents. Soldiers were going out there to get in between people who were killing each other, and I was one of those soldiers. I just didn't want to fuck up or let anyone down. There was no reason why that should happen, but times like those could cause self-doubt in anyone.

Two Scots medics were sat behind me discussing the pros and cons of battering and deep frying a Cadbury's Cream Egg, whilst a bloke to my left was reading that night's TV guide – maybe he knew something I didn't. The only annoying person was a two-shits sat in front of me, telling some poor lass about how great his car was. Fortunately, she shut him up for the rest of the flight by saying, 'I bet you go on fucking holiday to Elevenarife.' Classic! She must've been Int Corps.

The lack of windows gave an unsettling feeling of dislocation, like we were sat in an aircraft simulator. I had zero sensation of what the aircraft was doing, but when the engines roared and the cabin started shaking I knew we were off down the runway. The slight dipping sensation in my gut signalled that we were in the air.

In the time it would take me to drive back home from camp on a Friday afternoon, I'd be landing in Bosnia.

Jesus, the last time I'd flown from Brize was for an eight month jolly, on the piss, single, shagging, not a care in the world save for catching something off The Dalek. For once the recruiting office posters had been right. Now I was going to a war zone, worried about my girlfriend, with responsibility of all sorts on my shoulders.

All this, and pay as well!

Also from Monday Books

Picking Up The Brass / **Eddy Nugent**
(ppbk, £7.99)

IT'S 1985, The Smiths are in the charts and Maggie Thatcher is in No10. Eddy Nugent's in Manchester, he's 16 and he's slowly going out of his mind with boredom. Almost by accident, he goes and joins the British Army. Overnight, he leaves the relative sanity of civvie street and falls headlong into the lunatic parallel universe of basic training: a terrifying (and accidentally hilarious) life of press ups, boot polish and drill at the hands of a bunch of right bastards.

Picking Up The Brass is a riotous and affectionate look at life as an ordinary young recruit – the kind of lad who doesn't end up in the SAS or become an underwater knife-fighting instructor.

'Eddy Nugent' is the nom de plume of two former soldiers, Ian Deacon and Charlie Bell. Closely based on their own experiences, it's a must-read for anyone who has served, anyone who is planning to join up or anyone who's ever thought, 'Surely not every soldier in the Army is trained to kill people with a toothpick?'

'Laugh-out loud funny' – *Soldier Magazine*
'Hilarious' – *The Big Issue*
'FHM- approved' – *FHM*

In Foreign Fields / **Dan Collins**
(ppbk, £7.99)

A staggering collection of 25 true-
life stories of astonishing battlefield
bravery from Iraq and Afghanistan...
medal-winning soldiers, Marines
and RAF men, who stared death in
the face, in their own words.

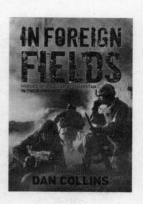

'**Enthralling and awe-inspiring untold stories**'
– *The Daily Mail*

'**Astonishing feats of bravery illustrated in laconic,
first-person prose**' – *Independent on Sunday*

'**The book everyone's talking about... a gripping account
of life on the frontlines of Iraq and Afghanistan**'
– *News of the World*

'**An outstanding read**' – *Soldier Magazine*

**From all good bookshops, online from
www.mondaybooks.com or via 01455 221752.**

Watching Men Burn - A Soldier's Story / **Tony McNally**
(ppbk, £7.99)

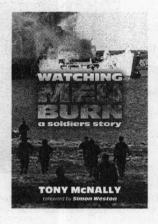

++ The Falklands ++ 1982 ++ Tony McNally is a Rapier missile operator, shooting down Argentinean planes attacking British troops and ships. And it's a tough job - the enemy pilots are fearless and they arrive at supersonic speed and breathtakingly low altitude.

But Tony's war is going well...

Until they bomb the Sir Galahad - a troop ship he is supposed to be protecting. His Rapier fails and he watches, helpless, as bombs rain down on the defenceless soldiers. Fifty men die, and many are left terribly injured.

Tortured by guilt and the horror of the bombing, Tony has relived the events of that day over and over again in his mind.

Watching Men Burn is his true story of the Falklands War - and its awful, lingering aftermath.

From all good bookshops, online from www.mondaybooks.com or via 01455 221752.

Wasting Police Time / **PC David Copperfield** (ppbk, £7.99)

The fascinating, hilarious and best-selling inside story of the madness of modern policing. A serving officer - writing deep under cover - reveals everything the government wants hushed up about life on the beat.

'Very revealing' – *The Daily Telegraph*
'Passionate, important, interesting and genuinely revealing' – *The Sunday Times*
'Graphic, entertaining and sobering' – *The Observer*
'A huge hit... will make you laugh out loud' – *The Daily Mail*
'Hilarious... should be compulsory reading for our political masters' – *The Mail on Sunday*
'More of a fiction than Dickens' – **Tony McNulty MP, former Police Minister**
(On a BBC *Panorama* programme about PC Copperfield, McNulty was later forced to admit that this statement, made in the House of Commons, was itself untrue)

From all good bookshops, online from www.mondaybooks.com or via 01455 221752.

Perverting The Course Of Justice / Inspector Gadget

(ppbk, £7.99)

A senior officer picks up where *Wasting Police Time* left off. A savage, eye-opening journey through our creaking criminal justice system, which explains what it's really like at the very sharp end of British policing.

'Exposes the reality of life at the sharp end'
– *The Daily Telegraph*

'No wonder they call us Plods... A frustrated inspector speaks out on the madness of modern policing'
– *The Daily Mail*

'Staggering... exposes the bloated bureaucracy that is crushing Britain' – *The Daily Express*

'You must buy this book... it is a fascinating insight'
– Kelvin MacKenzie, *The Sun*

From all good bookshops, online from www.mondaybooks.com or via 01455 221752.

When Science Goes Wrong / Simon LeVay
(ppbk, £7.99)

We live in times of astonishing scientific progress. But for every stunning triumph there are hundreds of cock-ups, damp squibs and disasters. Escaped anthrax spores and nuclear explosions, tiny data errors which send a spacecraft hurtling to oblivion, innocent men jailed on 'infallible' DNA evidence…just some of the fascinating and disturbing tales from the dark side of discovery.

'Expertly-narrated… beautifully understated… LeVay has a decided verve for storytelling' – *The Guardian*

'This book will intrigue you to the very last sentence' - *The Daily Mail*

'Spine-tingling, occasionally gruesome accounts of well-meant but disastrous scientific bungling' – *The Los Angeles Times*

From all good bookshops, online from www.mondaybooks.com or via 01455 221752.

So That's Why They Call It Great Britain / **Steve Pope**
(ppbk, £7.99)

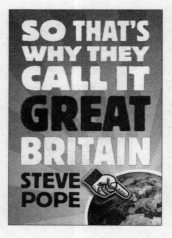

From the steam engine to the jet engine to the engine of the world wide web, to vaccination and penicillin, to Viagra, chocolate bars, the flushing loo, the G&T, ibruprofen and the telephone... this is the truly astonishing story of one tiny country and its gifts to the world.

A must for proud Brits from 8 to 108.

**From all good bookshops, online from
www.mondaybooks.com or via 01455 221752.**

A Paramedic's Diary / Stuart Gray
(ppbk, £7.99)

STUART GRAY is a paramedic dealing with the worst life can throw at him. *A Paramedic's Diary* is his gripping, blow-by-blow account of a year on the streets – 12 rollercoaster months of enormous highs and tragic lows. One day he'll save a young mother's life as she gives birth, the next he might watch a young girl die on the tarmac in front of him after a hit-and-run. A gripping, entertaining and often amusing read by a talented new writer.

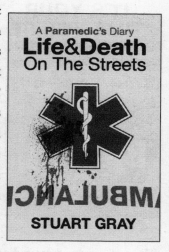

From all good bookshops, online from www.mondaybooks.com or via 01455 221752.

It's Your Time You're Wasting / Frank Chalk
(ppbk, £7.99)

The blackly humorous diary of a year in a teacher's working life. Chalk confiscates porn, booze and trainers, fends off angry parents and worries about the few conscientious pupils he comes across, recording his experiences in a dry and very readable manner.

"Does for education what PC David Copperfield did for the police"

"Addictive and ghastly" – *The Times*

From all good bookshops, online from www.mondaybooks.com or via 01455 221752.